THE DANCE OF LOVE

Jane hesitated for a fraction of a second, inexplicably terrified to touch him.

His eyes darkened at the perceived slight. "Does the prospect of dancing with me displease you so intensely?"

Jane's face flooded with heat, and she waved her fan, pretending to be affected by the room's warmth. "I . . . no. Of course not. It would be my pleasure," she lied, reaching for his arm.

She barely felt the floor beneath her slippers as she rested a hand on his shoulder, the other clasped tightly in his. His nearness positively unsettled her. She could feel his heat, warming her skin beneath the thin fabric of her gown and all but burning her hand through the layers of wool and kidskin that separated them. She thought of nothing save regulating her breathing as they began to glide across the floor to the strains of the waltz.

She was keenly aware that his touch, his closeness, affected her physically in ways she'd never before experienced, and the thought disturbed her greatly. Her eyes boldly sought his face, wondering if he was similarly afflicted. As if he sensed her appraisal, his eyes met hers.

Jane forgot to breathe.

BOOK YOUR PLACE ON OUR WEBSITE AND MAKE THE READING CONNECTION!

We've created a customized website just for our very special readers, where you can get the inside scoop on everything that's going on with Zebra, Pinnacle and Kensington books.

When you come online, you'll have the exciting opportunity to:

- View covers of upcoming books
- Read sample chapters
- Learn about our future publishing schedule (listed by publication month *and author*)
- Find out when your favorite authors will be visiting a city near you
- Search for and order backlist books from our online catalog
- Check out author bios and background information
- Send e-mail to your favorite authors
- Meet the Kensington staff online
- Join us in weekly chats with authors, readers and other guests
- Get writing guidelines
- AND MUCH MORE!

Visit our website at
http://www.kensingtonbooks.com

Unveiled

Kristina Cook

ZEBRA BOOKS
Kensington Publishing Corp.
http://www.kensingtonbooks.com

ZEBRA BOOKS are published by

Kensington Publishing Corp.
850 Third Avenue
New York, NY 10022

All Kensington titles, imprints and distributed lines are available at special quantity discounts for bulk purchases for sales promotion, premiums, fund-raising, educational or institutional use.

Special book excerpts or customized printings can also be created to fit specific needs. For details, write or phone the office of the Kensington Special Sales Manager: Kensington Publishing Corp., 850 Third Avenue, New York, NY 10022. Attn. Special Sales Department. Phone: 1-800-221-2647.

Zebra and the Z logo Reg. U.S. Pat. & TM Off.

First Printing: May 2005
10 9 8 7 6 5 4 3 2 1

Printed in the United States of America

For my mom, Laurie,
for handing down her love of reading to me.

And in loving memory of my grandfather,
Dr. Edgar Long Lewis,
for handing down his love of reading to her.

I miss you, Papa Ed!

Prologue

Glenfield, Essex, 1810

It was happening again.

A blinding flash of lightning illuminated the dark space where Jane Rosemoor cowered. She shut her eyes against the burst of light, covering her ears with her hands as the crack of thunder rent through the night. The storm raged on outside, echoing the storm that raged within her.

"Jane," Susanna cried as she peered under the coverlet. "Please, what's wrong?"

Jane huddled farther still beneath the bedding, not wanting to talk to anyone, not even her sister. "I . . . I just wish to be alone, that's all."

"You've been hidden away for hours. Aren't you hungry? Won't you come out?"

Jane listened as rain and wind lashed at the windows, rattling the shutters. She said nothing. Hot tears scalded her eyes, burning a fiery path down her cheeks. If Susanna were to see her face, she'd surely glimpse the despair that gripped her. Jane couldn't explain it, wouldn't speak of it.

"No," she finally managed to say. "Please, just . . . just go."

She listened as Susanna sighed heavily and then made her way back across the room, her slippers shuffling across the bare floorboards. The reluctant footsteps paused a beat, then resumed their noisy path toward the door that separated the girls' bed-chambers. At last the door clicked shut as another flash of lightning lit the night.

Jane took a deep, steadying breath, trying desperately to quell her trembling hands as the accompanying clap of thunder reverberated off the walls.

It wasn't the storm that frightened her. No, it was the heavy veil of despair that had dropped across her heart, making her feel hopeless, helpless. It had happened before, more than once. What was wrong with her? But she knew. She *knew*.

She'd heard them whispering again, just last night, about Grandmama. Her parents only spoke of her when they thought no one was about, that no children were around to hear the hushed words. But Jane had heard them. She'd stood frozen, outside her mother's room, late at night and long after she was supposed to be tucked into bed.

"It's worsening," her mother had whispered behind the closed door. "Aunt Gertrude says Mama no longer leaves her room." Her mother sniffled loudly. Was she weeping? Her father made faint clucking noises, as if he were comforting her.

"And what of your poor sister Susan?" he'd asked.

"There's no doubt she's afflicted as well." Her mother blew her nose. "It's gotten progressively worse with the birth of each child, same as Mama. I just don't know what to do."

"There's nothing you can do, my dear. But I don't think you should take the children to Derbyshire this year."

"No, of course not. It will do no good for the children to see her in this state. We can no longer pretend she is ill each and every time we visit. They're getting much too old, and they're certain to ask questions. Especially Jane. She's so sensitive as it is, just like . . ." Her mother's last words were muffled by sobs.

"Jane is but twelve, Elizabeth, just an adolescent. All adolescent girls are sensitive and . . ."

Jane could no longer listen. She had fled on silent feet to her own room. She'd lain awake most of the night and remained abed all day, feigning a headache, unable to face her family's solicitous attentions.

Whatever was wrong with Grandmama? And with her Aunt Susan? She didn't know, didn't understand the words, but knew it was something awful. Something that couldn't be spoken aloud.

But what frightened her most was the thought that whatever it was, she was victim to it, too; that the occasional bouts of melancholy that all but paralyzed her were the first symptoms of some terrible, unspeakable affliction.

Her mind raced toward the obvious conclusion— they were mad, Aunt Susan and Grandmama. And if they were, was she doomed to madness as well? Was that what her mother meant to say—just like *them*? Jane pressed her face into the mattress as fresh tears flowed with a vengeance, her heart twisted into a knot of terror.

She would never speak of it, this darkness she felt from time to time. *Never.* It would remain her most tightly guarded secret. From this day forward, she would try her best to put on a cheerful face, no matter what she felt in her heart. No one could know that she was surely going mad, as mad as her grandmother and aunt.

And from the hushed conversations she'd overheard, it was obvious that the condition worsened with childbirth. There was only one solution, then. Her twelve-year-old mind resolved at once that she'd never marry, never have children.

The glass in the windows began to rattle against the storm's onslaught, and Jane shuddered.

She didn't want to end up like her grandmother, locked away in her room. Or worse yet, Bedlam. She'd heard about the mad souls locked away in that horrible place, screaming and rolling in their own filth. No, she couldn't go there.

All she had to do was smile.

Chapter One

Richmond Park, Derbyshire, 1824

"I'm at my wits' end, Tolland. The child needs more than I can give her." Hayden Moreland, the Earl of Westfield, dropped his head into his hands with a sigh. His stomach churned uncomfortably. He hated finding himself in such a position. He'd never been so unsure of anything in all his years. It was insupportable.

"Yes, you've definitely gotten yourself into a bind, haven't you, old boy?" Cecil Tolland chuckled, the sound pricking each and every one of Hayden's nerves.

Hayden reached up to squeeze his brow, hoping to ease the dull throb that was steadily increasing in strength and intensity. "Miss Crosley is a fine governess, but Madeline needs more. She needs the influence of a lady, a proper lady. Your wife has been wonderful to her, of course, but soon she'll be occupied with her own infant."

"Emily adores Madeline," Tolland offered. "No doubt her attentions will continue after our child is born."

Hayden rose and began to pace a circuit across the library's dark floor. His hands, balled into fists, were shoved roughly into his coat pockets. "I should never have taken Madeline in. I should have turned her right over to the foundling home as everyone reasonable suggested. There are no assurances she's even my brother's child."

Yet Hayden knew in his heart that the girl was his niece. One only had to look into her mossy green eyes to see the striking familial resemblance. "Damn Thomas. And damn Sophia. Why did she beg me to take her child?"

"Because she knew what kind of man you are, a far cry from your brother. She knew you'd give her a good home, send her off to a fine school. Because she was dying and didn't want her daughter to end up on the streets—or worse yet, a brothel."

"It was a rhetorical question," Hayden bit out through clenched teeth.

"You'll pardon me, then," Tolland retorted, an irritating smile visible at the corners of his mouth.

Didn't Tolland realize the graveness of the situation? As usual, Hayden's brother, Thomas, had made a mess of things, and Hayden had been left to tidy up. Things would be far less complicated if only Thomas had married Sophia. Hayden had taken an enormous risk, taking in the child. The entire *ton* had known of his brother's long association with the beautiful opera singer, yet Thomas refused to take any responsibility for his illegitimate offspring.

Hayden had found it impossible to deny the dying woman, to refuse the infant placed tenderly in his arms. He had the means, after all, and he didn't give a damn what the *ton* thought. Richmond Park was a far cry from Mayfair, and few took notice that he'd taken in his "niece." He'd hired a capable nursemaid, added a governess to his staff, and had rarely been aware of the child's presence in the enormous house. But as she grew older, he could no longer ignore her presence. Madeline was a fearful, cowering little thing, and he hadn't a clue what to do with her. She needed attention, a measure of affection, and he didn't know how to give it to her—*couldn't* give it to her for that matter

Hayden glared at Tolland and poured himself a sherry, downing the liquid with one stiff jerk of the wrist.

"Are you really so obtuse, Westfield? Don't you see the solution when it's so plain? A wife, old boy. You need a wife."

Hayden choked on the drink, sputtering amber droplets onto his starched white cravat. "Don't be absurd."

"Absurd? Why, it's the only solution, and a sensible one at that."

"I'm not marrying a fool," Hayden spat out, "and that's what they all are." At least it appeared that way of late. All a bunch of silly, giggling fools, batting their lashes at him whilst they greedily eyed Richmond Park. He wouldn't have it.

Tolland cleared his throat.

"Your own wife excluded, of course," Hayden added. "Anyway, I'm done with all that." He set down his glass and took out his watch, polishing its face with his coattails.

"Come now, Westfield, you're the richest man in all of Derbyshire. They can't help but beat down your door, all wanting to be mistress of Richmond Park. You can't blame them for seeing pound notes when they look at you."

"Katherine didn't," he said, his chest tight.

Tolland's gaze met his, and he waited a beat before replying. "Perhaps, but Katherine grew up with the certainty of becoming your wife."

And now she was gone, dead for almost a decade. The sweet, sensible girl Hayden had been betrothed to since infancy. Dead, just days before their wedding. Taken at such a tender age, like his sister Isabel. Like his mother. Like every woman he'd ever loved. Devil take it, he was cursed.

He snapped shut the watch and returned it to his pocket. "I'm not marrying." He strode to the window and gazed out, his chest swelling with pride as he took in the sight of his estate's vast park—rolling, manicured acres, giving way to dense wood. It was his, all his. As far as the eye could see. The finest land in all of Derbyshire.

"Not marrying? Balderdash." Tolland shook his head. "Of course you can, and you will. Do you truly want Richmond Park passing to your sorry excuse for a brother? The estate will be bankrupt in less than a year's time, and you know it. You need an heir. Madeline needs someone to mother her. Whether or not the child is your niece is immaterial. You've taken her in; she's your ward, your responsibility."

Hayden's mind cast about for another solution—anything else. Something more reasonable. He came up annoyingly blank. Bloody hell, as much as he loathed the idea, Tolland was right. A wife. He needn't love her—couldn't, in fact. But a sensible woman to produce an heir and mother his ward—perhaps it would do.

Hayden slumped into a worn, leather chair. "And where do you propose I find a wife? None of the maids in this district will do."

"What about Lady Millicent Sunderland?"

"Surely you jest? She's without a doubt the most insensible woman I've ever met."

"The Viscount Stanley's daughter, then? The eldest one. Very sensible girl, quite bookish, if that's what you want."

"A spinster with the face of a horse." Hayden brushed a speck of dust from his sleeve. "Surely I can do better than a woman no other man wants."

Tolland threw his hands up in obvious frustration. "Go to London, then. Make the rounds, meet the debutantes. Surely *someone* will do."

He tapped his fingers on the arm of the chair. "I suppose so. I don't normally partake in the social aspects of the Season, but perhaps I could." The very idea was distasteful at best.

"Well, chin up, old boy. Perhaps you'll get lucky and a promising candidate will waltz through your front door and offer herself up." Tolland threw his head back and laughed.

Hayden didn't find it amusing, not in the least. "Perhaps she will," he muttered with a mutinous glare.

Glenfield, Essex

"I'm going, Mama, and that's all there is to it. Nothing you can say will dissuade me." Jane folded the letter and sealed it.

"But you can't, dear, not by yourself." Her mother fingered the quizzing glass that lay between her ample breasts.

"I had no intention of going by myself. Bridgette will accompany me."

"But Bridgette—"

"Has no duties to attend to with me away from Glenfield. She's a perfectly acceptable chaperone. Cousin Emily's husband will meet the post chaise and escort me to Ashbourne. Come now, Mama. I'm only going to visit family. Emily nears the end of her confinement and she welcomes the company." Jane tapped on the page lying before her on the escritoire. "She says so quite plainly. Besides, it's a short drive from Emily's home to The Orchards, and it's been years since I've seen Grandmama and Auntie Gertrude. How can you deny me my own kin?"

"I'm not denying you anything, Jane. But surely you realize that your grandmama is not well—not herself. She is not fit for company. Her nerves cannot take it, cannot bear the excitement."

Her nerves. That was precisely why Jane must go— to see just what state her grandmother's nerves were in, just what truth lay behind the whispered words and veiled hints at a mysterious malady that plagued the women of Jane's mother's family.

It was time to learn the truth. Jane could no longer hide from it. She was six-and-twenty, a confirmed spinster by choice. She had turned down a shocking number of proposals over the years— perfectly acceptable offers at that—because she knew that marriage inevitably led to childbirth, and childbirth could push her over the brink toward some sort of madness. Oh, her own bouts of melancholy had mostly subsided once she reached womanhood, but she'd glimpsed the darkness, faced the frightening reality of overwhelming despair, and she feared anything at all could tip the balance.

No, she could not risk it. Not till she saw for herself what her future might hold. Her family in Derbyshire held the clues she needed to piece together the puzzle, as no one would speak plainly about the situation—at least not in her presence. She was forced to come to her own conclusions, frightening ones at that. She thought of her sister Susanna, perhaps the most happy, serene, even-tempered woman she knew. What were the odds that both sisters had escaped the family curse?

She was leaving, in three days' time, and she would face her demons herself. There was nothing else to be done.

"I'm sorry, Mama. My mind is made up."

Her mother sighed. "So be it. You're a sensible girl, Jane. I hope this isn't some sort of mission to . . . to . . ." She trailed off, her faded eyes welling with tears.

"Mama!" Jane reached over and patted her mother's plump hand. "It's only a visit, nothing more."

"I fear I'll never understand you, my dearest. You're so pretty, so popular. You've had men falling at your feet for years now, and you reject them all. Even William Nickerson, the dear boy. I thought for sure he would be the one to win your heart."

"I cannot explain it, Mama. Truly I cannot." At least she *would* not. Putting her fears into words was much too terrifying. "But I've no wish to marry. Especially now, with Papa gone." Jane's eyes misted. "How could I leave you alone?"

"Oh, posh!" Her mother waved away her protestations. "Haven't I Susanna and her brood just a half day's drive from here? And Lucy at Covington Hall, just at the top of the road? You needn't worry over me. Why, I've a mind to quit Glenfield altogether for most of the year, and spend more time in London with my friends. Sometimes I feel as if this house holds too many memories. It's almost a shame that Colin has taken up his own estate in Scotland and not forced us out."

Jane's heart twisted. Was her mother so unhappy? She'd been so wrapped up in her own worries, in formulating her own plan, that she hadn't even recognized her mother's discontent. She clasped her hands together, her head bowed and her eyes squeezed shut to keep the tears at bay.

Her mother planted a kiss on the top of her head. "Go, then, Jane. If it means so much to you, go."

Jane looked up, her eyes brimming. "Thank you, Mama. I'll join you in Town by midsummer, I promise."

Three months' time. She had three months to uncover the family's deepest, darkest secrets—to learn what fate awaited her if she married. Jane swallowed a painful lump in her throat.

She only hoped the truth wasn't worse than her imaginings.

Ashbourne, Derbsyhire

Jane looked up at the yellow stone façade of her cousin's home with a satisfied smile. It was charming, a lovely, vine-traced manor just down the lane from the reputedly grand Richmond Park. She'd yet to glimpse the impressive estate, but the vast park they'd passed in on the drive in from the village was nothing short of magnificent.

Emily's husband Cecil guided her up the steps of his home and across the threshold, a smile illuminating his handsome, fair features.

"Emily, darling. Look who I've brought you," he called out.

Jane heard a squeal of delight followed by the tapping of slippers across a freshly polished floor.

In seconds, Emily stood before her, round with child, her face flushed a pleasing pink.

"I can't believe it—is it really you? Cousin Jane, it's been so very long!" The pretty woman, a good head shorter than Jane, threw her arms around her shoulders and embraced her.

"It's so good to see you, Emily. Why, we were only girls when we last met."

"Yes." Emily nodded, strawberry blond curls dancing about her flushed face. "I was no more than sixteen, for it was just after Mama passed away."

Jane was taken aback, never having heard anyone speak so openly of her Aunt Susan's self-inflicted death. The news, only hinted at, of course, and never spoken of plainly in her presence, had shaken Jane to her very core. She could only wonder if Emily worried as she did about sharing the doomed woman's fate.

Yet Emily looked happy. Jane attempted to shake away her misgivings about her cousin's impending motherhood.

A stout woman with steely gray hair under a white lace cap bustled in, and Emily waved her away with a swish of one delicate hand.

"Oh, no, Mrs. Smythe. I'll show Miss Rosemoor to her room. Just see to her maid." Emily gestured absently toward Bridgette, who stood a few paces behind her mistress. "Come, Jane." She looked up and caught her husband's dubious look, one blond brow raised in censure.

"Cecil, dear, I'm perfectly well. I've been resting the better part of the day."

"If you insist. I'll leave you two to get reacquainted, then." He bowed to the women with a smile and disappeared down a narrow corridor.

"You've no idea how pleased I am to have you

here. I've grown so bored of late, lolling about all day awaiting this babe. I've been desperate for some sort of distraction. I do hope you'll be happy here."

Jane followed her cousin up the stairs and into a cheerful room done in soft shades of pale green and cream. "It's lovely," she exclaimed, standing in the doorway and taking in the unfamiliar surroundings. Green silk hung in wide windows that overlooked the garden, and delicate, hand-painted furniture was scattered about pleasingly—a tall dresser in one corner, a writing desk beneath a window, and a wardrobe opposite the door. A sprigged coverlet was spread invitingly over a beautifully carved maple bed, and Jane realized at once how exhausted she was from her journey. She reached up to stifle a yawn.

Emily peered up at her, her brows drawn over soft brown eyes. "Oh, I'm so sorry. How selfish of me. Of course you must be tired from your travels. I'll have your trunks sent up at once and you shall lie down and rest before dinner."

Jane blinked, yawning again. "Thank you. That would be lovely." Moments later, she sank gratefully to the bed, fully clothed, and fell into a deep, dreamless slumber.

When Jane awoke hours later, deep orange sunlight streamed in through the curtains, casting long shadows on the room's pale floorboards. She sat up with a start, rubbing the sleep from her eyes as Bridgette bustled in.

"Well, miss, it looks as if it's time to get up and start preparin' you for dinner. Shall I fetch a ba–sin?"

"Yes, thank you, Bridgette," she answered, her

mouth dry. "And perhaps a pitcher of cold water, as well?"

"Of course." The maid bustled out again.

Less than an hour later, Jane glanced at her reflection in the glass as Bridgette completed her ministrations. Her chestnut brown hair was piled atop her crown, encircled by a thick band of sapphire blue silk. She frowned, noting the dark smudges beneath her eyes. She looked pale, tired. She pinched her cheeks, hoping to infuse them with some color. Rising from her seat, she stepped into a simply cut evening gown of matching blue silk and waited as Bridgette fastened it up the back and tied the long organza sash beneath her shoulder blades.

Instinctively, she tugged up the neckline, which Bridgette always insisted should be pulled low and taut across her full breasts. No use spilling out of her dress and into her soup. She allowed the maid to fasten a pearl and sapphire choker around her neck, then gave her hair one final pat before heading down to the drawing room to await the summons into dinner.

Her stomach grumbled noisily as she glided down the stairs on satin slippers, breathing in the succulent scent of roasted fowl. Her mouth watered in anticipation. How long had it been since she'd eaten? It was a good thing she was amongst family tonight, for she was likely to bolt down her meal like a ravenous dog.

"Here she comes now," she heard Emily call out, her voice as sweet and melodious as a bell.

Jane stepped into the room, a smile pasted upon her face—a smile that quickly vanished.

Emily rushed to her side, exclaiming over her gown, while Jane stood, rooted firmly to her spot in the doorway as an impossibly tall man rose to stand beside Cecil, his gaze raking boldly up her form. At last his eyes met hers, the most mesmerizing greenish gray eyes she'd ever seen. Jane's lips parted in surprise, her heart accelerating at an alarming rate.

The man raised one brow and then turned away, a look of sheer boredom descending across his noble features.

Jane's mouth snapped shut, her brows drawing together. Why, he looked as if she displeased him! If she could have huffed without seeming rude, she would have done so.

"Miss Rosemoor," Cecil said, "let me introduce you to our distinguished friend and neighbor, Hayden Moreland, the Earl of Westfield. Lord Westfield, I present my wife's cousin, Miss Jane Rosemoor. She's come to us from Essex."

Jane's gaze dropped to the floor and she curtsied on stiff legs.

"A pleasure," the earl bit out stonily, as if her mere presence annoyed him beyond belief.

"Indeed," Jane managed to mutter, refusing to look up into those mesmerizing eyes again. Instead, she fixed her gaze over his shoulder—and what a broad shoulder it was. Silently she chastised herself for allowing her thoughts to travel that route. She let out her breath in relief as the gentlemen moved away toward the sideboard where Cecil poured two neat drinks into tumblers. *Blast it,* she thought. Why was it that her eye was so easily drawn to a handsome man?

"How was your nap?" Emily asked her, laying a hand upon her wrist.

Jane dragged her attention back to her cousin.

"Quite refreshing, thank you. I must say, I had no idea I was so tired until my head touched the pillow. I can't thank you enough for inviting me here, Emily. I'm so looking forward to renewing our acquaintance. It's been far too long."

"I agree. I hope you don't mind Lord Westfield joining us tonight." She glanced over at the men. "I think perhaps Cecil knew we'd be so involved in womanly chatter that he'd do well to have some masculine company. He's a bit gruff and standoffish, Lord Westfield, but he has the best of hearts."

"Is that so?"

"Without a doubt," Emily replied, with seemingly implacable assurance.

Jane stole one more glance at the man, perplexed. If anything, he appeared cold and haughty at first inspection. Well, perhaps that was too judgmental, she corrected herself. He appeared arrogant, that's all. Rude and arrogant.

Lord Westfield stood before the fireplace, one hand resting on the mantel. Her gaze traveled the lengthy route from the tip of his boots to the top of his head. His polished Hessians gleamed ebony in the candlelight, and tight-fitting fawn breeches accentuated muscular legs. A well-cut, dark jacket and striped gray waistcoat stretched taut across his broad chest. His snow white cravat was tied intricately about a long, proud neck. Dark, wavy locks curled just below his ears, not a hair out of place. Everything about his form and dress exuded wealth, nobility, and exceptional taste. But those soft green eyes . . .

She dropped her gaze to her slippers, refusing to allow herself to be drawn back to his eyes. She shook her head, attempting to get her wits back about herself.

At that moment, the butler mercifully stepped in

to announce dinner. Jane sighed in relief as she followed Emily out.

"Perhaps she's waltzed through *my* front door instead, eh, Westfield?" she heard Cecil mutter under his breath to his companion.

Jane paused just beyond the door, curiously awaiting the earl's response.

"I'm afraid not, Tolland," a deep male voice answered. "She won't do. Won't do at all."

Jane felt her cheeks burn. It took every last inch of her reserve to continue on to the dining room without turning and giving the insufferable man a severe dressing down, as he deserved.

She "wouldn't do"? She'd make him regret those words. She tipped her chin in the air and schooled her features into the most cheerful of expressions before taking her seat at the long dining table. Directly across from Lord Westfield.

Bloody arrogant fool.

Chapter Two

Hayden stroked his chin as he observed Miss Rosemoor from across the width of the table. She chatted vivaciously with Emily, obviously doing her damnedest to avoid looking in his direction. When she did slip up and catch his eye, she favored him with a bright smile—a false smile, as it did not reach her eyes. For the life of him, he couldn't figure the woman out.

She was dazzling, no doubt about it. As beautiful and alluring as any woman he'd ever seen. His instant physical attraction had caught him completely off guard. He'd reacted instinctively, made his face blank, unreadable, so as not to betray his interest. It was clear that Tolland requested his company tonight in order to parade his wife's cousin before him, and he ruffled at the insult. Miss Rosemoor was no less than five-and-twenty, if his judgment was correct. A spinster, long settled on the shelf. Was her visit nothing more than a carefully orchestrated maneuver to snare a husband? One in desperate need of a wife, perhaps?

How had she avoided marriage, he wondered, unclaimed at such an advanced age? She must have faults of character, he concluded. Serious flaws. He raised a brow as he considered the possibilities. Perhaps she was bookish, a bluestocking in the worst way. She *did* seem rather intelligent, although he found no fault with that. He preferred intelligence to silliness, no matter the current fashion. Maybe she hadn't any accomplishments to recommend her, though not all men preferred accomplished women. He did, of course, but not all men. He shook his head, perplexed. He could only conclude that it was something more critical, more serious, for her beauty and poise alone would likely be sufficient under normal circumstances to attract a suitable match.

He narrowed his eyes, studying her more intently while she ate. Glossy chestnut hair was swept back from her oval face rather severely, yet the result was striking—her high cheekbones were clearly defined, her regular features showcased by her alabaster skin. Her nose was straight and narrow, neither too large nor too small. Her lips were full, almost sensual, stained a pleasing petal pink. But her eyes were her true crowning jewel—darkly fringed eyes of a deep, sapphire blue. They were round eyes, inquisitive eyes that drew you to them, dared you to look into their dazzling depths. They were no doubt a window to her soul, and Hayden feared them with a staggering intensity.

"I say, Westfield, have you heard a word I've said?"

Hayden blinked hard, reluctantly drawing his gaze from Miss Rosemoor. "Pardon me, Tolland," he muttered. "You were saying?"

"Forget it. I'll not repeat a quarter hour's worth of idle chatter. Shall we shoot tomorrow? What say you?"

"Why not? The day should be fair and mild."

"Oh, Lord Westfield," Emily chimed in, "I'd almost forgotten about the assembly day after tomorrow. Will you attend?"

Hayden took a breath to respond negatively, but before he had the chance to speak, Emily continued on in her usual breathless manner.

"Why, I've got the most brilliant idea! Since I cannot go, perhaps you two could escort Jane to the assembly. Why should she not enjoy a pleasant evening of music and dancing, simply because I cannot go?"

"I'm afraid I cannot—"

"But of course we can," Tolland interrupted Hayden's protestation.

Hayden shot the man a volatile look.

"Really, Emily, I'd rather not," Miss Rosemoor interjected. "I'm here to visit *you*. I've no need of such entertainments, and perhaps Lord Westfield has other engagements, besides."

"Please, I insist," Emily said, her brow furrowed. "You must go, and I will not take no for an answer. Tell her, Cecil, darling. She must go, and then report back to me who dances with whom, and what all the ladies are wearing."

Tolland nodded. "I'm afraid my wife will give you no peace until you agree to go, Miss Rosemoor. Westfield and I make fine escorts, I assure you."

"Well, I . . . If you insist. I don't wish to disturb anyone's plans."

"Nonsense," Tolland said. "Westfield and I hadn't any plans, had we, old boy?" Tolland turned to him with a smirk. He was obviously enjoying this. Immensely.

"I suppose not," Hayden muttered. He looked up and his gaze collided with Miss Rosemoor's. For the first time, he noticed a dimple in her left cheek. His heart began to pound; a vein in his temple throbbed.

With an inward groan, he tore his gaze away. It

took a concentrated effort to force his usual mask of ennui to descend across his features before he spoke again. "I'm afraid Miss Rosemoor might find our local entertainments a bit provincial for her tastes."

"Why ever should I?" Miss Rosemoor shot back. "I'm not some missish debutante who turns her nose up at a country dance."

"No, a debutante you're not."

"With age comes wisdom, I always say, and tolerance, too. Why, I'm surprised a man of your *vast* experience hasn't learned such a lesson." She smiled sweetly at him, despite her sharp tongue.

"I've no doubt you could teach me a thing or two, Miss Rosemoor."

"Certainly nothing of interest to you," she retorted.

"I think you'd be surprised at my range of interests, especially where ladies are concerned." Hayden suddenly pictured the rapier-tongued Miss Rosemoor lying naked in his bed, her chestnut tresses falling enticingly across those full breasts she obviously took great pleasure in displaying. *That* raised his interest, among other things. It had been far too long since he'd enjoyed the pleasures of a mistress.

"You underestimate me, Lord Westfield. I wouldn't be surprised in the least." Miss Rosemoor shook her head with a scowl. "Perhaps it isn't such a good idea that we go to the assembly."

"No, I insist," he challenged, inexorably sealing his fate. "I'm certain Mrs. Tolland will vouch that I can be a perfect gentleman, when necessary."

"Of course. It's settled, then." Emily rose, placing her napkin on the table with a nervous smile. "Let's leave the men to their port, Jane. We've much to talk about."

Hayden looked away, his gaze fixed upon the wall

as the ladies swept out with a swish of silk. Devil take it, he thought. He had no choice but to go to the blasted assembly now. Perhaps he *had* underestimated her.

"Have you had an occasion to visit Grandmama and Aunt Gertrude recently?" Jane asked, then took a sip of her steaming tea. She peered at Emily over the rim of her cup. The warm brew soothed her nerves as well as her throat, still parched from her journey.

"I'm afraid not," Emily answered, shaking her head. "I haven't seen Grandmama in years. Aunt Gertrude always says she's not up to it. It was perhaps four or five years ago that I saw her last, and even then she barely knew me. Most disturbing."

Jane nodded, her throat constricting uncomfortably. Dare she broach the subject with her cousin? No, she resolved; perhaps some things were better left unsaid, considering Emily's condition.

Deep baritone voices startled her as the men strode in, and she set aside her teacup with a frown. Why didn't Lord Westfield take his leave? It was clear he found her company unpleasant, and his forced civility was wearing on her nerves.

"There you are, Cecil darling," Emily called out. Cecil came to stand behind his wife, his hands resting on her shoulders. Lord Westfield, silent now, took a seat at the far end of the room, beside the door. "Perhaps Jane will play for us," Emily said, hopeful eyes turned toward her. "You *do* play?"

"Of course," Jane replied. "Not as well as my sister, but I play."

"By all means, then." Emily tilted her head

toward the pianoforte. "It would please me enormously."

Jane rose and strode over to the instrument, a lovely one at that and obviously well cared-for. Its keys gleamed, the wooden case polished brightly. Jane took a seat on the narrow, embroidered bench and ran her fingers across the keys. She couldn't resist stealing a glance at the earl, who sat stiffly, his gaze fixed on the fire. His words echoed in her ears. *She won't do,* he'd said.

With a practiced smile, she began to play—Beethoven's "Fur Elise," the most difficult piece she knew, one she played flawlessly and effortlessly. Her fingers flew over the ivory, her heart soaring at the beautiful sounds emanating from the finely tuned instrument. Oh, "she'd do," she thought to herself with a smug smile. She wouldn't have him, wouldn't have anyone, of course. But "she'd do" just fine. She always did.

When her piece was finished, she looked up to her cousin's beatific smile.

"Oh, Jane, that was lovely. I had no idea you played so well. If your sister is better, then she must play magnificently."

"Susanna is quite talented," Jane agreed.

"Wasn't that lovely, Cecil?" Emily laid her hand on her husband's arm.

"It was," Cecil answered. "Eh, Westfield?"

Jane started in surprise as the earl rose from his seat and strode over to the pianoforte, leaning indolently against it.

"Indeed. You play tolerably well, Miss Rosemoor. And do your accomplishments extend beyond the pianoforte?"

Jane's gaze snapped up to meet his, her sensibilities pricked. "I read both Greek and Latin, speak four languages, and can quote the ancient Greek philosophers with ease. I paint quite nicely—landscapes as well as china—and I sit a horse very well. Does that rate to your satisfaction, my lord?"

One corner of Lord Westfield's mouth twitched, and he arched a brow in reply. "You speak your mind," he said, his jaw flexing perceptively. "Some might see that as a flaw in a lady."

"Indeed?" She tipped her chin defiantly as she rose to stand before him. "And have you ever considered that ladies might find rudeness and arrogance offensive in a gentleman?"

"Or is it solely the perception of rudeness or arrogance when none exists?" he countered.

"Why should I perceive such traits if at least a hint of them weren't painfully evident? It's not as if I go about expecting ill manners—"

"I say," Cecil cut in. "Perhaps we can convince Emily to play for us." He turned toward Jane, his pale eyes pleading. "She's modest, of course, but her voice is incomparable. She'll only agree if you insist."

Jane opened her mouth to speak but closed it again as Emily hurried over to her side.

"Oh, if you insist, Jane. Here, now." She patted the bench, her eyes practically goggled. "Sit back down and turn the pages for me." Jane watched as Emily exchanged a desperate look with her husband.

"Of course." Jane sat compliantly, the conversation effectively over. Lord Westfield moved away, back to his seat by the door.

As Emily began to play, Jane peered back over her shoulder. With a sharp intake of breath, she watched incredulously as Lord Westfield's mouth curved into an all-too-arrogant grin.

Actually *smiling* at her, the maddening man! She

smiled back brightly, maintaining her façade, and
then turned to face the keys with nary a tremor, despite her churning emotions.

Men. She'd never understand them.

Jane tried not to frown as Lord Westfield's carriage
pulled up before the assembly hall. Crowds of people
spilled out onto the street in their finery as con-
veyances jostled about, depositing their occupants
here and there on the cobbles below. As Jane took
Cecil's arm and stepped out into the cool night, the
lilting notes of the orchestra reached her ears while
the breeze caressed her cheek. There was a hum in
the air; the excitement was almost palpable.

She turned and watched as their silent companion alighted, joining her and Cecil on the street.
Lord Westfield hadn't spoken a single word the entire drive. Instead he'd sat in stony silence as Cecil
pointed out local landmarks and made idle chatter.
Jane had felt as if she would scream if they did not
accomplish their destination in due haste. Why
ever had she agreed to this?

Pushing through the crowd, their party at last
made their way to the door. Jane instinctively
reached down to smooth the skirts of her favorite
gown as they entered the assembly. She'd thought to
leave behind these yards of crimson watered silk,
thinking she'd not likely have the opportunity to
wear such a fine gown. She was thankful now for her
change of heart. She knew the cut of the gown, with
its deep, square neckline and high, tightly fitted
waist, showed off her figure to its best advantage. It
was impossible to feel anything but confident in this
gown, and she was grateful for the self-assurance.

They entered the main room, where long lines of

couples engaged in a lively country dance. It was an attractive room, ornate in décor, done in red and gilt with sparkling chandeliers providing warm light from above.

Jane glanced up at her escorts, faintly amused by the opposite expressions worn by the two men. Cecil's pale face was lit with obvious pleasure; he turned and bowed cheerfully in greeting as they made their way through the crowd. Lord Westfield, on the other hand, looked almost pained. He moved forward without moving his head, clearly avoiding eye contact with anyone and coming perilously close to cutting several attractive ladies who visibly strove to catch his eye and initiate conversation. Jane almost laughed aloud at his self-imposed discomfort.

For her part, she remembered herself and resolved to enjoy the evening despite her misgivings. No use fretting over nothing. This seemed an agreeable, fashionable gathering, and she enjoyed such amusements.

"I say, Miss Rosemoor, there's Sir Thomas Huxley and his three daughters. Come, let me introduce you. Delightful girls, just delightful."

"Of course," Jane murmured, following Cecil to a group clustered beside the refreshment table.

A quarter hour later, Jane eagerly moved away from the Huxleys, convinced that Cecil found the girls far *too* delightful. His flirtations had made her more than a little uncomfortable, especially when she thought of sweet Emily confined at home and so sorry to miss such a party. It took a conscious effort for Jane to remove the furrow from her brow and force her lips from a pursed position to a pleasant smile.

She and Cecil rejoined Lord Westfield, who stood

against the wall with his hands clasped behind his back. Suddenly half a dozen ladies flocked about them, all demanding introductions to Jane, while batting their lashes solicitously at Lord Westfield. Yet he rebuked all attempts at polite conversation with his demeanor alone. Jane couldn't help but roll her eyes heavenward, both for the ladies' silly and obvious behavior and for Lord Westfield's evident disdain. Clearly, he was a much sought-after prey.

One particular lady seemed far more interested in Cecil. All but ignoring Lord Westfield, the striking brunette sidled up to Cecil with a coquettish smile.

"My dear Mr. Tolland, you must introduce me to your lovely companion. I don't believe I have the pleasure of her acquaintance."

Lord Westfield eyed her coldly and turned away with a sneer.

"Lady Adele," Cecil gushed. "How lovely you look tonight. You must allow me to introduce my wife's cousin, Miss Jane Rosemoor of Essex. Westfield and I have the honor of escorting her tonight. Miss Rosemoor, I present Lady Adele Etheridge."

The two women curtsied to one another. "A pleasure," Jane said. "You look so familiar, Lady Adele. Perhaps we've met in Town?"

"It's quite possible." Her gaze traveled to Cecil's face. "My late husband and I frequently took residence in Mayfair during the summer months."

A widow, Jane thought. *How interesting.*

After what felt like an interminable time, Lady Adele finally moved away with a swish of silk and the lingering scent of rosewater. Jane's brows rose as the woman turned and glanced back over her shoulder once more, favoring Cecil with an inviting smile before disappearing through the crowd.

At last alone, Cecil turned toward Jane. "Will you dance, Miss Rosemoor?"

Jane returned his easy smile. "Of course. I'd be delighted." She reached for his arm, but he shook his head.

"Oh, I'm not much of a dancer myself. But I'm sure Lord Westfield will accommodate you."

Jane cringed as the music switched to a waltz. *Of all the bad timing.*

She looked up at Lord Westfield with trepidation, expecting an expression of distaste. Instead, not a trace of any emotion whatsoever showed in his countenance. He simply offered her his arm.

Jane hesitated for a fraction of a second, inexplicably terrified to touch him, to connect with him physically in any way.

His eyes darkened at the perceived slight. "Does the prospect displease you so intensely?"

Jane's face flooded with heat, and she waved her fan, pretending to be affected by the room's warmth. "I . . . no. Of course not. It would be my pleasure," she lied, reaching for his arm. She followed him to the center of the room on weak legs.

She barely felt the floor beneath her slippers as she reached a hand up to his shoulder, the other clasped tightly in his. His nearness positively unsettled her. She could feel his heat, warming her skin beneath the thin fabric of her gown and all but burning her hand through the layers of wool and kidskin that separated them. She thought of nothing save regulating her breathing as they began to glide across the floor, the sound of her heart overpowering the strains of the waltz. She was keenly aware that his touch, his closeness, affected her physically in ways she'd never before experienced, and the thought disturbed her greatly. Her eyes boldly sought his face, wondering if he was similarly afflicted. As if he sensed her appraisal, his eyes met hers.

Jane forgot to breathe.

Seconds later, she let out her breath in a rush, still unable to look away from the mossy depths of his eyes. She swallowed hard. *I should say something*, she thought in panic. Anything, to break this spell. But he spoke, instead.

"You did not include dancing on your list of accomplishments," he said, his tone clipped. "An oversight, I'm sure."

Jane sucked in her breath, averting her gaze at once. Was he insulting her?

As if he'd read her mind, he continued. "I meant that as a compliment. No use getting yourself into a temper. You're an exceedingly graceful dancer. I can't imagine a more lovely partner."

Her gaze flew back to his. "I would never indulge in a fit of temper in public," she replied coolly.

"Then I apologize for suggesting you would." He smiled down at her, almost patronizingly.

"In fact," she added, "I rarely indulge in such fits at all."

"Indeed?" His smile widened.

Jane knew she was speaking nonsense, but it was all she could manage in order to keep from dwelling on the fact that he'd complimented her. Had he called her lovely? No, she corrected. He'd only said she was a lovely dancer. Quite different.

The music ended. Jane tried to step away from him, but he only held her closer, refusing to release his grip on her. "Isn't it customary to engage a partner for two consecutive dances?"

"Perhaps two dances," she said, feeling foolish,

"but not necessarily consecutive." As the music struck up again, Jane's mind raced to find a suitable topic of conversation. "Do you not come to Town often?" she asked at last.

"I attend to my parliamentary duty, yes. Each year. Why do you ask?"

"It's just odd, isn't it, that we've never before met? I've come to London for, oh, eight Seasons now, and yet our paths have never crossed. I thought perhaps you were one of those men who preferred the country."

"I do prefer the country. But I don't dislike Town. Eight Seasons, you say?"

Jane sighed impatiently. "Well, of course I haven't actively participated in all eight. But I do come to Town each summer with my family. I find it amusing enough." He peered at her oddly, as if attempting to solve a riddle. "Why are you looking at me like that?"

His face went immediately blank.

Moments passed in silence.

"And have you figured it out?" she asked.

"I have no idea what you mean."

"Why I'm on the shelf. Have you figured it out yet? It's terribly obvious that the question is on your mind." He wouldn't be the first, Jane thought, nor was he likely to be the last.

His only response was a quirk of the brow.

"Because I choose to be, my lord," she supplied. "I've had a number of offers each year, offers that I chose to decline."

"And what were your reasons for declining them, if I might be so bold as to ask?"

She shrugged. "I suppose no one suited," she lied. "I have very discerning tastes."

"Is that so?"

"Indeed."

"I suppose, then, that one with such, what was the phrase? 'Discerning tastes,' that was it"—he cleared his throat, obviously suppressing a chuckle—"that one with such discerning tastes prefers the unmarried state, then?"

He made no effort to cloak his amusement, and Jane's hackles rose at once. "I find it interesting that every man assumes a woman prefers the married state over spinsterhood. I enjoy a great deal of freedoms that a husband would likely deny a wife."

"Such as?"

"Such as, well . . ." Jane was flustered, suddenly unable to think of a good response. Just what activities *would* a husband restrict, she wondered. "Such as being able to travel whenever I take a notion to visit relations, for one."

"Hmmm, I see," he murmured. "Yes, a husband would likely want to keep you at home, wouldn't he?" He smiled wickedly at her, his eyes lit with amusement.

Her cheeks burning yet again, Jane looked away, past Lord Westfield's broad shoulder. Her attention was immediately distracted by Cecil, who hurried along the perimeter of the dance floor just steps behind Lady Adele. The unpleasant idea that perhaps Cecil had lovers, that his considerate attentions to his wife were nothing more than a façade, startled her.

Jane pulled away from Lord Westfield, suddenly dizzy and a bit queasy. "I think I need some air."

He held her shoulders as she swayed against him. "Come, let's step outside." Without waiting for her reply, he took her elbow and steered her out, through a set of open doors and onto a wide, sweeping terrace. Crowds of people milled about, strolling arm in arm and enjoying the refreshing, crisp air.

Lord Westfield led her to a stone bench, where she sank gratefully. Jane blinked rapidly, attempting to regain her equilibrium.

"Wait right here," he said. "I'll get you something to drink."

She nodded dumbly in reply, feeling foolish yet again. Would this night never end?

Chapter Three

Hayden reached for a flute from a silver tray. Grasping it tightly in his gloved hand, he strode back out to the terrace. Miss Rosemoor sat just as he'd left her, perched on the edge of the bench and looking quite pale.

She took the proffered champagne and gulped it down. His eyes widened dubiously. He certainly hoped she was accustomed to the effects of ingesting half a flute of champagne so efficiently.

He stood uncomfortably, unsure what to do, while she closed her eyes and took several deep breaths. The swell of her breasts rose provocatively with each inhalation, tempting him with images of them spilling out of the scarlet-colored silk. The color of a temptress, he reminded himself. Was she trying to seduce him?

Her dress was close to indecent, hugging her curves in all the right places and displaying an ungodly amount of bosom. The rich, jeweled tone set off her skin to perfection, made her eyes sparkle like the finest polished sapphires. Not a single sane man in the room tonight had been able to take his eyes off her. Sir James Quigley had nearly tripped over his own feet, trying to reach her side as they quitted the dance floor moments before. Surely she knew what effect a frock like that had on a man. Unless the man were blind, of course.

At last she opened her eyes. Even in the moonlight their intense color reached out to him, capturing him in their hold. He looked down at once, pretending to study his fingernails.

"Thank you, Lord Westfield. I feel much improved. I have no idea what came over me. Perhaps I'm still weary from my journey."

"No need to apologize, Miss Rosemoor. I'm only pleased to see you so well recovered. Perhaps we should take a turn. Are you up to it?"

"I suppose," she replied, wariness evident in her voice. She stood and reached for his arm, placing her hand in the crook of his elbow. In silence they strolled the length of the terrace, then back again.

"Better?" he asked.

She nodded her assent. "Much." They ambled over to the stone railing and looked out at the garden below, where paper lanterns cast shadows beneath the old yews. Minutes passed in silence.

Sensing her presence like a warning bell, Hayden looked over one shoulder with a scowl as Adele hurried to his side, her dark brows knitted into a scowl.

"Westfield," Adele said, her voice sharp. "A moment, please."

He cast a scornful glance at the woman, but did not respond.

"Hayden, please," she repeated, her voice rising. Hayden saw Miss Rosemoor flinch at the sound of his given name on the woman's lips. *Damn Adele's impropriety.*

"It's Tolland," Adele added.

With an inward groan, he realized he'd better hear what she had to say. "If you'll excuse me for one moment, Miss Rosemoor?"

She only glared at him in reply.

He moved away with Adele, grasping her elbow much too firmly. "You'd better make this fast, Adele. I haven't the patience for your games."

She looked up into his eyes, her own pale blue ones full of bitterness. "I hate to disturb your pleasant evening but if you venture into the maze, you'll find your *dear* friend Tolland has injured his ankle—perhaps broken it. He needs your assistance at once. I was forced to leave him there."

"Need I ask how you managed to find yourself alone with a married man in the maze?" he asked through clenched teeth.

She tipped her chin in the air defiantly with a mutinous glint in her eyes.

"No, I suppose not. Smile, my sweet. That scowl isn't the least becoming."

Without looking back, Hayden strode away from Adele and back to Miss Rosemoor, who stood watching the exchange with unmasked curiosity.

"What's wrong? What's happened to Cecil?" Miss Rosemoor asked as soon as he reached her side.

"Nothing of any import. Just female theatrics, I'm afraid. Perhaps you should go back inside for a moment, and I'll rejoin you shortly." He placed one hand on the small of her back, guiding her toward the doors leading back into the assembly hall.

She twisted herself away from his grasp and turned angrily to face him. "I demand you tell me what is going on, my lord. This instant. Where is Cecil?"

His anger rose a pitch at her impertinence, the blood pounding at his temples. "If you must know, he's somewhere in the maze with a twisted ankle, the fool," he spat out. "And I'm sure word is spreading like wildfire as to where he was and just who he—"

"Let us go at once." She strode off toward the steps leading down to the garden.

"I'm afraid you're not going anywhere but back inside, Miss Rosemoor." He reached for her arm. "And that's not a request."

She spun to face him, her face livid. "Not a request?" she sputtered. "You're *ordering* me to go back inside?"

"Very astute, Miss Rosemoor. That's precisely what I'm doing."

Almost regally, she drew herself up to her full height, her face only inches from his. "I don't know what type of lady you're accustomed to dealing with, my lord, but let me assure you that I take orders from no man. My father didn't order me about, nor would my brother dare, for fear of having his ears boxed. Emily's husband is injured, and I'm going to see to his welfare. Whether or not you accompany me is immaterial—"

"And how do you suppose to find him? Are you familiar with this particular maze, Miss Rosemoor? It's enormous, as twisted as a labyrinth. Do you wish to find yourself lost in there, alone in the dark?"

Her arrogant gaze faltered. "Then after you, my lord." She gestured ahead of herself with the sweep of one graceful arm.

"Certainly you realize that we cannot be seen—" he broke off, clearing his throat. "You've just arrived here in this district and I should suppose you'd wish to keep your reputation intact. If I might say so, venturing out into the darkened maze in my company would not be the most prudent move on your part."

She shrugged. "Surely when they see us emerge with the injured Cecil in tow, they'll understand. Besides, I haven't time for such worries." She turned and skimmed down the steps, the red folds of her dress billowing out behind her.

Damn it to hell, he had no choice but to go after her.

Across the lawn they hurried, the lanterns barely illuminating the soft grass beneath their feet. Silently they entered the maze, high hedgerows reaching more than twelve feet on either side of them. "Tolland," Hayden called out.

"Cecil," Miss Rosemoor echoed.

Silence greeted them.

"There's a clearing in the center," Hayden said. "Follow me; it's three rights and then a sharp left."

"Are you certain?" She strode on ahead of him. "Perhaps we should split up—"

"So I can lose you in here? Stay close by my side. I know this maze well."

He was relieved to see her acquiesce, waiting for him to reach her side before matching her pace to his. They hastily followed the path, illuminated only by the full moon above them.

As they hurried on, she turned and cast him an appraising glance. "You know this maze well?" she asked with raised brows, a wry smile on her lips. "Dare I ask how you became so well acquainted with it?"

"It's probably best that you don't," he answered with a tight smile, vaguely remembering an assortment of trysts from his past, inconsequential encounters with experienced, willing women of little reputation. He cautiously eyed the woman walking by his side. "You've a very sharp tongue, you know. Perhaps your father *should* have ordered you around a bit."

"My tongue is only sharp when provoked beyond

measure. In fact, I'm generally known for my pleasant disposition."

"Is that so? Interesting. I suppose I'll have to take your word."

"Haven't you heard that you'll catch more flies with honey than vinegar, Lord Westfield? It's a very common adage. Perhaps you should take it to heart."

"But why settle for a mere fly when I can have a wasp instead? I'm growing rather fond of our verbal spars, Miss Rosemoor. You're a worthy opponent, indeed."

"Humph." She tossed her head, apparently rendered speechless.

They reached the clearing in no time, a bubbling fountain in its center shadowed by a towering yew. Splitting up, they each paced the area, peering into the shadowed recesses and calling loudly for the missing man with no response.

"Tolland, where the devil are you?" he called out. What game was the man playing?

Nothing.

"Any other ideas?" Miss Rosemoor asked acidly.

His nerves prickled at her tone. "I suppose we should follow the path to the end, and then double back to the entrance. It's possible he managed to drag himself out by now."

Miss Rosemoor's head swung left, then right. Two paths led away from the clearing. "Well? Which way?"

"This way." He set off to the left. "Tolland?" he called out, his hands cupped to his mouth.

"Cecil?"

Still no answer.

Hayden cursed under his breath, vowing to wring Tolland's neck when he found him. He'd like to wring Adele's neck, too, he thought, deepening the scowl that already darkened his features. *Insidious woman.* Adele had been his mistress for more than a year, nothing more than a casual dalliance with a willing widow. But then her true nature had revealed itself—Adele was a manipulative, petulant woman with designs on Richmond Park. Her demands were ever increasing, her unwelcome visits an annoyance. One day he'd returned from a brief trip to London to find Adele settled in the salon with Madeline, attempting to ingratiate herself with the girl. That had been the last straw.

He'd swiftly and unequivocally ended it. Since that time, Adele had tried every trick in the book, from feigning illness to parading her newest conquests beneath his nose, hoping to make him jealous. Her games had annoyed him, nothing more, until now. Now she'd gone too far. Hell, he didn't care if she shared her favors with every available man in Derbyshire, but Tolland . . . He grimaced, thinking of Emily. Anyone but Tolland. Tolland was easy prey with his roving eye and flirtatious manner. But Tolland's indiscretions had always been that—discreet. There was nothing discreet about Adele, and the devious woman would make certain that Emily knew of her husband's transgressions. She cut her teeth on such triumph. He wouldn't allow it.

Hayden looked up, surprised to find that they'd somehow worked their way back to the clearing again without accomplishing the far side of the maze.

"Well?" Miss Rosemoor was slightly breathless.

He scratched his head. Left, wasn't it? Or right? He couldn't remember.

"Can you not find your way out?" she asked.

"Of course I can. Let's try this again. Left here. Then right. Then two more lefts."

He continued on, hoping he was correct.

Moments later they stopped again, decidedly back at the same juncture as before.

"We're right back where we started," she cried, stating the obvious. "I thought you knew this maze well."

"It's been a while. Perhaps we should turn back. Tolland must've already made his own way out. Otherwise he'd have heard us by now."

She nodded in agreement and hurried back across the clearing.

"This way, Miss Rosemoor." He pointed to the left. "This will take us back to the assembly hall."

She frowned at him. "I'm afraid you're mistaken, my lord. This way will take us back." She pointed to the right.

"Having never been here before, I'm not sure how you can say that with such authority. It's left."

"I've a good sense of direction."

"As do I," he replied. "It's this way."

Both stood, glaring at the other.

Finally, she shook her head with a sigh. "If you insist."

Fifteen minutes later they were back where they had started. Again.

"Left, you said," she huffed. "Now I know never to listen to you. I *told* you it was to the right. Good sense of direction, you say?"

The exasperating woman flounced off to the right, and there was nothing he could do but follow her.

Right back to the exact same juncture.

"Oh, this is madness." She dashed to the center of the clearing and stood on tiptoe on the fountain's pedestal, bracing her hands against the circular trough. "Cecil," she yelled, her voice rising in panic. "Someone? Anyone?"

"Tolland?" he joined in. "Can anyone hear us?"

An owl hooted.

She turned on him, her eyes flashing in the moonlight. "Now what are we to do?"

"We rest for a moment, and then we try again. To the left."

She let out a rush of breath. "Perhaps I could use a rest. I *am* a bit winded." Her eyes were bright, her cheeks stained strawberry from the exertion.

Damnation, she was beautiful. Perhaps the most beautiful woman he'd ever met. His gaze met hers, his heart thumping against his ribs. He hadn't meant to find himself alone—unchaperoned—with the woman. In fact, he'd protested against the very idea. But now, here they were, all alone. Unwatched.

Caught in his gaze, she stepped away from him, backing against the solid wall of clipped yew like a cornered animal. As he moved toward her, he was conscious of the fact that his mind ceased functioning properly and instinct took over, all but clouding his sensibility.

"Almost a full moon," she said at last, breaking the charged silence. "At least it's a lovely night to get lost in."

His gaze followed hers, up to the bright orb in the darkened sky, a wispy cloud shrouding its lower quadrant.

He took another step toward her, no more than an arm's length from her now. She turned her head, biting her lower lip.

"We're sure to have a pleasant summer," she added, still averting her gaze. "Quite warm, too."

He wanted to kiss her. It went against all reason, against every rational thought—against his very character. She was a lady, after all. A virgin. An innocent. Emily's cousin, for God's sake. But damn it, he wanted to kiss her. Now. If, for no other reason, to silence her mindless prattle about the weather.

He closed the distance between them, placing his hands on the tree's trunk on either side of her head and effectively trapping her. He could hear her rapid breaths, see her eyes widen with something akin to fear. There were no other sounds save the gurgling of the fountain as water trickled from a stone cherub down to the trough below.

Indeed, they were decidedly alone.

"Whatever are you doing?" she asked, her voice a husky whisper.

"I thought perhaps to kiss you," he answered, unable to suppress a smile as her eyes widened a considerable fraction.

"Kiss me? Have you lost your wits?"

"I'm fairly certain I've my wits about me." He inched his mouth closer to hers, her breath caressing his lips, tantalizing him. "Shall I show you how it's done? I touch my lips, thus"— he brushed his lips slowly, seductively, across hers—"to yours." Her deep blue eyes, inky in the moonlight, widened a fraction more. "Like so."

Then she startled him by reaching a hand up to his head. "Here," she whispered, "you've got something . . . a bit of a leaf . . ."

He felt her fingers brush above his ear and he shuddered at the contact. With a quick movement, he reached up and caught her hand, brought it to his mouth as he breathed in her scent, an intoxicating mingling of spices. Cinnamon, perhaps, mixed with anise? His gaze sought hers as he pressed his lips against her palm. Her breath caught, but her eyes didn't leave his face.

Damn propriety—he had to kiss her. His head dipped toward hers and he captured her mouth with his own, his heart hammering in his chest. He reached down to her throat, felt her pulse jump beneath his thumb as her lips parted, allowing access to his plundering tongue. She tasted like champagne mixed with the sweetest honey.

He felt her hands tangle in his hair, drawing him closer still. He pressed himself fully against her, his urgent erection firm against her hip.

She pulled back at once from the intimate contact. In a flash her hand flew out and struck him solidly across the cheek. "How dare you!"

His hand rose to his stinging cheek, his mind reeling in shock. Most marriageable ladies would eagerly allow him to kiss them senseless if he'd taken a notion to it, the threat of being caught nothing more than an enticement. Which was precisely why he hadn't made a habit of it. What a foolish, imprudent thing to have done. Next thing he knew she'd be measuring windows for drapes at Richmond Park.

"I assure you it will never happen again." He would make damn sure of it.

She opened her mouth as if to speak, then snapped it shut.

"Come now, after eight Seasons it's surely not the first time you've been kissed," he drawled, still smarting with annoyance. At himself. At her.

"I'll have you know it *is*," she replied with surprising vehemence. "I am a lady, sir, and I don't go about kissing men thither and yon. Dear God, what if someone came upon us?" She looked around wildly, her face suddenly a mask of panic and confusion. "What if we were forced to wed? How could I be so stupid, so impulsive?" Her voice rose a pitch to near hysteria.

"We've been yelling with no response for more

than an hour. It's obvious there's no one about to witness your ruin."

She nodded mutely, visibly gathering her composure.

"I said it would never happen again, and you have my word as a gentleman that it won't. Now let's get out of here and find Tolland."

"Fine," she replied tartly, walking on ahead of him. Toward the *right*.

He followed her silently, a bit shaken by the terror he'd seen in her eyes. Damnation, he'd only kissed her. He'd said it would never happen again, and by God, he'd make bloody sure it didn't.

"To think I actually listened to you," she muttered as he caught up to her. "Good sense of direction, indeed. I think perhaps you must have dozed off during lessons explaining the difference between left and right."

"I can assure you I'm perfectly capable of telling left from right, Miss Rosemoor. Here, allow me to demonstrate. The lady to my *right* claims not to have fits of temper in public, yet clearly cannot hold her tongue when piqued."

"Oooh!" Her cheeks reddened. "If ever a man was undeserving of my confidence in—"

"Confidence?" he sputtered indignantly. "If *that* was a show of confidence then I'm—"

"Cecil!" Miss Rosemoor interrupted, calling out shrilly as she dashed ahead of him.

"Cecil?" He looked up in confusion, surprised to see that they'd somehow found their way back to the maze's entrance. There sat Tolland on a wrought-iron bench, a dazed expression on his face as he rubbed one visibly swollen ankle.

Bloody hell, more than his ankle would be in need of a poultice when he was through with the man.

Chapter Four

"I'm sorry, mum," Emily's lady's maid said. "I'm afraid you'll have to entertain yourself this afternoon. Mrs. Tolland's taken to her bed."

Jane's heart began to race. "She's not unwell, is she?" It was still more than a moon till the babe was expected.

"No, she's well enough, miss. Just a bout of the blues is all. Comes and goes with my mistress. Don't fret; it'll pass. It always does."

Jane's racing heart progressed to a full gallop. The blues? Emily seemed so merry, so cheerful. Fear raced through Jane's veins.

She could put it off no longer. She would find Cecil immediately and make the necessary arrangements for a visit to The Orchards. It was time to see her grandmama, to uncover the truth—to face it herself once and for all. She would go tomorrow, once she was assured of Emily's well-being.

An hour later the arrangements were made, and Jane hurried upstairs to fetch her shawl. She'd go for a walk, explore the grounds. The sun was high in the sky, with not a cloud in sight, and the air held the promise of warmth. A perfect afternoon for an invigorating stroll. From her bedroom window, she could see a shimmering lake in the distance—an inviting destination.

She set off with a scowl, drawing her shawl tightly about her shoulders as her thoughts returned to her cousin's plight. Perhaps she was wrong—perhaps Emily's maid was simply overstating it. After all, most women occasionally had mild bouts of the blues, didn't they? Perhaps it was nothing more serious than that, she assured herself as she ambled across the manicured lawn and headed toward the wood, densely shadowed by enormous trees. The rugged, untamed landscape filled her with awe as she walked on, sure that she'd never before seen such beautiful land. Something about Derbyshire felt *right* to her. She felt eerily at home here even though many years had passed since her last visit to this district.

She passed through two large boulders, amazed at their impressive size. There was nothing like this in all of Essex. For a brief moment she wondered where Cecil's land ended and Lord Westfield's began. *Dear Lord,* she thought, *don't let me accidentally trespass into his park.* She should've asked someone about the estate's borders before setting off so impulsively. The last thing she wanted to risk was accidentally bumping into the man.

Especially after last night. Her cheeks burned at the memory of his kiss. It was bad enough that she'd allowed it, but for a moment she'd actually allowed herself to enjoy it. She'd been so careful all these years, never allowing a flirtation to progress to anything physical. She'd dodged her fair share of kisses, turning her cheek and scolding eager young men for their boldness. But it had been different with Lord Westfield, as if he'd paralyzed her with his presence. She'd only meant to go into the maze in search of Cecil—nothing more. She should have heeded his protestations.

But she hadn't truly thought he would corner her like he had, his ardor catching her completely off guard. It was only when she'd felt the evidence of his arousal that she'd finally snapped to her senses.

Her initial instinct upon meeting Lord Westfield had been to act her most charming, alluring self. Just for spite, so she could summarily dismiss him as easily as he had dismissed her upon first inspection. Yet she'd been unable to do so—somehow he pushed her beyond her usual limits and forced her to match wits at each and every turn. What was it about the man that was so different from the rest— the ones whom she'd been able to smile sweetly at and keep a civil tongue around, despite the temptation to do otherwise?

She'd never fully understand the male species. It would seem she had defeated her purpose, lashing out at him as she had since the moment they'd met. But his response had been to kiss her. And instead of being pleased with her accomplishment and subsequently rebuffing him—as he'd deserved—she'd not only allowed the kiss, but responded with a terrifying, overpowering passion. She'd felt his kiss right down to her toes, and she'd wanted more—far more than any proper maiden should dare wish for.

She shook her head in frustration as a single tear escaped the corner of her eye. She wiped it away and hurried on, scolding herself as she quickened her pace. Whatever had come over her? More often than not she was satisfied with her life—with the choices she'd made. She'd enjoyed a fair amount of popularity, and the proposals she managed to garner each year served to validate her womanhood, to assure her of her desirability, to remind her that she was alone because she *chose* to be alone.

Other times she thought she'd die from longing.

She'd lie awake in bed at night, her heart in knots, wishing desperately to find the sweet, abiding affection her sister Susanna had found in Mr. Merrill, or the consummate joining of heart and soul that her dear friend Lucy had found with Lord Mandeville. But those things were not meant for her—she'd known it all along.

Forcing herself to dismiss her dour thoughts, she continued on, carefully picking her way through the foliage, ducking under branches and dodging stones in her path. At last she emerged from the dense wood, the lake finally in her sights. She quickened her pace in anticipation, but stopped short as she passed a clump of trees to her immediate right. Was she hearing things? She was almost certain she'd heard someone crying. She stepped closer, sure that her ears were playing tricks on her. But the sound got louder as she neared a towering fir, and she peered anxiously around its trunk.

And then she saw her—a small slip of a girl with tangled blond hair and a dirt-smeared face hidden amongst the drooping branches. Her gaze took in the child's dress—soiled, but certainly quality. Well cut from fine fabrics. Definitely a gentleman's daughter.

"Good afternoon," she called out. "Are you hurt, child?"

The girl turned toward her, eyes wide with terror as she shrunk back against the tree.

"N-no," she stammered, burying her face in her hands.

"Are you lost?"

The girl shook her head, then changed her response to an uncertain nod. "I thought to go to the fishpond but I must have taken a wrong turn," came her reply, muffled through her hands. "I was angry at Miss Crosley, you see, and—I—I can't find my way back," she sobbed.

"Well, perhaps I can help. My name is Jane. What's yours?"

"Madeline." The child peered out from behind her hands.

"A pleasure to meet you, Madeline. Now that we are friends, you must tell me who your mama and papa are. Perhaps I can help you home."

"I haven't a mama or a papa."

Jane's heart wrenched. The poor girl. Wherever could she have come from? As far as she knew, there were no homes in walking distance save Richmond Park.

"Uncle Hayden's going to be cross with me. I was frightened, you see, when I lost my way. Terribly frightened. Uncle Hayden wishes me to be brave."

Uncle Hayden? Lord Westfield? Could she possibly be some relative of Lord Westfield's, living at Richmond Park? She supposed it was possible, although no one had mentioned the child. *How odd.*

"It's all right to be frightened, Madeline. I'm often frightened myself."

"Truly?"

Jane nodded solemnly.

"But I'm afraid to go home. What if they send me back?"

"Send you back where?"

"I don't know. Wherever it is I came from. I've heard the servants whispering about me, miss. They call me a name, something I can't remember. Something must be terribly wrong with me, and I'm afraid they'll send me away."

Jane knew just how she felt, listening to hushed whispers and worrying that something was wrong with you. She knelt before the child and reached for her hands. "Have you asked your Uncle Hayden about this?"

"No. He's so very kind to me, always bringing me sweets and such. I don't want to make him angry."

"Your uncle will be happy to have you safely returned, Madeline. I promise you that."

"You know my uncle?" Madeline peered down at Jane curiously.

"I've made his acquaintance." Jane stood and reached for her small, dirty hand. "Will you come with me? I'll see you home. And please call me Jane. We're friends now, aren't we?"

"Oh, yes. Thank you, Jane. You're the nicest lady I know. Well, except for Mrs. Tolland. But you're almost as nice as her."

"Why, thank you. I take that as the highest of compliments." With a grin, Jane squeezed Madeline's hand reassuringly. She wasn't entirely certain, but she thought Richmond Park was beyond the lake, over the hill to her left. If the child had wandered here alone, then Jane felt sure the house must be within easy walking distance. At least if they got lost, they'd get lost together.

"It's just over there, beyond that rise," Jane said, setting off with a smile, but feeling less confident than she pretended to be. "And I'll have you know that the nice Mrs. Tolland is my cousin."

The girl rewarded her with a wide, gap-toothed grin that made Jane's heart soar.

A half hour later they came to a field directly in front of the lake. Jane stopped short, her mouth agape.

There, directly ahead on the far side of the lake, the most magnificent house she'd ever seen rose up from the ground in utter splendor, casting its reflection on the mirrored surface of the water. A columned portico, rising three stories in height, stood in the estate's center, two dogleg staircases reaching down to the graveled drive below. Two perfectly symmetrical, two-storied wings stretched on for ages on either side of the portico, the tall, evenly spaced windows crowned with graceful carved arches. The simplicity of the design was stunning; the effect, staggering.

"There it is," Madeline called out. "Home. You were right, Jane!"

Jane found herself unable to respond. Instead she stood there, blinking repeatedly as if she were looking at a mirage.

This was Richmond Park? Oh, she'd known it was reputed to be fine, the finest in the district, but this was the midlands, after all. She'd enjoyed the hospitality of some of the grandest homes in the districts immediately surrounding London, and none were as magnificent as this. Lord Westfield lived *here?* It didn't signify.

"Come now, Jane. I'll show you the way." Madeline tugged on her hand, her confidence obviously restored now that she was on familiar terrain.

Jane hurried after the girl. In less than a quarter hour they reached the front gates, the house looming larger and larger still as they approached. As they climbed the wide front stairs, Jane glanced down at her frock and for a moment allowed herself to wish she'd worn something—anything—but this dowdy, printed muslin morning gown. Worse yet, her boots were surely covered in mud. She looked down, her scowl deepening. Even the hem of her gown was soiled. *Please,* she pleaded silently, *let the master be away today.*

"Madeline!" Jane looked up as the enormous door swung open, a slight but pretty young woman standing framed in the doorway. "Oh, thank God." The woman knelt, and Madeline hurried into her arms.

"Oh, Miss Crosley," the child sobbed. "I'm so very sorry. Please don't be angry."

"Miss Madeline?" another feminine voice shrieked, and a reed-thin older woman appeared, pushing spectacles up on the bridge of a narrow, aquiline nose. "Dear Lord, it *is* her. Oh, the master will be so relieved! You naughty, naughty child," she scolded, even as tears appeared in the corners of her faded eyes. She retrieved a handkerchief from her apron's pocket and dabbed at her eyes as Madeline hurried to her side, wrapping her arms about the woman's legs. "Oh, Mrs. Pierce, I was so very frightened."

"There, child," the woman cooed, patting the top of Madeline's head. "There's nothing to fear. You're home now."

At last the women noticed Jane's presence there on the threshold.

"I'm Miss Jane Rosemoor," she offered. "Mrs. Tolland's cousin. I ventured out in the woods today for a walk and stumbled upon the poor child, lost and frightened. We managed to find our way here together."

"Then we owe you our thanks, Miss Rosemoor. We've been out of our minds with worry. I am Mrs. Pierce, Lord Westfield's housekeeper, and this is Miss Crosley, Madeline's governess. Welcome to Richmond Park. Won't you come in? I'll arrange for tea."

Jane hesitated before replying.

"Oh, Jane, you must," Madeline pleaded, tugging on her hand. "Please! I'll show you my pony."

"Well," Jane said with a laugh, "who could resist such an enticement as that?"

"Come, then, Miss Rosemoor. I'll show you to the salon and arrange for a tray of tea and biscuits. And you, young lady, shall explain yourself."

Madeline bowed her head, looking penitent.

"Miss Crosley, ring for Robards at once and inform him that your charge has been located at last," Mrs. Pierce said, her voice cool, as she reached for Madeline's hand.

The younger woman briefly cast a scathing glare at the housekeeper before nodding and disappearing from sight.

Jane stepped into the cavernous front hall and looked around in fascination as she untied and removed her bonnet. She couldn't help but gape at her surroundings, which were grand yet tasteful. The floor was inlaid marble, freshly polished and gleaming, and wide arches were flanked by pillars at either end directly across from door. Deep blue velvet settees lined the far wall, placed at perfectly symmetrical intervals. Matching blue velvet drapes framed floor-to-ceiling windows along the front wall, looking out onto the manicured drive. In the center of the hall, an enormous floral arrangement sat on a pedestal. The rich, fragrant scents—hothouse flowers, no doubt—perfumed the air, and Jane inhaled deeply.

As she followed Mrs. Pierce and Madeline across the hall and under the archway leading out, Jane's eyes skimmed over the two portraits flanking the arch—one a formal portrait of Lord Westfield himself, looking as arrogant and imposing as ever in fawn breeches and a dark blue riding jacket, a pair of hounds sitting at his heels, and the other depicting an older gentleman in a red jacket and powdered wig, no doubt the previous Lord West-field. The familial resemblance was striking.

"Look at your face, Miss Madeline," Mrs. Pierce scolded as they entered the yellow and gilt salon. She retrieved her handkerchief and vigorously scrubbed the grime from the girl's flushed cheeks. "Why, if the master were to see you now, what would he think? You're a fright. Tea first, and then the nursemaid will draw you a bath. Sit, Miss Rose-moor." She gestured to a sofa the color of the mid-day sun. "I'll fetch the tea at once."

"But I promised to show Miss Rosemoor my pony," Madeline wailed.

"Another time, dear. Have a seat, child, and entertain Miss Rosemoor while I see to the tea."

As Mrs. Pierce bustled out, Madeline launched into happy chatter—a far cry from the frightened girl Jane had first encountered. Not ten minutes later, Mrs. Pierce reappeared, pushing a heavily laden tea cart.

"Mmmm, apple tarts." Madeline reached for one with a smile as Mrs. Pierce poured the tea into delicate bone china patterned in blue toile. Jane reached for a biscuit and nibbled distractedly.

"Mary Ann's the prettiest ever," Madeline exclaimed, brushing pastry crumbs from her lap. "You'll see."

"Mary Ann?"

"My pony. Haven't you been listening?"

"How could she not, Miss Madeline, with you going on as you are? Shush now, child. Give poor Miss Rosemoor a bit of peace."

"Oh, no, Mrs. Pierce. It's quite all right. Why, Madeline reminds me of a dear friend of mine, Lady Mandeville. Lady Mandeville could go on all day about horses. So you've already learned to ride, then?"

"Oh, you should see young mistress ride," Mrs. Pierce interjected, her eyes shining with pride. "The master taught her himself, he did, to ride and jump."

"Did he?" Jane asked, surprised that a man like Lord Westfield would take such interest in his young ward.

"I want him to teach me to shoot, too, but he says I'm too young. Perhaps when I'm older—"

"Shoot, indeed. He most certainly will not teach you to shoot. It's not at all appropriate for young ladies. Simply scandalous." Mrs. Pierce shook her head, her lips pursed in censure.

Madeline looked crestfallen, and Jane almost laughed aloud.

Suddenly a door slammed, and heavy footsteps in the hallway jolted Jane from her quiet enjoyment.

"Damn it to hell," a deep voice boomed, reverberating off the walls. "I've searched every inch of the property with no sign—"

"Master," Mrs. Pierce interrupted, dashing out toward the hall. "She's home. Right here in the salon."

"Thank God," came the familiar voice, moving closer.

Jane found herself shrinking back into the cushions as Lord Westfield hastily strode into the room. Madeline flung herself into his arms as he knelt to one knee. His coat was half buttoned, his cravat askew. His dark hair was mussed as he doffed his hat. Jane watched in rapt fascination as he pressed the small child to him, eyes closed, his face buried in her hair.

"Don't ever do that again, poppet," he said hoarsely. "You've no idea how worried I was, how—"

He opened his eyes at last, and his gaze met Jane's over the top of Madeline's fair head. His shock was evident. He released Madeline and stood, straightening his coat as he did so. Then his usual mask of cool indifference took its rightful place upon his features.

"Miss Rosemoor," he said levelly, with a curt nod in her direction. "I see you've met my niece."

"I have, indeed," she replied, rising from her seat.

"Madeline is my ward." He placed one hand on the top of the girl's head. Something about the protective gesture touched Jane deeply.

She swallowed hard and attempted a polite smile, trying to make her tone light. "I was out walking in Cecil's park this afternoon and I fear I strayed a bit onto your property where I stumbled upon Madeline. We found our way here together."

"Oh, and she's the nicest lady, Uncle Hayden," Madeline added enthusiastically. "Please, can she stay for dinner?"

"Yes, I'm sure—"

"No, I'm afraid I cannot—"

Both spoke at once, and Madeline looked curiously from one to the other with wide eyes.

"Madeline, as much as I'd love to, I'm afraid I must get back to Mrs. Tolland. She's feeling poorly today, and besides, I'm journeying to Clifton tomorrow and must be up early in the morn."

"Is Mrs. Tolland unwell?" His brow creased, a frown suddenly darkening his face.

"Nothing out of the ordinary for a woman in her . . . ahem, current state." Jane's cheeks burned. She was astonished at her own candor,

yet his obvious concern had moved her to such
an admission.

"Ah, I see. Very well." The worried creases
smoothed from his brow. "And what of Tolland and
his ankle?"

"Still smarting, I suppose, though he's made no
mention of it. But he limps when he thinks no one
is watching." When Jane had gone to his study and
asked him about visiting The Orchards, he had
been overly generous and accommodating, promising to make the necessary arrangements himself.
Yet his eyes had never once met hers.

"Some escort he was, the fool."

Jane felt the heat rise again in her cheeks. She'd
blushed more in Lord Westfield's presence these
past few days than she had in her entire life, no
doubt.

"Anyway," he said with a wave of one hand, as if
he were shooing away a pesky fly, "perhaps you can
join us for dinner another evening."

"Of course," Jane replied.

Madeline, obviously feeling forgotten, tugged on
Lord Westfield's sleeve. His niece, he'd called her.
Jane's brows rose suspiciously, for one only had to
glance at the pair, standing beside one another with
the same green eyes and the same strong, proud
chin, to suspect a different relationship altogether.
Perhaps she was his daughter.

His bastard daughter.

Just then Miss Crosley stepped into the room, in-
terrupting Jane's musings on the child's parentage.
The governess entreated her charge to go upstairs
at once for her bath.

"I won't leave without saying good-bye, I give you
my word," Jane promised.

With one reluctant glance back at Jane, Madeline

obeyed. Jane listened as the pair's footsteps faded and then disappeared altogether, and then she and Lord Westfield faced one another, silent, for what felt like an eternity.

After a beat, he reached down and buttoned his coat with sharp, precise movements. "I apologize for my current state. I'm afraid I left in a bit of haste."

"No need to apologize," she answered as he straightened his cravat.

"Will you sit?"

"Of course." On shaky legs, Jane returned to her previous seat on the sofa. "I believe the tea is still warm. Shall I pour?"

"Yes. Thank you." He reached for the cup she offered.

"She's delightful, my lord."

"What? Who?"

"Madeline. Such a lovely child. Her liveliness must brighten your household."

"Liveliness? Oh. Yes. An orphan, my niece. She had nowhere to go and I, ahem . . ." He took a sip of tea. "She's been with us since infancy. Miss Crosley does a fine job. Madeline's a terribly clever child, but, I fear, in desperate need of a woman's influence. Your cousin is very kind to her. Madeline is usually timid among strangers. I've never seen her take to someone as quickly as she has to you. You must have made quite an impression on her."

"I . . . suppose so." A feeling of unease settled in her stomach. It was not prudent for her to remain alone in his company. "I'm sorry, my lord. I must go."

"Call me Hayden."

"An unusual name," she replied, stalling.

"My mother's maiden name. Lady Caroline Hayden of Kent, before marriage. Her father was the Duke of Umberton."

"I see." Jane fidgeted in her seat. She couldn't possibly call him by his given name. Despite their indiscretion, she'd only made his acquaintance what, two, three days ago?

"And perhaps I should call you Jane," he added.

"Perhaps not," Jane replied.

"Tell me, how do you find Richmond Park?"

"Extraordinary." She brightened at once, her mood lightened a measure. "I've never in all my life seen a house so pleasingly situated, nor so elegantly appointed."

"I agree, but then I'm prejudiced. I'm glad it pleases you." He leaned back in his chair and eyed her closely. "I think perhaps it could use a woman's touch," he said.

"Whatever do you mean?" Jane's heart began to thump noisily against her ribs.

"Richmond Park. It has been many years since the estate has seen a mistress."

"I must say, it certainly does not seem to suffer for the lack of one."

He shrugged. "I do my best. You said you were leaving tomorrow for Clifton?"

"Yes, to visit my great-aunt and grandmother at The Orchards. I haven't seen them in quite some time."

"When will you return?"

"It depends upon my grandmother's health. She's . . . unwell. A sennight at most, I suppose."

"When you return, you must fulfill your promise to Madeline or she will be sorely disappointed. You must join us for dinner."

"Of course." Where had the gruff, acerbic Lord Westfield gone, and who was this new, polite man in his stead? Her heart leapt in her breast as it suddenly made sense—she saw the truth with startling clarity. Appraising her like a brood mare at Tattersall's; assessing her accomplishments; and now, measuring her affection for his ward and her approval of his home. "She won't do," he'd said on first meeting her.

He wanted a wife.

Jane sprang to her feet and hurried to the window, gazing out at the lake with churning emotions. The sun was fast moving toward the horizon, casting a golden glow on the lawn below. No matter his designs on her, she would not have him. She couldn't, not even if she wanted to.

"I must go," she repeated, placing one palm against the glass.

And then she felt his warm breath on her neck, tantalizing her, drawing gooseflesh across her skin. How had he crossed the distance separating them on such silent feet? How had she not felt his presence behind her before it was too late?

His hand covered hers on the glass, his taut body pressed against her back. A shiver began at the base of her spine and worked its way up. His lips pressed into her hair, behind one ear.

"Jane," he murmured, so quietly it was little more than a sigh, his breath seductively warm against her skin. She could feel the beating of his heart through the layers of cloth that separated them. Involuntarily, she inhaled his masculine scent—sandalwood and leather.

More than anything, she wanted to turn around, to press her face into his broad, muscular chest, to gaze up into his mesmerizing eyes, to kiss him again as she had kissed him in the maze.

"Please," she pleaded, her voice a hoarse whisper.

"You mustn't." She stood stiffly, braced against the window, unwilling to give in to her inexplicable desires.

As stealthily as a panther, he moved away, as quickly and silently as he'd come to her. An unexpected pang of disappointment shot through her. When at last she turned from the window, he was standing stone-faced on the far side of the room, observing her with his hands clasped behind his back. For a moment Jane thought she'd imagined his touch, his presence; that he'd been there across the room all along. Maybe she *was* going mad.

"I'll summon a carriage to return you to the Tollands'," he said briskly, his voice cool and clipped. "In the meantime, I'll have the housekeeper show you to the nursery to bid Madeline good-bye."

"Thank you, my lord." She feared her legs would buckle beneath her at any moment if she did not get away from him at once.

Moments later, Hayden watched as the housekeeper led Jane out of the salon and upstairs to the nursery. As soon as she was gone, he went to the sideboard in long, angry strides and poured himself a whiskey. With a jerk of the wrist, he downed the drink in one swift motion. He slammed the glass back down, his gaze drawn involuntarily to the very window she'd stood at just moments ago, her cheeks flushed a healthy pink, her hand trembling beneath his on the cool glass.

He picked up the empty tumbler and threw it at the casings, sending shards of broken glass sailing onto the carpet below.

Bloody hell!

His tightly guarded self-control was slipping, and

slipping fast. She was positively maddening. Waspish and proud one minute, quivering beside him the next. Sharp as a blade, yet all womanly accomplishment. She was unlike any woman he'd ever met, and his desire for her could not be denied.

He sought only a pleasing, accommodating disposition for the wife who would share his home. Nothing more. Therefore, he'd immediately dismissed Miss Rosemoor—Jane—as far too alluring, much too tempting, and not nearly docile enough, besides. She would challenge him at every turn.

But since that kiss in the maze, he hadn't been able to get her out of his mind, much as he tried. His firm resolve was wavering. He wanted her in his bed. But she was a lady of breeding, despite her outspoken nature, and good *ton*, the sister of the Viscount Rosemoor. Not acceptable for the role of mistress, but perfectly suited for that of wife.

He couldn't deny that he desired her physically, but nothing more. His heart would remain immune to a woman with such a sharp tongue, a woman so quick to speak her mind. Lust was a far cry from love, after all. She was no different from the rest, he told himself; no doubt she had stood there at the window, surveying the grounds and envisioning herself mistress of Richmond. Even so, he felt certain that she'd be good to Madeline—that she would treat the child with affection and kindness. Naturally she'd have the skills to capably run his household; such skills came with good breeding.

Perhaps she'd do, after all. It would certainly save him the trouble in London. He nodded, his mind made up, and resolved to inform her of his decision immediately upon her return from Clifton. Dismissing any doubt that she would refuse his suit, he hastened out to summon the carriage.

Chapter Five

"Aunt Gertrude," Jane called out merrily, dashing up the front steps to fold the frail woman into her arms.

Her great-aunt released her and stepped back, bringing her spectacles up to rest upon her nose. "Is it really you, child? It's been so very long."

"It has, indeed, Auntie. How's Grandmama?"

"Unchanged, I'm afraid. Not at all up for visitors. I fear you've come all this way for naught."

"Come now, it would be worth the trip just for your pleasant company alone." Jane's cheerful tone belied her agitation. She had not traveled so far to be denied the truth. She'd come to see her grandmama, and see her she would.

"Come inside, dear. Trevors will get your traveling cases."

Jane followed her aunt into the great hall, shuddering at the deterioration of The Orchards since her last visit. The vine-embellished paper on the walls was peeled back at the edges, hanging loosely in places. Lacelike cobwebs sullied the hall's corners, and chairs with their stuffing peeking out from faded covers lined the wall. As they moved further into the house and settled into the drawing room, Jane noted that the rest of the house suffered a similar fate. The once-fine manor was in tatters.

Jane resolved at once to do whatever she could to smarten the place up a bit. Perhaps her brother would help with some funds. She would write to Colin at once.

Her aunt startled her with a papery-thin hand on her forearm. "I know, dear. I can see it in your eyes. Perhaps we've allowed the place to grow shabby. There's just never been a need, as we have very few visitors. Very few, indeed. We're happy here, your grandmama and I. Mrs. Carter is a fine nurse—we're in capable hands."

Jane shook her head sadly. "I . . . are you certain? Because if there's anything I can do, anything at all—"

"Just live your life, dear Jane. Knowing that you are happy and settled will give us both the greatest joy. Your mama writes that you come to us with questions, seeking answers. Truly, there's nothing to tell, nothing that should affect the choices you make. Your grandmama is ill, nothing more. A weak, sickly constitution. Her nerves give her trouble. Sometimes she's a bit confused, disoriented."

"But Aunt Susan—"

"Her accident was surely a tragedy."

Accident? Jane shuddered as a cold bead of sweat trickled down her back. Why would Aunt Gertrude say it was an accident when everyone knew the woman had taken her own life? She shook her head, perplexed.

"Aunt Gertrude, I must know. I've heard talk that this . . . this *malady* increases after childbirth. Do you believe that to be true?"

"Well, let me think." Aunt Gertrude pursed her mouth and pushed her glasses farther up the bridge of her nose. "No," she said at last, her thin lips drawn into a tight smile. "No, I do not. I recognize no such connection. Come now, this is not a pleasant topic of conversation, not for a young lady. Tell me, have you any new suitors? Surely a gentleman or two must have caught your fancy by now."

"No, I'm afraid not." Jane smiled indulgently at her aunt. Every conversation she had with well-meaning relations inevitably took this route, as though she wore her spinsterhood like a yoke about her neck.

"But how can that be? A girl as lovely and gay as you? Your mother tells me you've enjoyed a good deal of popularity over the years." She leaned forward and laid a hand on Jane's wrist, a knowing smile on her lips. "None of the young bucks managed to sweep you off your feet, did they?"

Jane could only shake her head, biting her lip to suppress an amused smile. *Young bucks?* Had her elderly aunt actually spoken those words aloud?

"A love match is a fine thing, dear," Aunt Gertrude continued on enthusiastically, "but in the absence of one, perhaps a nice, companionable marriage would satisfy?"

"I'm afraid not, Auntie. Besides, I'm perfectly content to remain a spinster."

"I must confess I've not minded terribly my own decision not to wed, but still . . ." She trailed off with a sigh. "Do not think I didn't enjoy a furtive kiss in the garden in my day."

Jane's eyes widened with surprise. "Goodness, Auntie! That's positively scandalous." She couldn't help but laugh.

"Oh, times were quite different in my youth, mind you. What you call scandalous today was simply . . . Well, never mind. Anyway, I haven't had much time to regret my unmarried state, as busy as I've been caring for your grandmama all these years. But how will you occupy your time? Your own sister is well enough, happily married at that."

"I haven't really thought about it," she confessed. "Besides, I have not said that I'm entirely set on spinsterhood. I thought perhaps to get some answers first, answers about Grandmama and—"

"Oh, dear, here I've prattled on and on, and look at you, barely able to sit upright, so overcome with fatigue. How very selfish of me." She rose and gestured for Jane to follow suit. "Come, let me show you to your room. We'll have plenty of time to talk in the days to come."

Clearly, Jane would get no answers from Aunt Gertrude. Not tonight, at least.

Jane set down her fork and reached for her napkin. "So, Aunt Gertrude, did you speak with Grandmama's nurse today? How is she faring?"

Her aunt's forehead furrowed at once. "I did indeed. Bad news, very bad news, I'm afraid. She's worsened, still not at all fit for company. In fact, it's possible that she will not have recovered enough for visitors before you must return to Ashbourne. I'm sorry, dear. I hope you've not grown tired of my company."

"No, of course not," Jane murmured, her heart sinking. As always, it was impossible to argue with the woman. As one day had passed into the next, Jane had grown more and more frustrated. All her pleas to see her grandmother had been rebuked, brushed off with one excuse after another. She'd found herself banished to the south wing of the house, entreated to leave her grandmother to her rest, to stay away from the locked west wing that housed the purportedly ill woman.

Aunt Gertrude herself spent a great deal of time resting, and Jane passed much of each day in solitude, sitting in the garden with a book or exploring the grounds on foot, often taking her midday meal in her own room, perhaps the tidiest in the house, thanks to Bridgette's attentions. She shared a quiet dinner each evening with her aunt, who almost immediately retired as soon as the dishes were cleared from the table.

The only subjects her aunt seemed willing to discuss at length were fanciful tales of her own youth, stories which Jane had to admit were highly entertaining, albeit shocking. Why, her mother would surely swoon if she knew Aunt Gertrude was regaling her with stories about stolen kisses and transparent gowns worn without proper undergarments!

Yet she couldn't listen to her aunt's talk without her thoughts being drawn reluctantly to the mysterious and confounding Lord Westfield. Every time she remembered the kiss they'd shared, her cheeks burned with renewed shame and mortification. Thank goodness she had come to her senses when she did. She wished more than once that she'd never met him, never felt the stirring of longings that he'd stoked within her. For she had to admit that he *had* awakened something inside her, something she could not explain or understand. Surely with some fortitude she could push such feelings from her mind, as she'd always done when any gentleman had piqued her interest in the past.

"Anyway, dear. Where was I?" Her aunt continued on, her eyes shining brightly. "Oh, yes. Major Barnaby. Of course. Now then, my sister and I were desperate for the major to take notice of us, for he was the handsomest officer we'd ever laid eyes on and there were so many pretty girls in Bath that summer. We had heard that he would be attending the theater that evening, so we dampened down our dresses to the point of transparency and left off our shifts." She covered her mouth with her napkin and giggled like a girl, delighted by her memories.

"Oh, Auntie, did you really?"

"We did, indeed. Of course, so did half the girls there that night. Why, everywhere you looked you could see . . . ahem." A coughing fit overtook her.

Jane felt her cheeks flush. "And what happened? Did the major notice you?"

"I'm afraid he did not. But it was that very same night that the baron first noticed your grandmama, and they were wed before St. Michaelmas."

"Fascinating." Jane reached for her goblet and took a sip of sweet wine.

"Well, I'm afraid I must retire now. You're a dear, though, allowing a silly old lady to prattle on all night. I hope you'll forgive me."

"On the contrary, Aunt Gertrude. I'm enjoying your delightful tales. Are you sure you wouldn't like to join me in the drawing room? I see you've a harp in there, and I can play tolerably well."

"No, dear. Perhaps tomorrow. But you should feel free to play if you so desire." She rose and crossed over to Jane, planting a kiss on her cheek. "Good night, then."

"Good night, Auntie." Jane dropped her hands into her lap with a sigh as the woman strode out.

It was too early for Jane to retire, and she didn't feel at all like sitting alone in the drawing room, so instead she hurried upstairs, changed into her nightclothes, and began a letter by candlelight to her sister Susanna. She knew Susanna would adore

Aunt Gertrude's tales, so she attempted to retell as many of the shocking details as she could remember. But her attention was flagging, her ability to fill the page with cheerful words waning.

She knew in her heart that something must be wrong in this house, terribly wrong, for such secrecy. Why else would her aunt go to such lengths to keep her away from her own flesh and blood? As her frustration increased, so did her determination. Looking up from her letter, she saw the full moon framed in the window, the line of trees along the drive illuminated by the silvery glow.

Her resolve gathered. She would not allow her concerns to be brushed off so easily. She'd come all this way, allowing herself a flicker of hope. For years she'd been shielded from the truth, denied the knowledge she needed to effectively chart the course of her life. She stood, tightening the belt of her dressing gown with grim resolve.

She would find out. Now.

She reached for the candle and held it aloft as she padded across the room and pushed open the door, listening for any signs of movement in the darkened house. There were none. She hurried down the curving stair and across the great hall, one hand cupped in front of the candle's flame.

Reaching the entrance to the west wing, she reached for the cut-glass doorknob with a trembling hand. Her eyes widened with surprise. It was unlocked.

She struggled to turn the handle, her palm slippery with perspiration. At last, she stepped into a long hall lined with floor-to-ceiling windows all draped in musty, worn plum velvet. The brilliant light of the moon crept in between the seams, casting long, slanted beams across the bare floorboards. She took two tentative steps forward, her heart pounding in her breast. *Just breathe,* she told herself.

Along the left side of the corridor, a row of doors lined the wall. At the far end, a cantilevered staircase rose in a graceful, curved sweep. Her grandmama was likely housed upstairs, she reasoned, as most of the bedchambers seemed to be on the first floor, one flight up.

Struggling valiantly to regulate her breathing, she moved forward on silent feet, her eyes darting about to take in the fleur-de-lis pattern on the walls, which was peeling at the edges. From somewhere in the house, a cool breeze stirred, caressing her calves and sending the hem of her dressing gown aflutter. Jane turned with a start as the heavy door that she'd left ajar rattled shut on creaking hinges behind her. Her heart leapt, accelerating at an alarming speed.

"Oh!" she cried, one hand rising to her mouth. An icy coldness flowed through her veins, and she shivered almost violently.

The heavy silence was broken by footsteps—quick, efficient footsteps, gaining in speed and volume. Jane stood frozen in terror, unable to move a muscle or utter a single sound.

"Miss Gertrude?" a sharp, feminine voice called out from the direction of the staircase. "Are you about?"

A stout old woman appeared at the end of the hall, her hair tucked neatly under a crisp, white cap. When her gaze flitted to Jane, one plump hand rose to her breast. "Oh, miss, you frightened me. You must be Lady Bassford's granddaughter. Here now, hurry back to your own room like a good girl. This is no place for a lady such as your-self."

Jane swallowed hard. "You . . . you must be Mrs. Carter, my grandmother's nurse."

"I am, dear. And I'm quite busy at the moment, so you must hurry on back." She reached for Jane's arm and wheeled her back toward the hall's en-trance. The blood rose at once in Jane's cheeks, and she stopped short, tugging her arm free from the woman's grasp.

"No. I won't go. I've come for answers, and I *will* get them. If you won't take me to my grandmother, then I'll find her myself. I *must* see her."

"Now, child—"

"I'm not a child. I'm a woman, fully capable of understanding her condition. I will no longer be pushed aside and denied the truth. I request—no, I demand—that you take me to my grandmother at once."

Mrs. Carter pursed her mouth into a scowl, her eyes narrowed at the impertinence. "As you wish, miss. Follow me."

Jane's heart thumped loudly in rhythm to the tapping of Mrs. Carter's heels as they climbed the stairs and passed through several doors, then across a wide gallery. She noted with satisfaction that the corners were free of cobwebs on this floor, the white walls mostly unblemished. They turned into a narrow anteroom, and at last the woman paused before an intricately carved door. She turned to Jane with a frown. "You're sure, miss?"

Jane nodded in reply, unable to speak. She held her breath as the woman reached into her apron and produced a key, then slid it into the lock and turned the door handle.

Jane's nostrils were assaulted at once by an as-

sortment of unpleasant odors—astringent medici-
nal smells intermingling with the faint scent of un-
washed body. A large four-poster bed dominated
the dim room, and there, lying against the ivory pillows, was her grandmother. At last.

Black hair streaked with gray escaped a single
plait and fell across her thin shoulders. Darkly
shadowed, pale eyes stared ahead at the wall—
unblinking, unseeing. Deep lines ravaged her
once-smooth face, all but obscuring her cheekbones. Her features displayed not the slightest bit
of emotion—no perception, no awareness whatsoever as her eldest granddaughter approached
the bed. Only a hint of the woman Jane remembered remained in this empty shell.

Jane's heart beat so loudly in her breast that all
other sounds were blocked out as she moved toward her grandmother's side. Jane shuddered as
she reached for the woman's hand, frail and fragile
as the finest bone china, lying on the sheet at her
side.

"Elizabeth?" her grandmother croaked, spittle is-
suing forth from thin lips and landing on Jane's
hand. She fought the urge to recoil.

"No, Grandmama. It's Jane, Elizabeth's eldest
daughter."

Suddenly, the woman pulled her hand from her
grasp and began to tremble, her eyes widening as
she shook her head wildly about.

Mrs. Carter placed a hand on her charge's forehead. "Shhh, Lady Bassford. Quiet, now. Here, have
a spoonful of this." Her grandmother allowed the
woman to spoon a dark liquid into her mouth.
"There, now. We'll leave you to your rest."

Her grandmother moaned, a deep guttural
sound, and began to rock from side to side as a

rivulet of frothy drool made its way down her chin. Jane flinched at the sight, but Mrs. Carter efficiently retrieved a handkerchief and patiently wiped her mouth.

"Come, Miss Rosemoor." Mrs. Carter laid the square of linen on the bedside table as her charge's eyes drooped shut, her erratic motions stilled at last. "Any interruption of her usual schedule disturbs her greatly. She does not welcome visitors. Let us leave your grandmother in peace."

Jane nodded her assent, then turned back toward the bed once more. "Good-bye, Grandmama," she murmured. "I love you."

With one last look over her shoulder, Jane followed the bustling Mrs. Carter out to the chamber's anteroom. Only once the door closed behind them did she find her voice, however small. "I had no idea it was so dreadful. How long has she been like this?"

"For many years, I'm afraid. I've been her nurse for nearly two decades, and she's gotten progressively worse as the years have passed. At first she'd have long bouts of melancholy that could stretch on for weeks, followed by periods of almost maniacal energy. She'd clean the house from top to bottom, empty her purse in the village's shops, stay up till the wee hours pacing the floors, rearranging knickknacks and such until she dropped from exhaustion. But over the past several years, she's retreated more and more into herself, and she grows weaker by the day."

"Do you know how long she's suffered from this terrible affliction?"

"From what I've been told, she's always suffered, since girlhood. It worsened after the birth of her first child. But it was only after her third child, I'm told, that she descended into true madness. Very sad, very sad indeed. And such a shame. Why, I remember when Lady Bassford was the young mistress of Bassford Hall, just at the top of the road. The current baron lives there now—your uncle, I suppose, with his wife. Yes, Lady Bassford was a fine lady, a diamond of the first water. Such a shame." Mrs. Carter shook her head sadly, a faraway look in her eyes. "It was kind of your uncle to allow his mother and Gertrude to live out their days here at The Orchards. Always a lesser estate, but perfectly comfortable for Lady Bassford and Miss Gertrude, and later for poor Susan as well, God rest her soul."

"Aunt Susan was . . ." Jane couldn't bring herself to say the words.

"Yes, similarly afflicted. Although I'm told your own mother has escaped the family curse. You must be much relieved of that."

"I am," Jane murmured. But was she truly immune? It was obvious that Susanna was—her sister's disposition remained sunny and bright at all times. But as to her own disposition, she couldn't help but remember the terrible bouts of suffocating melancholy she'd experienced as a girl—bouts that had worsened with adolescence. What would happen if she were to have children?

She closed her eyes, remembering the image of her grandmother lying just on the other side of the door, drool running unchecked down her chin. Even worse, her Aunt Susan had flung herself from a third-floor window and broken her neck.

Scalding tears burned her eyelids. No, she wouldn't risk it. Couldn't risk it. Just as she'd always supposed, she was sentenced to the life of a childless spinster. And strangely enough, just as this thought crossed her mind, so did the image of Lord Westfield, his arms wrapped protectively around young Madeline. Jane reached a hand up to wipe away the tear that coursed down her cheek.

No, it could never be. Love was meant for others, not for her. She'd been right all along.

"Thank you for your candor, Mrs. Carter. I should get back at once. Is it possible for you to refrain from mentioning this visit to my Aunt Gertrude? It would only upset her to know that I've violated her wishes."

"Of course, miss." The woman nodded solemnly.

Jane turned to go.

"Miss Rosemoor? If I might . . . Before you go, I feel I must say this to you."

"Yes?" Jane turned back curiously.

"I hope you don't find it presumptuous of me to say so, but you must know you're nothing like them."

"Pardon me?"

"I can see it, in your eyes. You're nothing like them. Your aunt tells me that you come seeking answers, wishing to discuss things she's not at all comfortable discussing. She's told me that, as a girl, you were sensitive, given to short bouts of the blues. Although it's not my place to speak so freely, I must tell you that from the sound of it, you have not inherited this terrible affliction. It would have manifested itself by now, I'm sure."

"How can you be so sure? It's true I suffered from melancholy as a girl. I still do, on occasion, though I'm able to overcome it rather quickly with some fortitude. I've shielded my family from the true extent of it."

"That is your answer, then. Your grandmother and your Aunt Susan were never able to shield the truth from their families. Their suffering was acute, and painfully evident to those who loved them. Much more than simple melancholy. No, as I said before, the melancholy was followed by periods of maniacal energy—the inability to concentrate, to focus. Quite frightening. Have you ever encountered such as that within yourself?"

"N-no," Jane stammered. She hadn't. "Nothing like that. As soon as the melancholy lifts, I'm right back to my own cheerful, composed self."

"You see, then? There's nothing to fear."

Jane shook her head, unconvinced. "Still, I can't be sure."

"I'm sure. I've spent many years in the service of your family, Miss Rosemoor. I can recognize it in an instant. No, you've been spared."

"I hope you're correct, Mrs. Carter. Indeed I do." But could she risk it? No, she shook her head. It was far too dangerous. Besides, she'd yet to meet a man worth the risk—a man who touched her heart enough to make her believe she could tempt fate.

And then she remembered the way she felt, backed against the tree's wide trunk, caged in by Lord Westfield's powerful arms, his insistent mouth pressed against hers, his tongue invading spaces never before explored. He was a man who wasn't afraid to say what he thought, to act as he felt, to take what he wanted. Prideful, yes. Arrogant, without a doubt.

Perhaps I've met my match. The thought sent a shudder down her spine.

Chapter Six

"Jane, it's so good to have you back," Emily called out, waddling over to embrace her. "I've missed your company most dreadfully."

"As I've missed yours." Jane recognized the truth in the statement.

"I'm so sorry I wasn't able to see you off. I wasn't quite myself for a few days, but I'm much better now."

"I'm delighted to see you so well recovered. I hope you didn't mind my taking off to The Orchards like that."

"No, of course not. How was Grandmama?"

"The same, I'm afraid. Not quite well enough for visitors." Jane would never share the horrifying images of the madwoman with her delicate cousin. "But Aunt Gertrude seemed well."

"I'm glad to hear it. Aunt Gertrude has been so good to Grandmama, sacrificing her own independence to devote herself to her care."

"Yes, she's lucky to have her."

"So, what shall we do today? I was thinking perhaps to head to the garden and paint. It's a beautiful day, mild and sunny. The light is perfect."

"That sounds lovely. I'll join you, then." Jane reached for her shawl.

"Wonderful. I'll have Mrs. Smythe fetch the supplies and send them out. Oh, there you are, Mrs. Smythe." Emily looked up as the housekeeper bustled into the room.

"Madam, you have a visitor. Lord Westfield is requesting your company."

"Lord Westfield? Did you tell him that Mr. Tolland is not at home? And not expected back for several hours?"

"I did, indeed, madam, but his lordship insists it is your and Miss Rosemoor's company that he desires this afternoon."

"Strange," Emily muttered. "I could have sworn Cecil said he was going into the village today with Westfield." She shook her head. "Show him in, then."

Jane reached down to smooth her dress with a frown. She couldn't deny that she longed to see him. As she traveled back from The Orchards, she'd barely been able to think of anything save finding herself in his presence once more. Like a magnet, she felt involuntarily drawn to him. It terrified her, her intense longing for someone she barely knew—someone she could never have.

She forced a smile as he strode into the drawing room, hat in hand. Her heart fluttered against her breast like butterfly wings as he stood before her at last, just as tall and intensely handsome as she'd remembered.

"Mrs. Tolland, Miss Rosemoor." He bowed to them, then stood stiffly, refusing the seat that Emily gestured toward.

"Mrs. Tolland, if you'll indulge me, I'd hoped for a private word with Miss Rosemoor."

Emily's mouth popped open, her eyes round. Jane, standing just behind Lord Westfield and out of his line of vision, madly shook her head. She had no wish to find herself alone with him again. It was dangerous, far too dangerous.

"Why, of course," Emily said brightly. "I'll just be out in the garden, then."

Again he bowed to Emily with stiff formality before she hurried out. Finally Lord Westfield turned to face her, as if just remembering her presence.

"Won't you sit?" Jane murmured, ignoring the racing of her heart.

"Yes, thank you." He settled himself into the gold brocade chair by the window, his long legs stretched out before him. As always, Jane was amazed at the size of him.

"How was your journey to Clifton?" He balanced his hat on one of the chair's arms.

"Very well, thank you. I believe I accomplished what I set out to accomplish."

His brows drew together. "Is that so? Well, it's good to have you safely returned."

"Thank you, my lord."

A moment of uncomfortable silence ensued. Jane found herself fidgeting in her seat, unable to meet his questioning gaze.

"You're comfortable here in Derbyshire, then?" he finally said.

"I am, indeed."

"I'm glad to hear it." He leaned forward in his chair. "Miss Rosemoor, I won't beat around the bush. Madeline is in dire need of feminine companionship, and I'm finding it increasingly difficult to raise the child on my own. What's more, Richmond Park is in need of a mistress, a capable mistress. It's time I take a wife and produce an heir. You must realize, of course, that I seek onlycompanionship—nothing more. A partner, of sorts. I'm not offering love, nor will the relationship ever progress to such a state."

Jane refused to allow her astonishment to show in her countenance. She raised one brow, hoping to affect a haughty posture.

"You sound as if you are offering me a position in your household, Lord Westfield."

"Well, in a way, I suppose I am. But given your circumstances—"

"What circumstances would that be?" she asked, her temper flaring.

"Your age, of course." He waved one hand at her. "You're a sensible girl; surely I needn't pretend you're not well past the age most women marry."

"No, you surely needn't," she said through clenched teeth.

"This arrangement will no doubt benefit you greatly," he continued, obviously completely unaware of her discomfort. "I'm told your brother, the Viscount Rosemoor, makes his home in Scotland, but what if he later decides to take up residence at your family's estate in Essex? What then? Will you be content to make your home with your brother and his wife? Wouldn't you prefer a home of your own?"

Jane remained silent in reply.

"Besides, I think we'll suit nicely," he added, sounding almost cheerful.

"Do you, now?" she asked, her tone decidedly cool.

"Yes. I had meant to go to London, much as I loathed the idea, and choose from amongst this Season's debutantes. You've saved me the trip."

"Is that so?" she sputtered, no longer able to hide her indignation. Why, the arrogant fool! "I've saved you the trip?" Had he truly thought she'd accept such an offer—one so thinly cloaked in insult?

"Will you give me your answer?" He drummed his fingers on his knee.

Jane rose to her feet. "Indeed I will, my lord. My answer is a resounding no."

His forehead creased, his eyes widening perceptively, though he remained seated. "I might ask whatever would induce you to decline such an advantageous offer."

"And I might ask what would induce you to make such an insulting offer."

"You are protesting much too vehemently for a woman who allowed my kiss."

"If I remember correctly, my lord, my response to your kiss was to soundly strike you."

"Eventually, yes." One corner of his mouth twitched. "But not before you returned the kiss. Quite passionately, I might add."

Oh, he was positively infuriating.

Jane watched as he rose and reached for his hat. "I'm offering to rescue you from the sad state of spinsterhood and make you mistress of the finest estate in Derbyshire. To make you a countess, for God's sake."

Jane peered up at him with narrowed eyes, her face burning with anger and humiliation.

"I've no intention of taking a husband, Lord Westfield, but let me assure you that if I were, you would be the last man I'd consider. Now if you'll excuse me, I believe our business here is concluded."

"Indeed it is, Miss Rosemoor." He tipped his hat back onto his head.

In their haste to quit each other's company, they found themselves tangled together at the door. "Oooh," Jane exclaimed, elbowing her way past the hateful man and out toward the garden without a backward glance.

Oh, the insufferable man! The nerve. Jane stormed down the hall, flinging open the pair of French doors leading to the garden. *How dare he?* She crossed the terrace in angry strides, practically flinging herself down the stairs to the garden in haste. "How dare he!" she repeated, her voice rising in pitch.

"Dear Lord, Jane, whatever is the matter?"

Jane looked up to see Emily rise unsteadily from a wrought-iron chair, a canvas on an easel behind her.

"The nerve of that man, Emily. You'd never believe—"

"Lord Westfield?"

"Yes, Lord Westfield. The most arrogant, prideful, insulting man I've ever met."

"Whatever did he say to you? Why did he wish to speak with you privately?" Emily's normally smooth brow was knitted into a frown.

"To ask for my hand in marriage, that's why." Jane all but spat out the distasteful words.

"No," Emily said, her face beaming.

"Oh, yes."

"Then why are you angry? Surely you accepted his offer?"

"Why would I accept his offer? I declare, never in my life have I been so insulted."

"By an offer of marriage? From an earl with an enormous income? I confess I'm astonished. Why, he's perhaps the most eligible bachelor in all of Derbyshire. Everyone for miles about has speculated on whether or not he'd eventually be lured to the altar. Many have tried, none successfully. You've accomplished what no other woman has been able to." Emily came to her and laid one hand on her sleeve. "You should be honored by the compliment he has bestowed upon you."

"Honored? By his insults?" Jane shrugged off Emily's touch and paced a circuit before the easel. She thought of all the offers of marriage she'd received in the past—polite, sometimes passionate, declarations of abiding affection and admiration. Some—William Nickerson, for one—actually professed to love her. They'd acted as if Jane would be bestowing the greatest honor on them if she accepted their suit, and it had been with great regret that she'd had to refuse them. But never, *never* had a man acted as if *he* were doing *her* a favor.

He didn't want *her*—he wanted a mother for the child he called his niece, a vessel to carry his heir. A brood mare. Nothing more. She would save him a trip to London, that's all. She was convenient; he hadn't even felt the need to properly court her. He'd only expected her gratitude. He could have at least pretended admiration; it would have been so much less offending. She would have refused him either way, but at least her pride would have been spared.

Jane reached her hands up to her temples. Oh, what a confounding mess she'd gotten herself into. She wasn't able to think rationally, hadn't been able to since she'd come to Derbyshire. Perhaps it was time to go home. She'd gotten her answers, after all.

"Cousin Jane? It's time."

Jane realized Emily was speaking to her. She shook her head in confusion. "I'm sorry, Emily. Time for what?" Emily was standing behind the

chair, leaning against it, gripping the curved back
with white knuckles and a mysterious smile.

"The babe. It's time. My water just broke."

The impertinent woman had actually refused
him. Hayden could barely believe the insult. Damn
Tolland and his brilliant ideas. He laid the crop on
Andromeda's flanks, spurring the stallion into a
gallop as he crossed the wide-open field on the far
side of the wood.

She must be mad. Wasn't there some mysterious
mental illness that plagued her mother's family?
She seemed rational enough on first inspection,
but perhaps he'd misjudged her. Had she expected
flowery professions of love? He only believed in
speaking the truth, and she seemed a sensible girl,
not the type to expect pretty words and false
promises. Whatever was the matter with her? He'd
made a perfectly reasonable offer, one which any
sensible woman in her position would gladly accept. He was utterly and completely confounded by
the absurdity of it.

At last he reined in the horse. He'd been riding
aimlessly for more than an hour, and it had done
nothing to ease his wounded pride. He needed a
drink. Badly.

He swung down from the saddle as a groom hurried over to take the reins, Vlad loping alongside
the boy. The enormous white dog hurried to its
master's side, leaning against him with his tongue
lolling out. Hayden reached down to stroke the
thick, wavy coat. "Good afternoon, old boy. Out for
a run? Where's your flock?"

Vlad answered by taking Hayden's hand in his
muzzle, chewing his master's fingers with delight.

The ferocious dog's gentleness never failed to amaze its owner. Hayden had bought the dog as a pup on the Continent, impressed by the loyalty and intelligence he'd seen in the breed. He hadn't been disappointed. Vlad took to his beloved sheep at once, defending the flock with his life. Hayden knew with unflagging certainty that the dog would similarly protect his master—or Madeline—should the need arise.

The pair set off together across the park toward the house. Hayden bent and retrieved a sturdy stick from the lawn and threw it ahead, into the tall grass for the dog to fetch. Vlad lunged after it, disappearing from sight and then racing back to drop the stick at Hayden's feet. He threw it again, enjoying the game. Yet several minutes later, the dog had yet to return to his side. Puzzled, he increased his stride, anxious to see what had distracted him.

Cresting the last rise before the drive, Hayden heard Vlad's raucous bark and craned his neck, searching for the cause of the excitement. His brows drew together at once. Tolland's coach was in the drive. Strange, as he'd thought Tolland had gone into the village for the day.

"Why, what a beautiful boy you are," he heard a familiar voice call out. An unmistakably feminine voice.

What the hell?

And then he saw her—Miss Rosemoor, eagerly stroking the intimidating dog's ears as if he were a lapdog. What was she doing here, so soon after he'd quitted her company? Had she come to tell him she'd reconsidered his proposal?

His chest swelled with anger. Did she honestly think he'd repeat the offer?

He walked indolently to her side and bowed. "Miss Rosemoor. What an unexpected surprise."

Her eyes visibly sparked. "Yes, well, you'll pardon the inconvenience." She cleared her throat and cast her gaze down to the pebbled drive. "I've only come to ask for your assistance on behalf of Mrs. Tolland. The baby . . . ahem . . . her time has come and we were hoping you could be convinced to go into town and fetch Mr. Tolland at once. Mrs. Tolland is quite desirous of his presence at home."

Devil take it, he hoped there weren't complications. "And Mrs. Tolland . . . she is well? No problems, I hope?" Women were so damned close-mouthed about childbirth; he knew he'd never get a straight answer from her.

The color rose in her face at once. "Oh, no, everything seems very well. She only wishes for her husband's company."

He hoped she spoke the truth. He'd find out for himself soon enough. "And no servant could be spared to request my assistance?"

Her cheeks flushed a lovely pink. "The household was in a bit of disarray. I volunteered to come myself."

"Did you?" he asked, masking his surprise. "How very charitable of you. Very well, I'll try to locate him at once."

"Thank you, my lord." She curtsied politely, that same false smile of hers on her face.

Hayden dismissed her with a bow and watched as she climbed back into the coach. As the conveyance rattled off down the drive, his humor faded. He summoned his own carriage with trepidation, hoping he could locate Tolland without trouble. First he'd try the gaming hells, then the brothel. And then, he thought with a grimace, if worse came to worst, Adele's house.

"A girl? Oh, how wonderful. Has Mr. Tolland seen her yet?" Jane clapped her hands in delight.

"Yes, mum," the midwife said with a satisfied smile. "He's just left 'er bedside to pour himself a celebratory drink. Mrs. Tolland has asked for you."

"Of course. Thank you." Jane pushed open the door to Emily's bedchamber, a smile slowly spreading across her face as she saw mother and child curled together on the bed. Jane hurried to Emily's side and peered down at the tiny infant cradled in her arms.

"Oh, Emily, she's beautiful. What will you call her?"

"We were thinking we'd call her Amelia."

"Amelia." Jane tested the name. "It's lovely." She felt tears well in her eyes, joyful tears.

Jane saw a shadow pass across Emily's features. "Cecil's angry I presented him with a daughter, no matter how beautiful. He was desperately hoping for a son."

"Cecil's disappointed, perhaps, but I'm certain he's not angry. It's only natural for men to wish for sons. The next one will be a boy," Jane reassured her.

"Perhaps," Emily answered, pushing back the blanket from the babe's forehead. "Look at her hair. Isn't it lovely?"

Downy hair the color and texture of cornsilk dusted the child's head. "It is, indeed. She's perfect, Emily. I'm so very happy for you."

"Thank you, Jane. I hope one day soon you'll be similarly blessed. Perhaps you'll reconsider Lord Westfield's—"

"There's no possibility of that. No, I'm perfectly content being everyone's favorite aunt," Jane lied, at once overwhelmed with the desire for a child of her own.

"I hope you'll change your mind, Jane. I . . . I cannot begin to describe the way I feel right now. So complete. I've risked . . ." Emily shook her head. "I would risk anything for such a blessing," she corrected, placing a kiss on the sleeping babe's forehead.

A knife twisted in Jane's heart. Did Emily recognize the same risk she did, but just refused to speak of it? *Please,* Jane pleaded silently, *please let Emily be spared.*

Chapter Seven

"Emily, dear," Jane called out, "are you almost ready? The guests have all assembled in the drawing room." She peered anxiously around the door that stood ajar and saw Emily sitting motionless at her vanity, staring at her own reflection. "Emily?"

The seated woman didn't move a muscle.

With a frown tugging at the corners of her mouth, Jane hurried to Emily's side and laid a hand on her shoulder. Their eyes met in the glass, Emily's at last flickering to life.

"Jane?" Her voice wavered, sounding slightly disoriented.

"Your guests have arrived. Shall we go down together?"

"I'm just so very tired."

"Of course you are. It's only natural." Jane patted her shoulder. "With poor Amelia so colicky, you haven't gotten much sleep these past weeks."

Jane saw a shadow waver across her cousin's eyes, and she felt her own muscles tense in response. Her worries for her cousin increased daily. Emily seemed to go about in a daze, her brow furrowed and her mouth pinched. She'd grown paler each day since Amelia's birth.

"It's more than that," Emily said, her hands shaking as she clutched the vanity's marble top. "My nerves . . . I'm so anxious, so irritable. Amelia does nothing but cry, no matter what I do for the child. I don't . . . I don't know what to do for her."

"Many infants suffer so. It will pass with time; didn't the apothecary say so?"

"I suppose." Emily sighed heavily. "Has Lady Adele arrived?" she asked, her voice flat.

"I believe so. You've quite a number of guests. Perhaps we should—"

"Cecil's never forgiven me for presenting him with a daughter, you know. He thinks it entirely my fault."

Jane swallowed, unable to reply.

"The day I gave birth to Amelia, he came to my bedside reeking of perfume. Cheap perfume."

"I'm sure you're mistaken, Emily."

"I'm not. No doubt Lord Westfield dragged him from some woman's bed."

Jane gasped. "Emily, you shouldn't say . . . We shouldn't speak of such things."

"Cecil has many lovers. He thinks I don't know, of course. Lady Adele is no doubt his latest conquest."

Jane shuddered, remembering the night of the Ashbourne assembly—recalling the come-hither look the woman had given Cecil, and then the following debacle in the maze. No doubt Emily was correct. But to speak of such matters . . .

"Ours was not a love match," Emily continued, her voice hollow. "Still, it pains me. There are times when I cannot get out of bed, so paralyzed am I by fear and despondency."

Jane reached for her shoulder. "But why did you not tell me this before? Perhaps there's something to be done—"

"What's there to be done? I'm just like my mother,

don't you see?" Emily cried out vehemently. "Sometimes I fear that Amelia would be better off without me."

"No, that's not true, Emily." Jane shook her head.

"Other times I've listened to her inconsolable wailing, nothing I can do to comfort her, and I've . . . I've wished she had never been born."

Jane's hand rose to cover her mouth. Emily's gaze met hers once again in the glass, her eyes silently pleading for help.

Jane dropped her hand, resolved to conceal her fears, to show nothing but support. She would help her cousin through this. "Emily, if you ever experience such doubts, such thoughts again, I implore you to come to me at once. I'll do whatever I can to help you. Will you promise me this?"

A single tear escaped to trail down one cheek as Emily nodded her assent. "Thank you," she choked out. "I'm so frightened."

"Don't be frightened. Perhaps a change in scene would do you good. Cecil spoke of going to London next month—perhaps we can convince him to bring us all along."

"Perhaps," Emily answered, a faint smile appearing at last. "It's been so very long since I've been to Town. My cousin Harriet is being presented this year. It would be lovely to attend her come-out."

"I agree. But what shall I tell your guests? Are you well enough to come down to dinner?"

"I believe I am." Emily allowed Jane to thread her arm through hers. "I cannot tell you how much better I feel for having shared my fears. Thank you, Jane. I . . . I don't know how I'd get through this without you."

"There's no need to find out. I'll stay with you as long as you want my company."

* * *

"At last, my lovely wife," Tolland said.

Hayden looked up from his port as Emily and Jane appeared together in the doorway. Tolland strode over to join them, taking Emily's arm in his. Jane's icy gaze met his, and he immediately looked away.

Hayden wished he were anywhere but there in Tolland's drawing room, surrounded by the cream of Ashbourne society. And yet, this was meant as a celebratory dinner, and he would not insult Emily by his absence, no matter his personal discomfort. It was bad enough that Adele was there, pretending to be Emily's friend while shamelessly casting sultry glances at the woman's husband every time her back was turned. But worse still was suffering Jane Rosemoor's company. It was insupportable. Hayden tipped back his port, draining the glass in one long draught.

Impertinent chit. It wasn't as if she had any other prospects, as far as he could tell. He turned to eye her coldly as she perched beside Emily on the sofa. Her butter-colored frock skimmed her figure enticingly, stretched taut across her bosom. Alabaster skin, flushed the palest pink, spilled from the deeply cut neckline, beckoning to his eyes. He forced his gaze up to her face, her dimpled cheek flushed, her blue eyes fringed by thick lashes. A band of cream-colored lace encircled her chestnut tresses, one lock brushing a perfectly curved shoulder. He leaned against the wall, his arms crossed, watching her curiously as she hovered protectively over an usually wan Emily.

"I hear Amelia is a darling," Adele said, leaning

toward Emily, her tone patronizing at best. "Why, just last night Tolland was telling me—"

"Last night?" Emily interrupted, her brow furrowed.

"Yes, last night. I had the pleasure of meeting him in the village last night, isn't that so?" Adele simpered, smiling seductively at Tolland.

"It's true," he answered curtly. "A very unexpected surprise, of course."

"Of course," Adele murmured.

Emily's face went white.

Everyone in the room fidgeted visibly in discomfiture.

What the hell was Adele doing?

"As I was saying, Tolland was telling me what a dear she is. Very disappointing not to have a son, of course, but—"

"Lady Adele, might I request a private word with you?" Hayden crossed the room in several strides.

The look of sheer delight that crossed Adele's features sickened him as he reached for her arm. In stone silence, the pair made their way across the room, every eye trained on them. Hayden could barely contain his rage, which simmered just beneath the surface, threatening to boil over before they reached a private spot.

As soon as they crossed the threshold and the door swung shut behind them, Hayden tightened his grip on Adele's arm, practically dragging her down the hallway and into the first room they encountered. Tolland's library.

"Ouch," Adele cried, wrenching her arm from his viselike grip. "You're hurting me, Hayden."

"What the bloody hell do you think you're doing?" he barked.

"I have no idea what you're talking about." Her cold eyes met his.

"You know exactly what I'm talking about. Listen to me, Adele, and listen well. I want you to go back into that room, make your apologies to Mrs. Tolland, and take your leave at once. Make up some excuse—I don't care what you say. But I want you out of this house within the half hour, do you understand? And if I ever see you again in Mrs. Tolland's company, I'll—"

"You'll *what*, Hayden? Bring physical harm on me? I doubt it. Sully my reputation? Why, you've already done so. Your idle threats don't frighten me. But I will promise to stay away from your precious Mrs. Tolland if you'll admit that you're jealous." She reached for his sleeve. "Admit it, Hayden. You miss me in your arms, in your bed. I'll do whatever you ask of me, don't you see? You'll never find another woman so willing, so eager to please. No one has set your blood racing as I have. I know you'll never forget that night in your carriage—me straddling you, riding you like—"

"You're wrong, Adele. I have forgotten. Your memory has been easily erased." It was the truth, as it had taken very little effort to remove the memories of their ill-considered affair from his consciousness. He wanted no reminders of his poor judgment where she was concerned.

"Do you mean to say that another woman . . . that you've . . ." Adele sputtered.

Hayden's only response was silence. Yes, someone else had surely set his blood afire, far more than Adele ever had. Images of Jane flashed in his mind, her hands entwined in his hair, drawing his head toward hers, her warm, honeyed mouth so pliant, so welcoming.

"No, I don't believe it. You want me," Adele said silkily, obviously misinterpreting the lustful look in his eyes. She advanced toward him like a cat stalking its prey, her sheathed claws enveloping his neck before he'd had the chance to react. Her hard, demanding mouth was on his before he knew it.

The door swung against the wall with a thump.

Hayden roughly shoved Adele aside, stunned to see Jane standing in the doorway, one hand covering her mouth, her eyes round with surprise.

"Why, Miss Rosemoor," Adele called out sweetly. "Did you come to see where the brutish Lord Westfield dragged me off to? I assure you no damage has been done." Her smile was a triumphant one.

"My—my shawl," Jane stuttered, pointing to a square of lace lying across the back of one chair.

Hayden strode over to the chair and picked up the shawl, inhaling the faint, spicy scent that wafted from its folds. He handed it to Jane, who snatched it from him as if she were terrified of her hand meeting his. As if he were a leper. A monster.

"It's not what you think, Miss Rosemoor," he said, amazed by his words. He owed her no explanation.

She met his gaze and held it for a moment, her eyes seeming to gather in intensity like sapphire storm clouds. Her lips were parted ever so slightly, and he could hear her quick breaths, could feel the heat from her cheeks across the distance that separated them. Without another word, she spun on her heel and fled.

"Jane," he called out after her. "Miss Rosemoor," he corrected, just as the door banged shut.

Hayden's blood turned cold as Adele threw back her head and laughed. "Badly done, Hayden. Badly done, indeed."

He couldn't agree more.

* * *

Jane hid behind the cards she held in her hand, fearing that the color in her cheeks would betray her emotions. Try as she might, she could not erase the image of Lord Westfield and Lady Adele pressed together, joined in a passionate embrace. Of all the rooms in the house, why had they chosen the exact one where she'd left her shawl for their little tryst? She knew she shouldn't care, that Lord Westfield's amorous attentions were none of her concern, and yet she felt somehow . . . violated. It hadn't been so many weeks since he'd offered her his hand in marriage, after all. Just what kind of man was he? she wondered. Was this some sort of game he played, toying with a woman and then quickly moving on to the next? Was Lady Adele his lover? She had addressed him by his given name the night of the assembly, after all. Could they not cool their ardor long enough to pass an evening in polite company without removing themselves for a romp?

And to think she had allowed herself to believe that he'd dragged Lady Adele out of the drawing room in a rare act of gallantry—that he would administer a severe dressing-down to the woman. She'd thought it an almost heroic gesture.

But no, he'd only pulled Lady Adele out of their company to kiss her. Clearly, it was something he made a habit of, despite his assertion to the contrary. An unfamiliar pang of jealousy shot through her heart as she tossed a card to the green felt table. Thank goodness the loathsome woman had taken her leave so abruptly.

Jane sighed, glad she was not hanging out for a husband. What if she'd been swayed by her indisputable attraction to the rakehell? For she could no longer deny that the attraction existed. She longed for the return of her sensibilities. She wasn't herself these days, and it frightened her.

"Have you any news from your brother, Mrs. Tolland?" Lord Westfield asked. Jane looked up from her cards with surprise. She hadn't realized Lord Westfield was acquainted with Emily's family.

"Why, yes," Emily answered with a bright smile. "I received a letter from Anthony just yesterday. He's getting on well in Hertfordshire."

"I'm very glad to hear it. I hope to pay him a visit on my way to London in a fortnight."

"A fortnight?" Emily asked with a grimace. "So soon?"

"Yes, I'm afraid I have some, ahem, pressing concerns to take care of in Town." He directed his gaze toward Jane. She answered it with a scowl and then returned her attention to her cards.

Ah yes, she thought. That trip to London to secure a bride. He was no longer spared that trip after all. Unless, of course, Lady Adele had agreed to fill the position.

"Wait till you see his two eldest boys, Lord Westfield," Emily continued. "They've grown so big and boisterous. I declare, they remind me of you and Anthony when you were lads, always at fisticuffs."

Jane looked up over her cards again. "I didn't realize your acquaintance went back so many years," she murmured.

"Oh, yes," Emily answered. "Why, I've known Lord Westfield all my life."

"My family has a lesser estate in Gloucestershire," Lord Westfield explained. "Neighboring Mrs. Tolland's childhood home. My brother lives there now. As children, we spent most of the winter months there, as the climate was more suited to my sister's weak constitution. Mrs. Tolland's brother and I went to Eton and Oxford together."

"And, I must say, Lord Westfield was my greatest champion. Anthony was horrible to me most of the time, relentlessly teasing and torturing me. Lord Westfield soundly boxed his ears a few times on my behalf." Emily smiled shyly at the earl.

"Is that so?" Jane asked curiously.

"Mrs. Tolland was my late sister's dearest friend, and spent almost as much time at our home as her own. I came to think of her as a sister," Lord Westfield said softly.

"Imagine my delight as a bride when I learned that Cecil had taken a residence neighboring Lord Westfield's ancestral estate. Friends *and* family in such close proximity." Emily was beaming, and Jane was relieved to see her spirits so lifted.

"I confess I imagined that you only came to know Lord Westfield when you married Cecil." Jane shook her head. Why, Lord Westfield became more and more complex as the days wore on. She was surprised by the sudden thought that perhaps he *had* pulled Lady Adele out by her ear as a protective measure toward Emily. After all, he'd never been anything but kind and gentle toward her cousin. Of course, the end result had been the same—he'd still managed to find himself in Lady Adele's arms, shamelessly kissing her.

No longer able to concentrate on her cards, she tossed them onto the table and excused herself. The blasted man did nothing but unsettle her, confusing her thoughts and stirring her emotions. She scurried across the room and took a volume of poetry from the shelf. She found a quiet corner and took a seat on the red velvet settee that sat beneath a wide window, flanked by an enormous potted palm. With trembling hands she opened the leather-bound book and began to scan the pages, unable to focus on a single word.

Tentatively, she glanced up, peering over the pages. Her heart practically leapt from her breast as she saw Lord Westfield standing directly across the room from her, leaning against the pianoforte. His gaze was trained on her, a puzzled look darkening his features, as if he were studying her like a specimen under a glass. She shivered and shrunk back behind the palm, returning her attention to the book. The words on the page were nothing but a blur.

Seconds later, she felt the hair on the back of her neck rise and gooseflesh cover her arms. Heart pounding, she lowered the book and looked to the floor, watching in trepidation as a pair of polished Hessians moved toward her. Her hands began to tremble, and the book slipped from her lap and onto the floorboards beside her slippers with a thump. Holding her breath, she reached for it, just as another hand snatched it up and held it out to her. She was afraid to raise her eyes and yet, at the same time, couldn't resist the strong, compelling pull to do just that.

She finally tipped her chin in the air, boldly meeting Lord Westfield's gaze.

"Byron," he drawled, his face an irritating blank. "I find his work overly sentimental."

For a moment she couldn't move, couldn't respond. She sat as still as a statue, gazing into the bottomless depths of his eyes, wondering just what kind of hold the man had on her senses.

At last she came to her wits, shaking her head as if to clear it. "As do I. Frightfully oversentimental."

She reached for the thin volume, his hand brushing hers as he placed it in her palm. Somehow, inexplicably, she felt his fingers stroke the back of her hand as he released the book into her grasp. She sucked in her breath, amazed both by his boldness and by the very sensuality of the gesture.

"May I join you?" he asked, his voice rough.

"I . . . of course." Had she any choice? He had seated himself by her side before she'd even spoken the words.

"I feel compelled to explain to you what you witnessed tonight in the library."

"There's no need for explanations, my lord. It was quite obvious what I'd stumbled upon and not at all proper to discuss it."

"Miss Rosemoor, I fear that you've made some unfortunate judgments about my character and I'd like to set things straight once and for all."

"Why? I'm a fair judge of character. I was quickly able to sketch yours, and nothing you say now will change that. Initial impressions are telling, my lord, and very often correct."

He balled his hands into fists by his sides. "You mean to tell me that your initial summation of character is implacable, regardless of the truth in it?"

"Yes, that's exactly what I'm saying." She refused to budge.

"Surely you realize the nonsensical nature of that statement? You cannot possibly be correct each and every time you so hastily judge someone."

"More often than not, I am."

He turned his head away from her, his jaw flexing, before turning to face her once more.

"What you witnessed this evening in the library was nothing more than a desperate woman's unwanted attentions. I would have immediately removed her person from mine whether or not you had entered the room when you did. Her embrace was unwelcome, uninvited, and unpleasant at best."

"I cannot say it looked that way," she replied. "Nor is it any of my concern."

"You're correct on that count. It isn't your concern, except that I recently made you an offer of marriage, one which you declined. I don't wish tonight's misunderstanding to further serve your need to justify such a foolish refusal. Think what you wish about your own reasons for refusing me, but don't think my offer anything but honorable and respectful."

"Respectful? You call that respectful? If I might refresh your memory, my lord, you managed to insult me while you offered yourself up as if you were some prize. I've received many proposals of marriage, and none phrased as unprettily as yours."

"And yet," he said softly, "my proposal was perhaps the most honest, most sincere of the lot."

Jane swallowed hard, astonished by the truth that resonated in his words.

He reached for her hand and drew it from her lap. "If I offended you, Miss Rosemoor, I apologize. I do not tolerate falsehood or pretense. I thought we might suit, yet did not want to mislead you with pretty words and false promises of love. I hope that someday you will come to appreciate that."

Her cheeks burned and she silently cursed her own stubborn pride—her vanity. She endeavored to speak the truth at all times; why did she not value that trait in others? Was she so far above him, playing games, hoping to lead him on a chase that would inevitably end in his disappointment?

Her eyes misted as she looked up at him, still clasping her hand in his. A slow smile spread across his face—the mask of indifference lifted, the curtain drawn from his eyes. She looked into their depths and saw only honesty, integrity, and sound moral character.

He spoke the truth about Lady Adele—she was surprisingly certain of it. When he gave her hand a gentle squeeze, she returned the pressure, a bittersweet, regretful smile tugging at the corners of her mouth.

"I say, Westfield, what are you and Cousin Jane speaking of so secretly over there?" Cecil called out.

Lord Westfield released her hand at once, resting his beside hers on the settee, his fingers just barely grazing hers.

"Nothing secret at all," he called out in reply. "Poetry."

"Byron," Jane answered brightly, perhaps too brightly. She lifted the book from her lap and held it aloft, aching at the loss of contact with Lord Westfield's hand.

She felt her stomach flip-flop, keenly aware that something had shifted between them, something subtle but substantial nonetheless. She only hoped it would not make their next meeting all the more difficult.

Chapter Eight

"She's a beauty, Tolland, the finest horseflesh I've seen in quite some time. A bargain, too, at that price." Hayden lowered the brim of his beaver hat as the noon sun rose high in a clear, cloudless sky. "How did you ever get Billingsly to part with her without paying dearly?"

Tolland smirked as he joined Hayden on the narrow, dusty lane that led back to the house. "It would appear that Billings House has found itself in dire straits. Too many unsuccessful nights at the poker table for poor Billingsly, I'm afraid. Being the generous soul that I am, I naturally offered to take the beast off his hands. He jumped at the first price named. I think for five quid more, he would've thrown in his wife, as well."

Hayden chuckled. "Surely she's worth more than five quid?"

"Well, if she's anything like her eldest daughter, then she is indeed worth a fair price." Tolland's brows rose suggestively. "I can say from experience that the delightful Mrs. Williams is a delectable morsel, indeed."

At once the fine afternoon was spoilt. Hayden's chest tightened, unbidden anger flooding his veins. It was all he could do to restrain himself from bloodying the fool's nose with one perfectly placed punch. But such an action would no doubt require an explanation to Emily, and he would do everything in his power to make sure she remained mercifully unaware of her husband's infidelities. As it was, he tried his best to rein in the man's lustful appetites, steering him away from temptation when he could. But he couldn't spend every bloody moment of his life keeping Emily's errant husband from straying.

Emily deserved better. He'd been furious when he'd learned of her arranged match with Cecil Tolland, his brother childhood chum. Tolland was a far cry better than Thomas, but still, he was not nearly a fine enough man for Emily. Indeed, Emily was a rare jewel—brilliant on the outside, fair and sweet, yet strong as the finest diamond.

He'd never have made it through those dark months following his sister's death if it hadn't been for Emily sitting by his side and offering him comfort when he thought there was none to be had. She'd been only a girl then, but possessing the quiet wisdom of a woman.

Years later, when Katherine had been snatched from him, he'd thought he would surely go mad with grief. Emily's family had been there, guests at Richmond Park for his wedding, and again it was Emily who had eventually pulled him from the blackness when no one else could. It had also been there at Richmond Park, in the wake of Katherine's death, that Emily had first met Cecil Tolland.

Hayden had been unable to convince Emily's father against the match, as Tolland was heir to a respectable fortune, even with no title to accompany it. Her father had been more than satisfied. He had three other daughters to worry about, after all.

Hayden found a measure of relief when the

newly wedded Tolland and Emily settled just down the lane from him, allowing him the opportunity to shield Emily as best as he could from her husband's true nature.

He clenched his hands into fists by his sides and took a deep, fortifying breath. No, boxing Tolland's ears wouldn't help, no matter how dearly he deserved it. Hayden was better served acting as Tolland's friend, not his adversary. It allowed him to watch over Emily without difficulty. With some effort, he managed to subdue his anger as he followed Tolland to the house for a drink.

Silently, he hurried up the front steps and entered the front hall, feeling a surge of anticipation quicken his heart. Would he catch a glimpse of Jane? Five full days had passed since they last met, and his desire to see her grew more insistent, harder to ignore, with each passing day.

"Mr. Tolland?" The stout housekeeper appeared before them, her mouth pursed.

"Yes, Mrs. Smythe?" Tolland doffed his hat, and Hayden followed suit.

"Mr. Winston came while you were out, and desires a word with you. He's asked that you come to his office in Ashbourne straightaway." The housekeeper bobbed a curtsy and disappeared down the hall.

"Too bad, Westfield," Tolland said, replacing his hat on his head. "We'll have to have that drink another time. Important business, this is. I should go at once."

Hayden refused to acknowledge the raw disappointment that washed over him. He would not get his wish today.

Tolland rushed out without another word, leaving Hayden standing there alone in the entryway.

"There you are, Cecil. I'm so worried about Emily—you must come at once . . ."

Hayden turned to face Jane, who stood halfway down the stairs, her face grave and one hand gripping the banister so tightly that her knuckles were white.

"Oh, Lord Westfield. I'm so sorry, I thought you were Cecil." Slowly, she descended the remaining stairs and stood on the landing.

"So I see. Your disappointment is evident."

Her brows rose, and she paused before responding. "You must forgive me, my lord. I'm afraid I'm not fit company today."

Indeed, she looked tired, her features drawn, her brow creased with worry. About Emily, she'd said, when she thought him to be Tolland.

He took a step toward her, his mouth curled into a frown. "Is Mrs. Tolland unwell?"

Jane shook her head. "No, she's . . . I'm afraid she's not at all herself today. I can't . . . I'm not certain—"

"Shall I send for the physician? I'll ride for him myself." He had taken three strides toward the door before the words were out of his mouth.

"No, I don't believe she needs the physician. I'm not sure what she needs. Her health seems well enough; it's her disposition that worries me." She shook her head again. "Forgive me. I shouldn't speak of such private matters to you." Her eyes welled with tears.

He hastened to her side and reached for her hand. "I beg your pardon, Miss Rosemoor, but if you have serious concerns about Mrs. Tolland's well-being, I implore you to share them with me at once. My friendship with your cousin goes back many years and she's been a comfort to me in dark times. If there's any way that I can similarly aid her, you must let me do so. May I see her?"

"She won't see anyone, not since yesterday afternoon. Not me, not the nursemaid with Amelia. She hasn't taken a single meal today and her door remains locked. I think that Cecil—"

"Take me to her."

"Lord Westfield, you know I cannot. It isn't at all proper."

"I don't give a damn about propriety. Take me to her," he demanded, the blood rising in his face.

"But Cecil—"

"Has just left for his solicitor's office in Ashbourne. He won't return for several hours." Without waiting for permission, he tossed his hat aside and sprinted up the stairs, taking two at a time. "Emily?" he called out, pausing before a door where a pair of maids stood, wringing their hands before it.

He rapped sharply on the door with his knuckles. "Emily? It's Lord Westfield. I'd like to speak with you. Please unlock the door."

There came no reply.

"Please, Emily." He rattled the doorknob in frustration.

Finally, a faint voice answered from the other side of the door. "Lord Westfield?"

"Yes. Won't you please let me in?"

"What if she's not decent?" one of the maids wailed, and Hayden silenced her with an icy glare.

Relief washed over him as footsteps shuffled toward the door. The key turned in the lock with a resounding click.

Pushing the door open a fraction, he saw Emily standing there, decently attired in a somber gown, a heavy shawl wrapped about her. He turned to glance over one shoulder at Jane, who stood motionless in the hall, her eyes wide with shock. She couldn't possibly think that anything untoward would occur—not between him and Emily. Surely she knew better. With a shrug, he entered the room and closed the door behind him. Any explanation would have to wait.

Time seemed to stand still as Jane waited for Lord Westfield to emerge from Emily's room. She'd sent the maids away and asked the housekeeper to prepare a tray for Emily, in case he was able to talk her into eating something.

Whatever could he be saying to her? And why would she agree to admit him, and no one else? Their conversation was muted by the thick, oaken door, but occasionally a snippet escaped. She distinctly made out the words "Amelia" and "Isabel," but then Emily's sobs muffled her words.

A pang of guilt shot through her for eavesdropping on what was obviously a personal conversation. Yet she was angry, too—angry at Lord Westfield for so blatantly disregarding propriety. Good Lord, he was a bachelor, ensconced in a married woman's bedchamber! She could barely believe it. Even so, she was certain that nothing untoward was happening on the far side of the door. But what if Cecil should arrive home? Would Cecil be so certain?

Maybe I should knock on the door, she thought, *and ask that they take their counsel to a more respectable location.* She shook her head. No, she couldn't do that. She couldn't very well leave, either. Overwhelmed with indecisiveness, she remained there, wringing her hands before the door for what felt like hours.

At last the door opened and Lord Westfield appeared. "Emily has agreed to take a meal in her room."

"Very good," Jane answered, then hurried down to summon Mrs. Smythe. When she returned, the door was ajar, and she entered to find Emily sitting on a chaise longue by the window, dabbing her eyes with a handkerchief. Lord Westfield stood by her side, one hand resting on her shoulder. Mrs. Smythe bustled in and silently placed a tray on a side table before exiting.

At last, Emily looked up at Jane and smiled weakly. "I'm so sorry, Jane dearest. I don't know what came over me. Please don't be angry at Lord Westfield."

"I'm only glad to see you well, Emily." Jane looked up to Lord Westfield with grateful eyes. Whatever he had said to her, it had done wonders. Emily was back again. Jane smiled at him, relief coursing through her.

Lord Westfield averted his gaze. Clearing his throat, he moved toward the door. "I'll leave you in Miss Rosemoor's care."

"Thank you, Lord Westfield," Emily said with a sniffle. "I'll not soon forget your kindness."

"Nonsense. You've shown me equal kindness when I was in need of it myself. I owe you much. I only hope that if you find yourself in such a state again, you will send word to me at once. I'll do everything in my power to help you, in any way I can."

"I know that you will, Lord Westfield. Thank you again."

He bowed, then strode out, closing the door softly as he went.

Jane turned back to Emily, who held out one

hand to her. "I'm so sorry, Jane. Can you ever for-give such silly behavior?"

"There's nothing to forgive." Jane sat down be-side her on the chaise. "I only wish I could bring you such comfort as he has." Jane shook her head in amazement.

"I was so overtaken by melancholy. It was terrify-ing, Jane. I was all but paralyzed. It's difficult to ex-plain."

"You don't have to, Emily. I know from my own experience. I suffer from bouts of melancholy my-self."

"Do you? Then you know. It's gotten so much worse since Amelia's birth. Lately I have to force myself from bed each morning, so gripped am I with fear."

"Can you tell me what you fear?" Jane probed tentatively.

Emily shrugged. "So many things. That I'm a terrible mother, a terrible wife. That when faced with my shortcomings, I'll lose all hope." Emily squeezed her eyes shut, and a tear trickled down one cheek. "That I might suffer my mother's fate."

Not again, Jane thought with a shudder. She squeezed Emily's hand reassuringly. "You're not your mother, Emily. You can either choose to give up, to give in to your dark thoughts, or you can choose to challenge them, to fight them with all your might."

"I'm not as strong as you, Jane. Sometimes I can-not fight it." She blew her nose into her handker-chief. "Lord Westfield thinks I'm strong, but he's mistaken. If he only knew . . ." Her voice broke as she trailed off. "He gives me such comfort, but still, I could not tell him."

Jane's heart thumped so hard against her ribs

that she feared it might burst. "Could not tell him what?"

"If I tell you, will you promise not to tell a soul? Not Cecil, not Lord Westfield. No one."

"Of course, Emily. You have my word." Jane's palms dampened in anticipation of what dreadful thing Emily might divulge.

"Yesterday afternoon I had the nursemaid bring the baby to me. Amelia was so happy, so cheerful, so I thought to spend some time alone with her in the garden. She started to fuss right away." Emily dabbed at her eyes. "I tried everything I could; I refused to give up. I brought her inside and tried to calm her, to get her to sleep. The nurse came and I sent her away, determined to prove to myself that I could do it, that I could soothe my own child. I rocked her, I held her, I fed her—I did everything possible. When I could take no more, I laid her on my bed and sat beside her, covering my ears, as she wailed on and on. I picked up the pillow and held it in my hands, and I actually thought to cover her with it, to silence her, if just for a moment."

A terror filled Jane's heart. *No,* her mind cried. "You wouldn't do it, Emily. I know you wouldn't."

"No, but I *did* have the thought, and it's not the first time. Remember?" Emily looked up at her with pleading eyes as she twisted the square of embroidered linen in her hands.

"I remember, but still, I don't believe you'd ever do such a thing." Dear God, she hoped not!

"Oh, Jane, I don't deserve to be a mother. I'm sure Cecil knows it and that's why he won't . . ." Emily's voice trailed off miserably, her tears renewed.

"He won't what?" Jane said, then immediately wished she could withdraw the words.

"He won't . . . he doesn't . . . he hasn't come to

my bed once since Amelia's birth." Emily smoothed her hands across her abdomen. "I'm as plump as a Jersey; look at me."

"Don't be ridiculous, Emily. Your figure is lovely. Come now, you're just exhausted and overwrought; you try to do too much. The nursemaid is here to care for Amelia; just take care of yourself. I know how it feels to despair, to have terror grip your heart. Let me help you," Jane pleaded.

"I know you're right. It's just so very difficult."

"I know. Shall we go to London, as we discussed before? Cecil is at his solicitor's office now, but as soon as he returns, I will speak with him about it."

"It won't do any good." Emily shook her head with a frown. "He wishes to go alone."

"I'll tell him that it's necessary to your health. Surely he won't refuse. We'll bring Amelia and the nurse, and you'll be able to meet my dear friend Lucy, Lady Mandeville. Why, she has a daughter not much older than Amelia, her third child. It will be lovely."

Emily nodded solemnly. "If you can convince him, it will be lovely indeed."

Oh, Jane would convince him, all right. She wouldn't take no for an answer, not with Emily's well-being at stake.

"Oh, and Lord Westfield has asked us to dinner at Richmond tomorrow night. I'm to remind you that you promised Madeline."

Indeed she had. "Will it please you to go, Emily?"

Emily nodded in reply. "Certainly. I'll be sorry to see him leave for Town."

As will I, Jane added silently, surprised by the thought.

* * *

"Mrs. Tolland, Jane!" Madeline ran into the drawing room, barreling toward them with her ribbons streaming out behind her.

"Miss Rosemoor," Hayden corrected.

"It's perfectly all right, Lord Westfield. I gave her leave to address me as Jane, did I not, Madeline?"

"She did," the child answered before wrapping her arms about Jane's legs. "I'm so glad to see you again."

Jane knelt and gave the girl a proper embrace. "I'm glad, too. It was kind of your uncle to invite us." As she stroked Madeline's hair, she looked up and met Lord Westfield's penetrating eyes.

He held her gaze but a moment before clearing his throat and looking away. "Just a few moments more, Madeline, and then you must allow Miss Crosley to take you upstairs to bed."

"Must I?"

"I'm afraid so," he answered with a shrug, then turned his attention to Cecil. The men moved toward the sideboard and the pleasures of their brandy.

Madeline turned her attention to Emily. "Mrs. Tolland, I've missed you dreadfully. Why haven't you come to call?"

"Didn't your uncle tell you that I've a babe at home now?"

"I suppose he did," Madeline said with a sigh, sounding bored.

"Her name is Amelia and she's still quite small," Emily offered. "She keeps me very busy these days, but soon I'll be able to call more regularly."

Madeline frowned. "Jane, you're not going to have any babies, are you?"

Jane looked up in surprise and saw Lord Westfield freeze, his drink midway to his mouth. She spoke quickly before he had the chance to chastise the child. "Most definitely not, Madeline. I haven't even a husband, you see." She smiled brightly at the child as the sound of Cecil's guffaws reached her ears.

"I'm glad. I hope you never get a husband." Madeline planted her small fists on her hips. At once, her face lit up and her lips parted with a small gasp. "I've an idea! You could marry Uncle—"

As if he'd anticipated her words, Lord Westfield was at her side in an instant. "Enough, Madeline. It is time for you to scamper off to bed. Come now, take Miss Crosley's hand." He steered her toward her governess, who had appeared in the doorway almost magically. "Off you go."

The heat in Jane's cheeks subsided, and she recovered her voice. "Lord Westfield, if you don't mind, might I see Madeline upstairs?"

"Yes, can she?" Madeline pleaded, tugging on his hand.

"I suppose so," he answered uneasily—as if he feared that the girl might continue with the same train of thought once out of his earshot.

"You can tell me more about your pony," Jane supplied, hoping to put his mind at ease.

The plan worked well. Madeline took Jane's hand and led her away toward the great stairs, chattering on enthusiastically about her beloved Mary Ann.

Halfway up the stairs, Jane flinched as Cecil's hearty laugh reached her ears. "You should've let the poppet speak her mind, old boy. Perhaps she has the right idea."

With a sigh of exasperation, Jane hurried her step.

* * *

For the third time in the past few minutes, Hayden glanced toward the drawing room's empty doorway, wondering what was keeping Jane. He set down his glass and took out his watch, flipping open the lid with a scowl. How long had she been gone? Fifteen minutes? Twenty? He snapped the lid closed again. Bloody hell, there was no telling what the child might be saying to her at this very moment. Clearly, the governess needed to have a talk with Madeline about appropriate topics of conversation with a lady.

"Don't you agree, Westfield?"

He realized Tolland was speaking to him. "Of course," he replied distractedly, having no idea what he'd agreed to.

"It's no use, Westfield. It's obvious you haven't heard a word I've said. Why don't you go upstairs yourself and fetch her back down here. I can't bear to watch you stare at the doorway another minute."

"I don't know what you mean." Hayden brushed away a speck of lint from his sleeve. "It's well past eight o'clock. I'm going to see when we will be called in to dinner." He strode out without waiting for a response.

No doubt his guests knew exactly where he was headed. He stormed up the stairs, feeling like a fool. This was madness. He hadn't the slightest idea what had induced him to extend the dinner invitation yesterday. He wanted to think it was concern over Emily's well-being, that he wanted to assure himself that her mood had improved before he left for London. But he knew it was more than that. He'd wanted to see Jane again. He should have known better.

Halfway up the stairs, he paused. He thought he saw a flash of pale blue silk on the landing above, moving toward the gallery, yet the nursery was one floor up. Curious, he took the remaining stairs two at a time. What was she doing, creeping through the house alone? Perhaps his initial impression had been correct, after all. Perhaps she *was* measuring windows for drapes. A sharp sense of disappointment startled him. He'd thought better of her.

Silently, he rounded the bend of the first-floor landing and turned into the wide gallery, stopping midstride as he saw her standing there, gazing up at a portrait on the wall.

"My grandfather," he called out, and she spun around sharply to face him.

"Oh, Lord Westfield." One slender hand rose to her throat. "You startled me." A flush stained her cheeks strawberry red.

"I suppose I did."

"I saw the gallery on my way back down and I'm afraid my curiosity got the best of me."

"You look lovely tonight." Would she simper at the compliment, as most ladies would? He spoke the truth, however. She was a vision in blue silk the color of the morning sky. "That color suits you."

She didn't respond. Instead, she turned back to his grandfather's portrait. "He looks just like you."

"Does he?" he asked. "I've never seen the resemblance."

"Well, the hair color is different, of course. But the eyes are the same." She turned to peer at him curiously. "Madeline's are the same unusual shade. Not quite green, but not really gray, either."

"Perhaps." Hayden shrugged, wondering at her sudden interest in familial resemblance.

"In fact, it's amazing how much she favors you," she said boldly, turning back to the portrait.

"Is it?" he asked in growing annoyance. "If it will

put your mind at ease, Miss Rosemoor, allow me to assure you that Madeline's father has the same eyes, just as my father did, and his father before him. She is my niece, and it should not surprise you that we favor one another in some respect."

"I didn't mean to imply—"

"Of course you did. If you'd like, I'll tell you how she came to be my ward."

She turned to face him, shaking her head. "No, it's none of my concern. Please forgive me, Lord Westfield. We must go down to dinner at once."

He held up one hand to stop her. It didn't signify, but he wanted to tell her—needed to tell her. "Dinner can wait. Madeline's mother was dying, and she brought her here when she was just a babe. Sophia was an opera singer, and she had been my brother's mistress for many years. They lived together openly in London, until Madeline was born. By then she was already quite sick, and he had tired of her. Thomas certainly had no interest in the child. He put them both out on the street, and she turned to me in desperation. She begged me to take Madeline, and against everyone's advice, I agreed. What else could I do? She stood there on my front step, clutching the babe to her breast while she retched pitifully into a bloody handkerchief."

"You did a very noble thing, Lord Westfield," Jane murmured, her blue eyes luminous.

He did not desire her approval. "There was nothing noble about it. I did not offer Sophia my protection. I took her child and sent her off to die. I never thought what it would mean to Madeline. I've raised her in a world that will never accept her. Who will marry her, the bastard child of my wastrel brother and his lover? How will she feel when society rejects her, after being raised in such privilege, shielded from her true position in this world? I've done her no favors."

"That's untrue." Jane laid a gentle hand on his sleeve. "Of course you have. You've given her a safe home, a secure bed to sleep in each night, the hope of an education."

"Yet I've denied her the one thing a child needs most."

"Whatever do you mean?" Her eyes narrowed perceptibly.

"Love, Miss Rosemoor," he answered softly.

She shook her head so hard that one chestnut tendril escaped its binding and fell across her alabaster cheek. "I don't believe that. I've seen you with her. Your love for her is evident."

"What you see is an illusion you've created in your own mind. You see what you want to see. I'm fond of her, yes, but I am no longer capable of loving anyone."

"That's nonsense, Lord Westfield. I do not believe it."

His chest tightened painfully. "What do you know of me, Miss Rosemoor?"

"I know that you care for Madeline, regardless of what you think," she entreated him. "You care for Emily, too. A kind heart beats in your chest, a generous heart."

"That's where you are mistaken." He offered his arm and nodded toward the stairs as the dinner bell sounded below. "In fact, I think you'll find I haven't a heart at all."

Chapter Nine

Jane balanced a wicker basket in the crook of her arm and set off across the park toward the wood, humming a tune as she walked. She tipped her chin in the air, allowing the sun past her bonnet's brim to warm her face. It was a fine day for a walk, and she'd come to love the dramatic Derbyshire landscape. Emily had sent her off with tales of an enchanting pool fed by a waterfall deep in the woods. She'd brought along the basket, as Emily had specifically mentioned that wood lilies often bloomed in abundance in a glade beside the pool, even as early as late spring when the winter had been as mild as the one they'd just had.

She took the path leading toward the right, just past the standing boulders, as Emily had instructed, and hurried her step in anticipation. The sound of rushing water grew louder as she walked on into the dense brush, and Jane knew the falls that emptied into the pool must be close by.

As she walked, her thoughts inevitably turned to Lord Westfield. "I haven't a heart at all," he'd said, and Jane could only wonder at those words. Odd words, especially spoken by a man who had so gallantly taken in a dying woman's child, a child who was his brother's illegitimate offspring. A foolish thing to do, perhaps, but certainly not heartless.

Madeline would never be accepted into society, but she'd have a good life, nonetheless, far better than the lot she'd have on London's streets. He'd no doubt send her off to a fine school, and then perhaps she'd find a position as a lady's companion or governess. A marriage into the gentry could still be accomplished, even for a girl with Madeline's dubious origins. No, despite his words, Lord Westfield loved his niece. Jane was certain of it. He had his faults, the arrogant man. But heartlessness was not one of them.

Jane raised her skirts and stepped carefully over a downed tree, its trunk covered with spongy green moss. The water's roar grew louder still, and she pushed by a veil of ferns, their fronds angling across the barely visible path. At last the falls came into her sight, a narrow cascade tumbling over a stand of rocks perhaps twelve feet high and falling into a wide pool of shimmering blue-green water.

Jane quickened her gait, enthralled by the tranquil setting. As she approached, the water rippled strangely. Something slick and dark surfaced, displacing the water with a rush.

Jane's hand rose to her mouth, the basket dropping to the mossy ground beside her boots with a thud. *Oh, dear God.* It was a man, his backside facing her. Sunlight pierced the thick canopy above the pool, bathing the water in a ray of light and clearly illuminating the swell of the man's bare buttocks above the waterline. She sucked in her breath, immobilized by shock. She knew she should turn and flee at once, but she was positively mesmerized by the sight before her.

Fat droplets of water dripped from his dark head and down his back in tiny rivulets. Muscles rippled across the length of his back as he propelled himself forward, back toward the foam-tipped water that tumbled down the greenish rocks.

At last her limbs obeyed her command, and she took a step backward, right into her basket. With a yelp, she fell to the ground in a heap, one boot tangled in the wicker handle.

In stunned horror, she watched as the man spun around, a spray of water accompanying the motion. *Lord Westfield.*

"Oh!" she cried out.

She saw his eyes widen in surprise. "Dear Lord, Miss Rosemoor! Are you hurt?" He moved rapidly through the water, toward her.

"No," she managed to say, attempting unsuccessfully to gain her feet with a modicum of grace. Her eyes flew involuntarily to the length of his torso, and followed the trail of dark hair down his stomach where it disappeared beneath the surface of the water. Her gaze flew immediately back up to his face. "Good heavens, my lord! You're unclothed!" At last, she disentangled herself from the basket and rose on unsteady legs.

"A fine observation, Miss Rosemoor. I was not expecting spectators."

"B-but," she sputtered, "you're right out in the open. Anyone could stumble upon you."

"On my own property, I might add."

"Your property? But Emily said—she said—"

"Emily sent you in this direction, then?" His mouth curved into an arrogant smile. She attempted to look anywhere but at him, standing there glistening in the sunlight, utterly and completely nude. Thank God he remained modestly immersed in the water. Even so, she'd never before seen a man shirtless—not even her brother Colin. Her own curiosity made her cheeks burn with humiliation even as she secretly allowed herself to admire his spectacular male form. She swallowed hard before finding her voice. "Yes, Emily specifically sent me here in search of wood lilies. I had no idea this was your property."

"That line of trees behind you marks the property line, although I've always been happy to share this pool with the Tollands. With forewarning, that is, as I make a habit of bathing here in the falls. Unclothed. A fact I'm certain Emily is aware of. Wood lilies, eh?"

"Are you suggesting that Emily sent me here on purpose, hoping that I'd encounter you in such a state of . . . of dishabille?" The heat in her cheeks rose.

"That's exactly what I'm suggesting, Miss Rosemoor. Your cousin is a clever woman. Never underestimate her."

"That's nonsense," Jane protested with a wave of one hand. "Whatever would it accomplish?"

"Need I spell it out for you? We're alone, together, and as you so astutely pointed out, I am unclothed. To what conclusion does that lead you?"

She felt the flush spread from her cheeks down her neck. "Emily is aware that you have already offered your hand in marriage and that I declined your *kind* offer. What would she do, send the vicar here in search of wood lilies, too, hoping he'd find us together?"

"There's no vicar at Richmond," he countered. "The post has remained empty for many years now."

"Well, then, what purpose would such maneuverings serve on her part?"

"What if you were to find yourself in my arms,

Miss Rosemoor? In a compromising position? What then? Would you still refuse my suit?"

"You wouldn't dare," she said breathlessly. He took two steps toward the shore. "Stop!" she called out. "For the love of God, my lord. This is indecent."

"You're blushing, Miss Rosemoor. Furiously. Does my 'state of dishabille,' as you so delicately put it, unsettle you so?"

"What do you think?" she snapped. "Of course it does. Need I remind you that I am a lady? It's not every day that I find myself in such a position. Why, even Colin wouldn't dare to . . . to . . . well, to so blatantly parade about in such a state."

"I must confess, I'm finding a great deal of enjoyment in your discomfort. What you call 'blatantly parading about in such a state,' Miss Rosemoor, I call enjoying the outdoors, bathing in the privacy of my own grounds. And, I might add, no one is forcing you to remain here in my presence. You should see yourself; you look like a frightened fox, cornered by the hounds."

"I'm not frightened."

"Aren't you? You're terrified that I might walk out of the water at any moment."

"Don't be absurd. It's not as if I haven't seen a . . . the . . . the male form before," she lied. Foolish talk. Hadn't she just said that she'd never before found herself in such a position?

A deep, booming laugh echoed off the trees. Clearly he saw through her words. "Is that so? Then you won't mind if I come out now. It's getting a bit chilly, standing here having this conversation with you, no matter how pleasant." He moved toward the shore, the water behind him forming a V as he pushed through it. "My clothes are right there on that branch, just to your right. Would you mind—?"

"I most certainly *would* mind." Jane spun around with a huff, her back to him. "You're positively barbaric, you know. Completely uncivilized." She heard his footsteps on the soft earth, followed by a faint rustling sound. She sighed with relief, hoping he was retrieving his clothing. She reached blindly for her basket, knowing it must be somewhere around her feet. "I should go. What if what you say is true, and Emily has sent someone out here to witness us together?"

"Who would she send? Tolland? I wouldn't worry. I'm sure she was counting on your own sense of duty, once you found yourself unable to resist my charms."

"Ha!" She rolled her eyes heavenward, her back still facing the sound of his movements. "You overestimate your appeal, I'm afraid. I'm in no danger of succumbing to your so-called charms."

"An assertion I'd sorely like to test," came his reply.

Jane knew she should go—immediately. What on earth was stilling her feet and holding her in this dangerous spot? She was surely turning into a silly fool, and she didn't like it one bit.

"You may turn around now, Miss Rosemoor," Hayden said, pulling on his boots. "I'm sufficiently clothed as to no longer affront your maidenly sensibilities." He saw her spine stiffen in reply.

"I really should be going." She reached for her basket, her hand visibly trembling. She turned so her profile faced him, obviously avoiding looking in his direction, yet remaining rooted to the spot, not moving a muscle to flee as she insisted she must.

"Miss Rosemoor?" Finally her gaze flicked toward him, her mouth set in a tight line of disapproval.

"You could at least button your shirt, you know," she snapped. "Do *try* for civility."

He glanced down at his unbuttoned linen and shrugged. "I'm not yet dry. Shall I help you locate the highly sought-after wood lily? I believe it's generally found over here in abundance, although I'm not certain any are yet in bloom." With a gesture to the right he moved off toward the small glade just beyond the falls. "Watch that root there, it'll surely—"

Thud. He spun around in time to see the usually composed Miss Rosemoor fall into a heap of muslin for the second time in one day. He couldn't help the laughter that issued forth at the sight of the fuming woman, her cheeks flushed delightfully pink and her eyes flashing angrily.

"I suppose you find this funny?"

"I'm sorry. Not very chivalrous of me, is it? Here, let me assist you." He reached a hand out to her and she took it warily, rising unsteadily. He saw her wince as she put weight on her right foot, her leg buckling beneath her.

His arms went around her instantly, his brow drawn in concern. "Are you injured?"

"No, I . . . ahhhhh." She bit her lower lip. "Yes. My ankle. It's smarting a bit."

In a swift motion, he lifted her off her feet and into his arms, carrying her back to the side of the pool. He set her gently on a smooth stump and began to unlace her half boot.

"What are you doing? Remove your hands at once." She clutched at the sides of the stump.

"I'm checking your ankle, Miss Rosemoor. You might have sprained it. If I don't get the boot off now, the swelling might force me to cut it off. The boot," he added. "Not the foot."

"Don't be ridiculous. It's nothing. Just a twinge."

She peeled off her gloves and stuffed them into her apron pocket.

The boot slid off, and he circled the span of her delicate ankle, running his fingertips across the curved arch of her foot and back to the ankle again. He decidedly felt a shudder run through her, and he smiled inwardly. Despite her protestations to the contrary, she clearly enjoyed his touch.

"Please," she protested. "You really mustn't. Ouch!" A hand flew out and gripped his shoulder. The linen slid down the slope of his shoulder, and her fingers made contact with his skin, still damp from the pool. Her hand slipped, sliding down over his breastbone, her palm flat against his bare chest. A jolt ran through him, startling him, at the intimate contact. There was no denying that he enjoyed *her* touch.

She pulled back her hand as if burned. He rocked back on his heels, steadying himself against the onslaught of lustful thoughts running through his mind. Bloody hell, it wasn't often that he found himself half clothed in the middle of the woods, alone with a woman as tempting as Eve herself. More than anything, he wanted to strip off her maidenly gown and make love to her beneath the falls. In seconds, his mind formed a picture of her standing naked, her skin bathed in sunlight as the foamy water tumbled over her shoulders. It took a great deal of fortitude to push the vision from his mind.

"Please, Lord Westfield. This is highly irregular. I really must go."

"As you've said. Numerous times. But look, your ankle is already swelling. Definitely a sprain, or a strain at the very least. The water in the pool is quite cold. I suggest you dip your ankle into it. That might keep the swelling down till you can get some ice. Here, can you pull down this stocking? I'll carry you over to the pool."

She clutched at her stocking, her eyes filled with terror. "Of course I can't. You shouldn't even mention such things."

"Good God, woman, your ankle is swelling up right before my eyes, and you're quibbling over whether or not to remove your stocking? I can assure you it would not be the first time I've seen a woman's bare limb. But, if you insist, put your foot in the water with your stocking on, then." He gathered her in his arms and carried her toward the pool's bank, lowering her to the grass beside him.

Without a word, she tentatively lowered her injured foot into the water, gasping as her stocking-clad skin broke the surface.

"There, how's that?" he asked after a moment of silence.

"Cold. Better."

"Good. Leave it there for a few minutes. It'll reduce the swelling and numb it some."

She shivered and wrapped her arms about herself. "However did you bathe in this water? It's positively frigid."

"I find it refreshing." It *was* cold. Despite his threats to the contrary, he never would have emerged from the water in her sight, not with what the cold did to his body—it certainly wouldn't have showcased his assets to their best potential. Of course, now that she sat beside him, her body brushing enticingly against his and the delicious curve of her ankle bared to his gaze, warmth was flooding to his nether regions, almost uncomfortably so. Before long he'd have to cool himself off again or his arousal would become evident.

"When do you leave for London?" she asked conversationally, jarring him from his lustful thoughts.

"In two days' time. I'll stop briefly in Hertfordshire to visit Emily's brother and arrive in Town shortly thereafter. Just in time for the resumption of Parliament following the Easter break. Why do you ask?"

She shrugged, and his eyes were involuntarily drawn to the swell of her breasts. "I'm just making polite conversation."

"And do you expect to come to Town yourself?"

"I'm not certain. I'd planned to join my mother there by midsummer, but now I'm thinking it might be good for Emily's spirits if we traveled there together as soon as possible. I shall speak to Cecil about it."

"Hmm, a fine idea. I'm sure she would prefer it to remaining here alone while her husband spends time in Town. You're a good friend to Emily."

"It would seem we have that in common, Lord Westfield. She admires you greatly."

"Yes, well, perhaps," he replied uncomfortably.

"Why does my pointing out your kindness to Emily make you uncomfortable?"

"Why the impertinent question?"

"That wasn't the least bit impertinent."

"Why haven't you married, Miss Rosemoor?" The question continued to burn in the back of his mind.

"I told you. No one suited." She looked off toward the horizon, her features hard.

"I don't believe you."

"Believe what you wish. I don't owe you any explanations."

"Perhaps you're hoping for a love match?"

"Of course not. I'm a sensible woman." She

swirled her foot in the water, sending an arc of ripples to the far side of the pool.

"Here, let me see." He reached for her foot, pulling it from the water. "The swelling's down. How does it feel?" He cradled it in his lap, massaging it.

"Much improved, thank you. That's not necessary." She tried to pull her foot from his grasp, but he only tightened his hold.

"Do you fear my touch, Miss Rosemoor?" He continued to massage her ankle with his thumbs.

"You're talking nonsense again. I'm not afraid of you, Lord Westfield."

"I think you are. I think you fear that I might kiss you again, and that you might like it."

She gasped as he released her foot and moved toward her, his mouth slanting toward hers. He saw her eyes widen, her pupils dilated. He softly brushed his lips against hers, his erection straining against his breeches' flap. With a groan, he took her mouth with his, his lips crushing hers, his tongue boldly seeking entrance.

He felt her hands move against him, as if she were going to draw him closer. With one sharp shove, he felt himself tumbling backward, right into the water below with a splash.

His feet found the sandy bottom and he came up, sputtering in indignation. Jane sat on the bank, watching him, her arms folded across her breasts, a smug smile on her face. "And you thought I couldn't resist your charms," she called out. He glared at her as she rose on unsteady legs and retrieved her discarded boot, limping as she went.

Blast it; he couldn't let her walk home, not in such a state. Her ankle would never hold out. He quickly gained the bank and climbed out. Without another word, he came up behind her and lifted her off her feet. His clothes sopping wet, he silently carried her back through the woods and right into the Tollands' front hall, a trail of water dripping in his wake.

Emily looked up from her needlework in surprise as he carried Jane into the salon and deposited her, now almost as wet as he was, onto the blue sofa.

Emily arose, her needlework still clutched in her hands. "What on earth?"

"Don't ask," Jane muttered.

With a nod to Emily, Hayden turned and strode out, bristling at the sound of feminine laughter behind him.

"Enjoy your time in Town," Jane called out gaily, just before the front door slammed shut behind him.

Chapter Ten

Mayfair, London

"Isn't this lovely, Emily?" Jane smiled at her cousin, who stood by her side holding a flute of champagne in one hand and looking happy and relaxed for the first time in ages. "Her Grace throws the most lavish balls."

Emily reached over to squeeze her hand in reply. "Coming to Town was a brilliant idea. I'm so glad you talked Cecil into it."

Jane looked around the crowded ballroom, filled with the *ton*'s most fashionable ladies and gentlemen, and sighed appreciatively. The Duke and Duchess of Falmouth's annual ball was perhaps the most sought-after invitation of the Season. She knew she had her close association with the Mandevilles to thank for their presence there. Already Lucy and Emily had become fast friends, and their first few days in Town had passed much too quickly, a pleasant blur of rounds of calls, dinners, and soirees. Now that she was here, in familiar circumstances and enjoying the Season as she always did, Jane would be very sorry indeed to return to Derbyshire in a month's time.

"Jane, Mrs. Tolland," a voice rang out through the crowd, and Jane looked up to see Lucy headed their way, her husband, Lord Mandeville, in tow.

"I thought I'd never push my way across the room," Lucy huffed. "What a crush tonight."

"Isn't it?" Jane replied. "You look positively radiant, Lucy."

Lord Mandeville reached his wife's side and bowed. "Miss Rosemoor, Mrs. Tolland. A pleasure, as always."

Jane curtsied in reply. "Why do you suppose it is that whenever Mandeville enters a room, it suddenly appears smaller?" The ladies laughed easily. Jane had once teased Lucy that Lord Mandeville wasn't so hard to look at, and it remained true. He cut a fine form indeed in his dark dress coat and perfectly knotted cravat. He was tall, dark, and imposing, and yet he gazed at his wife with such evident adoration in his indigo eyes that he set hearts aflutter wherever he went. Every woman wanted to be worshipped the way Lord Mandeville worshipped his wife.

"Where is Mr. Tolland tonight?" Lucy asked, her emerald eyes luminous in the candlelight.

"He went off to the refreshment room some time ago. I expect he'll eventually find his way back," Emily answered.

"If you ladies will excuse me one moment, there's someone I wish to speak with." Lord Mandeville raised his wife's hand and placed a kiss on her palm before striding off, the crowd seeming to part for him as he made his way through it.

Jane turned toward her friend with a smile. "So, Lucy, tell us the latest *on-dits*. Which debutante are they calling this year's *Incomparable*?"

"Without a doubt it's Miss Dorothea Upshaw. A very sweet-tempered girl. Have you made her acquaintance?"

"I don't believe we have," Jane answered.

"Who are her parents?" Emily asked.

"The Viscount and Viscountess Pemberton, from Surrey. I'm sure they're here tonight." Lucy rose on tiptoe and peered over Jane's shoulder. "There, that's Miss Dorothea dancing the Scotch reel with Sir John Astor. The lovely blonde in pale rose. I had the pleasure of speaking with her last week at Lady Stanley's luncheon, and I confess I was surprised by her intelligence. Perhaps the tastes of the *ton*'s gentlemen are improving at last."

"One can only hope," Jane replied with a grimace.

At once the lively music quieted, and then struck up again with a waltz.

Cecil reappeared at his wife's side to claim her for the dance, and Emily took his arm and followed him onto the floor with a delighted smile. Jane glanced over at Lucy, selfishly hoping that Lord Mandeville would remain engaged in his conversation a bit longer so that Lucy didn't disappear as well, leaving her to stand there alone, without a partner.

"I wonder who was lucky enough to secure Miss Upshaw's first waltz," Lucy asked, rising up on tiptoe again. "There she is, but I don't recognize the gentleman. He's uncommonly tall. I can't quite make out his face. You look, Jane. You're a good head taller than I am."

Jane couldn't understand Lucy's sudden fascination with the girl, but looked nonetheless. "Where? In rose, you said?"

"Yes, the pale rose crepe. There." She cocked her head as a twirling pair glided by.

Jane lost sight of the girl in question, then craned her neck rather indecorously in an attempt to find her again. "Wait, there they are. If they'd just spin back around so I could see his face. The backs of dress coats all look the same. Oh, there . . ." Jane stilled, her breath caught in her throat.

Dear God. It was Lord Westfield. She could only stare, openmouthed, as Miss Upshaw tilted her head to one side and gazed up at him, her dimpled cheeks stained pink, her bow of a mouth curving into the most charming of smiles. Jane suddenly felt as if she might be ill.

"Well," Lucy asked, reaching for her wrist. "Do you recognize the man?"

"I—no," Jane stuttered. "I'm afraid I don't." She looked around frantically as the waltz ended, seeking an escape as the dancers left the floor in pairs.

"Jane, whatever is wrong? You're acting so strangely."

"Nothing's wrong. I'm just . . . I could use a lemonade, perhaps."

Lucy peered up at her curiously, her brows knitted.

"Lucy," Lord Mandeville called out, shouldering his way through the crowd. "There's someone I'd like you to meet." He turned, and another man appeared at his side.

Jane's stomach lurched yet again.

"Lucy, I present Hayden Moreland, the Earl of Westfield. Westfield, my wife, Lady Mandeville."

Jane watched in horror as Lord Westfield took Lucy's proffered hand, bowing and placing a kiss on her knuckles as she curtsied. Hurriedly, Jane ducked behind Lucy, prepared to flee.

"A pleasure, Lady Mandeville," she heard Lord Westfield say.

Wherever were Emily and Cecil? Jane scanned the cavernous space, hoping desperately to locate them amongst the faces crowding toward the refreshment room. Purposefully, she dropped her fan and bent to retrieve it, glancing about nervously as she did so.

"Westfield and I went to Oxford together," Mandeville offered. "He's my regular opponent at the fencing club, a fixture at White's and an ally in Parliament, but until this year, I've not seen him actually enjoy the Season's entertainments."

Dear Lord, please don't let him recognize my back, Jane thought as she reluctantly straightened, still directly behind Lucy. She could not face him—not yet, not in this state of discomposure.

"Your husband has spoken highly of your talents," Lord Westfield said, deftly changing the subject. "Veterinary arts, he says, and I hear your stables are the finest in all of Essex."

"I like to think so. It *is* my passion," Lucy replied, her voice full of pride. "Are you acquainted with my dear friend Miss Rosemoor?" She felt Lucy turn, presumably looking at the empty space beside her. "Jane?" she called out.

"Miss *Jane* Rosemoor?" Westfield asked.

Jane had no choice but to step forward. "Lord Westfield. What an unexpected surprise."

He reached for her hand, and she obligingly raised it. His eyes never left her face as his lips grazed her knuckles. Jane averted her gaze, her cheeks burning as she saw Lucy's eyes widen with surprise.

"Then you've met Miss Rosemoor?" Mandeville asked.

"Indeed, I've had the pleasure." Hayden held her hand far too long before releasing it.

"Yes," Jane added, finding her voice at last. "We met in Derbyshire. Lord Westfield is Mr. and Mrs. Tolland's neighbor."

"What an interesting coincidence," Mandeville said.

"In fact, it is on account of Miss Rosemoor that I'm here tonight, forced to endure such nonsense, is it not?" Hayden asked.

"Is it?" Jane asked crisply. "I'm sure I don't know what you mean."

"Don't you?"

Lucy's head swung back and forth, from Hayden to Jane and back again, her curiosity evident in her expression.

"How is your ankle?" he asked.

"Completely healed, thank you. And have you fully recovered from your unfortunate spill into the pool?"

She saw a vein throb in his temple. "Indeed I have. If you're not otherwise engaged, Miss Rosemoor, might I request your next two dances?"

Jane resolutely shook her head. "I'm afraid—"

"She's not been engaged," Lucy cut in.

Jane shot her a mutinous glare. "Very well," she murmured, reaching for his arm and allowing him to escort her toward the dance floor.

"How dare you speak in such innuendo before my friends?" Jane hissed, as soon as they were out of earshot.

"I only spoke the truth," he said as he placed his hand at the small of her back.

"Yes, well . . . have you ever thought perhaps there's a time to simply hold your tongue? Now I'll never hear the end of her questions."

"Lady Mandeville seems charming. I'm amazed at her accomplishments. Does her husband exaggerate her talents?"

"Not in the least, I'm sure. Lady Mandeville has a special gift with animals."

"Fascinating."

"I agreed to dance, not make pleasant conversation," Jane snapped, feeling peevish. She fixed her gaze over his shoulder, refusing to meet his eyes. "And you're holding me much too closely," she added.

She distinctly felt him pull her closer still.

Just to vex her. Just as before, his touch made her heart race, her skin tingle. Every time she looked at him, she remembered the sight of him standing in the pool, bathed in sunlight, his chest bared to her curious eyes. She couldn't erase the image of his broad back, powerfully muscled, and the visible swell of pale buttocks peeking above the waterline. Her legs went wobbly at the memory, and it was all she could do to remain steady in his arms. Her weakness angered her, made her ill-tempered. She had no reason to be cross with him, after all. He was perfectly free to court whomever he wished, to dance with every debutante in the room if he so desired. Hadn't he come to London to do just that, to find an appropriate bride?

She allowed her gaze to flit to his face, recognizing the risk. What she saw there took her breath away. His gray-green eyes bored into her very soul. She felt her heart skip a beat as she tore her gaze away. He looked at her now just as he had that day by the pool, just before he'd kissed her. She'd desperately wanted to return his kiss, to feel his arms around her, but she'd known she couldn't. Even as the delicious taste of his mouth had tempted her almost beyond reason, she'd managed to come to her senses and do the only thing she could think of to prove that she was immune to his charms—shove him into the water. Drawn back to the present, she took a deep breath and returned her gaze to his face. Never before had someone looked at her with such unconcealed desire, such longing. It was positively indecent. As the orchestra's last strains faded away, Jane pulled away, barely able to catch her breath as her heart pounded erratically.

"I believe I've engaged you for *two* dances, Miss

Rosemoor. I suppose your friends would be curious as to why you quitted my company after just one."

"Oh, very well." She reluctantly returned to his arms as another waltz struck up. "Haven't you some debutante to trifle with?"

"I thought we were refraining from conversation," he said, one corner of his mouth twitching. No doubt he was enjoying this exasperating game.

Hayden gazed down at Jane, fuming in his arms as they glided about the room. He studied her face as she did everything she could to avoid looking at him. He'd pressed each and every one of her lovely features to memory these past weeks, summoning her visage before him whenever he closed his eyes. She was every bit as beautiful as he'd remembered. Her glossy hair reflected the warm candlelight, and her skin almost appeared to glow. Her eyes appeared a richer blue than he'd remembered, the flicker of the flames above reflected in their depths. He inhaled her intoxicating scent, reminding him of honey mixed with exotic spices—a far cry from the usual rosewater or lavender that always seemed to emanate from the fairer sex. Her touch, her scent, her warmth—her very presence—heightened his every sense, prickled his skin, set his blood afire. While he held her in his arms, he came more fully alive. The very idea disturbed him greatly, and he refused to allow himself to ponder the implications.

He'd been going through the motions, meeting the debutantes and assessing their wifely potential. His efforts had been met with success. He'd been deemed "mysterious" and "aloof," both desirable qualities to the silly girls of the *ton*. Yet only one had captured his reluctant attention.

Miss Dorothea Upshaw. She was brighter than most and attractive enough, suitably accomplished and impeccably bred. She'd made it perfectly clear that her attentions were driven by the desire to secure an advantageous match, and he admired her sensibility. Not a half hour ago, he'd thought her well suited.

And then Jane had to go and dispel the illusion. He'd felt nothing more than bland satisfaction as he'd held the childlike Miss Upshaw in his arms, nothing like the fierce fire that raced through his veins as he held Jane. He peered curiously at her face, her eyes downcast, her lashes casting shadows across her cheekbones. Her brow remained furrowed, her lips pursed. No doubt she was angry with him, and he hadn't any idea why.

"Perhaps you'll sate my curiosity and tell me why you're so angry with me?"

"I'm not angry," she said with a shrug. "I'm just surprised to find you here."

"Indeed?" He'd been equally surprised to see her. He could only wonder why Tolland hadn't seen fit to inform him of their arrival. "Might I remind you that I'm only here, forced to endure the dreaded marriage mart, because you refused my suit?"

"And how relieved you must be. You certainly looked as if you were enjoying yourself."

"I don't know what you mean." He hadn't been enjoying himself, not in the least.

"With Miss Upshaw. The Season's *Incomparable*, I'm told. What good fortune I *did* turn you down."

He froze, his blood beginning to boil as he stepped back from her. She was confusing the hell out of him, and he didn't like it one bit. He'd given her a fair chance, after all, and she'd thoroughly rejected him. Yet here she was, acting like a spurned lover. She knew he sought a match, after all. He'd made that quite clear. "What is it you want from me, Jane?"

"Miss Rosemoor," she ground out.

"Pardon me?"

"Please do not address me so informally, my lord. It's 'Miss Rosemoor.' And people are staring."

Indeed they were, but he didn't give a damn. "Very well, *Miss Rosemoor.*" He reached for her arm and led her off while the orchestra played on. He bowed stiffly before turning on his heel and stalking away from her, leaving her standing alone on the edge of the dance floor.

Jane stood frozen in utter and complete shock as she watched Hayden disappear through the gaping crowd.

"Miss Rosemoor," Lord Mandeville said, stepping in at once. He took her arm and led her back amidst the dancers where they picked up the waltz without missing a beat. "Dare I ask what just transpired?"

"I'm not quite certain myself," she muttered.

"I'll have a word with Westfield. There's no excuse for treating a lady so grievously, and in such a public forum."

Her gaze snapped up to meet his at once. "No. I'd prefer if you said nothing. In his defense, I spoke rather sharply to him, something I seem to do frequently in his company. Not that he doesn't deserve it, insufferable man," she added with a scowl.

"He'd best have a care. Lucy's fit to be tied. I sincerely hope he doesn't cross her path again tonight. I don't presume to know much about the ways of women, but I would suggest that perhaps you smile, as everyone is looking your way right now. No use in fueling the tabbies."

He was right. Jane responded by smiling brightly, tipping her head back and laughing as if Mandeville had just told her something most amusing.

"Good girl," he murmured as the music ended at last.

Jane continued smiling gaily as she laid her hand in the crook of his arm and followed him back to Lucy, amidst a hum of whispered speculation. Hadn't they anything better to do, the gossips?

Back at Lucy's side, Jane's confidence was instantly bolstered. "I'll explain it all later," she murmured to her friend in response to Lucy's questioning gaze.

"I certainly hope so," Lucy replied. "It's all I can do not to throttle the man myself. Whatever was he thinking?"

Jane looked up as Emily hurried over to her side, a frown on her face. Was the news of her slight traveling so quickly?

"Jane, dearest, I heard what happened. I can barely believe he'd do something so abominable, and to my own cousin. Shall we take our leave?"

"No, there's no need for that. In fact, I plan to thoroughly enjoy the rest of the evening."

"Very good, Jane," Lucy said, nodding in agreement. "And what lovely timing, too. William Nickerson is headed your way."

"Is he, now?" Jane couldn't help but smile as the one man who'd almost tempted her into marriage strode to her side and bowed.

"Lady Mandeville, Miss Rosemoor. What a delightful surprise. I had no idea you were in Town, Miss Rosemoor."

"I only arrived a few days ago, with my cousin, Mrs. Tolland." She gestured toward Emily. "Emily, I present Mr. William Nickerson, a very old and dear friend of mine. Mr. Nickerson, my cousin, Mrs. Cecil Tolland."

"A pleasure, Mrs. Tolland," he replied, bowing his fair head in her direction.

"It is, indeed," Emily answered.

"Miss Rosemoor, will you favor me with a dance?"

"Of course," she answered, taking his arm with a smile. There was nothing unsettling, nothing disturbing or frightening whatsoever about agreeing to dance with Mr. Nickerson. What a far cry from her last partner. She felt safe in his arms, secure. She was only glad they had remained on friendly terms since her refusal of his marriage proposal. She briefly wondered how he'd managed to remain unattached all these years. He was handsome, charming, a gentleman in every respect.

Once on the dance floor, she reached for his hand with a smile—a smile that quickly vanished. Over Nickerson's shoulder, she watched as Lord Westfield claimed his own partner.

Miss Upshaw, of course. Inwardly, she groaned.

Averting her gaze, Jane smiled up at her own partner as she followed his lead. She tried her best to avoid watching Lord Westfield from the corner of her eye, but it was no use. She could physically feel his presence each time he neared—a magnetic pull that made gooseflesh rise on her skin, made her cheeks burn. Even through the cacophony of music and voices, she could distinctly make out his deep voice and Miss Upshaw's lilting laughter. Was he deliberately edging closer? She felt her temper rising.

Minutes later, Nickerson pulled her from her thoughts with an easy laugh. "Tell me, Miss Rosemoor, are you still committed to the notion of remaining unmarried?"

"I'm afraid so," she answered. "If anyone could have swayed my firm resolve, it would have been you, Mr. Nickerson. Nothing has changed on that count."

"Are you certain?"

"Of course. Why do you ask?" Lord Westfield was

definitely moving closer, she was sure of it. Just to irritate her, no doubt.

"Well, if you'll pardon me for saying so, it seems you can't take your eyes off Lord Westfield."

"I don't know what you mean." She shook her head, the heat rising in her cheeks. Had she been so obvious?

"Oh, I think you do," he answered good-naturedly. "Hayden Moreland, the Earl of Westfield. I heard what happened earlier tonight, and I can't help but wonder."

"Wonder what?" she bit out, more sharply than she intended.

"Why, if he's tempting your resolve. If he's succeeding where I could not."

"I assure you, my resolve is as firmly in place as ever. I'm not so easily trifled with."

Nickerson grinned down at her. "Perhaps someone should warn him, then. He's positively simmering with jealousy at this very moment, even while he holds the lovely Miss Upshaw in his arms."

"Don't be ridiculous."

"I'm feeling a bit reckless tonight. Perhaps I should hold you closer." He did just that, pulling her dangerously close.

Jane couldn't help but smile.

"Hmmm, maybe not." He slackened his hold on her. "He's a good deal larger than I am, after all. I *do* value my limbs."

"Come now, Nickerson, you're teasing me. Hasn't anyone told you it's cruel to tease a spinster?"

"I wouldn't dare tease you, Miss Rosemoor." His eyes danced mischievously. "Especially with such a powerful and, I might add, *enormous* man glowering at me. You'd best put your heart under lock and key. I fear you may lose it at last."

Jane threw back her head and laughed. "I assure you my heart is safe from the likes of Lord Westfield."

The music ended, and Jane stepped back from her partner, right into something solid. "Oh, pardon me," she said, spinning around. She sucked in her breath as she raised her gaze to Lord Westfield's brooding glare.

Refusing to be cowed, she turned back to her partner with a practiced smile. "Perhaps I could use a breath of fresh air, Mr. Nickerson. It's decidedly stuffy in here."

"Of course," he replied with a slight bow, offering her his arm.

Without a backward glance, she followed him out, feeling Lord Westfield's gaze boring through her as they made their way across the ballroom.

Only once they'd reached the doors did she dare turn, searching the crowd for him.

He stood just where she left him, his dark head bent toward Miss Upshaw's fair one. She almost stomped a slippered foot in frustration as she watched him whisper something into the girl's ear and then pull her into his arms for the next waltz. He'd already engaged her for two dances—as many as propriety allowed. Wherever was the girl's chaperone?

"Shocking, isn't it?" Nickerson murmured, his gaze following hers.

"Indeed," she answered, feeling decidedly old and irritable. She was no longer a young debutante, no more the darling of the *ton*. She reached one hand up to her temple, surprised to find that the realization bothered her so.

"Some air?" Nickerson asked.

Jane could only nod in reply.

Chapter Eleven

"Hurry now, Jane. You'll be late." Emily waved her hands toward the door.

"Are you certain you won't go? Lucy will be sorely disappointed." Jane was loath to leave her there alone, fearing another bout of despondency threatened her cousin's fragile state.

Emily smiled. "I'm certain, dear Jane. It's nothing more than the headache. I could use a quiet evening at home. Please go, and enjoy yourself. The gardens are said to be lovely this time of year."

Indeed they were. Jane longed for the entertainments at Vauxhall. Still, she worried about leaving Emily. But then a disturbing vision of Cecil prowling about Vauxhall's secluded lanes flitted through her mind. She shook her head resolutely, her mind made up. She would go.

An hour later, their party settled themselves into their supper box. The meal was lively and festive, the accompanying music delightful.

As soon as the remaining bits of ham, tiny capons, assorted biscuits and cheese cakes were cleared away, Cecil stood and reached for his walking stick. "If you'll excuse me, I think I'll take a brief turn. It's a lovely evening."

"Isn't it?" Jane added, quickly rising to her feet. "If you haven't any objection, perhaps I might join you."

She saw his eyes darken as he offered his arm. "Of course."

"Make certain you return in time for the fireworks, Jane." Lucy waved a hand at the sky. "You get a much better view here than out on the walks."

"Of course." Jane placed her hand in the crook of Cecil's arm as she followed him out. They strolled aimlessly for more than a half hour, their conversation held to a bare minimum. They traversed the length of the elm-lined Grand Walk, then over the Cross Walk and finally to the South Walk. At last Jane began to feel a bit winded, and she looked around for a place to rest.

Spotting an alcove ahead, she tilted her head toward it. "Perhaps I might sit and rest a moment."

"Of course," Cecil replied, leading her to an ornamental bench, where she sank gratefully.

He removed a handkerchief from his pocket and dabbed his brow. "I say, Miss Rosemoor, you do look a bit peaked." He scowled as he stuffed the handkerchief back into his pocket. "In fact, you look frightfully pale, if I might say so. You must remain here and let me fetch you a lemonade."

"No, there's no need." She shook her head. "I'm perfectly well."

"Oh, but I insist. I fear I've allowed you to overexert yourself. However will I face Emily if you fall ill because of my carelessness?"

"I assure you I am well. You cannot leave me here—"

"It will only be for a brief moment," he interrupted. "I promise to return at once with a lemonade. You look as if you sorely need one."

Jane lost her desire to argue with the irritating man. Whatever his true intention, the idea of a moment of quiet solitude suddenly pleased her. She did not object again as he strode off, back in the direction from where they had come. Surely he would do as he said and return promptly. Wouldn't he? A shadow of doubt flitted across her consciousness.

The night was unseasonably warm, and she reached for her fan, flicking it open with one sharp movement of the wrist. She looked up to the sky, then lowered her gaze to her immediate surroundings, where the silvery moon cast a metallic glow across the greenery. Absently, she began to stir the air before her.

The strains of the orchestra filled the warm night with its rich tunes, and she felt herself tapping her toes. Several couples strode by, no doubt headed for the darker and more secretive Lovers' or Druid's Walks. Ah, to be young and in love. Jane couldn't help but smile at their boldness. For a moment, she closed her eyes and breathed in the rich, earthy scents around her, the air redolent with the first blossoms of summer. Whatever was taking Cecil so long?

She heard approaching steps, far too brisk and purposeful to be those of a lady, and she looked up from her fan, thinking the errant Cecil had returned at last. Her heart leapt in her breast as she took in the familiar figure headed her way instead, his looming shadow perfectly outlined in silver moonlight. Lord Westfield.

She twisted her torso away from the path, raising the fan to her face. Even as she shrank into the alcove's shadows, she couldn't help but peer over the top of the pleated silk as the footsteps hurried by her at a brisk clip. Her heart beat wildly, mimicking the rhythmic tapping of his boots. And then he paused.

Jane held her breath as he stood motionless, not twelve feet away, his back to her. Her breath let out in a rush as he slowly but deliberately spun around, as if he sensed her presence. Even in the dim shadows, she could see his gaze trained directly on her. She lowered her fan to her lap.

Several seconds passed before he spoke. "Miss Rosemoor? Whatever are you doing there, cloaked in shadows?"

"I was out for a stroll with Cecil," was all she could say in reply.

"And where is he now? Do not tell me he has left you alone?" As he moved silently toward her, she could see the firm set of his jaw.

"I thought I was being so clever, forcing my company on him to keep him from mischief. It seems he found a way around my watchfulness."

"Indeed? And what excuse did he find for depositing you here and disappearing?"

"A lemonade, my lord. He went to fetch me a lemonade. Quite some time ago."

"I'll break his neck when I see him." He balled his hands into fists by his sides, and for a moment Jane feared he might do what he threatened.

She cleared her throat uncomfortably. "Yes, well, until that time, perhaps you'll escort me back to our supper box? I've come with Lord and Lady Mandeville and they must wonder where I've disappeared to."

"Actually, I've just come from their box myself. It seems Lady Mandeville has taken a notion to dislike me. I cannot for the life of me fathom why, as we've only just met."

Jane arched a brow. "Can't you?"

Understanding lit his eyes, and he smiled ruefully. "Hmmm. The Falmouth ball?" he offered. "My abominable behavior?"

Jane nodded.

"I suppose I further piqued her ire just now, talking politics on a night like this. Beautiful, isn't it?"

"It certainly is. So, Lord Westfield, Mandeville tells me you are a political ally. What are your feelings on the Combination Acts? Will you vote to repeal them?"

Now it was his turn to quirk a brow. "A lady, interested in politics? Most unusual."

"I think you'll find I'm unusual in many respects, my lord." She wasn't a simpering miss like Miss Upshaw, for one, she thought acidly.

"There's no doubt of that, Miss Rosemoor. Suffice it to say I've never before met your equal. Although," he said, scratching his chin, "I wouldn't be surprised to find that Lady Mandeville comes close, should I have the opportunity to know her better."

Jane laughed. "Wherever do you think I pick up my revolutionary tendencies? You'll never meet a lady as keenly intelligent and accomplished as she."

"Then I suppose I must apologize to you at once for my boorish behavior at the Falmouth ball. And, of course, you must convey to Lady Mandeville that I've done so."

"She won't be satisfied by an apology made simply to gain her favor. No, it won't do at all, I'm afraid, Lord Westfield. You must try harder."

He looked at her with a mischievous grin, then dropped to one knee, clutching her hand to his breast. "My dear Miss Rosemoor, you must accept my most earnest, most heartfelt apology for treating you as unspeakably as I did at the Falmouth ball."

Jane reached a hand up to stifle a giggle.

"But you see," he continued, "I confess that your very presence alone sends all rational thought and gentlemanly behavior out the window, as you might have already noted."

Jane found herself laughing aloud. "Do get up. What if someone were to see you?"

He dropped her hand and rose to his feet, towering over her once again. "Does that mean you accept my apology?"

"Yes, of course. Anyway, Lucy was angrier at you than I was. I'll admit to my role in provoking you."

His face was all seriousness now. "Admit to nothing. My behavior was inexcusable, and no fault of yours. I hope you will forgive me."

Jane's gaze dropped to her slippers. She nodded silently, suddenly unable to speak.

"Thank you. Now, to answer your question, yes, I'll vote to repeal the Combination Acts, not that I have strong sentiments about the trade unions. Like Mandeville, my concern lies mainly with social reforms, namely education."

"I confess I was a bit skeptical at first of Mandeville's convictions toward educating the street urchins," Jane said. "After all, in what manner can we educate them? 'The most effective kind of education is that a child should play amongst lovely things.' How can you accomplish that in London's roughest neighborhoods?"

Lord Westfield stared at her, his brow furrowed. "Did you just quote Plato?"

"Of course." She shrugged. "But after listening to Mandeville's arguments, I've concluded that it's worth trying. As to the street urchins, pickpockets and the like, 'For if you suffer your people to be ill-educated, and their manners to be corrupted from their infancy, and then punish them for those crimes to which their first education disposed them, what else is to be concluded from this, but that you first make thieves and then punish them?'

Therefore it's our responsibility, wouldn't you agree, Lord Westfield?"

He blinked and shook his head, but said nothing in reply. "Lord Westfield?" She peered up at him curiously.

"Sir Thomas More."

"Yes, *Utopia.* Have you read it?"

"I have. What amazes me is that *you* have."

"Why shouldn't women have the equal education of men? 'If women are expected to do the same work as men—'"

" . . .'we must teach them the same things.' Plato again."

A smile spread across Jane's face. "Yes. Oh, I realize that women aren't truly expected to do the same work, but still . . ." He was studying her face intently, his mouth slightly agape. "Why are you looking at me like that?"

"You are, without a doubt, the most extraordinary woman I've ever met," he replied, his tone almost reverent. Jane felt a blush creep up her neck. She rose and stood before him, waiting for him to offer his arm.

Instead, he peered down at her curiously, his brow furrowed and a smile tugging at the corners of his mouth. Only when he reached for her shoulders did she realize her mistake. She'd held the handle of her fan to her lips, a blatant request for a kiss.

She backed away from him, shrugging off his hands as she shook her head. "You must excuse me. I'm not myself tonight." She silently cursed her carelessness, her foolishness. Whatever made her do such a thing?

High above them, a spot of white light zigzagged across the sky, erupting into a starburst of twinkling light that drifted down toward the treetops. When the last light faded into nothingness, his eyes sought hers, and she met them with equal determination.

"Come with me," he commanded, holding out a hand to her.

Without thought, she took it. Her heart soaring, Jane hurried beside him, her hand clasped in his.

Brilliant displays of color lit the sky, one after another, as they raced down Druid's Walk. Slowing his pace at last, he ducked behind a row of hedges, pulling her with him into the most shadowed, secret place. Without a word, he pulled her into his arms as a burst of fireworks fell from the sky above them. She could see the purple points of light reflected in his face, in his eyes, as his mouth descended on hers, taking it roughly, possessively.

The explosions of color and sound above only fueled her desire as she yielded, opening her mouth to meet his, kissing him with a hunger she didn't recognize. She felt her knees buckle as his tongue parted her lips, teasing her own with light flicks before plunging inside. She stumbled back, pulling him with her against the trunk of a sturdy old oak.

Her heart accelerated, echoing the booms from above, as his hands coarsely moved down her bodice, across her breasts, her stomach, around to cup her bottom in his grasp. It felt as if her skin were afire, burning with an unfamiliar, terrifying heat.

She reached her hands up to his broad chest, running her fingertips across the hard planes while she explored his mouth with her own traitorous tongue. She slid her palms up his flat, taut stomach, up to his heavily muscled chest, feeling wicked, wanton, even as she did so. If only she could see him shirtless once more, touch him this time as she longed to do by the pool, trace the path of hair down his stomach.

His mouth retreated from hers with a groan, his hands seemingly everywhere at once as his lips sought her throat. "Dear God, Jane," he ground out, and then she felt his tongue tantalize her skin behind her ear and down to her collarbone, his breath warm against her skin. She inhaled his scent, unmistakably masculine, an intoxicating mix of cedarwood and sandalwood; perhaps a bit of bergamot.

Before she knew it, he'd reached around to cup one breast, his insistent mouth seeking the hardened peak through the fabric of her bodice. Jane threw her head back as a shiver raced from the back of her neck down to her toes. "Oh," she cried out as his teeth found the nipple, teasing it, taunting it.

She knew these wondrous feelings were wrong, very wrong, yet she was unable to find the strength to fight it. She wanted his touch. She wanted *him.*

But she could never have him. The thought echoed in her ears as she summoned the will to drop her hands and push him away. "My lord, we cannot do this."

"Hayden," he said hoarsely, gripping her shoulders as he met her gaze with his.

"Hayden, we cannot do this. You must stop. At once."

He dropped his hands to his sides.

Her hand rose to her breast, to the place his mouth had possessed only moments before. "We can never do this again," she said, her voice hoarse. "Never."

"Change your answer, Jane," he demanded, gripping her shoulders. "It's not too late. Marry me."

She couldn't meet his eyes, focusing instead on the tips of her slippers. "No. I can't." She shook her head. "I won't."

"Very well." He hastily straightened his waistcoat and jacket. When he looked at her again, his face was guarded. His implacable mask had returned to shield her from his thoughts, his emotions. "What I've done here tonight is inexcusable and cannot be repeated."

"I—of course," she stammered.

"Tomorrow I will ask for Miss Upshaw's hand in marriage."

She froze, unable to speak. The pounding of her heart reverberated in her eardrums, nearly deafening her.

"I presume she will accept," he added, unnecessarily, his face a stony mask.

Still, she said nothing. She looked into his eyes, wondering if this would be the last time she could study them so closely, the last opportunity she'd have to see how the gray and green intermingled seamlessly, how a ring of darker green encircled the irises.

With trembling hands she smoothed down her dress and nodded.

Without another word, she allowed him to lead her back to the Mandevilles' supper box.

Her fate was sealed. She would die a spinster.

Devil take it, Hayden thought with a scowl. Now he had no choice but to ask for Miss Upshaw's hand in marriage. He dismissed his valet with the wave of one hand and roughly untied his cravat. He tossed the length of starched cloth to the chair before the hearth and began shrugging off his waistcoat. Pacing before the cold fireplace, he hastily undid the buttons on his shirt. He shuddered as his fingers made contact with his skin, remembering the touch of Miss Rosemoor's hands on his torso just hours before. His groin stiffened at the memory.

In frustration, he strode to the window and gazed out at the night, wondering what had possessed him to speak such ill-considered words. He'd said he would ask for Miss Upshaw's hand tomorrow, and now he must, no matter how unpalatable the idea seemed upon further thought. He'd hoped Miss Rosemoor—Jane—would beg him to reconsider; that she'd confess her regret at having refused him; that she'd ask for a second chance. But no, she had refused him yet again.

What was the woman about? He was baffled. He leaned his forehead against the cool glass and exhaled sharply. He supposed it was possible that she was hoping to make a love match, despite her assertion to the contrary. Love matches were becoming more fashionable of late, after all. Hell, even Mandeville had succumbed a few years back, improbable as it had seemed at the time.

He turned away from the window and leaned against the wall, his boots crossed indolently as he stroked his chin. If she were waiting for a love match, then it was best this way. It wouldn't be fair to her, for he could never love her.

He dropped his hands to his sides as his heart accelerated. Cold fear raced through his veins. Unbidden, the memories of his beloved Katherine flashed before his mind—her clear green eyes staring, unseeing, as he'd lifted her lifeless, broken body from the rocky ground and pressed her to his heart. The blood had darkened her fair hair to the color of wet bricks and soaked through his coat, staining his skin—marking him. He had loved her. Not a passionate, all-consuming love, but a quiet, deep love borne from years of close association, nurtured over the years and encouraged by their parents, who had betrothed them in childhood. Katherine had been warm, sensible, her inner strength belied by her delicate, almost angelic appearance. She had been taken from him most cruelly.

Even then, he had been no stranger to despair. He had watched helplessly as the life ebbed from his mother, following a miscarriage when he'd been but a boy. A well-meaning servant had brought him in to bid her farewell, and he could still smell the metallic scent of blood that had hung heavy in the air as he'd sobbed on her breast, begging her not to leave him.

And then, years later, Isabel. He had done everything in his power to see to his frail sister's health, her comfort. To save her. But his efforts had been for naught. Only weeks into his first term at Oxford, Isabel had slipped away. He hadn't even been there to hold her hand, to ease her into eternal rest.

He couldn't fathom what he'd done to deserve such a curse—that every woman he loved was taken from him—but never again would he let down his guard and freely give his love to anyone.

With each successive loss, a part of his heart had been torn away until he feared there was nothing left—no heart, no soul. He had nothing left to give of himself. When Madeline had come into his life, he had vowed to protect her from his curse. Yes, he had a certain fondness for his niece, but he'd distanced himself from her, sustained a certain detachment that had served them both well.

And that was exactly what he must do with his future bride. Distance himself. Remain detached. The more he thought about it, the more certain it seemed that Jane was not the type of woman who would abide by that. So it was best that she had refused him, even though he wanted her. Physically. He reached up to squeeze the bridge of his nose. Dear God, how he wanted her. More than he'd ever wanted any woman. It was senseless, ridiculous even, but he craved her physically with a desperation he'd never before experienced.

When he'd seen her at the Falmouth ball in William Nickerson's arms, smiling up at him with a genuine smile, he'd been infused with a suffocating rage. He'd wanted to storm over to the couple and pull her back into his arms, to demand to know why her eyes lit up and her cheeks flushed pink when she smiled at Nickerson. For when she smiled at him, the show of pleasure rarely went past her mouth.

When Nickerson led her out of the ballroom for a breath of air, had she allowed him to kiss her? Had Nickerson's hands roamed her luscious body the way his had in the gardens? Even now, the thought blinded him with anger. Ever since he'd met the woman, she'd set his carefully ordered existence spinning. He wouldn't stand for it.

With an oath, he strode angrily across the room and collapsed in the chair before the hearth, sprawling inelegantly.

Damn it to hell. He'd ask for Miss Upshaw's hand tomorrow, just as he said he would, and be done with it.

Jane Rosemoor would remain safe from his curse. He would make bloody sure of it.

Chapter Twelve

It was done. Hayden straightened his cravat and reached for his whip as he called for his curricle. Miss Upshaw's father had accepted his suit, and all was settled. By autumn he and his new bride would return to Richmond Park. Yet he found no joy in the arrangement. Instead, he felt strangely hollow, resigned to his fate. He sighed as he stepped up into the curricle and took up the ribbons. He gently slapped the horses' backs, and the conveyance lurched off. He was not the first man to marry one woman while desiring another; certainly he would not be the last.

Glancing up, Hayden noted the perfect sky, clear blue with wisps of clouds drifting lazily toward the horizon. How could the day seem so tranquil when inside he felt anything but? He grimaced at the irony of it.

The day was warm—not unpleasantly so, but enough to draw a thin film of perspiration across his brow as his curricle rattled along the streets of Mayfair. He reached for his handkerchief and dabbed at his forehead, suddenly thinking to head to Gunter's for an ice. If he was lucky, most of the *ton* would remain in Hyde Park, enjoying the weather, and he would be left mercifully alone.

With a nod to himself, he reined the matched pair of grays toward Berkley Square.

Minutes later, he entered the establishment with a satisfied smile. Very few patrons crowded the counter, and only a handful of carriages sat across the bustling street, awaiting the return of gentlemen ferrying ices, sorbets, and sweets to the eager ladies inside.

Once he had his own lemon ice in hand, he headed back outside to enjoy it in the sunshine. Leaning against the railing, he took an enormous bite, savoring the tart, tangy coldness on his tongue. For a flickering moment, he wished that Madeline were there with him, for the child greatly enjoyed ices. He shook off the thought. Madeline couldn't accompany him to London. It simply wouldn't do. There were too many questions about her parentage that must remain unanswered. Yes, Madeline was best tucked safely away in the countryside, away from the prying eyes and wagging tongues of the *ton*'s notorious gossips.

Before he'd asked for Miss Upshaw's—Dorothea's—hand, he'd told her about his ward, confessed the shocking truth that she was his brother's bastard child. She hadn't blinked an eye at the news, and he'd made it clear that he would entertain no further discussion regarding her unfortunate origins. Still, she'd accepted him with a triumphant smile and sent him straightaway to her father, her pale blue eyes dancing and her alabaster cheeks flushed pink.

The arrangements had been completed in the most businesslike manner, and he'd left without bidding his affianced good-bye. He feared she might have expected a chaste kiss or some other display of affection, and he could not oblige her— not yet. Not till he somehow managed to erase the memory of Jane's touch, Jane's kiss, from his mind. No longer did he think of her as Miss Rosemoor; she was now Jane. *His Jane.* And yet she'd never be his, outside his dreams.

He swallowed a spoonful of his ice and almost choked as the frigid lump made its way uncomfortably down his throat.

A clear, feminine voice pulled him from his dark thoughts.

"I'm so glad you happened upon us in the park, Mr. Nickerson. What a delightful idea. I'm positively parched."

"I confess, Miss Rosemoor, the lure of Gunter's was simply a ruse in order to squire you off. I've something important to discuss with you. I hope you'll forgive the falsehood."

Hayden froze, his spoon poised midway between his mouth and the ice he clutched in one hand.

"Perhaps a plateful of sweets and a dish of sorbet will repay . . ." Jane's voice trailed off as she and William Nickerson stopped directly in front of him. Nickerson's brows drew together at once, and Jane's eyes widened in surprise. "Lord Westfield," she said brightly, bobbing a curtsy in his direction.

"Westfield," Nickerson echoed, tipping his hat.

Hayden paused a beat before replying, noting how Nickerson's scowl deepened with each passing second.

Finally, Hayden bowed. "Miss Rosemoor, Mr. Nickerson." As he straightened, his gaze sought hers, involuntarily seeking the warmth of those sapphire depths.

"What a surprise." Her cheeks pinkened ever so slightly, and he saw her tighten her grasp on Nickerson's arm.

"Indeed," he replied. "You look radiant today."

"Thank you. Tell me, are felicitations in order as of yet?"

"They are," he bit out. A shadow, barely discernible but there nevertheless, flickered across her eyes, and something tightened in his chest in response. This was madness. And yet he was certain to run into her at some point. Mayfair was small. Best to get it over with.

"My heartiest congratulations, then." Her mouth curved into a forced smile. "I wish you much happiness."

Nickerson loudly cleared this throat, his growing annoyance evident in his countenance. Hayden looked to the man with a frown before returning his gaze to Jane. More than anything, he wanted to reach out to her, to run his finger along her jawbone, to tease her lower lip with his thumb. It took every ounce of his reserve to keep his hands by his sides, his ice still firmly in his grasp. At last, he managed to tear his gaze from hers.

"Good day, Miss Rosemoor," he managed before spooning another bite of ice into his mouth, welcoming the cold distraction. "Nickerson," he added with a curt nod.

For a moment, a troubled look gathered on Jane's features. At once, she shook her head as if to clear it. "Good day." With a bob of her straw bonnet, she dismissed him and allowed Nickerson to steer her into the shop, the mint green folds of her dress billowing out on the breeze behind her.

Hayden inhaled sharply as her familiar spicy scent wafted past his nose, then dispersed. A groan of frustration tore from his throat as he headed for his curricle.

* * *

"I'm so sorry, Mr. Nickerson." Jane reached for a tiny tea cake. "I'm afraid neither Lord Westfield nor I can keep a civil tongue in each other's presence." She took a bite, then licked a dollop of custard from her fingertips.

"Don't apologize, Miss Rosemoor. I only wish we'd managed to avoid him, arrogant brute. But the discourse *was* quite civil, really."

"Too civil, I suppose." The lump of cake felt like a stone in her stomach. *He was marrying Miss Upshaw.*

"Dare I ask why you offered felicitations?"

Her heart skipped a beat. "He's asked for Miss Dorothea Upshaw's hand, and she's accepted."

"Is that so? Well, that will surely quiet the tabbies who've been speculating that he would ask for yours, instead. They're gossiping still about the Falmouth ball, saying that he held you far too closely and that a lover's spat led him to cut short your waltz."

"Is that what they're saying, whispering behind their fans like cowards?" Jane frowned, the blood rising in her face. "I suppose they'll all pity me now, thinking I've been cast aside."

She pushed the unpleasant thought from her mind. She wouldn't think about it. Not now. "Anyway, enough about Lord Westfield. You've piqued my curiosity. What did you wish to discuss with me?" She took a sip of chamomile tea, hoping it would settle her stomach a bit.

Nickerson stared back at her eagerly, a hopeful expression illuminating his noble features. "I'd hoped to enlist your aid in a bit of . . . well, deception."

"An intrigue? How exciting! Tell me more."

"Are you at all acquainted with Miss Evelyn Adare? Lord Astley's niece?"

"Of course. Lovely girl." Jane knew her slightly.

She was several years her junior, only come out last
Season.

Nickerson took a deep breath, his gray eyes dancing merrily with some sort of mischief. "We're secretly engaged."

"No," Jane gasped.

"Yes, for many months now. We met in Kent. She
was there visiting her aunt, and we became well acquainted away from her parents' watchful eyes. I'd
hoped to gain the approval of her father and uncle
before asking for her hand. Of course, they were
hoping for a more advantageous match for her, but
we're desperately in love."

"I cannot believe it." Jane reached for his hand.
"I am so very happy for you. But what can I possibly
do to aid your cause?"

"Perhaps pretend an attachment? Allow me to
squire you about to parties where Miss Adare will be
in attendance?" He raked one hand through his wavy
blond locks. "It will give me an opportunity to curry
favor with her family while not appearing to court
her. Your family is held in high esteem, and with your
connection to the Mandevilles . . . Well, being seen
in your company can only show me in a positive light,
and perhaps allow for some secret assignations with
Miss Adare, as well. Will you do it?"

A slow smile spread across Jane's face. "Of course
I'll do it." How wonderful that Nickerson had
found love. Somehow she felt immediately easier in
his company, knowing that he did not pine for her.
And with Lord Westfield engaged to Miss Upshaw,
she would be relieved to have the company of a
pleasant escort. Logically, she didn't know what
Lord Westfield had to do with it, but at least it
would prove to him that she would not want for
male companionship. Perhaps a small part of her

hoped to make him jealous. Whatever the case, she'd do everything in her power to aid Nickerson and his beloved. "It would be my pleasure," she added, giving his hand a conspiratorial squeeze.

Nickerson's face lit up with a smile. "You've no idea how much this means to me, and to Miss Adare as well. I must send word to her at once. You and I can begin our mock courtship tomorrow night, at Lord and Lady Pemberton's ball."

"But the Pembertons are Miss Upshaw's parents," Jane stammered. Surely the girl's engagement would be announced at the ball. She could barely stomach the notion.

"They are indeed. You see, my plan will serve your needs as well as mine." Nickerson smiled slyly. "Why, what better way to show the *ton* how unaffected you are by Westfield's engagement than by allowing me to escort you there, and by looking pleased with the news."

Jane smiled grimly. He was sharp, indeed. She would do it. She would make herself do it, she corrected.

"Jane, dearest, you look lovely. Stop fretting." Emily patted Jane's shoulder. "Remember, it's only an *imaginary* courtship, after all."

Jane laughed. "I wish I could tell you everything, Emily. But I gave my word; I'm sworn to secrecy. I only told you what I did so you didn't get your hopes up, imagining my feelings for Mr. Nickerson had changed. Besides, you must help me with the ruse."

"Of course I will. As will Lady Mandeville. You can count on our discretion."

"I'm lucky to have friends such as you." Jane reached over to kiss Emily's soft cheek. Amelia's cries pierced the air, and the pair turned toward the door. "Your little one awakens. You're sure I look acceptable?"

"Oh, to be so unaware of such beauty!" Emily laughed as she headed off in search of the nurse-maid.

Jane took one last look into the glass. She'd worn her newest gown, ordered upon her arrival in Town from the most fashionable modiste. The ice blue satin under the layer of filmy tulle was not a color she wore often, yet Lucy had insisted it suited her. She hoped she was right. She must look her best—and most cheerful—tonight as the *ton* learned of Lord Westfield's engagement to Miss Upshaw.

A pang of regret twisted her heart as she thought of Miss Upshaw, mistress of Richmond Park. To think, it could have been hers instead. She tried to picture the doll-like Miss Upshaw reigning over the long dining table at Richmond, sharing walks through the estate's grand park with her husband, sharing his life, his bed. Jane struck the vanity's cool marble top with one fist. It should be hers! Hot tears burned her eyelids, and she felt her stomach lurch uncomfortably.

The disturbing images of Miss Upshaw at Richmond faded away and were replaced instead with visions of herself sitting across the long table with Lord Westfield opposite her. "Hayden." The name rolled off her tongue, spoken in the merest whisper, and gooseflesh rose on her skin. *Such a lovely name.* So masculine, so unique, like the man himself. How would it feel to lie with him, to allow him to touch her most secret, unexplored places? To carry his child? A sob tore from her throat, and she reached one gloved hand up to suppress it.

The beast of despair stirred in her breast, and she

vowed to thwart it. No point giving in to melancholy, allowing it to rule her actions, her emotions. She stared back at her own pale face, valiantly willing herself to composure. *Smile*, she told her reflection. *Just smile*.

"Dear Lord, Miss Rosemoor. You're stunning tonight." Nickerson looked pleased as he presented his arm. "Perhaps too much so. I fear you'll make Miss Adare jealous."

"Nonsense," Jane answered, laying her hand in the crook of his elbow. Nickerson's beloved stood not ten feet away, a dazzling smile upon her face as her eyes met his and lit with excitement.

"Miss Jane Rosemoor and Mr. William Nickerson," the butler's baritone voice boomed out. Jane looked down and smoothed the folds of her dress, running her fingers lightly across the smooth pearls that ornamented the bodice. She readjusted the filigreed gold armlets encircling her arms as she scanned the cavernous ballroom, searching for Lucy and Lord Mandeville. She would need every bit of her friends' support tonight.

She found them near the entrance to the refreshment room, and with a tip of her head led Nickerson in their direction. As soon as the initial pleasantries were dispersed with, Jane and Lucy excused themselves to the ladies' retiring room.

"It was cruel of Mr. Nickerson to make you accompany him here tonight," Lucy said with a scowl as the door closed behind them. "Especially if what you say is true. The announcement, I mean."

"Oh, it's true. But it's best that I'm here, putting on a good face. Nickerson's right. Honestly, Lucy, you mustn't fret over me."

Lucy looked skeptical. "I still don't understand why you didn't accept his suit. Lord Westfield's, I mean. Henry likes him immensely, and it's clear you've formed an attachment of some sort. He's rich, he's sinfully handsome, and his estate in Derbyshire is nothing short of magnificent by your own account. I fear I'll never understand your reticence about marriage."

"I wish I could explain it to you. Truly, I do. But you must trust my judgment when I say it's best this way."

"Best for whom?"

"For me. And for Lord Westfield," Jane added.

"But you love him," Lucy insisted.

"I do not love him. I . . . I don't know what I feel toward him." She looked around surreptitiously and lowered her voice to a whisper. "I fear it's indecent."

Lucy bit her lower lip, then laughed. "I felt much the same about Henry when we first met. Everyone but me realized I was in love with him, including you, I might add. Why can you not see the truth in yourself, when it's so plain?" She sighed in exasperation.

"Because it cannot be," Jane snapped, then reconsidered. She sighed heavily. "I'm sorry. I didn't mean to speak so sharply."

Their conversation ground to a halt as a pair of giggly young ladies—debutantes no doubt—rushed into the room with their faces aglow, whispering behind their fans.

With raised brows, Jane allowed Lucy to thread her arm through hers, and the pair hurried back to the ballroom.

She wasn't the least surprised to find Hayden at Mandeville's side and Nickerson nowhere to be seen. She swallowed the painful lump in her throat as she joined them.

She felt his eyes on her, prickling her skin, as she curtsied in greeting. "Lord Westfield."

"Miss Rosemoor, Lady Mandeville." He bowed sharply. Several seconds of uncomfortable silence ensued.

"I believe I need some refreshment," Jane announced, and turned toward the refreshment room.

"I'll join you," Hayden said.

Jane almost stomped a foot in frustration as she turned back toward her companions. Why didn't Lucy or Mandeville offer to accompany them? Instead, a smug smile passed between the two, and Jane was left with no choice but to accept Hayden's offer of escort.

Her head held high, Jane stalked off, Hayden at her heels. As he reached her side, she gave him a sidelong glance, attempting—unsuccessfully, of course—to assess his intentions. His veil of ennui was firmly in place, betraying nothing. "I won't dance with you," she snapped out.

"I hadn't any intention of asking you to."

"Oh," she inhaled sharply.

"Don't be offended. I shan't dance with anyone tonight save my betrothed."

The taste of bile rose briefly in her throat. "I'm not in the least offended," she lied.

He turned and looked over his shoulder, grimacing as Nickerson rejoined the Mandevilles. "You seem to frequent William Nickerson's company."

"I do, indeed. We have quite a history together, Nickerson and I."

"So I've been told." His eyes narrowed, and a muscle in his jaw flickered. "Mandeville tells me you refused his hand several years ago. Perhaps you've reconsidered?"

"Perhaps," she replied noncommittally before attempting a bright smile. Was he jealous? She saw him ball his hands into fists by his sides.

With a trembling hand, she reached for a flute of champagne, just as Hayden reached for the same one. Their fingers met on the stem. In an instant, his thumb covered hers, subtly massaging it. Jane sucked in her breath, unable to move.

"Jane," he said, so hoarsely, so quietly, that Jane feared she had imagined it.

She drew back her hand at once.

He picked up the flute and held it out to her, but she dared not take it. Instead, she reached for another, refusing to meet his gaze. She took a sip of the bubbly liquid, shuddering as it traced an ice-cold path down her throat. "Why did you follow me?"

He shook his head, his brows drawn together. When he spoke, the words were soft, gentle—almost apologetic in tone. "I haven't any idea."

"Lord Westfield," a voice pealed. Miss Upshaw hastened to them, golden blond ringlets bobbing around her heart-shaped face. She looked up at Hayden with the largest, most perfectly round brown eyes Jane had ever seen—eyes the color of drinking chocolate. "There you are. I couldn't find you anywhere," she chastised, laying a hand on his arm.

"Are you acquainted with Miss Jane Rosemoor?" he asked.

"No," she answered, "but I've heard much about you from Lady Mandeville. What a pleasure to meet you at last."

"A pleasure, Miss Upshaw." Jane curtsied. In comparison to Miss Upshaw's petite proportions, she felt large, ungainly. "If you'll excuse me, I must rejoin my companions."

"Of course," the girl replied good-naturedly, happy to return her attention to her betrothed.

Without chancing a look at Hayden, Jane spun around and hurried back to her friends as quickly as decorum allowed.

"There you are," Nickerson called out to her. "Shall we dance?" He held out a white-gloved hand, and she reached for it with a nod.

"Of course." Jane followed him onto the floor as the sets formed for the opening quadrille. It was only when the music struck up that she noticed her unfortunate position in the square. Somehow, she and Nickerson had managed to find themselves in the third couple's spot, opposite the top couple—Hayden and Miss Upshaw. She nearly groaned aloud as the opening figure commenced. It wouldn't be long before she'd be forced to join hands with Hayden.

Seconds later, she placed her palm against his, refusing to meet his eyes.

"Miss Rosemoor," he said with a nod, his voice full of formality.

"Lord Westfield." She glanced over her shoulder and watched as Miss Upshaw smiled up prettily at Mr. Nickerson, her pastel curls dancing about her flushed cheeks.

Jane didn't breathe again until she was returned to her own partner. Nickerson shrugged helplessly in reply to her icy glare. Did he not realize how painful this was for her? But no, he was far too busy making calf's eyes at Miss Adare, who, with her partner, was strategically positioned directly opposite them in the nearest square.

The next figure required Jane to join hands with Miss Upshaw and circle about. As she reached for the girl's delicate hands, Miss Upshaw smiled up at her warmly.

"Miss Rosemoor, you must tell me which modiste you patronize. That dress is enchanting."

Jane glanced down at her filmy blue skirts. "Madame Villency, on Oxford Street. She's yet to disappoint me." She stepped back, allowing her gaze to briefly flit over to Hayden's face as he reached for Miss Upshaw's hand and led her through the next figure. She saw not a flicker of emotion, not the faintest spark of desire as he looked at his betrothed. If anything, she sensed a reluctance, an expression of resignation in his countenance. Why, then, would he wish to marry her? He could likely have any woman he chose. She shook her head. She'd never understand the man. Probably for the best.

At last it was her turn to move through the next figure, and she forced a smile upon her lips as she took Nickerson's hand.

"Alexander Clifton is staring at you," Nickerson whispered into her ear. Jane's gaze followed the tilt of his head toward her immediate right.

Indeed he was, the rogue. Clifton leaned indolently against the wall, his hands shoved into his pockets as his eyes boldly skimmed the length of her figure. He had been a suitor of hers several years past, before he'd ruined Miss Portia Butler and been forced to marry her. Yet his marriage had done nothing to curb his rakish behavior, and his many conquests were legendary. Luckily, he had paid her very little heed the past few years, preferring the bloom of youth to aging spinsters. But now

he looked at her with a predatory glint in his eye.
Jane shuddered.

"I say, he's looking at you almost indecently."
Nickerson tightened his grasp on her hand. "Shall
I call him out?"

Jane laughed. "I don't think that's necessary,
Nickerson. He is, after all, only looking at me."
Prickles rose on the back of her neck as the corners
of Mr. Clifton's mouth rose into a lascivious smile.
"I do wish he'd stop, though," she muttered as she
returned to her place in the square.

Again she was forced to join hands with Hayden.
She heaved a sigh of frustration as she reluctantly
met him in the center for a brief promenade.

"Another of your spurned suitors, I suppose?" he
drawled, his eyes boring into hers.

"I don't know what you mean."

"Oh, I think you do. Clifton. Odd, as I didn't
think he bothered with women over the age of consent."

"Nor did I," she answered dryly. She risked a
glance in the man's direction, and her heart leapt
in her breast. Dear God, she distinctly saw his
tongue flick across his lips suggestively. Her breath
caught in her throat.

"Shall I call him out?"

"No, and besides, *William* has already offered." As
she released him and stepped back to her place opposite her partner, she watched in grim satisfaction
as Hayden's expression changed from incredulous
to mutinous in a matter of seconds.

Not for the first time, she silently cursed Lady Jersey for ever introducing the interminable quadrille.

An hour later, the tension knotting her stomach
had eased only a bit. While her dance card had
filled respectably, she felt like the fox in the hunt,

dashing this way and that, trying her best to avoid crossing paths with Hayden or Mr. Clifton. Nickerson's lighthearted company was her saving grace, along with Lucy's comforting presence.

"Allow me to fill your plate, Miss Rosemoor."

Jane couldn't help but smile at Nickerson as she nodded her assent, watching as he filled her plate with slices of roast beef and ham so thin you could nearly see through them, savory pastries, and an assortment of cheeses.

"Mmmm, the lobster pastries are delicious," Lucy murmured at her side.

Jane sampled one from the plate Nickerson handed her and nodded appreciatively. "Decidedly so. Thank goodness for small favors. At least the food is pleasurable."

"And what of your escort?" Nickerson asked, feigning insult.

"Oh, certainly the most pleasant of sorts. If only he'd be more careful in choosing our position on the dance floor, I might forgive him." Jane laughed easily, her mood lightened a bit.

"Look, there's Henry, conversing with poor Mrs. Clifton. I suppose he's trying to distract her while her husband nearly mauls Miss Anderson over there in the corner." Lucy shook her head, a disgusted frown upon her face. She moved off toward her husband, Nickerson right behind her. Jane started to follow.

"Miss Rosemoor?"

Jane turned toward her name. A manservant stood by her elbow, peering at her curiously.

"Yes?" Jane answered curiously.

Without another word, the man reached for her hand and slipped something inside before disappearing through the crowd. She could only stare at his retreating form in puzzlement.

Opening her palm, she saw a small square of paper lying there. She blinked in astonishment. *How strange.*

Abandoning her plate on the buffet, she hurried to the ladies' retiring room, anxious to see what news the curious missive bore. Once the door closed behind her, she unfolded the slip of paper with trembling hands. Three words were scrawled in obvious haste.

Rose garden. Midnight.

Perhaps this had something to do with Nickerson and his Miss Adare—some secret arrangements for an assignation. Or perhaps it was something else altogether. Her heart began to pound in anticipation as her eyes skimmed lower, looking for a signature. *Please, not Clifton.*

And then her heart skipped a beat.

At the page's lower right corner, there was a single, elegant letter. "W." Her palms dampened as the missive fluttered to the carpet at her feet.

Westfield.

Chapter Thirteen

This was madness. Hayden knew it to be so, yet he'd been unable to stop himself from hastily scribbling the note. His own engagement was to be announced at the close of the ball, for God's sake, and yet here he stood, secretly awaiting another woman among the darkly shadowed, fragrant bushes. He paced between the thorny branches, reaching one hand up to tug at his cravat. The damn thing felt like a noose around his neck.

He retrieved his watch and flipped open the case. Two minutes till midnight. He snapped it shut again and shoved it back into his pocket. Would she come? He reached down and pinched off one single rose, its velvety petals the same shade of pink as Jane's lips, and equally as soft. He ran a fingertip lightly along the petals' rim, deeply inhaling the rich scent as he did so.

"Lord Westfield?"

He spun around in surprise, at once amazed and relieved to find Jane standing there, even if her countenance showed nothing but annoyance. "I asked you to call me Hayden," he said at last, dropping the blossom to the grassy carpet below.

"And yet you know how inappropriate my doing so would be, Lord Westfield. Need I remind you that you are a betrothed man? The honor of addressing you so informally belongs to Miss Upshaw, and Miss Upshaw alone." Her mouth was set in a hard line, her brow furrowed in obvious irritation. "Why did you ask me to meet you here?"

"I need to speak with you, nothing more."

"Then speak quickly. I must return at once before my absence is noticed."

His well-rehearsed words abandoned him, leaving him momentarily speechless. This *was* madness, and he should allow her to leave before Nickerson came looking for her. Roaring silently in frustration, he started to return to the ballroom posthaste.

But as he brushed by her, he felt her fingers clutch at his sleeve. He stopped dead in his tracks and inhaled deeply before turning toward her.

She looked up at him pleadingly, her eyes glowing in the moonlight. "What did you wish to say? Speak now, and let us end this maddening game, Lord Westfield." Something was different about her gaze, as if a shrouding veil had been lifted from her captivating eyes, and he recognized pain in their depths. Deep, tortured pain—a pain she'd hidden from the world. He was suddenly aware of her suffering, sensing it as if it swirled around her like a dense fog, enveloping her in its shroud.

He closed his eyes and took a ragged breath. Had he played a part in her suffering? A knife tore through his heart at the thought.

"I fear I've treated you badly, Miss Rosemoor," he said, his voice hoarse.

She said nothing, but her lower lip trembled perceptibly.

"I've no excuse," he continued, his heart racing, "except that my judgment clouds in your presence."

Still, she said nothing.

He allowed one of his hands to stray to her side,

to lightly brush the soft fabric of her skirts with his fingertips. This gown was so very different from any other he'd seen her wear. It was more virginal, almost fairylike, with delicate silk leaves appliquéd near the hem, even as the fashionably low-cut bodice revealed an ample amount of her breasts. The opaque tulle over the icy satin lent an ethereal look to her fair skin, making the deep color of her eyes even more intense.

She looked like an enchantress.

"Did you wear this dress tonight to torture me? It suits you perfectly. Innocent yet sensual, beautiful and intriguing all at once."

Her eyes narrowed as her cheeks flushed angrily. "As hard as it might be for you to comprehend it, your tastes do not dictate my choice of gowns. I wore this dress tonight because Mr. Nickerson's favorite color is blue, if you must know." She tipped her chin into the air.

Something inside him snapped. "Are you in love with him?"

"It's none of your concern," she bit out, then spun around. She took no more than two steps before turning to face him once more. "And what if I am? He's a gentleman in every respect, more noble than you despite his lack of a title. Mr. Nickerson doesn't try to—to—" she sputtered, "to seduce me, to risk my reputation at every turn. He's honest and guileless and—"

"No need to go on," he interrupted, the blood rising in his face. "I wholly understand."

"Do you? Then why are we out here, hidden amongst the shadows, sneaking about like lovers? When will it end? I've made it clear that I've no wish to marry you and now you're betrothed to another. You owe me no explanation, Lord Westfield."

"You say the words convincingly, yet your kiss at the Gardens betrayed you. I felt the desire in your kiss, desire that matches mine."

She shook her head vehemently. "Your arrogance misleads you. Your kiss caught me unawares, that's all." She dropped her gaze and shrugged. "I confess I was perhaps a bit curious, nothing more."

He reached for her chin, grasping it between his forefinger and thumb, forcing her gaze to meet his. "You're lying. Tell me the truth." His eyes scanned her face, witnessing her inner struggle. "You want me. Say it." She closed her eyes and shook her head weakly, but he didn't release her. "Say it," he commanded in a low growl.

He tipped her head back, his mouth moving to her throat. Her pulse raced beneath his hungry lips, and it took every ounce of fortitude to tear himself away. "Say it," he whispered, refusing to take his eyes off hers.

"I want you," she murmured, so quietly he barely heard the words.

Triumph filled his heart and set his blood racing through his veins. He felt the stirrings of desire in his loins heighten a pitch, the length of him suddenly straining against his trousers.

"I want you," she repeated, more loudly this time, her gaze boldly meeting his. "But I will never have you," she added defiantly. "What would you have me do? Become your mistress? Because I would not—"

"No. That would never do." *Dear God.* That would be just as dangerous as taking her as his wife. More so, perhaps. How could he possibly explain, when he barely understood it himself?

"You're the most beautiful woman I've ever met—intelligent, charming, accomplished." He swallowed a lump in his throat and reached out to her, stroking her cheek with his knuckles. "You are perfection."

She turned her head aside, but he saw one glistening, crystal tear trace a path down her cheek. "Why must you make this more difficult?" she whispered.

"When I offered for you, I was acting rashly, prematurely. I did not know you well enough to see the threat. Marrying Miss Upshaw is the right thing to do, to protect you, to keep you safe from my curse. I'm a strong man, Jane, but I cannot go through it again." His voice broke, and he cleared his throat. "I simply cannot."

She shook her head. "You speak in riddles."

He reached for her shoulders and pulled her toward him, gazing down into her tortured face, his own contorted with despair. "I am no longer capable of love. I have no heart to give, and my affections are nothing but a curse to anyone I bestow them on. Nothing but tragedy follows in its wake. You must remain safe from that. That's why I must marry Miss Upshaw. I asked you to meet me here because I felt you must know my reasons." He released her, as if her flesh burned his hands. "Never before has my resolve been tested as you have tested it."

"We are more alike than you know, then, Hayden," Jane said quietly, her mouth curved into a mysterious, sad smile.

So deeply mired was Hayden in his own pain, in his own intensely felt regret, that he didn't even begin to wonder what Jane meant by those mystifying words until she left him standing there alone in the pale moonlight. Sighing heavily, he shoved his hands into his pockets and glanced down. Moving one foot aside, he saw the lovely pink bloom he'd held so tenderly, trampled and bruised beneath his boot. With a primal groan, he stormed back inside.

Back to his betrothed. He reached up to readjust his cravat as he stepped into the ballroom. The noose was tightening.

"Jane, dearest, you're as pale as a ghost. What's wrong?" Emily set down her coffee with a frown.

"Am I pale? I must be tired. I suppose I'm not as young as I once was. I'm finding the Season frightfully exhausting." She would never confess that she'd lain awake the better part of the night, painful images from the evening's ball replaying in her mind, over and over, till she thought she'd surely scream.

Only moments after she'd returned from the rose garden, Lord Pemberton had joyfully announced his daughter's engagement to Lord Westfield. Jane had raised her glass with the rest of the guests, gripping Nickerson's forearm with her other hand as if her life depended on it. Across the length of the room, Hayden's eyes had met hers over the rim of his flute, and her heart had momentarily stopped beating. The look of longing, of regret, touched her like a physical blow.

"You are perfection," he'd said. She reached one hand up to her burning cheek at the memory. *Perfection.* No one had ever said such a thing to her. If only he knew the truth—that she was horribly flawed; that madness lurked somewhere within her, simmering, just waiting to rear its ugly head. He was cursed, he'd said. Well, she was equally cursed.

Yet she didn't quite understand what he meant. Why ever would he think himself cursed? She turned to Emily, who sat at her side, nibbling a piece of toast while she read the latest gossip sheet. Emily had known him her whole life—did she have the answers? Dare she ask?

"Emily?"

"Yes? More coffee?" Emily reached for the silver pot.

"No, thank you. I'm a bit, ahem, curious about Lord Westfield's past. He's hinted at some tragic history of which I know nothing."

Emily's eyes widened with surprise. "Somehow I thought you knew."

Jane shook her head. "I'm afraid I've no idea."

Emily looked uncertain for only a moment. "I suppose there's no harm in speaking of it, especially if he's hinted at it. Perhaps he thought I'd told you. Well, it all began when his mother died. A miscarriage. He was only a boy, but it's been said that they brought him in to bid her farewell as she lay on her deathbed, and the poor child witnessed her final moments. And then you've heard that he had a sister?"

Jane nodded. "Yes, I've heard her mentioned. She was your friend."

"Indeed she was. Isabel was my dearest friend. She was the sweetest girl one could ever hope to know. She was kind and generous, as unselfish as could be, and blessed with the most endearing sense of humor. But she was sickly and frail from birth—a weak heart." Tears gathered in the corners of Emily's eyes. "Lord Westfield adored her, and she worshipped him in return. He did everything in his power to make her life as comfortable, as happy as possible. I believe that his vigor, his vitality gave her strength. His father insisted, of course, that he go to Oxford, and not two months into his first term, she slipped away."

"Oh, how dreadful." Jane's heart sank.

"I'm not certain Lord Westfield ever recovered from her death. He's been a changed man since. I fear he holds himself responsible, for having left her."

"But it wasn't his fault."

Emily nodded her agreement. "And then there was Katherine."

"Katherine?"

"His fiancée, Lady Katherine Holt. They were betrothed as infants, by their parents, yet they grew to love one another on their own accord. I think that, after Isabel's death, Lord Westfield found comfort in Katherine. It was such a relief, to see him smile again. Their wedding was to be held in Derbyshire, in the rectory at Richmond Park. Guests traveled from near and far, the district filled with a festive atmosphere. And then, just days before their wedding, Lord Westfield accompanied her family to a dinner in Ashbourne, a feast in honor of their upcoming nuptials. Their carriage lost a wheel on the way home and was sent flying over an embankment. Everyone survived, mostly unhurt, except for poor Katherine who was thrown from the conveyance. She broke her neck, I'm told. It was Lord Westfield who retrieved her, and it took several men to pry her broken body from his arms. Quite tragic."

"Poor Lord Westfield." Jane struggled to grasp the full meaning of his words, and her mind raced to the obvious conclusion. Did he truly think that everyone he loved would die?

She shuddered at the thought.

"I think I'll take a walk," Jane announced, rising on shaking legs.

"So early?" Emily's brow furrowed. "It isn't even noon."

"I must get some air at once. Please excuse me." She hastened out of the room without a backward glance.

A half hour later, Jane found herself standing outside a gray stone town house on Upper Brook Street, her lady's maid at her side. This was Richmond House, Hayden's accommodations in Town. Emily had pointed it out to her days ago as their carriage had sped past, and Jane was glad for the opportunity to study it more closely, admiring the fine details.

The structure rose five stories high, a Venetian window gracing the first floor just above the shiny black front door. The keystone in the arch above the door depicted a lion's head, intricately carved and amazingly detailed. A dogleg staircase doubled back from a single landing, its railing an elaborate scroll of ironwork painted a brilliant lapis blue. The house bespoke of great wealth and excellent taste, and Jane couldn't help but admire the lovely Palladian style architecture.

Bridgette peered up at her curiously. "Are you planning to call on someone, miss?"

"I'm not certain," Jane confessed with a shake of the head.

"Might I ask what lady resides here?"

"No ladies at all, I'm afraid."

"I implore you to reconsider, then. I would surely lose my position for allowing such an impropriety. Please, miss, let's return at once to Leicester Square." Poor Bridgette stood on the walk, wringing her hands in desperation.

Bridgette was right, of course. She could not call on a gentleman, a betrothed one at that. She hadn't a clue what had come over her. She'd needed some air, and she'd started walking aimlessly toward the park, her gaze lowered to the walk beneath her feet. When she'd looked up, Richmond House stood before her. For a moment, she'd allowed herself to consider going inside, giving her name to the butler and awaiting Hayden's surprise at finding her there. She only wanted to tell him that she understood.

But it was folly. With a nod, she turned and headed back toward the Tollands' more modest residence as Bridgette's dramatic sigh of relief reached her ears. They walked toward Leicester Square at a brisk pace, Jane's heels tapping the cobbles in rhythm to her racing heart. Whatever had she been thinking, standing on the walk and gaping at his house?

A half hour later she skimmed up the stairs of the Tollands' rented town house and breezed into the foyer. "Where is Mrs. Tolland?" she asked the housekeeper as she handed over her bonnet.

"She's gone out, miss," the woman answered. "Not a quarter hour ago. Mr. Tolland arrived home, and they left in the carriage. Shopping, I believe."

"Very well. Perhaps I'll rest, then." Jane hurried to her room, but instead of lying down, she sat down at her small escritoire and began a letter to her mother. Her mother had hoped to join her in Town by now, but her youngest grandchild had taken ill and kept her in Essex. The poor child had the whooping cough, and Susanna had been happy for the extra pair of hands. Not for the first time, Jane realized how desperately she'd missed her family.

Voices below in the drawing room drew her attention away from her task before she'd yet filled the page. Curious, she rose and went to the door, pulling it open and peering out into the hall. The housekeeper appeared at the top of the stairs.

"Have we callers?" Jane asked.

"Indeed. Lord Westfield is in the drawing room. Shall I tell him you are not at home?"

Jane swayed against the door frame. Had he seen her standing outside his home? The blood rose in her face. Oh, if only Emily and Cecil had returned so that they could receive him. She pressed her fingertips to her temples, unable to decide what course to take. She took a deep, steadying breath and dropped her hands, straightening her spine. She would face him.

She took her time descending the stairs, her hand firmly gripping the banister for support. Her feelings of trepidation increased as she neared her destination, and it was all she could do to force herself to breathe normally.

She stepped into the room on silent feet. Hayden stood with his back to her, gazing out the window as the sun rose high in the sky. He held his hat in one hand, resting it upon his hip. She could see his black kid gloves folded neatly inside the hat. Her gaze skimmed across his broad back, the dove gray wool of his jacket stretched taut across the impressive width. Dark locks curled against his collar, and Jane suppressed the urge to reach out, to feel his silky hair between her fingers. Unable to speak, she cleared her throat in an attempt to gain his attention.

He spun around in unmasked surprise. "Miss Rosemoor."

"Lord Westfield."

He bowed stiffly. "I'd expected to find Tolland at home. We have some business to discuss."

Jane shrugged. "I'm afraid you've found only me. Will you sit?"

"I should go." He retrieved his gloves from his hat.

Jane gestured toward an oversized chair covered in wheat-covered velvet. "Please, Lord Westfield. Sit. I'll ring for tea. Do not be uneasy on my account."

His gaze sought hers, and then he nodded. Moving aside his coattails, he sat in the chair she'd indicated and stretched his long legs out before him.

"Are you hungry?" she asked. "Perhaps I'll ask for some sandwiches and cakes with the tea."

"That sounds very well, Miss Rosemoor." His voice was stilted with formality, and it made Jane flinch.

In silence, she rang the bell. Only after she'd made her request to the housekeeper did she take a seat opposite him.

"And how is baby Amelia faring?" he asked at last.

"Very well. She's much less colicky these days and becoming quite a delight."

"I'm glad to hear it. Mrs. Tolland is well?"

"Yes, exceedingly so. Town has done wonders for her spirits."

Five full minutes passed in uncomfortable silence until the tea tray was laid before them.

Jane was happy to busy herself with spooning sugar and stirring cream into her cup. Hayden did the same. The food sat untouched.

At last Jane found her courage. "The Pembertons' ball last night was lovely."

"It was tolerable," he responded.

She took a deep breath and spoke quickly. "Emily

has told me a bit about your past. Your sister and your betrothed."

"Oh?" he asked, one brow raised. "How very forthcoming of her."

"I only questioned her because you spoke so mysteriously. Please don't be angry with her."

"I'm not angry."

He certainly *looked* angry. His mouth was pinched, and his eyes looked like storm clouds about to burst.

"Perhaps now you understand," he added, folding his arms across his chest.

"But you cannot blame yourself for their deaths. You cannot believe yourself responsible."

"I can believe whatever I wish to believe, Miss Rosemoor."

Jane swallowed hard. "I understand," she said quietly.

"Do you?" He rose and stood towering over her. "Do you understand? Do you know what it's like to know you're cursed, forced to deny your will, compelled to go against your own desires? To protect yourself and those you might love? Can you possibly understand what it's like to live in that hell?"

A tear coursed down Jane's cheek. She reached up to brush it away. "I *do* understand. You see, I'm similarly cursed myself."

He stepped back from her and she saw his face blanch. "What do you mean, 'similarly cursed'?"

She shook her head. "I cannot tell you."

"Cannot or will not?"

"Both. I could not speak the words, even if I wanted to. It's far too dreadful." She stood to face him, her gaze challenging his.

He reached for her shoulders, taking them roughly in his grasp. "Tell me," he commanded.

Jane took a deep breath before replying, fighting

for the courage to say the words aloud. "I will not have children. Therefore I cannot marry. Not you, not anyone," she whispered, feeling as if her heart might break in two.

"Not even William Nickerson?"

"Not even him," she answered, a bubble of hysteria rising in her breast, threatening to topple her composure.

"But you seem so fond of Amelia. You were so good to Madeline. How can you not want children?"

"I didn't say I don't want children, my lord. I said I cannot have them."

"Cannot? But how can you know such a thing? And even if it's true, you can still marry."

"No." She shook her head wildly. "You don't understand."

"Then make me understand."

"Oh, Lord Westfield," a voice called out, and he released Jane at once. She looked up as Emily entered the room, her eyes wide with surprise.

"Westfield, old boy. Sorry to keep you waiting." Cecil strode into the room and clapped Hayden on one shoulder. "Why, we just ran into your betrothed, buying her trousseau I suppose."

Jane's heart contracted painfully as her eyes met Hayden's one last time. As long as she remained in Town, she'd be forced to endure reminders of his impending nuptials. No doubt she'd continue to run into him or Miss Upshaw wherever she went. It was unavoidable. However would she bear it? Already her fragile heart could take no more.

She turned and fled from the room.

Chapter Fourteen

Jane pulled her shawl more tightly about her shoulders as she stepped out of the carriage and walked toward the grand, columned façade of the Theatre Royal Haymarket, Nickerson's hand resting lightly on her elbow. She sighed heavily. She loved the theater, of course, but no doubt Hayden would be there, Miss Upshaw on his arm. Tonight marked the opening of Mrs. Centlivre's *The Busy Body,* and everyone was suddenly abuzz about it. No doubt the *ton*'s finest would be in abundance tonight.

As they entered the theater and made their way through the lobby to their box, Lucy turned and smiled weakly at her. "I hope you don't mind," she said brightly, speaking loudly to be heard over the din of the crowd, "but Henry has asked Lord Westfield to join us tonight."

Jane was sure that her shock was evident in her countenance. Why had no one mentioned this to her until now—now that it was far too late for her to decline the invitation?

Lucy moved closer and whispered in her ear, "What could I say, Jane? You asked me not to speak a word of it to Henry."

Jane forced herself to smile in reply. It was the truth; she had exacted such a promise from Lucy, and she was glad and a little surprised that her friend had actually honored the request. She must suffer through it, all five acts. Her head began to pound in anticipation as she settled herself into her seat between Lucy and Nickerson. Emily and Cecil took seats behind them, next to the two empty seats directly behind Jane. Awaiting Hayden and his betrothed, of course.

Nickerson tipped his fair head toward hers. "There she is," he whispered. "Miss Adare. With her parents, and that's her uncle, Lord Astley, behind her."

Jane sat forward in her seat, her eyes trained on the box across the width of the theater from them. Miss Adare wore a gown of pale yellow, and she smiled sweetly across the way at them.

Jane was moved into action. "Come, then. There's still time before the curtain. Let us go and pay our respects."

"Are you mad? I can't just walk over there and start conversing with her."

"No," Jane whispered with a smile. "But I can. Lucy," she said, tapping her friend on the wrist with her fan, "if you'll excuse us for one moment, there's someone I'd like to speak to. Come, Mr. Nickerson. I won't be but a moment."

"Of course," he answered, taking her arm with a delighted smile.

It seemed they'd never make their way across the lobby, so thick was the crowd, all trying their best to see and be seen before the evening's actual entertainments began. At last they made their way to Lord Astley's box. With her head held high, Jane stepped in, delighted by Miss Adare's expression of joyful surprise at finding her beloved in her company.

"Miss Adare, how lovely to see you again." Jane

reached out to grasp the girl's hand in hers. "I'm so glad we had the chance to get reacquainted at the Pembertons' ball last week. I knew I must come pay my respects when I saw you sitting directly across the way."

"Oh, Miss Rosemoor." Miss Adare stood, her dark eyes shining brightly. "What a delightful surprise." She couldn't seem to keep her gaze from trailing longingly to Nickerson's beaming face.

"You must meet my escort for the evening, Mr. William Nickerson. He's been a friend of mine for many years. Mr. Nickerson, this is Miss Evelyn Adare."

"Miss Adare, a pleasure." He reached for the girl's hand and bowed, his gray eyes dancing with mischief. "I believe we have met, albeit briefly, in Kent."

"Of course," Miss Adare answered, her cheeks flushing pink. "At my aunt's estate. That's why you look so familiar, then."

Her parents rose and joined them. "Miss Rosemoor, how lovely to see you," Lady Adare trilled. "How is your dear mother? When will she be coming to Town?"

"Soon, I hope. I'm afraid my sister's youngest has been quite ill and my mother has remained in Essex to lend a hand. But she does hope to spend some time here before the Season ends. Have you met Mr. Nickerson?"

"I don't believe we have," Sir Alan answered with a smile.

"Mr. Nickerson, Sir Alan Adare and his wife, Lady Adare. I present Mr. William Nickerson, a longtime Rosemoor family friend. My father thought very highly of Mr. Nickerson," she added.

Sir Alan stroked his whiskers. "Is that so? Well, then, it is a pleasure to meet you, Mr. Nickerson."

The men shook hands, and Nickerson bowed gracefully to Lady Adare.

"Well, Miss Adare, I'm afraid I must hurry back across to the Mandevilles' box. It's such a pleasure to see you again. I hope you enjoy the evening."

"Oh, I'm sure to," she murmured, casting a shy glance at Nickerson from beneath her lowered lashes.

Jane congratulated herself smugly as they made their way back across the lobby to their own seats. That had gone perfectly, just as she'd anticipated. As they stepped into the privacy of the box, Nickerson reached earnestly for her hand and squeezed it.

"That was brilliant, Miss Rosemoor, simply brilliant." He raised her hand to his lips and brushed a kiss across her knuckles. "You are surely the most extraordinary woman I know."

Jane laughed merrily, pleased with herself for aiding his cause.

Someone cleared his throat loudly, and only then did Jane notice Hayden sitting there, a frown darkening his face.

"Good evening, Lord Westfield," she said with forced cheeriness as she took her seat, noting the still-empty one by the earl's side. "Where is Miss Upshaw tonight?"

"She accompanied her parents to Surrey for a sennight."

"Really?" Nickerson took his own seat beside Jane. "A newly betrothed girl taking off to the countryside? Not sticking around Town to bask in her accomplishment? I'm astonished."

Hayden only raised a brow in reply.

"Jane, who is that watching our box with opera

glasses?" Lucy leaned toward her with a frown. "Right there, down below in the pit? He just lowered the glasses and is staring right up at . . . at you, I believe."

Jane squinted to make out the form in dark dress coat leaning indolently against the row of seats in front of him, and smiling up at her lasciviously. She sucked in her breath. Clifton. Down there in the pit, amidst the *demimonde,* his wife nowhere in sight. He kept his eyes trained on her until a woman in a shockingly transparent dress leaned over to him and whispered something in his ear, affording him an ample view of her breasts as she did so. Jane watched in disgust as he whispered something in return, and then reached a hand out to tweak one nipple through the thin cloth of her bodice. He briefly threw his head back and laughed, then sought Jane out in the crowd once more, his eyes pausing briefly on her face before lowering blatantly to her décolletage.

Dear God, Jane thought in horror. *The nerve of the man.* She turned toward Nickerson, who'd obviously watched the exchange. His face was scarlet.

"How dare he?" Nickerson sprang to his feet. "I'll have a word with that scoundrel."

"Oh, no, you won't." Jane reached for his sleeve and pulled him back to his seat. "Really, Nickerson, what has he done besides look at me?"

"Indecently, Miss Rosemoor. He looks at you as if you weren't a lady, and I won't stand for it."

The houselights dimmed. "Shhh. The play is set to begin. No more of this."

He took his seat with a scowl. Jane couldn't resist turning and stealing a glance at Hayden behind her. The murderous look on his face made her blood run cold. His hooded eyes were narrowed and flashing, his hands flexing menacingly. She spun back to face the stage with a gasp, forcing herself to think of nothing save the play. It was a losing battle, of course. She flicked open her fan and nervously stirred the air, hoping to cool her flushed cheeks as she trained her eyes on the stage.

When the first intermission presented itself, Jane's neck was stiff with tension. It had taken a great amount of concentration to keep her gaze forward, to resist the sharp pull to turn in her seat and peek at Hayden. She could physically feel his eyes on her back, burning her skin, prickling her neck, throughout every minute of the first act. Again, she set her fan in motion, the heat rising in her face.

"A lemonade, Mr. Nickerson," she managed to say, her voice strangled. "Might you fetch me one?"

"Of course." He leaned toward her. "Who knows who I might encounter out there, eh?"

Jane forced herself to smile up at him. He exited with a smile, all thoughts of Clifton's offense obviously long forgotten.

"Jane, we'll return shortly," Lucy said, rising to her feet and taking her husband's proffered arm. "Henry and I are going for a stroll. Poor man," she said with a laugh. "He finds the theater almost as unbearable as the opera. We'll return in time for the third act."

As soon as the Mandevilles departed, grinning at each other with mischievous glints in their eyes, Emily rose and reached for Cecil's arm. "Cecil, darling, I think I could use some air myself. Jane, can we get you anything?"

"No, Nickerson's fetching me a lemonade," she answered before she thought. Blast it, now she had no excuse but to remain here in the box with *him*.

What was this, she thought, as Emily and Cecil took their leave—some sort of conspiracy?

Glancing at Hayden, she saw that he looked as uncomfortable as she felt about finding themselves alone in such a small space. He stood abruptly and moved toward the back of the box, his arms folded as his eyes scanned the double circle of boxes.

Just then, Alexander Clifton appeared in the open doorway. He bowed, then faced her with a roguish smile, his white teeth flashing in his face. "Miss Rosemoor. What a pleasure to see you. The first few weeks of the Season seemed somehow less bright without your presence."

"Good evening, Mr. Clifton," Jane said, rising to her feet. "And how is Mrs. Clifton?"

He shrugged. "I wouldn't know, nor do I care overmuch. She lacks your spirit, Miss Rosemoor. Courting you a few years ago has spoilt me for other ladies, I'm afraid. I was hoping perhaps we could renew our acquaintance."

From the corner of her eye, Jane saw Hayden move out of the shadows. Surprise registered briefly on Clifton's countenance, replaced immediately with a knowing, cocky grin. "Once you tire of your current paramour, that is."

"What are you suggesting, Clifton?" Hayden challenged, his voice clipped. He moved toward the much smaller man, his hands clenched and his massive chest thrown out menacingly.

Clifton stepped up, seemingly not the least intimidated. "Come now, we're all adults here. Miss Rosemoor is no longer a debutante, well past the marriageable age. There's no shame in it. A woman has certain needs, after all. I saw the two of you, stumbling out of the dark lanes at Vauxhall not so many weeks ago, your clothing in a shocking state of disarray. I'm offering to set you up, Miss Rosemoor. To give you *carte blanche*. I know for a fact I'm offering you more than Westfield here has. I've asked around, you see. What say you, Miss Rosemoor?" he asked with an arrogant smile. "Are you game?"

Jane was utterly shocked into silence, barely able to believe her ears. And then it registered in her mind . . . he'd seen them—seen her and Lord Westfield together at Vauxhall Gardens. What must Clifton think of her? Worse still, what if he told? She had always held dear her sterling, exemplary reputation. Never before had it been threatened, not even the slightest bit. Her hand rose to cover her mouth, bile rising in her throat at the thought of ruin.

"Well?" he asked, and only then did Jane notice Hayden's silence.

Suddenly Hayden's fist flew out, connecting with Clifton's jaw with an unnaturally loud crack. Jane recoiled in shock as Clifton sank to the ground, a spot of bright red blood appearing at one corner of his mouth.

She looked over at Hayden, who stood, his feet planted firmly apart, his hands in fists by his sides, breathing raggedly. Defending her honor, even though he was betrothed to another.

Clifton struggled to sit, one hand reaching up to feel the wetness that dripped from his mouth, staining his cravat. He looked to his blood-covered hand with surprise, then up to Westfield.

"Apologize to the lady at once, Clifton," Hayden barked.

"Apologize?" He rose unsteadily to his feet.

"Unless you want me to make your life miserable, I suggest you do as I ask. Together with Lord Mandeville, I can make things particularly difficult for you in this town. I know you owe an enormous debt to a number of creditors, some more, shall I say, *unreasonable* than others. I won't think twice about insisting that your loans be called in. You will apologize, and you will never speak a word of this. In fact, you'll never speak to Miss Rosemoor again, nor will you as much as utter her name to anyone. Understood?"

Clifton looked from Hayden to her, and back again before nodding his assent. "Understood." He turned toward her, his gaze dull and lifeless. "Miss Rosemoor, I apologize for my behavior and hope that someday you will find it in your heart to forgive this, ah, misunderstanding on my part."

Jane only nodded.

"Now get out." Hayden pointed to the doorway.

Clifton acquiesced, nearly tripping over a chair in his haste to quit their company.

Jane's eyes met Hayden's the moment they were alone again. "Thank you," she murmured.

"He'll remain silent, have no fear. His debts are far too substantial to risk it. If it weren't for his poor wife, I'd call him out. Although now that I think about it, it's not such a bad idea. She'd be substantially better off without him."

"She'd be left without a shilling to her name," Jane said quietly.

"Hmm, you're right. No matter. It's settled. He won't bother you again; I'd stake my life on it." He ruefully rubbed his knuckles, which were already turning an alarming shade of blue.

"Oh, dear. Your hand. Let me see." Jane reached for it. "You might have broken something."

He pulled his hand from her grasp. "Nothing save his teeth. Far less than he deserved."

"You must let me see," Jane insisted. Reluctantly he assented, wincing as she took his hand in hers and ran her fingertips lightly across the swollen knuckles. "You should get something cold on this at once." She couldn't help but allow her fingers to linger on his, unable to release him, to break the physical connection. As the theater darkened once more, he interlaced his fingers with hers, covering their joined hands with his free one. Looking around, he shrugged. "Where has everyone gone off to?"

Jane smiled thinly. "Purposefully leaving us alone, I imagine."

He tilted his head toward hers. "Do you suppose anyone would notice if we slipped out of here?"

"Together? Without a doubt." She nodded. Her hand remained firmly clasped within his.

"Even for a moment?"

"Are you willing to risk it? As it is, Clifton managed to spy us together at the Gardens. No, we cannot. Besides, what would come of it?"

He shook his head. "I do not know. I only know that I want it more than anything." His voice was soft against her ear, his warm breath caressing her skin.

"I should leave London at once, before we cause further talk, before your betrothal contract is endangered."

"I want to kiss you, Jane," he murmured against her ear. "I want to touch you. I *need* to touch you."

"Not here," she said vehemently, roughly shaking her head.

"Where, then?" His voice was rough, filled with a need that matched her own. They were so much alike, after all. She understood his torment, and it made her feel closer to him than she'd ever felt to anyone. When she spoke, the words surprised even her.

"I'm told there are places, here at the theater," Jane whispered. "Dark places, secret places."

"Follow me," he whispered huskily, reaching for her hand.

Minutes later, Hayden turned into a darkened hallway, reaching for a door that led to an abandoned dressing room. Jane followed close behind. Looking around to make sure no one was about, he pulled her roughly inside, closing the door and turning the lock before taking her mouth with his—roughly, desperately. She moaned against his lips, hers held firm, then yielded, her hands finding his linen shirt as her tongue met his. With several tugs, she released the fabric from his trousers, and he shuddered as he felt her bare hands slide up his torso, her fingertips brushing his skin with exquisite softness. In an instant his staff hardened, straining against the wool barrier that separated them. He pressed himself fully against her as her hands circled to his back, her nails digging into his flesh as she drew him closer.

Abandoning her hot, sweet mouth, he sunk to his knees, his hands pushing up her skirts while he simultaneously pulled down her stockings. "Hayden," she cried out, "please." He groaned at the invitation, and his lips found her warm skin immediately, his tongue tracing a path upward, toward her silky thighs. Cloaked in darkness, his hands replaced his mouth on her bare legs, his fingers stroking her flesh, moving steadily toward the apex of her thighs. She gasped as he found her mound of soft curls, her entrance slippery and wet. Ready for him. He ran his thumb over the hardened nubbin of flesh nestled between her folds, and her whole body shuddered convulsively at the contact. Bloody hell, it would be so easy, so very easy to take her right then and there.

But it would also be wrong, for so many reasons. Too many reasons to name. Struggling valiantly to squelch the riptide of desire coursing through him, he dropped his hands and pressed his face against her thighs as he tried to catch his breath. "I can't do this," he muttered, his voice ragged. "God help me, I can't."

"Look at us, Hayden," she gasped, her whole body trembling against him. "Look what I've become. I am exactly what Clifton supposed I am. Nothing but your—"

"Don't say it." He rose on unsteady legs, placing a finger across her lips. "It isn't true."

"What are we doing, then? Why did I allow this?"

He reached blindly for her hands. "I cannot explain it myself. We got carried away, that's all. But it will go no further."

"I'll leave London at once. This isn't fair to Miss Upshaw. Were I in her position, I'd never . . ." She swallowed hard, her remorse evident in her halting voice.

"It isn't fair to *you*, either, Jane. I'm a sorry excuse for a gentleman." Hell, he'd boxed Clifton for nothing more than insulting Jane's honor, for assuming her virtue was lost, yet here he was, doing everything in his power to take that virtue, to steal her virginity even while he was betrothed to another.

He bit back the sour taste of self-hatred, not for the first time, and found his usual steady, commanding voice. "Go, Jane." He moved away from her. "Leave me. Get away from me, before it's too late."

With a whimper, Jane did exactly that. He'd never forget the pained look in her eyes as the door swung open and she fled from him, no doubt hating him every bit as much as he hated himself.

Chapter Fifteen

Derbyshire

"I'm so glad you insisted we leave Town when we did, Jane." Emily looked up from her needlework with a smile. "I feel much restored already. I'm grateful to you for looking after my health."

A wave of guilt washed over Jane, for her reasons for fleeing Town had little to do with Emily's well-being.

"Besides," Emily added, "I see the bloom has returned to your cheeks. There's nothing better than the clean, pure Derbyshire air. It acts like a tonic every time."

"I believe you're right." Jane smiled indulgently, not wanting to remind her that they'd only gone to London in the first place to cure Emily of a terrible despondency that began there in the Derbyshire air. "And how is Amelia faring? I know the journey must have been tiring for such a little one."

"Very well, actually. None the worse for the wear. The nurse was hoping to take her out today; it's too bad the weather has turned so abysmal. I'm a firm believer in the restorative powers of fresh air, even for an infant."

"I agree. The dark skies make me want to curl up

in bed all day." Jane reached a hand up to stifle a yawn.

Emily nodded in agreement. "It was all I could do to get out of bed this morning. Oh, not because of melancholy," Emily added, waving a hand. "It's just that the sound of rain makes me so very sleepy, that's all."

Jane studied her cousin's expression closely, but could find no sign of artifice. *Thank goodness.* She sighed in relief.

In the days since their return, Emily's moods had swung wildly from delight at being home again to a quiet melancholy, and back again to apparent cheerfulness. Jane desperately longed to leave these parts, to return to Essex and the family she'd left behind. The knowledge that Hayden's home lay just beyond the woods outside her window unsettled her greatly, even though he remained in Town. She was plagued by the memory of his touch at the theater, mortified by her own wanton behavior.

She needed to get away, far away, from any reminders of him. Yet she did not quite feel ready to leave Emily alone, especially as Cecil had spent less time at home and more time away since their return.

Jane set aside her own needlework and rose from the settee. She crossed the room in several strides and stood at the window, gazing out at the misty twilight shrouded in a drizzling rain as her sense of self-preservation battled against her love for her delicate cousin. She ran her fingers across the heavy brocade drapes and shivered, feeling a chill even though none survived in the warm, humid air that wafted in the window.

At once an odd, low-pitched sound reached her

ears, growing louder and more intense. The hair rose on the nape of her neck in response to the eerie noise. Suddenly an enormous white dog moved into view on the edge of the wood, barking raucously.

Emily rose and joined Jane at the window. "Whatever is that?"

Recognition dawned on her. She'd seen the dog before. At Richmond Park, the day she'd gone to ask Hayden to find Cecil and bring him home for Amelia's birth. "Isn't that Lord Westfield's dog?"

Emily squinted, leaning closer to the window, then nodded. "It is. Vlad, he's called. But I've never seen him so far from home. How odd."

The barking grew louder, more insistent, and then the animal turned toward the woods and let out a loud, plaintive whine before turning back toward the Tollands' house. He continued barking, pacing back and forth and moving closer to the house.

"Is Cecil home?" Jane asked her cousin.

"No, he left this morning for Shropshire. I don't expect him back for a fortnight."

Jane headed for the door.

"Where are you going?" Emily followed her. "You can't go out in this weather."

"Where is my cloak?" Jane looked around distractedly, then hurried to the entrance hall, where she found her black cloak hanging on a peg beneath a gilt-framed mirror.

"But you can't mean to go out in this drizzle, not in those slippers."

"I must. I have this terrible feeling that something is not right." She fastened her cloak and pulled the folds of the hood over her head.

"Jane, I beg you to reconsider." Emily stood in

the doorway, wringing her hands as Jane hurried out toward the distressed dog.

Moisture seeped into her slippers at once, but Jane didn't heed the discomfort. She almost swore she saw relief light the animal's intelligent brown eyes as he spotted her and loped to her side. He ran in circles around her, barking and whimpering as he attempted to herd her toward the woods.

"What's wrong, Vlad? Shall I follow you?" The dog whined in reply. "You've something to show me, haven't you, boy? Come then, lead the way. And make haste!"

Jane set off, following the dog's path through the dense wood that she now knew led to Richmond Park. Vlad hurried on ahead, barked in agitation, and then circled back to her side before leading her off again.

At last she saw him stop in a thicket ahead, crouched down on his haunches. He let out a blood-curdling howl. Breathless and soaked through, Jane ran the distance separating them.

Her blood turned cold. There, lying on a bed of mossy earth beside a downed tree limb, was little Madeline, her eyes closed and a deathly pallor across her features. A gash above one eyebrow was caked with blood and a goose egg distended her brow. Most frightening of all, her lips were a dreadful shade of blue.

In sheer terror, Jane knelt to the ground and laid her head on the girl's chest. *Thank God!* The child was breathing. But she was cold, so very cold. However would she warm her?

She stood and hastily unfastened her cloak, then knelt again to wrap the girl in its folds. As gingerly as possible, she lifted Madeline's limp body and held her close, hoping the heat from her own body would help warm Madeline's blood.

"Please, Vlad," she pleaded, "I know you cannot understand me, but you must lead me back to Emily. I cannot do it alone."

As if he perfectly understood the words, Vlad trotted off, back in the direction from which they'd come. Nearly blinded by the misty rain mixed with her own tears, Jane raced after the dog, clutching the child to her breast. Somewhere along the way, she lost a slipper, but she dared not stop to retrieve it.

Relief washed over her as she saw the Tollands' house take form through the foggy mist. She increased her pace, her lungs positively burning from exertion. The door swung open, and Emily ran down the steps, her delicate features twisted with fear.

"Dear God, whatever has happened? Madeline?"

"Vlad led me right to her, lying in the woods."

"She's unconscious?"

Jane nodded. "It looks like a blow to the head. You must summon the surgeon at once!"

"Of course." Emily turned and headed back inside at a run, Jane following close behind.

When she reached the salon, Jane gingerly laid the child down upon the sofa and began to inspect her thoroughly for other wounds she might have missed. Breathing a sigh of relief, she tightened the cloak about her small form. She saw no additional injuries, at least none visible to the eye. She laid a hand across Madeline's brow and gasped as her hand made contact with the child's skin. She was burning with fever.

Emily reappeared at last, carrying a basin of water and a cloth. "I sent word to Westfield's surgeon to come straightaway."

"Good. A fever has set in."

"Then let us pray he comes quickly."

Jane nodded solemnly. *She must recover,* her mind screamed out. *She must.* She realized with a start that her concern extended beyond that of the child's welfare. She thought of Hayden, as well. *I cannot go through it again,* he'd said, just weeks before. However would he manage if Madeline was taken from him? She closed her eyes and shuddered.

Hurry, she thought. *Please hurry.* If only she could summon the surgeon to her side with her thoughts alone. She reached down and clasped the child's small hand in her own, watching helplessly as her tears splashed onto their wrists and rolled off.

"Her condition is grave, indeed." Mr. Allan wiped his hands on a bloodstained cloth. "The cut and concussion are the least of it. It's the fever that might take her. Under no circumstances is she to be moved to Richmond Park. She must remain here."

"I'll ready a room for you, then, Mr. Allan. But first I'd best send word to Richmond Park." Emily bustled out.

"It's lucky she is that you stumbled upon her when you did, Miss Rosemoor. Another hour exposed to the elements and she would not have survived."

Jane looked at the huge white dog that remained planted firmly in the chamber's corner, his curly coat matted from the rain. He'd saved the child's life. *What a remarkable animal.* She resolved to go to the kitchen and find a meaty bone for him as soon as she could slip away.

"As it is, I'm not certain she'll live through the

night," the man continued dourly, shaking his head. "Lord Westfield has suffered enough misfortune as it is. This is terrible, very terrible indeed. I will remain here and do everything in my power to aid her recovery, of that you can be sure."

Taking the child's hand in her own, Jane sat wearily, massaging Madeline's palm with her thumb. "Please, Madeline," she murmured. "You must fight. You cannot leave us." Her eyes misted with unshed tears.

"Come, Jane," Emily spoke from the doorway a quarter hour later. "I'll sit with her a spell. You're soaked and you're shivering. I've had a warm bath sent up to your room."

Jane shook her head silently. She couldn't leave her. Not now. Not with her condition so tenuous, her hold on life so fragile.

"You'll be of no use to her if you catch your own death from the dampness. Please, Jane. I insist that you do as I ask." Emily moved to her side, laying one hand on her shoulder.

"Mrs. Tolland is right," the surgeon added, looking up from his tray of supplies. "'Else you'll end up abed yourself, I'm afraid, and I'll have two patients to tend instead of one."

Jane shivered, suddenly aware of the damp cold that permeated her dress. Droplets of water fell from her hair to the floor at her feet, silently splashing against the floorboards. She looked down, surprised to see she wore only one mud-caked slipper, her other foot in nothing but a soggy, stained stocking. A puddle had formed beneath her, slowly increasing in circumference, even as she watched.

At last, Jane nodded. They were right. She couldn't remain here in this state. She allowed Emily to wrap a blanket around her shoulders.

"Thank you, Jane. I know Lord Westfield would want you to see to your own health." Emily smiled a weak smile, her eyes full of understanding. "He would not suffer such stubbornness, you know."

Jane reached for her hand and squeezed it in reply. Emily knew him well.

"Besides," Emily continued, "someone must write to him in London. I'm sure the staff at Richmond Park will do so, but one of us should send word as well, and assure him we will do everything we can to see to her care. My eyes grow tired, Jane. Perhaps you will write the letter?"

Seeing right through her cousin's ruse, Jane smiled. She had underestimated Emily; clearly, she recognized more than she let on.

"I will write to him on your behalf, Emily. As soon as I get myself out of these wet things and warmed up a bit, that is. Will you stay here with her until I return?"

"Of course," Emily answered.

Jane leaned over Madeline's still form and placed a kiss on one burning cheek.

"Fight, little soldier. He needs you."

"I still can't believe you braved Almack's. I wish I had witnessed it with my own eyes." Lord Mandeville picked up his glass with a grimace. "Allow me to retract that statement. Witnessing it would have required my presence at Almack's."

Hayden drained his own glass and signaled for the waiter to bring him another. Tonight's Parliamentary session had run late, and White's was teeming with weary gentlemen, all hoping for a restorative meal and drink before heading home. It was all Hayden could do to catch the attention of the harried young man dashing between tables with a heavy tray balanced on his hands.

"Mark my words, Mandeville. Never again shall I allow myself to succumb to the pressure to go there. If Miss Upshaw wishes to go, then she can go alone."

"Hmmm, will you accept a wager on that? Let's put it in the betting book, then," Mandeville said with a grin. "I fear you'll make my pockets heavy."

"Your pockets are heavy enough." Hayden tiredly spooned a bite of hearty stew into his mouth. He was exhausted. His sleep of late had been plagued with troubling dreams; nightmares that awoke him in the dead of the night, his heart pounding and his body bathed in sweat. Even in his waking hours, he could barely assuage the lingering feelings of unease stirred by the dreams. With such little restful sleep, his Parliamentary obligations alone were enough to tire him without being dragged about to social events each and every night of the week. "Miss Upshaw's social schedule is relentless. Now that we're betrothed, I don't see why I can't slip back into obscurity and await the wedding date in peace."

"Makes perfect sense to me. How's the stew?"

"Superb."

"You've made an appropriate match, I suppose." Mandeville stroked his chin thoughtfully. "Miss Upshaw is a comely little thing, and my wife tells me she's bright enough. Still . . ."

"Yes?"

"Never mind. I need another drink." Mandeville signaled to the waiter.

Hayden's temper flared. "If you've something to say about my choice of bride, say it and be done with it."

Both remained silent as the waiter appeared at last and filled their glasses with whiskey.

"I've nothing against Miss Upshaw," Mandeville said as the waiter moved away. "It's just that Jane—"

"Jane?" Hayden set down his spoon. "Miss Rosemoor?"

"That's the one. I thought perhaps there was something between you two. I was more than a little surprised to learn of your betrothal to Miss Upshaw. I realize Jane's no longer a young debutante, but she is everything a sensible man should want in a wife. You can find no fault with her. I realize my connection with her leaves me a bit biased, but—"

"What has your wife said to you about me and Miss Rosemoor?" Hayden couldn't stem his curiosity.

"Nothing, not a word. She's as silent as a tomb where you are concerned. Which, of course led me to the obvious conclusion that there is something between you and Jane—er, Miss Rosemoor. That you would prefer Miss Upshaw over her surprises me."

"I do not prefer Miss Upshaw to Miss Rosemoor." Hayden drained his glass with a stiff jerk of the wrist. He muttered a silent oath as his traitorous heart accelerated. "In fact, entirely the opposite is true. Which is precisely why I've chosen to marry Miss Upshaw." He reached up to loosen his cravat.

"Ah, I see, then." Mandeville nodded his understanding.

Hayden was relieved that he did not need to explain himself further.

Mandeville cleared his throat. "I'll admit to harboring similar sentiments, before I married Lucy. I almost married the Duke of Corning's daughter instead, you know. Lady Helena. She's since wed the Viscount Bradley, the poor chap. Marrying her would have been the single biggest mistake of my life, no matter how appropriate she might have been in theory. As ridiculous as I feel saying it, there's something to be said for love."

Hayden stared at him in utter astonishment, wondering if marriage had made him lose his mind. "I think perhaps you've been reading too much Byron."

"Lord Westfield?"

Hayden looked up in surprise at the sound of his footman's voice. "Yes, Michaels?"

"An express messenger just brought this, milord. I thought you might wish to have it right away." He held out a letter sealed with red wax, the direction written in an unfamiliar hand.

Hayden took it. "Thank you, Michaels."

Michaels bowed, then turned and made his way back through the thick crowd.

Hayden broke the seal and unfolded the page with a scowl, smoothing the paper with damp palms while Mandeville looked on curiously. Rarely did an Express bring glad tidings.

His eyes hastily slid over the page, searching for the signature. *Jane.* What could she possibly want, and with such urgency? With mounting trepidation, he read.

Ashbourne, Derbyshire

Dear Lord Westfield,

Please excuse the urgent nature of this correspondence, but I write with a heavy heart on behalf of Mrs. Tolland. I assume that word of this misfortune has by now reached you from Richmond Park, but in case it has not, forgive me for being the bearer of ill tidings. Your niece, Madeline, is gravely ill. I do not know under what circumstances she found herself there, but she was found alone in the dense woods surrounding your home with an injury to her head. Your loyal dog Vlad is to be credited with her rescue, as he led me to find her.

Madeline was taken at once to the Tollands' home, where a vicious fever set in. Your own surgeon, Mr. Allan, is attending her, but her condition is grave, indeed, and she cannot be moved to Richmond Park. Please be assured that the Tollands and I will do everything in our power to see to her care and comfort. Nay, my lord, I will not leave her side until I see her well; that I promise you. I will send word of her condition immediately upon the morn.

With Sincere Regret,
Miss Jane Rosemoor

"Well?" Mandeville asked, his brow furrowed.

"My niece. I must go at once." Hayden shoved back his chair and rose. He dashed to the door without a backward glance, his stomach knotted with dread.

He didn't have a moment to lose.

Chapter Sixteen

"Mrs. Tolland?" a faint voice whispered. Jane sat up at once, blinking the sleep from her eyes. She reached for Madeline's feverish hand as the first light of day shone through the part in the drapes, allowing pearl gray light to filter in and cast long shadows across the floor.

"No, Madeline. It's Miss Rosemoor. Jane. Do you remember me?" From the corner of her eye, Jane saw Mr. Allan stir in his chair by the fireplace.

"I . . . it's so hot, so very hot in here." Her blond head tossed from side to side on the pillow, her cheeks flushed scarlet.

"Shhh, dearest Madeline. You must rest." She gently stroked the child's cheek as Mr. Allan hurried to the bedside. He felt Madeline's forehead and frowned, shaking his head sadly as he reached for her wrist and felt her pulse.

Jane rose, turning to the table beside the bed where a blue-rimmed ceramic bowl sat beside a matching pitcher and a stack of thick, absorbent squares of cloth. With trembling hands, she poured water into the bowl and then took a cloth, which she dipped into the cool water. Gently, she wrung out the excess moisture. Not wanting her fear to show, she schooled her features into a cheerful expression. At last composed, she turned back to the child and laid the cloth across her brow. "There now, that should cool you down a bit."

Madeline's eyes flew open, slowly focusing on the face that loomed above her. "Jane, is that you?"

Jane smiled, tears welling in the corners of her eyes. She'd forgotten how much Madeline's mossy green eyes looked like Hayden's. "Yes, it's me. It is so good to see you again."

Madeline's eyelids fluttered shut, her long lashes resting against her darkly shadowed, sallow skin. "You've come to dinner, then? Oh, Uncle Hayden will be so pleased."

Jane shook her head, her brow furrowed. "No, child. You're here at Mrs. Tolland's home."

"We'll have a pudding for dessert. Uncle Hayden said . . . he said you would come to dinner again." She turned her head so that one cheek rested against the damp pillow, tendrils of wet, golden hair clinging to her face. Her mouth curved into a frown, her bottom lip trembling. "Where is Uncle Hayden?"

Jane took her hand and stroked it softly. "He's not here, Madeline. Shhh, you must rest."

Mr. Allan shook his head. "She's delirious, poor child. Her fever holds. Perhaps I should bleed her again." He bustled off to retrieve his supplies.

Jane stood silently, watching as Madeline at last eased into a fitful sleep, her chest rising and falling with each rasping breath.

If only Hayden would come! Five full days had passed since she'd first sent news of Madeline's condition, and two more letters had followed. They hadn't yet received any reply. Was he so preoccupied with his upcoming nuptials that he couldn't spare the time to write a few lines in inquiry of his niece? Was he so cold, so heartless, so self-absorbed?

Jane shook her head as she released Madeline's hand and laid it gently on the sheet. No, Hayden was not so cold, so cruel. She knew in her heart that he wasn't. Even if he had immediately written a reply, they should only now be receiving it. Perhaps the afternoon post would bring his response.

She scurried to the chair by the door as Mr. Allan returned and began the dreadful procedure of bleeding Madeline—first making a small incision in her forearm, then holding a bowl beneath it to catch the warm, metallic-scented blood. Despite this invasion, the child didn't stir.

Jane clutched her fingers to her temples, refusing to look as Madeline's lifeblood spilled noiselessly into the bowl.

Leaning back against the chair, she stifled a yawn. She was tired, so very tired. She stretched her legs, wincing at the ache that spread from her calves up to her shoulders. When Emily awoke, she'd ask her to sit with Madeline for a spell, and perhaps she could rest a bit.

Her eyes drooped, and she reluctantly allowed them to close. *I'll rest now,* she thought sleepily. Just for a moment, till the surgeon is done with his awful procedure.

Voices in the hall forced her eyes open again. Groggy, she looked to the window and noted the bright midday rays streaming in through the drapes. Madeline lay just as she had before, her lips parted slightly, her chest rising and falling in a regular rhythm. The surgeon was nowhere to be seen. How long had she slept? Jane rubbed her eyes and licked her parched lips. Goodness, she felt positively drugged.

She jumped in fright as the door rattled open, flung against the wall in haste. Her eyes widened in surprise as Hayden entered, followed closely by Mr. Allan and Emily. The earl had clearly sought his niece in haste—he still carried his hat in one hand and his camel-colored greatcoat billowed behind him, dusting his ankles as he strode purposefully across the room. His clothes appeared rumpled, as if they'd been slept in, and his face was lined with worry, his mouth pinched.

"Madeline," he called out, his voice edged with emotion, as he bent to place a kiss on the sleeping child's forehead.

Jane averted her gaze, a sigh of relief escaping her lips as Emily came to stand beside her.

"Jane, dearest, you must go lie down. Please, I beg of you. You're exhausted."

Jane nodded wearily in reply. Casting one last glance over her shoulder at Hayden, she allowed Emily to take her arm and lead her to her room. Hayden was here at last; all would be well. Without bothering to undress, Jane sank onto the down-filled mattress and slept peacefully for the first time in days.

When Jane awoke at last, it was well past midday. She sat up, wincing at the aches and pains that seemed to be everywhere at once. Her stomach grumbled noisily. When had she last eaten? She shook her head, unable to recall her last meal. Summoning Bridgette, she changed her clothes and did her best to tidy herself up a bit. Bridgette arranged her hair in one simple plait, coiled and pinned neatly against her crown. It would have to do. She hurried down the hall, but paused before Madeline's room. The door was slightly ajar, and she pushed it open a fraction to peer inside, not wishing to disturb Hayden if he remained by his niece's side.

What she saw made her breath leave her lungs in a rush. Hayden sat in the chair by Madeline's side, his bowed head resting in the crook of one arm on the bed beside Madeline's small form; his other hand clasped the child's hand in his. Emily stood beside him, her fingers lightly stroking his dark head as she whispered soft, soothing words.

"Shhh, now, Lord Westfield. It's not your fault. You arrived here as quickly as you could."

Jane froze, holding her breath. She knew she should leave at once, that she shouldn't compromise their privacy. Yet she couldn't make her limbs move—she stood rooted to the spot, unable to move a muscle.

"No, you don't understand, Emily," came his muffled reply. "It is my fault, just as it was my fault with Isabel, with Katherine."

Emily shook her head. "No, and I won't listen to these foolish words. Stop now. You cannot blame yourself." She continued to stroke his head. "I won't have it."

He raised his head at last. The anguish in his countenance took Jane's breath away. He reached for Emily's hand and clasped it tightly in his own. "You've always been so strong, Emily."

Emily laughed softly. "I am not as strong as you think, my lord. Haven't you seen the proof of it?"

He shook his head. "Do not underestimate yourself, little Emily. I thank you from the bottom of my heart for the kindness you've bestowed upon Madeline." He raised her hand to his lips and placed a soundless kiss on her knuckles. "You should not have this burden, especially with your husband away."

"It is Jane you should thank. I've done what I can

to see to Madeline's comfort, but it is Jane who followed your dog out into the woods to find her, who has stayed by Madeline's side day and night. I fear she's exhausted herself with worry—not just worry over the child, but over you, as well. She cares for you far more than she'll admit."

Jane found herself unable to breathe, awaiting his response. He only shook his head in reply. "I see where your words lead, Emily, and allow me to satisfy your curiosity. It will never come to be. I was a fool to think otherwise. I am betrothed to Miss Upshaw and I will uphold my end of the bargain struck with Lord Pemberton. My honor demands it. I know you will not understand, but trust me when I say that Miss Rosemoor is better off without me in her life. The sooner she returns to her home in Essex, the better."

Jane's heart twisted painfully. At once a bitter jealousy sprang forth from her soul, surprising her with its rancor. She was envious of Emily, of the close camaraderie she so obviously shared with Lord Westfield. She was equally envious of Miss Upshaw. One woman he called friend; the other he would call wife. She was nothing to him. *Nothing.*

No longer able to bear listening, she slunk away from the door, drowning in sorrow and shame.

"Is that what you truly desire, Lord Westfield? For Jane to return home, cut from your life forever?" Emily looked up at him plaintively, her brown eyes shining with unshed tears.

The pain inflicted by her words cut Hayden deeply, wounding him in ways he'd never imagined. He inhaled sharply. "It must be so."

"Then you are correct. I do not understand. I see

the way your eyes light whenever you're in her presence. I haven't seen that light since Katherine. Can you deny that you love her?"

A terror gripped him. He swallowed hard before he spoke, carefully measuring his words. "You've overstepped your bounds, Emily. This conversation has gone far enough. I do not love her, and that's the last I will say on this matter."

"I'm sorry," Emily murmured, her eyes downcast as she fiddled with the coverlet.

Bloody hell, he needn't have spoken so sharply. Not to the one woman who understood him best, God bless her soul. He cleared his throat uncomfortably as he reached for her hand.

"Forgive me. I don't mean to be a brute, Emily, not to you. No one deserves it less."

"You're exhausted, Lord Westfield, and worn with concern. I cannot hold your words against you." Her forgiving gaze rose to meet his, and she smiled. "Come now, let me get you something to eat, and perhaps a brandy would do you well."

"No, I must stay here." He shook his head and rested his palms wearily on the bed, leaning against it. "I cannot leave her."

"Of course you can, for a half hour, no more. Mr. Allan will return straightaway and remain by her side long enough for you to have a much needed drink and a bite to eat. Please?"

He looked to Madeline, still sleeping fitfully, and back to Emily's pleading gaze as he weighed his options. His empty stomach grumbled in reply, and his throat was dry. Finally, he nodded his assent.

He followed Emily back down the narrow stairway to the entry hall, where he finally allowed his coat and hat to be taken from him. She led him into the cheery breakfast room, and he stopped in his tracks as Jane laid down her fork and looked up at him in surprise.

"Jane, dearest," Emily called out. "I'm so glad to see you take a meal at last. Did you sleep?"

"I did, thank you. I feel much improved." Her expression remained flat, unanimated. Her features spoke of her exhaustion. Dark circles marred the fair skin beneath her eyes, and all color had fled her usually rosy cheeks. Still, she looked lovely, and his eyes devoured the sight of her. He hadn't thought he'd see her again; at least, not till he brought his bride home to Richmond Park. Only tragedy had swayed the fates. He knew he should take no joy in beholding her, not under the circumstances. Yet he couldn't help his hungry gaze, even as he was riddled with guilt for the pleasure.

Jane's hair was dressed simply, knotted on the back of her head, but a few stray tendrils escaped, caressing her cheeks. She wore a pale yellow morning gown, simple of cut, yet elegant nonetheless. Her sapphire eyes retained their normal luster, the one spot of brilliant color in her pale face, even as they avoided his gaze.

She pierced a lump of scrambled egg with her fork and brought it to her mouth with trembling hands, and he watched as she swallowed the bite with obvious difficulty. *I should leave her in peace,* he thought.

"Perhaps you should send a tray to Madeline's room for me," he said to Emily. "I do not wish to disturb Miss Rosemoor's solitude."

"Please do not leave on my account." Jane gestured to the chair at the end of the table. "Sit, my lord. I'm finished here. I'll return to Madeline at once."

"No," Emily cried. "You've barely touched your

meal. Sit, Lord Westfield," she commanded. "I will
have some food brought out at once. In the meantime, may I fetch you a bottle of Cecil's brandy? Or
would you prefer tea?"

"Tea will suffice for now. Thank you, Mrs. Tolland. Don't trouble yourself; I can pour." He waved
her away and reached for the teapot.

"Very well. Let me find Mrs. Smythe and arrange
for your meal. Miss Rosemoor will keep you company in my absence."

Jane looked up in surprise as Emily bustled out.
After a pause, she cleared her throat. "What news
has Mr. Allan of Madeline's condition?"

"Her condition remains grave at best. The fever
is holding fast and weakening her considerably. I
fear for the worst." He took a sip of steaming tea,
hoping to ease the ache in his throat.

"She's a strong girl; a fighter, 'else she'd have
long been taken. I'm sure your presence brings her
great comfort, even if she cannot acknowledge it. I
choose to hope for the best." Jane stubbornly
tipped her chin in the air.

He set down his cup, his chest uncomfortably
tight. "Thank you, Miss Rosemoor. Mr. Allan tells
me that she would not be with us still if you had not
found her when you did."

"No, the credit belongs entirely to that magnificent animal of yours. Vlad appeared suddenly on
the edge of the wood and barked furiously for our
attention. I knew somehow that he wanted me to
follow him, and I'm glad I followed my instincts.
Your steward had to come and forcibly remove him
from Madeline's room, 'else he'd still remain, lying
patiently in the corner." Jane's mouth curved into
a gentle smile.

"I'll reward him greatly when next I see him, you

may count on that." Yes, Jane had saved Madeline's life, but Vlad had played an important role. "But I'm deeply indebted to you. How can I ever thank you?"

"Madeline's full recovery will be thanks enough, my lord. I know it sounds silly considering she's been unconscious most of the time, but I've grown quite fond of her these past few days."

Inexplicably, his heart felt a measure lighter. The women in this house were remarkable, the finest in all of Derbyshire, he thought with a smile. Perhaps in all of England.

Jane knocked tentatively on the door. "Lord Westfield?"

"Come in," he called out, and Jane pushed the door open and peered inside. Hayden sat slumped in the chair by the bed, his long legs stretched out before him. Mr. Allan remained in his usual corner, snoring softly.

"It grows late, my lord," she whispered. "Won't you go to bed?"

He looked up at her, his face drawn with exhaustion. She shivered, physically feeling the whisper of his gaze as it swept across her face and down her body, to her slippers, and back up again. She clutched the book she carried tightly to her breast, hoping he could not hear the furious pounding of her heart. Crossing to the window, she pulled aside the heavy drapes, revealing the hazy crescent moon that hung amidst the stars, casting a faint glow upon the lawn.

He stood and joined her at the window, his arm barely brushing hers, yet she felt it with exquisite keenness. They stood side by side for several minutes, silently watching the clouds that drifted across the moon, deepening the night, cloaking the proud oaks and yews in eerie shadows.

Jane turned to face him, closely studying his noble profile in the warm candlelight that bathed the room. His eyes stared straight ahead, unblinking under drawn brows. How she longed to smooth his creased brow with her lips, to press his shadowed face, deeply in wont of a shave, against her breast and stroke his hair as Emily had! Her traitorous hands itched at the very thought, and she clutched her book tightly in restraint, her nails digging viciously into the leather spine.

As if drawn by her gaze, his head slowly swung toward hers, his mesmerizing eyes questioning hers. She dared not speak. As if spellbound, their gazes searched wordlessly for answers, speaking phrases that must remain unspoken.

He held out one hand to her, in invitation. She bit her lower lip in indecision, till she tasted the faint, salty tang of blood. Tremulously, she reached out her hand to meet his, and he clasped it firmly in his grasp, his hand warm and strong. She could think of nothing save the scent of him, warm and powerful beside her.

A tremor ran through her and the book she grasped in one hand clattered to the ground. They both turned toward the surgeon, who snuffled loudly and then resumed his regular snoring. With a bitter reluctance, she pulled her hand from his grasp, unable to meet his eyes, and she knelt to the ground to retrieve her book. At the same time, he knelt beside her, and his hands found the thin volume before she could.

He stood and turned it over in his hands, a slow smile spreading across his face. "Mary Shelley?" he asked. "I'm astonished. You do not strike me as the type to enjoy horror stories."

Jane smiled wryly as she rose to face him. "*Frankenstein* is far more than a horror story, my lord. I find that Shelley does a fine job of exploring the duality of human nature. Besides, I find Victor Frankenstein a fascinating character—intelligent and kind, driven by passion, yet when faced with the monster he has created, he turns selfish, unsympathetic. The book itself is an apt treatise on society's readiness to judge character based on nothing but appearance alone."

"Very well said, Miss Rosemoor." He held out the book to her, and she quickly snatched it from his grasp. "Do you have a great love of reading? You speak with such passion."

"I suppose one might say I'm a passionate reader. It is indeed my most beloved pastime, as it gives me much pleasure. What of you, Lord Westfield? Where lies your passion?"

She moved to Madeline's bedside and brushed one golden lock from the child's forehead.

"The people of Richmond Park are my passion. Heavy toil has made the estate what it is today, and I take great pride in it. I believe that the satisfaction and happiness of my tenants is vital to the estate's well-being. No one at Richmond goes without a soft bed to sleep upon, without adequate wood for fires or food for their cupboards. Any child who wishes an education will get one. I do not credit the myth that education creates discontent; Richmond is proof otherwise. Lord Mandeville and I have worked stridently to change public opinion about education for all, but still, many refuse to listen to reason. The road ahead is long and hard, but I will not give up so easily. There, I suppose, is your answer."

"And a fine one, at that. I'm much impressed by your convictions."

He shrugged, and Jane noticed again the lines of exhaustion that marred his face.

Nodding toward the still-sleeping Mr. Allan, he grimaced. "Why does he bother to remain here, if he sleeps so soundly? What is his purpose? Someone should wake him and send him to his own room."

Jane looked at the man with a fond smile. "No, leave him be. He feels it's his duty. Mr. Allan is quite devoted to your family, it seems. But you, Lord Westfield, must get some rest. Please. I'll stay right here with her, till the sun rises."

"I cannot ask that of you, Miss Rosemoor. You've done enough."

"Come now, you've been awake for hours. I slept at length this morning and am now fully rested, eager to read." She held up her book. "Leave me. I'll send for you if there's any change."

"You're certain?"

"I'm certain."

With a weary nod, he acquiesced. Once he'd left the room, Jane sank into the chair by the bed and sighed, keenly aware of his absence in every fiber of her being. More disturbing was the thought that something inside her had changed fundamentally these past few months; that never again would she feel peaceful contentment. Instead, the days ahead would be plagued with unfulfilled yearnings, with unsatisfied desire tinged with regret. She could only shudder at the thought. Struggling to force the dark feelings away, she opened her book and began to read.

Chapter Seventeen

"Where's Lord Westfield?" Jane asked, looking up as Emily came in, followed by Mrs. Smythe, who carried a tea tray.

"I've sent him off to bed. Here, I've brought you some tea and cakes. I thought you might need some nourishment if you insist on sitting up through the night again." Without a word, Mrs. Smythe set down the tray and bustled out.

"Well," Jane said, "we've established a nice pattern, haven't we?" Hayden sat with Madeline throughout the day, and Jane throughout the night. It had worked well for the past two days, and kept them from each other's company as much as possible. She was satisfied with the arrangement.

Emily turned toward Mr. Allan, who busied himself by the washbasin, cleaning his instruments with a scowl. Finding him suitably occupied, she turned back to Jane and spoke in a hushed whisper. "Oh, Jane, I fear for Lord Westfield. His patience is wearing thin and his spirits are dreadfully low tonight. I do believe he's lost hope. Mr. Allan has told him that she cannot hold on much longer and that he should prepare himself for the worst."

Jane shook her head sadly. "Poor Lord Westfield."

"I cannot even imagine . . ." Emily shook her

head, her eyes squeezed shut. "I promised him that should her condition deteriorate in the night, you would summon him at once. He wishes to be with her at . . ." She sniffled into her handkerchief. "At the end."

Hot tears blurred Jane's vision as she looked at the child who lay so still and pale, the rising and falling of her chest now barely perceptible. "Of course. Go on to bed, Emily. I will do as you ask."

"Very well. Good night, then, dear Jane."

"Good night, Emily."

After brushing a few golden strands from Madeline's cheeks and readjusting the light coverlet that lay over the child, Jane settled herself into her chair and took out her needlework. She had begun an embroidered gown for Amelia weeks ago, and was anxious to finish it before the child grew too large to wear it.

More than an hour passed before she stopped and examined her progress. The candle had burned low; she moved it closer and held up the gown for inspection. Very pretty, she thought, pleased with her work. If her eyes held out, she'd finish it by sunrise.

A faint movement from the bed stirred her attention. She carefully set aside the gown and needle, rising on weary legs to peer down at the child. Were her eyes playing tricks on her? She held her breath, willing Madeline to stir. And then she saw it again; one thin arm moved against the coverlet, pale fingers grasping at the cloth. "Madeline?" Jane's voice trembled with excitement. "Can you hear me?"

The child's tongue darted out to wet her lips. "Thirsty," she croaked, her voice rusty with neglect.

Jane's breath escaped with a rush, and her hands

began to tremble. *Oh, thank God!* "You're thirsty? Here, let me get you some water." Jane clumsily reached for the pitcher and filled a glass, spilling a fair amount in the process.

"Here you are, just open your eyes, Madeline. Come now, you can do it!"

Jane's heart accelerated as the child's eyes fluttered open, her blond brows drawn in puzzlement. "Jane?"

"Yes, it's me. Here"—Jane reached around Madeline's thin shoulders and propped her up before bringing the glass to her lips—"drink."

Madeline sipped obligingly, coughing and sputtering as the liquid made its way down her parched throat. Panic rose in Jane's breast, and she almost dropped the glass, trying to pat the child's back. Once quieted, Madeline reached again for the glass and took a long, gulping draught with no ill-effects. Jane's pulse settled at last as Madeline leaned back against the pillows, smiling wanly.

She raised a hand to the child's forehead and almost wept with relief. It was cool! A thin film of sweat beaded on Madeline's forehead.

"Mr. Allan!" Jane cried, quaking with excitement.

The surgeon roused himself at once and hurried to her side, rubbing the sleep from his eyes.

"She's cool!"

"Very good, very good indeed." He felt Madeline's forehead, then her pulse. "Her fever has broken."

"So sleepy," Madeline murmured.

"Yes, child." Mr. Allan patted her hand, smiling broadly. "You need a great deal of rest."

They watched as she slipped back to sleep with a faint smile on her lips, her breathing far easier than before. Mr. Allan retrieved his stethoscope, putting one end against his ear, the other against Madeline's chest. Jane held her breath as he listened intently. At last he straightened, removing the single earpiece from his ear. "This is good, indeed. Her heart sounds strong, her lungs are clear. I believe she'll make a full recovery," he proclaimed, looking very pleased with himself. "Let her sleep. We'll see how she fares by morning."

"I must go tell Lord Westfield. Perhaps the news will bring him a peaceful sleep." Her heart singing, Jane headed for the door.

"Yes, yes," Mr. Allan said absently, settling himself into the chair by the bed. "Go at once."

Jane blinked back the sleep that threatened to overcome her as she hurried to Hayden's room. She hoped he'd managed to get some rest. Lord knew she needed some herself. Stepping up to the door with a sigh, she rapped sharply. "Lord Westfield," she called out. "Are you awake?"

The door opened at once, startling her. She stepped back and caught her breath. He reached for her wrist and pulled her inside, his face contorted with despair. She'd never before seen him so disheveled, so discomposed. He wore no waistcoat, no coat—only a simple, white cambric shirt that was pulled haphazardly from the waistband of his trousers. Even his hair, usually so neat, tumbled about in unruly dark waves.

"By God, has she worsened?" he asked, his voice thick with emotion.

"No, Lord Westfield. I've come to tell you she's much improved. Her fever has broken at last."

She saw the relief wash over his features as he grasped her hand in his so tightly that she feared he might crush the bones.

At last he dropped her hand and strode to the chair beside the hearth. Flinging himself onto the worn leather, he dropped his head into his hands. "If she had been taken, I would never have forgiven myself," he said, his voice thick with grief.

Jane tiptoed to the doorway and looked out into the hall, listening sharply for any sign of movement within the house. All was silent. As quietly as possible, she pulled the door shut and hastened to his side.

She knelt beside him and laid a hand tentatively on his arm. "You cannot say that, my lord. This was not your fault. Besides, she's better. Mr. Allan says she should recover fully, now that the fever's gone. Please don't blame yourself."

He raised his head, and Jane flinched at the sight—his cheeks were dampened with tears, his eyes red-rimmed. He was weeping. Her stomach twisted in knots. She'd never before seen a man weep, and she had no idea what to do. She swallowed, trying desperately to retain her composure.

"It *is* my fault," he continued, his voice breaking. "I love her, God help me. I knew the risks, yet I allowed myself to love her nonetheless." He dropped his head again. "Madeline was all I had left."

His words, so full of pain, ripped at Jane's heart. "Come, now, Madeline's much improved. Do not despair. You still have her, my lord."

"Hayden." He stood abruptly, nearly knocking Jane to the carpet. "My name is Hayden, and you can bloody well start calling me that."

She rose and drew herself to her full height, facing him with her chest heaving in indignation. "I only meant to help," she said, tears threatening her eyes. She spun toward the door, but he reached for her hand to stop her flight.

"Jane." His voice was a hoarse whisper. "Please don't go."

Guilt washed over her. She couldn't leave him alone, not in this state. He didn't know what he was saying, so torn was he with worry and grief. One look into his tortured eyes told her so.

She reached up to stroke his cheek, rough with several days' worth of stubble. "Oh, Hayden," she murmured, moving dangerously close to him. Her feet moved of their own volition, and before she knew it, she was standing just inches from him, peering up into his face, the heat from his body warming hers. In seconds his hands were on her flushed cheeks, one thumb tracing her lower lip. Her whole body quivered in anticipation.

With a groan, his mouth took hers, more greedily than ever before. Her skin tingled, her back arched, and she pressed herself against him. This time she didn't flinch at the blatant evidence of his arousal. Instead, it fueled her desire, made her moan against his mouth as his tongue flicked teasingly against hers. It felt as if the world had stopped spinning, as if time were suspended and nothing— *nothing*—signified except the feel of his mouth possessing hers. Their bodies melded into one, their hands moving in unabashed exploration. He somehow managed to release her hair from its pins, and she felt the weight of her tresses brush her shoulders. His fingers combed through her hair before moving lower, working the fastenings on the back of her dress.

The breeze stirred against her bared back as her dress parted at last. His mouth moved from hers, and his hands found her neckline, roughly shoving the fabric from her shoulders in one motion. In an instant, he had unlaced her stays, and they fell to her feet with a swish. She shuddered convulsively as a warm, moist heat gathered between her legs. His mouth, hot upon her skin, moved to her neck, tracing a path from behind one ear, down the curve of her shoulder and across the swell of her breasts. Lower still, his mouth moved, to one taut nipple. She tipped her head back, arching herself into him, desperately wanting him to suckle her.

Instead, he froze. His gaze rose to hers, his eyes glazed, half lidded. They swam into focus, his struggle for self-control evident in his countenance.

A sharp sigh of frustration escaped her lips. *Don't stop*, her mind screamed. *Not now. Not this time.*

"I know I must stop," he said hoarsely, "but I haven't the strength, not tonight." He shook his head and stepped away from her. "Go, before it is too late."

"No, Hayden," came her reply, her gaze boldly meeting his. "I can no longer deny my desires. I no longer wish to."

He hesitated, his eyes seeking affirmation in hers. She only smiled. He nodded slowly and drew her toward him, his hands clutching at her chemise. He paused, his head dipping down toward her ear. "Thank you," he murmured, then fiercely tore away her chemise.

She gasped as the fabric fell to the floor. Somehow she managed to kick off her slippers and step out of the folds of her dress, pushing aside the tattered remnants of her chemise with her stocking feet. She straightened, bared to him in the candlelight. His gaze raked over her body appreciatively, his eyes smoldering with desire. A shy smile formed on her lips in response, even as her heart fluttered in anticipation.

"You are the most beautiful woman I've ever seen," he said, his voice rough. "Do not ever doubt it."

Without taking his eyes off her, his fingers flew furiously over his shirt's buttons, and in seconds he pulled it over his head. Roughly, he removed his boots before stepping out of his trousers and standing proudly before her, his body entirely bared to her curious eyes.

Her cheeks burned as her gaze slid over his form in fascination, following the path of the dark dusting of hair that covered his finely sculpted chest and narrowed to a fine line, bisecting his taut stomach and tapered hips, and widened again at the source of his erection. She swallowed hard, amazed by the frightful size of him in arousal. Her heart skidded and her eyes quickly flicked back to his face, dark with desire, his eyes burning intensely with need. *Dear God, he's beautiful.* More beautiful than she'd dared to imagine. Jane's legs grew weak, threatening to buckle if he didn't take her in his arms quickly.

As if he'd read her mind, he gathered her in his embrace and lifted her off her feet, cradling her against him as he carried her across the room to the heavily draped bed. She laid her cheek against his warmly scented skin, where his heart slammed against his ribs, echoing her own.

Gently—almost reverently—he lowered her to the bed. His hands roamed the length of her body, sending flames of desire leaping from her skin at his touch. She felt his fingers stroke her legs, barely aware that he was untying her garters and sliding her stockings down until she felt his warm breath caress the curve of her calves. She closed her eyes as soft, featherlike kisses rained from the tips of her toes to the top of her head. His scent—tobacco mixed with sandalwood and the faintest hint of bergamot—enveloped her, sent her senses reeling, her head spinning. Turning her head to one side, she moaned softly against the bedcovers.

At last his mouth found her breasts, his teeth nipping at one swollen nipple until she cried out, arching her back off the bed as she did so. She tangled her hands in his hair as he took her in his mouth and suckled her, gently at first, then more insistently, as his hand trailed down to her most secret place, his fingers searching through her nest of curls for entrance.

She thought she'd surely die from pleasure when he found it. First one finger, then another parted her slick folds and entered her. Moaning in sheer delight, she ground herself against his hand as a mysterious pressure welled inside her. This was wicked, sinfully wicked, yet she did not want him to stop.

She whimpered when his hand withdrew, but soon his mouth followed the path of his fingers, down her stomach, across her thigh. She gasped as he parted her legs with his head, and her breath caught in her throat as she felt his tongue flick across her womanhood. Her soft moans increased, and she bucked her hips in reply, moving toward something inexplicable.

Just as she felt herself teetering upon some unknown precipice, he shifted his weight and moved atop her, straddling her. And then she felt it, the tip of his swollen member, pressing insistently against her entrance. Instinctively she flinched as he pressed against her barrier.

"Jane, my sweet, this will surely hurt a bit." He stroked her flushed cheek with his knuckles.

"No," she whispered, shaking her head with complete assurance.

"I'm afraid it will," he insisted, raising himself up on one elbow to peer down into her face. His gaze was steady, honest, his jaw firmly set. "But only for a moment, nothing more. And then, I promise you, you will feel nothing but pleasure."

She bit her lower lip and nodded. She trusted him, with all her heart.

In one swift motion, he sheathed himself within her and she gasped sharply—not from pain, but instead from the sheer rapture of feeling him, deep inside her. This was *right*. This was meant to be. The certainty of it flooded her veins, brought tears to her eyes.

He stilled, clutching her against him as he reached up to brush away a tear that rolled toward her ear. "Forgive me. I couldn't control—"

She covered his lips with her fingertips. "Shhh. These are tears of joy, Hayden."

He nodded, and then a smile slowly spread across his features. He began to move against her, slowly and subtly at first, establishing a rhythm as he plunged into her, again and again. Jane allowed herself to move with him, their bodies one, the blissful sensations inside her building to a crescendo once more until she thought she might scream.

Instead, she cried out his name, over and over again as something inside her exploded into blinding flashes of rapturous pleasure, her insides pulsing against the length of him in undulating waves of pleasure. Before she'd even had the chance to recover from her own release, he threw back his head and uttered a primal groan intermingled with her name as his hot seed spilled forth into her. Fighting for breath, he collapsed against her. Their bodies remained entangled, slick with perspiration, as he rolled onto his side, taking her with him as he went. He pressed his lips against her neck, his breath warm and comforting.

No wonder people took such great risks for such an experience, Jane thought with a smile of utter and complete satisfaction. It had been nothing short of exquisite.

"My sweet Jane," Hayden murmured sleepily against her ear, burying his face in her tousled hair as she slept against him, her even breathing making him smile in contentment. Making love to her had been the single most sensual, enjoyable experience he'd ever known. He'd never felt so complete, so spent, so sated in all his years.

A smile lingered on his lips as he drifted into a deep, satisfied slumber. But the same haunting dream that had plagued him for weeks pervaded his consciousness, causing him to toss and turn uncomfortably.

He stood in a dim, candlelit drawing room papered in flocked red silk. The muffled sound of tears surrounded him, cries of anguish piercing the quiet. He was compelled to move toward the far side of the room, toward the dark, shadowed corner. He moved reluctantly, on wooden legs, as hands reached out to clutch at him as he passed.

Shrugging off the grasping fingers, he moved closer, closer still. Upon a bier sat a heavily carved oak box, a coffin. "No," he shouted, but no sound came from his lips. His blood ran cold.

"Open the lid and look," cried a disembodied voice over his shoulder, the breath hot against his neck. "See what you've wrought." Again, he tried to cry no, but instead he felt a suffocating dread tighten

his windpipe, making him sputter and gasp. Per-
spiration ran down the side of his face, making his
hands slippery as he reached for the lid and pulled
it back.

Blue velvet lined the box—sapphire blue. He in-
haled deeply, paralyzed by fear, refusing to look upon
the face that lay pale and ashen against a white
satin pillow. At last, he raised his gaze and howled
in pain as Jane's face swam before him, sharply com-
ing into focus in his mind's eye.

With a start, Hayden's eyes flew open. Fully awake,
his heart raced. Never before had he been allowed to
see the face; instead, he'd always awakened to a
vague sense of dread. With painful clarity, he now understood the dream's meaning. It was a warning.
God's teeth, he couldn't love her. Hadn't he learned
anything from Madeline's brush with death? His
palms damp, he forced himself to glance down at the
supine form lying naked beside him, her face deathly
pale in the moonlight.

And then she stirred. He almost wept with relief
as she stretched her arms high above her head,
sighing sleepily as she did so. Suddenly the pain of
possessing her and then losing her seemed far
greater than the pain of never possessing her at all.

Her eyes fluttered open. "Hayden?" she mum-
bled, her voice heavy with sleep. His arm stole
around her waist protectively, drawing her against
him. He bent his head toward hers, inhaling the
fragrant lavender scent of her hair.

"Rest, my sweet. The sun's not yet come up.
There's plenty of time for you to get back to your
own room before anyone else stirs." Reluctantly, he
released her and stood, pulling on his trousers. "I
must go to Madeline and see how she fares." He

pulled his shirt over his head and hastily tucked the shirttails into the band of his trousers.

Jane stared at him silently, her eyes widening as the seconds ticked by. Her lower lip began to tremble, and she sat up abruptly, clutching the bedcovers to herself. A look of absolute terror gripped her features.

"Dear Lord," she gasped. "Do you realize what we've done? What risks we've taken? What if we've started a child?"

"Started a child?" He hastily buttoned up his shirt, trying to conceal his trembling hands. Damnation, he hadn't even allowed himself to consider that possibility, not while the other one, far worse, loomed in his mind. *Jane, lying lifeless on the blue velvet, her pale, stiff hands folded across her breast, clutching a small posy of flowers.* He squeezed his eyes shut against the vision, swallowing the bile that rose in his throat. Taking a deep breath, he opened his eyes again. "But you said you could not have children—"

"I'm sure I'm perfectly capable of doing so," she interrupted, her voice rising in near hysteria. "No, I meant I *would* not have them. Don't you see?"

"No, I'm afraid I *don't* see. I'm a man of honor, Jane." He raked a hand through his hair. "If we've started a child, I will not abandon you." Somehow, he would provide for her and the child. He couldn't begin to imagine how, not now, not with his signature on Lord Pemberton's betrothal agreement, the ink barely dry. He'd face a breach of promise suit, but he'd not abandon Jane.

She shook her head wildly. "It doesn't matter if you abandon me or not." Her eyes darted about wildly, her hands visibly trembling. Clearly she was terrified, by something far worse than the thought of being forced to wed, or even bearing an illegitimate child. It was something else, something altogether more terrifying. *But what?*

He reached for her hands, prying them from the sheets, and gripped them tightly in his own. "You must tell me what you fear."

Her lip trembled again, and he saw her swallow hard before taking a gasping gulp of air. "If I have a child, I might go mad," she cried, the words spilling out of her mouth. "Just like Grandmama, just like Aunt Susan. Mad as a hatter, don't you see?" Her face was ashen, her eyes as wide as saucers. "Grandmama has been locked away for years, spittle running down her chin, her eyes a hollow shell. My Aunt Susan took her own life, threw herself out a window. Did you not know?"

He shook his head, confounded. He'd only heard that her death had been a terrible accident. "Why does that mean you should suffer the same fate? What does having children have to do with it?"

"It has everything to do with it. You've seen what's happened to Emily since Amelia's birth. Her moods swing wildly, from melancholy and despair one day to cheerful brightness the next."

"But Emily's always been like that," he countered. She had always been mercurial. Nothing more.

"No, it worsens with childbirth." She raised a hand to cover her mouth, then dropped it. "Emily said such awful things—that Amelia would be better off without her, that she'd thought of silencing Amelia's cries—forever. She wished her own daughter had never been born."

He shook his head. "No. I will not believe that. Not of Emily."

"It's true. I could never have a child of my own, worrying all the while that something inside me might snap, that I might bring harm to my own flesh and blood." Her voice broke into sobs. "I cannot even tolerate the thought."

He pulled her against his chest. "You cannot believe that of yourself. You would bring harm to no one. I trust that with all my heart."

"Your heart?" she cried, pulling away from him. "How can you say that—you who say you *have* no heart? What of *your* curse? Have you forgotten?"

"I haven't forgotten," he bit out through clenched teeth. He rose to his feet as a fierce battle waged within him. A part of him wanted to comfort her, to reassure her that she would never become the woman she feared. Whatever illness ran in her family's bloodline surely hadn't tainted her. He would bet his life on it. Yet he knew that to remain by her side would risk endangering her, damn his curse. He had to distance himself, no matter the cost, to keep her safe, to thwart the prophecy he'd glimpsed. He'd come too close, far too close.

"I must go to Madeline now." He strode angrily to the door, pausing with one hand resting on the cut-glass doorknob. He turned to her, his face set in a stony mask. "We'll speak later and decide what must be done. That you would find yourself with child is unlikely at best."

She nodded, a single tear slipping down one cheek. Clutching the bedsheet about herself, she slid to the edge of the bed, revealing a small spot of darkened blood where she'd lain.

His eyes were involuntarily drawn to the damning spot, demanding that he acknowledge her ruin. He forced himself to breathe, willing the air to expand and then leave his lungs. Dear God, what had he done? What terrible, unforgivable sin had he committed? His blood ran cold, and he was overcome with self-loathing. How had he the nerve to call himself an honorable man, when clearly there was no honor left in him? He ached to take her in his arms again, to wipe away her tears and tell her that all would be well. But he couldn't, he reminded himself. *For her sake.*

Instead, he simply opened the door and strode out, despising himself as he did so.

Chapter Eighteen

Two days later, Hayden was amazed to find Madeline well enough to sit up in bed, hungrily devouring the broth laid before her. Since leaving Jane in his bed, he'd only left Madeline's side to sleep. He'd held her hand and told her stories of the old knights of the realm, of dragons and wizards and other fanciful tales he pulled from his memory.

Anything to keep his mind from Jane and the horrible way in which he'd misused her. He'd glimpsed her only twice since that fateful night, passing her in the hallway with nary a word spoken between them. He'd had to invent an injury to his person to explain the bloodstain on his sheets before the servants had the opportunity to speculate on its origin.

He hated himself with a vengeance, yet there was no way to right the wrong, not without putting Jane in great peril. Madeline would be moved to Richmond Park in the morn, and then he'd be rid of the temptation.

He would busy himself with securing a new governess, as he'd sent word to his steward to dismiss Miss Crosley at once. Whatever excuse she had for losing her charge—not once, but twice now—was irrelevant. It was intolerable.

And then he must return to London and prepare for his wedding. He no longer wished to wait till the Season's end to make Miss Upshaw his bride; instead, as soon as he was satisfied that Jane was not with child, he would obtain a special license and insist that Miss Upshaw wed him at once. Surely Pemberton would have no objection, and they could travel to Surrey and accomplish it posthaste. Then—and only then—would Jane be safe.

For he knew with certainty that once he spoke the vows, he would never stray. It went against everything he believed in, no matter the current fashion for adultery. Any ties remaining with Jane would be permanently severed the day Miss Upshaw became Lady Westfield. Surely the memory of Jane would fade from his heart with time.

His future looked bleak, indeed.

"Uncle Hayden?"

Pulled from his dark thoughts, he looked at his niece as she set aside her spoon, a scowl darkening her features.

"What is it, poppet?"

"Aren't you listening to me? I asked why you look so angry."

He forced all expression to flee his features. "Do I look angry?"

She squinted, tilting her fair head to one side as she appraised him. "Well, perhaps now you don't."

"I'm happy, Madeline, happy to see you well. More than you'll ever know. Tomorrow we shall go home. Will that please you?"

"Must we go?" she asked with a pout.

"We cannot remain here forever."

"I know. It's just . . . just . . ." She looked as if she might cry.

"Just what? Won't you be happy to sleep in your own bed again? To see your dolls? Your pony?"

"Yes, but I'll miss Jane and Mrs. Tolland terribly. Mrs. Tolland brought Amelia in here to see me this afternoon—what a sweet baby."

He smiled at her enthusiasm.

"And last night, after you went to your own room, Jane came in and sat with me till I fell asleep. We had the loveliest time."

He raised one brow. "I thought you were asleep when I left you."

"Well," she said sheepishly, "not quite. But you looked so tired that I pretended I was. Jane read to me, and then she told me all about London and the wonderful sweetshops there." Her green eyes lit with excitement.

"She shouldn't tire you so. You need your rest," he said with a scowl.

"Truly, Uncle Hayden, I've done nothing but rest for days and days. You must let her come to me again tonight," she pleaded. "She promised she would."

"Well, then, I suppose so. Promises are meant to be kept. But first you must answer a question, and you must answer it honestly. What were you doing alone in the woods that day? Why had you run off, when I asked you so plainly not to?"

Her lip trembled, and she bowed her head, her hands clasped in her lap. "I will tell you, but you must promise not to get angry."

"You have my word." He reached out to stroke her cheek.

"Miss Crosley and I went into the village that morning, and I overheard Mrs. Tanner, the shop-keeper, you know, at the shop with all the lovely ribbons and bonnets?"

"Yes, I know the one. Go on."

"She was talking about you. I was hidden behind a bolt of cloth, you see, and she was telling Mrs. Robards that you were soon to marry. She said you were bringing a bride to Richmond Park come autumn. I asked Miss Crosley about it on the drive home, and she refused to tell me anything. I asked if I could go to Mrs. Tolland's house to see if she had any news, but Miss Crosley wouldn't let me. She told me I had to take a nap instead. I *had* to go, don't you see? I do not want you marrying! At least, not to someone I've never met. I was hoping that Mrs. Tanner was mistaken, that perhaps it was Jane—"

"No, Madeline. I am not marrying Miss Rosemoor. It is true that I am taking a bride, a young woman named Miss Dorothea Upshaw. I know you will like her."

Madeline crossed her arms with a defiant glare. "I won't. She sounds dreadful."

"But I haven't told you anything about her. Anyway, you're changing the subject. You wanted to go to Mrs. Tolland's, but Miss Crosley said no. So you set off without her knowledge?"

"I'm sorry, Uncle Hayden. Please don't be too cross. I . . . I thought I knew the way, but I got lost and I was frightened and crying, it started raining and I was so very cold." Her eyes scrunched up, and she started to cry.

In an instant, Hayden moved to the bed and cradled her in his arms. "Don't cry, little one. There's nothing to be frightened of now. You're as good as new, aren't you?"

He felt her nod against his chest, sniffling as she did so. "I'm so very glad you're here, Uncle Hayden. Will you stay long? Must you return to that dreadful ol' London?"

"I'm afraid I must, and London's not so dreadful. Remember the sweetshops Jane told you about? Well, there's one called Gunter's that has the most delicious ices in all of England. I'll take you there one day."

"Will you?" she asked, brightening at once.

"I will. Soon enough Miss Upshaw will be your auntie, and we'll both take you."

"No." Madeline shook her head vehemently. "I only want you to take me. Besides, I don't need an auntie. Haven't I Mrs. Tolland and Jane? They're like aunts to me. I don't need that nasty Miss Upshaw."

Hayden shook his head in exasperation. This would be harder than he'd thought. "Anyway, I'm sure Jane will be returning to her own home soon. She shan't stay here forever; she has family far away, in Essex." He looked down at her and saw tears well in her eyes.

"Then I should like to go to Essex to visit her one day."

Hayden sighed. He would not fight this battle now, not today. "Perhaps," he muttered, noncommittally, knowing full well it would never come to pass.

No, Jane must stay as far removed from their lives as possible. One single night of perfect, unparalleled passion would have to sustain him through a lifetime of nights bereft of passion. That thought alone made his gut wrench.

"Oh, Jane, I'm going to miss you most dreadfully!"

"I'm going to miss you, too." Jane clasped Madeline's head to her breast, holding her little body tightly against her own. Unshed tears burned her eyes.

"Won't you come to Richmond Park to visit? Every day, if you'd like."

"I'd like that, Madeline, but perhaps I will give you some time to settle back at home first. Then Mrs. Tolland and I will both come to see you, I promise." As soon as Hayden returned to London, she mentally added, and not a day before. Surely he wouldn't tarry long in Derbyshire, not with Madeline's health restored and his affianced back in London, preparing for their wedding.

And surely not after . . . She refused to allow herself to think the words, to remember the night spent so recklessly in his arms, in his bed. A heat inflamed her cheeks as she struggled to vanquish the memory of his skin against hers, of the wicked things she allowed him to do to her, of the exquisite feeling of him buried deep within her.

More than anything, she had to forget the way in which it had felt so *right*—for there was nothing right about it, nothing at all. He was promised to another, for one thing. She was ruined, nothing but spoilt goods as far as the *ton* was concerned, for another. Yet she knew with certainty that the loss of her virginity would remain a tightly guarded secret. Hayden would not tell a soul, and since she would never marry, no one would be the wiser. Her guilt over making love to another woman's betrothed was far overshadowed by the terror that gripped her heart at the thought that his seed might have sowed a child, growing now inside her womb. She placed a trembling hand on her abdomen.

At least she wouldn't have long to worry over it, she thought, relieved at the providential timing. Her monthly courses were due in less than a week's time. Soon she would know if she was headed down the long road toward madness or if she'd managed to tempt fate and escape unscathed. Would she be punished for her sins? Would she end up like her grandmama?

What a pair we make, she thought, shaking her head. *Me, afraid that bearing a child will mean the certain doom of madness, and him, convinced that anyone he loves will be cruelly snatched from him.* If ever two people were meant to avoid an attachment, then surely they were. What a cruel twist of fate that they'd become entangled as they had.

"Jane?"

She looked up, surprised to see that Madeline was speaking to her. She'd almost forgotten her presence, so lost was she in her own thoughts. "I'm sorry." She patted Madeline's hand affectionately. "You were saying?"

"I was asking you if you'd ever been to a sweetshop in London called Gunter's. Uncle Hayden was telling me about it last night. It sounds grand."

Jane flinched, remembering the last time she had patronized Gunter's, remembering the uncomfortable exchange she'd had with Hayden, right there on the walk in front of the shop.

"I have been there, and it *is* lovely," Jane agreed, her chest tight. "The most wonderful ices in London, I'd say."

"Uncle Hayden!" Madeline cried out.

Jane looked up to find him standing in the doorway, his face an unreadable blank.

"Must we leave now?"

"I'm afraid we must, little one. But first I must have a private word with Miss Rosemoor."

Madeline looked up at him curiously.

"Will you allow me a moment of your time?" he asked Jane, his voice cool.

"Of course." Not meeting his eyes, she rose unsteadily, reaching for the bed for balance. "I'll be back to see you off," she offered, giving Madeline's hand a squeeze.

She'd known this moment would come, that they must speak before he took his leave, yet the knowledge did nothing to ease the discomfort that gripped her now as she followed him out and down the stairs to Cecil's study. She winced when he closed the door behind them.

Smiling weakly, she clasped her hands in front of herself and reluctantly met his gaze. That he looked as uncomfortable as she felt gave her a measure of satisfaction.

"Will you sit?" he said at last, gesturing toward Cecil's leather wing-back chair.

"I'd prefer to stand. Whatever we have to say to one another should be said in haste, Lord Westfield."

"Hayden."

"Hayden, if it pleases you."

"None of this pleases me, Jane, I can assure you of that." His usually soft eyes flashed angrily, and he began to pace, treading back and forth before the bookcases like a man possessed. "I cannot find words to excuse my behavior, and I have no hope of receiving your forgiveness. I don't deserve it. I've committed one of the most grievous sins imaginable, dealt you an inconceivable injury."

"Lord West—Hayden. Let me speak plainly. You owe me no apology. You gave me ample opportunity to leave that night and I stayed willingly, of my own volition. I have no one to blame but myself. It would be unfair to hold you accountable."

He turned on her furiously. "You don't understand, do you? You were an innocent, unable to make such a choice. I should have known better."

He jabbed his chest with one finger. "I should have been stronger. Now I will have to live with this the rest of my life. Can you understand that? Can you understand how it will feel to take my bride to our marriage bed, wishing she were you? Forced to close my eyes and pretend it's your body I drive myself into, instead of hers? And knowing that even as I do so, even as I hold your memory in my heart, I put you in danger?"

All breath left her body. Quickly, she spun around to face the wall, unable to meet his tortured eyes as her mind reeled from the revelation. She struggled to find her voice. "I don't know what you mean."

"That I must exorcise you from my mind, that's what. I must forget you, forget that night, forget that you exist, if I am ever to have any peace."

She closed her eyes and inhaled deeply, hoping to quiet her racing heart. "Then it must be done." Turning to face him again, she opened her eyes and gazed into his mossy ones. "I should be glad that my task is simpler. I do not have to forget you, nor do I have to forget that night. I'll hold it close to heart, savoring it for as long as I live, if indeed I'm spared and no child has been conceived. No, my task is only to resist you, to keep myself apart from you." She shook her head sadly. "But forget you? *Never.*"

Hayden's hands shook as he leaned against Tolland's desk, digesting the full meaning of her words. The blood drained from his face, and he felt cold, stunned. He closed his eyes, and the horrible vision returned—Jane, lying cold and lifeless in a wooden box. No, his mind countered. No. He couldn't give in to it. Nevertheless, her words hewed out what was left of his heart. He'd come perilously close to loving her, but he'd never dared to hope she might return the feeling. He snuffed out the desire to rejoice in it, for it mattered not. It only meant she would suffer.

He straightened, drawing himself up to his full height with as much dignity as he could muster. Their business was not yet complete. There was yet one more thing they must discuss.

"There's something I must ask, and I fear there's no delicate way to phrase it."

"Then ask plainly and let us be done with it."

He pressed his hands against his temples, hoping to dull the ache that grew more and more unbearable. "When do you expect to know whether or not you carry my child?"

She didn't flinch. Her features were stony, betraying not her thoughts. "By the week's end I should have evidence to the contrary. I would expect to know with some certainty in a fortnight."

"I must ask that you send me word, once you have . . . er, evidence that you are not with child."

"What would you have me write, Hayden? The bare, vulgar words? And what if the missive should find itself in the wrong hands? What then?"

"Then we must agree on some sort of code." He took out his pocket watch and ran his finger along the grooved circumference, unable to look at her. "A simple word will suffice, and no signature is necessary. I want to hasten the date of my marriage, but I won't till I have word from you that I'm free to do so."

"Perhaps a simple congratulations will suffice, then?" she offered coldly.

He looked up, and her expression cut him to the quick. Anger mixed with fear, anguish and regret all fought for dominance in her fair face. It was more than he could bear.

"That will do," he choked out.

"It's settled, then."

With a groan, he reached out to her, cupping her chin and forcing her to look at him. "Jane," he said, his voice hoarse.

She twisted from his grasp and turned toward the window, her head bowed. "Farewell, Hayden."

A searing pain shot through his chest. "Farewell, my lovely Jane," he countered softly. Straightening his shoulders, he strode out and closed the door.

A part of him died right then as he paused for a moment, his back pressed to the door, listening to her sobs.

With a vicious oath, he slammed his fist against the wall and stormed off to collect his niece.

Chapter Nineteen

The day had come at last. Hayden glanced up at the bright blue sky, mocking him as he walked up the steps of the parish church near Pemberton's estate in Surrey. He paused halfway up, raggedly breathing in the humid morning air redolent with the overpowering scent of roses from the manicured beds surrounding the old stone structure. A lone bird arced across the glittering sun.

How would he do it? Every instinct told him it was wrong, that he was making a terrible mistake. With an oath, he reached up to rub his temples. Damn it, he hadn't any choice. What a bloody mess he'd gotten himself into. With a sigh, he ran one hand across his coat, barely discerning the folded paper tucked into his breast pocket. Jane's letter. One simple word, written in a neat, feminine script: "*Congratulations.*" The single word—their agreed-upon code that she was not with child—weighed heavily on his mind. He'd carefully examined the page time and again since its receipt, looking for any hint, any clue to the author's state of mind. Did the pen appear to waver, held by tremulous hands? Could the uneven patch near the top possibly be a teardrop, splashed onto the page?

No matter his close scrutiny, he'd not been able to discern a thing. The writing was clear and strong, the page crisp. The missive betrayed nothing except one fact, and one fact alone—Jane did not carry his child. He realized the news should bring him great relief, yet it did not. Instead, he felt an empty, almost raw disappointment. Completely irrational, he'd told himself, over and over again. And yet, there it was.

Startled, Hayden looked up as the church bells began to peal the hour. It was time. He had no choice but to move forward into the church and fulfill his obligation. Nothing was holding him back—nothing, that is, except his reluctant heart. What was left of it shattered into jagged shards as he pulled open the heavy door and entered the church's dim, shadowy interior.

Moments later, he silently took his place before the altar, awaiting Dorothea's hand. Taking in the sea of unfamiliar faces watching him expectantly from the wooden pews, he reached up to readjust his cravat. The past few weeks had been hellish. He tried to blink back the unpleasant memories, now a blur in his mind.

He'd paid a visit to Lord Pemberton only hours after receiving Jane's reassurances. As he anticipated, he'd had no problems convincing the viscount to hasten the date of the nuptials, and so Hayden had secured a special license and removed to Surrey at once.

Yet one impediment after another had arisen—Dorothea's wedding gown required a difficult-to-obtain Spanish lace; the parish clergyman had been away in Hertfordshire, visiting family; a dear relative's arrival from Scotland had been delayed. His patience had grown thin, and each passing day had chipped away at the armor of his resolve. At last he'd been forced to put his foot down, to name the date that the joining would take place or else he'd drag Dorothea off to Gretna and be done with it. He had to protect Jane, his mind screamed.

He absently brushed a bit of lint from the crisp lapel of his dark frock coat, his thoughts dragged dangerously back to the night he'd spent in Jane's arms. His flesh warmed at the memory of her flawless bare skin, her chestnut tresses falling enticingly over her beautifully curved shoulders and resting upon her full, rose-tipped breasts.

A virgin, he thought with a remorseful shudder—the first virgin he'd ever bedded. For all her inexperience, their coupling had been more sensual, more satisfying than he'd ever thought imaginable. Flames of heat licked at his loins, and he forced himself to breathe deeply. Bloody hell, he was waiting for his bride to walk down the aisle, and all he could do was lust after another woman, a woman he could never possess. He raked a hand through his hair and looked up at the faces before him. His brows flew together at once.

No longer smiling up at him contentedly, the guests appeared restless, concerned. With a scowl, he retrieved his watch and checked the time, then snapped it shut in annoyance. Where was she? The appointed time had long since passed. Looking to the back of the chapel, he saw Lord and Lady Pemberton engaged in an animated conversation, both gesturing wildly with their arms.

What the hell? In long, angry strides he hastened back down the aisle. "What's happening Pemberton?" he whispered sharply. "Where's Dorothea?"

Lady Pemberton reached up to cover her mouth with a handkerchief, her eyes brimming with tears.

"She's here," Pemberton snapped. "In the vestibule."

"Then what the hell's going on? Get her out here at once," Hayden barked.

"She's a bit . . . uh, well . . . discomposed, you might say, at the moment, but she'll be out shortly. Margaret"—Pemberton turned toward his wife, his face now a mottled red—"get in there and tell that girl she has exactly three minutes to present herself." Pemberton clenched his beefy hands into fists by his sides. "I will drag her down the aisle by her ear if I must."

Hayden heaved an impatient sigh. Female theatrics. He would have a word with his intended. "Take me to her," he commanded.

Lady Pemberton's face flushed scarlet. She shook her head. "I don't think—"

"Take me to her," Hayden cut in.

"Very well," Pemberton said. "Perhaps you can talk some sense into the silly chit. Follow me." With a wave of his hand for Hayden to follow, he set off back through the double doors at the end of the aisle.

Hayden followed the man down a narrow hallway. He paused before a heavily carved door, where the sound of desperate sobs reached his ears. He looked to Pemberton with a frown.

"Have no fear, Westfield. She will honor our agreement, either of her own volition or not."

Hayden nodded as Pemberton opened the door and strode inside. Dorothea stood by the window, her back to them. Her whole body wracked with noisy sobs.

"Enough, Dorothea," Pemberton called out. "Westfield here will have a word with you, and then I expect you to take your place at the altar."

Dorothea spun around to face them, her fair face a blotchy red, her eyes swollen. "You cannot

make me, Papa." She vigorously shook her blond
curls, sending her lace cap to a dangerous tilt
upon her head.

"I can and I will. Enough of this nonsense. You
have a duty to attend to."

"But what of Jonathan?" she wailed. "How can I?
Not when we've—"

"Damn your loose lips, Dorothea." Pemberton
reached for his daughter's shoulders and shook
her. "Enough!" he growled.

"Leave us," Hayden ordered, favoring Pemberton
with an angry glare. "I will have a word with
Dorothea. Alone."

"As you wish," the man muttered reluctantly. "I
suggest you not say anything you will regret, Daughter." With that last threat, Pemberton turned and
strode out.

Hayden went to the window, laying one hand on
the sill while he exhaled slowly. "Tell me what's
going on, Dorothea. Forget your father's threats; I
want the truth. I have no desire to marry an unwilling bride." He thought he saw a movement beneath the window. With an impatient grunt, he
threw open the sashes. A slight man in a dark coat
scurried along the side of the wall, breaking out
into a full run once he reached the corner.

Hayden turned toward his betrothed, who stood
opposite him, wide-eyed, a handkerchief pressed to
her trembling lips.

"Who is he?" he asked.

Dorothea shook her head, but said nothing.

Hayden's ire rose at once. What kind of fool were
they playing him for? "Damn it, Dorothea. You'll
tell me who he is." He saw her eyes widen with fear,
and he changed tactics. "Perhaps I can help you,"

he said, his voice softer. "I won't force you to marry me if you're in love with someone else."

Fresh tears coursed down her cheeks as she eyed him suspiciously. Then she nodded. "Jonathan Banks. The son of Papa's steward."

"Steward?" Hayden blurted out in shock, then bit back his words. He shook his head.

"I've loved him since I was a girl. I . . . I tried . . ." She trailed off miserably.

"Tried what?"

"Tried to do what Papa asked of me. I knew I could never marry Jonathan. I was pleased with our match, yours and mine, truly I was. But when we came here to Surrey for the wedding, Jonathan begged me to run off to Gretna with him. I couldn't do it, couldn't disappoint my family like that."

"Then why the change of heart?"

Dorothea's lower lip trembled and her tears renewed, flowing freely down her cheeks. "Because—" she stammered, "because now I might carry his child." Her chin dipped to her chest, her eyes downcast.

"Good God, Dorothea." He sighed heavily. What had the foolish girl gone and done? Immediately, his sympathy was replaced by anger, anger at her father. What the hell had Pemberton been thinking? Had he honestly meant to silence the girl and force her hand on him, even while she might carry another man's child? The child of his steward's son? His hands balled into angry fists.

"You'll marry your Mr. Banks, Dorothea. I'll see to that."

"But how? Papa will never allow it. Never. Jonathan hoped to enter the clergy, but he hasn't the funds to support us, not now. Whatever shall I do?" She began to wail, and Hayden thought he might scream if he had to listen to her weeping for one more second.

At once he seized upon a plan. The rectory at Richmond sat empty, the last vicar having passed away several years ago. Since then Richmond's tenants had gone into Ashbourne for religious services. Richmond's rectory and the vicar who was employed there depended entirely upon the largesse and patronage of the Earl of Westfield, and Hayden had not seen fit to bestow such an honor since the old vicar's death. He would offer it to this hapless Mr. Banks, along with the small but well-maintained parsonage. Hayden would see that Dorothea got Pemberton's consent, even if it meant threatening the man with breach of contract. He hadn't signed on to marry a woman who might carry another man's child.

Of course, Hayden didn't miss the irony of the situation. He'd taken Jane's virginity, and fate had seen fit to have his betrothed's taken by another man. A steward's son. He almost laughed aloud.

"Your father will allow it. Trust me. Wait here and I'll go inform him that there will be no wedding today."

Without another word, he went in search of Lord Pemberton, a smile spreading across his face. Like a doomed man who'd narrowly escaped the gallows, he'd been spared.

"Must you go, Jane? I cannot tell you how sorry I will be, how much I will miss your company." Emily flopped onto the chair beside the bed with a sigh as Jane directed Bridgette in packing her trunks. With a pout, Emily picked absently at the embroidery on her sleeves.

"You know I must go. Oh, Emily, I'll miss you

dreadfully. You must promise to bring Amelia to Glenfield soon." Jane desperately needed to return home. She missed her mother and her sister Susanna, and the comfortable life she'd left behind.

Besides, there was nothing more she could do for Emily here. Her cousin had blossomed in the past few weeks, grown more confident in her mothering skills and more acclimated to her new role. Apparently fallen from Lady Adele's favor, Cecil spent more and more time at home, and Jane sensed a renewed affection between him and his wife. Suddenly she felt in the way. Worse yet, the Season would officially close in a fortnight, and it wouldn't be long before Hayden returned to Richmond Park with his bride. It was essential that she be long gone from these parts by then.

The thought sent her mind reeling dizzily. *Do not think about it.* It was too painful to bear, too painful to consider her future circumstances. She'd only made it through the past few weeks by refusing to allow herself to think about anything save Emily, Amelia, and Madeline. As she'd promised, she'd dutifully paid a visit to Richmond Park each day since Hayden's departure, and it took every ounce of her resolve to steel herself against thoughts of him while she remained in his home with his niece. *What am I going to do?*

She glanced up at the window, drinking in the flawless blue sky as she valiantly fought to force the dark thoughts away. Her temples began to ache with the effort. Perhaps some air would help clear her head.

"Will you join me for a walk, Emily? Or better yet, a trip into the village? I'd like to bid farewell to Miss Benson and to Mrs. Tanner at the shop."

Emily brightened at once. "Of course. What a

lovely idea. I'll send for the carriage, then." She
rose with a smile and hurried out.

An hour later, Jane found herself fingering a
lovely blue silk-covered bonnet in the draper's
shop, admiring the fine workmanship and detail.
She shivered as she brushed her palm across the
dyed feather on the bonnet's crown. It would look
lovely with her pale blue frock—the one Hayden
had admired at the Pembertons' ball. Her mouth
went dry at the memory, and she swayed against the
display as her legs began to shake.

The bell jangled in the door, and she looked up.
All breath left her body at once. There, framed in
the doorway and smiling broadly at her, was Miss
Upshaw. Lady Westfield, she corrected herself, feeling as if she might retch. Emily was next door at the
glove maker's, and Jane bolted toward the exit, desperate to find her cousin and insist they return
home at once.

"Miss Rosemoor," the beautiful blonde sang out
gaily as Jane approached her. "What a surprise."

Jane paused, barely able to find her voice. She was
shocked by the sudden, inexplicable urge to strike
the woman. She swallowed the lump in her throat
and forced herself to breathe. "Yes, isn't it? I offer my
heartiest congratulations on your marriage."

"You've heard, then?" The dimples in her rosy
cheeks deepened. "Thank you ever so much. Richmond Park is lovely, far exceeding my expectations.
Lord Westfield has made me the happiest woman
alive. Such a generous man he—"

"Good day," Jane cried out, stumbling past the
woman and into the street, blinded by hot, bitter
tears. She had to get away, as quickly as possible.

As she reached the glove maker's, she paused,

stepping back to catch her breath as her heart twisted in bitter agony.

The door opened, and Emily stepped out. Her initial smile quickly faded, replaced by a worried frown. "Jane, dearest, are you unwell? You're terribly pale." Emily reached for her arm. "Come, let's sit." She gestured toward a bench.

Fearing that her legs would buckle, Jane shook her head. She couldn't sit, couldn't remain here. She couldn't risk seeing Hayden's wife leave the draper's, her cheeks aglow with a new bride's happiness. She shook her head. "No, the carriage. Please," she pleaded.

With pursed lips, Emily nodded her agreement. "Come, then. We'll go at once. Here, take my arm."

Jane obliged. Only once they'd reached the sanctuary of the carriage's shadowy interior did Jane's tears turn into uncontrollable sobs, wracking her body as she dropped her head into her hands.

"Dear Lord, Jane, whatever has happened?" Emily asked, sliding across the seat to Jane's side and reaching one arm around her heaving shoulders.

"Miss Up—Lady Westfield, I mean." Jane hiccupped. "At the draper's."

Emily's eyes widened. "What did she say?" she whispered.

"That . . . that Hayden has made her the happiest woman alive." Jane's throat ached miserably.

"No. Oh, no, Jane. I never thought he'd actually do it. How could he? It's *you* he loves, the foolish, stubborn man," Emily whispered.

Jane choked on a sob, her tears renewed.

"Poor Jane." Emily stroked her hair. "Always so strong. Go ahead and cry. You've earned the tears."

The enormity of it hit her then, with the suffocating weight of bricks. She'd made a mistake, a terrible mistake, and now it was too late—now he belonged to someone else. The thought took her breath away, the pain almost too exquisite to bear. How could she have been so foolish? Why hadn't she realized he was worth the risk before it was too late?

She laid her head on Emily's shoulder and gave in to the wretched despair that lanced her heart. Emily stroked her hair, whispering soft, soothing words, as if she were comforting a hurt child. It was only when the Tollands' home came into view that Jane at last reined in her anguish and managed to staunch her tears.

"Look, a traveling coach," Emily said as they turned off the road and into the lane.

Indeed it was, clattering out of the drive in a puff of dust. As their own carriage accomplished the drive, Jane's eyes were drawn to a stack of trunks before the door.

"How very odd." Emily shook her head. "I wasn't expecting guests."

The carriage rolled to a stop and the footman handed the women down as a plump figure appeared on the front stairs with the housekeeper.

"Mama!" Jane cried, her slippers flying over the pebbled drive. She flung herself into her mother's arms, breathing in her warm rosewater scent as her angry tears returned with a vengeance.

"Dearest daughter, whatever is wrong?" She clasped Jane to her ample bosom.

"Oh, Mama, I'm so happy to see you," Jane murmured, her voice muffled. It was true. She'd never in her life been so happy to see her mother's familiar, comforting face.

"And this must be little Emily, all grown up. I can

barely believe my eyes! Why, you look just like Susan, only more beautiful. Come give your Auntie Eliza a hug." She released Jane and reached for Emily, folding the slight woman into her arms.

"Aunt Eliza," Emily said. "What a delightful surprise. Welcome to Ashbourne."

"Why, thank you, dear. You must forgive me for arriving unannounced like this. Something in my daughter's last letter . . . Well, dear"—she turned toward Jane—"I must confess something in your letter alarmed me, and I set off at once. Now I'm glad I listened to my instincts. I'll accompany you and Bridgette back to Essex, but first I must spend a couple of days getting reacquainted with dear Emily and meeting my grandniece. I cannot wait to see little Amelia." She rubbed her hands together in anticipation.

"But I'd planned to depart first thing in the morning."

"Nonsense. Only a few more days. Indulge your mother, Jane dear."

Jane's gaze was involuntarily drawn to the north, where Hayden's home lay just beyond the wood. A few more days. Surely she could avoid him for that long. After all, he was a newlywed. Her eyes fluttered shut, images of Hayden and his wife tangled together upon his bed flashing across her mind's eye. Bile rose in her throat and her surroundings began to spin.

"Very well," she managed to murmur, then slid soundlessly to the ground.

Chapter Twenty

"Jane, Jane . . . can you hear me?"

Jane's lids fluttered open at the sound of her name. Her mother's face swam into focus, looming over her with a worried frown. She clutched a vinaigrette in her hand, waving it rapidly before Jane's nose. Emily hovered nearby, her face drawn and her lips pursed.

"I . . . what happened?" Jane sat up in her own bed, feeling dizzy and disoriented. She pushed away the vinaigrette.

"You swooned, dearest." Her mother ran a cool hand across her brow. "The footman carried you upstairs."

Jane shook her head in disbelief. She never swooned—*never*. Not once in all her life.

"You nearly frightened me to death," Emily chastised, laying a gentle hand on her wrist.

Had she really swooned? It didn't signify.

"I'll go and ring for a pot of tea. Chamomile and bergamot, Jane. Your favorite."

Jane merely nodded, sinking back against the pillows with a sigh as Emily hurried from the room.

Her mother rose and stood at the foot of the bed, studying her intently as she wrung her hands. She crossed to the door and shut it softly before turning to face her once more. "Are you unwell, Jane?" she inquired, laying the back of her hand across her brow.

"I'm well enough, Mama."

"Nonsense. I've never before seen you so discomposed. It is so unlike you to swoon like that."

Jane swallowed hard as she laid a hand on her still-churning stomach. She moved it lower still, to her abdomen, and inhaled sharply.

What had she done? Little more than a fortnight ago, she'd written Hayden the one word he needed to go through with his marriage to Miss Upshaw—"*congratulations.*" Their agreed-upon code that her monthly courses had signaled she did not carry his child. She'd written the word with nary a tremble, her script firm and controlled, and directed it to his London town house. She had posted it quickly, before she could rethink her decision.

She'd lied.

All this time, she'd refused to consider the implications, refused to believe it could possibly be true even as her physical symptoms begged her acknowledgment. She hadn't even begun to consider what she'd tell her family or, worse yet, what her life would be like as a ruined woman with a bastard child. Just how long would it take till the madness set in, till she could no longer recognize those she loved? Would they send her off to The Orchards to be cared for by Mrs. Carter? Would they lock her away in Bedlam?

The only thing she was certain of was that she could never tell Hayden. *Never.* To protect him from her own inevitable madness; to protect her babe from a father who refused to love, who could not acknowledge the child, besides. *He deserves to know he has fathered a child,* a part of her mind screamed out. But she ignored it and pushed aside the insistent thought. She simply could not bear it.

A single tear traced a path down her cheek. She closed her eyes, then opened them, meeting her mother's questioning gaze at last. She took a deep, fortifying breath before she spoke, her voice no more than a whisper.

"I'm with child."

"No," her mother cried out.

Jane swallowed the painful lump in her throat. "God help me, it's true. I don't know what to do, Mama."

Her mother's lower lip began to tremble. "Oh, Jane." She shook her head in disbelief. "No, this cannot be true."

Jane remained silent as she nodded her assurance. She watched as her mother strove to compose herself, now clearly convinced of the truth and rallying to find the strength to acknowledge it.

"Well, perhaps it's not so bad, after all. There are worse ways to get a reluctant groom to the altar." She reached over to pat Jane's hand. "I will send for Colin. He will ensure that the gentleman in question marries you. Oh, Jane, please tell me he is a gentleman." Her voice rose to a wail. She retrieved a handkerchief from her apron and pressed it to her mouth.

"He's a gentleman," Jane assured her, her voice flat. "A peer, in fact. But he cannot marry me."

"He can, and he will. Colin will see to it. A dueling pistol will serve as a sufficient prompt, if necessary." Her mouth was set in a tight line.

"No, Mama, you don't understand." Jane shook her head, another wave of queasiness washing over her. "He cannot. He is married to someone else."

"A married man?" she said with a gasp, her

cheeks flushing a deep scarlet. "No, you cannot tell me this. Not you. Not my Jane." In silent horror, Jane watched as her mother succumbed to jagged sobs, her face turned away from her.

"I'm so sorry, Mama," Jane whispered. Unable to bear her mother's disappointment, her despair, she squeezed shut her eyes and focused on the sound of her own irregular breathing until her mother's wails subsided enough for her to regain her voice, however tremulous.

"I cannot believe it. I would expect this from someone like Susanna, perhaps, but not you." She shook her head vehemently. "Never you. You're far too sensible to find yourself in such a bind. Dear Lord, I think I'm going to swoon." She retrieved the vinaigrette that lay on the table beside Jane's bed.

"Please don't swoon." Jane's voice was sharper than she intended. She reached a hand out to her mother, laying her trembling hand upon the woman's plump one.

Her mother pulled away at once. "I will send for Colin. He will have a word or two with this *gentleman* and see what plans he has for supporting you and your child."

"I will not tell him, Mama."

"Of course you will. It will not be the first arrangement of its kind, Jane. Nor will it be the last. He's left you ruined, without the hope of a husband, and he must take responsibility for that. If he's a gentleman as you say, a peer, he will understand this."

"No. You must see—it's better this way. I love him, Mama, and I will not have him bound to me by duty. I can't." Her voice broke on a sob. "I won't have his money or his pity as he watches me turn into a raving madwoman."

"Madwoman? Whatever do you mean?"

Jane shook her head wildly. "You cannot pretend that you don't know. This family malaise, Mama, this madness no one will speak of, that increases after childbirth. I saw Grandmama, with my very own eyes! It was dreadful, far worse than I ever imagined. It's why I never married, why I turned down every offer I received. I could not take such a chance."

"You cannot mean to think you suffer from the same condition as my mother? As poor Susan did?"

"I do. I might," Jane corrected. "I've tried my best to hide it all these years, but you've suspected as much yourself."

Her mother shook her head. "Never."

"Oh, but you did. Long ago, I heard you say as much to Papa. I couldn't have been more than twelve. You were speaking of Grandmama and Aunt Susan, and you said I was just like them."

"No, Jane. Not 'just like *them*.' Just like *me*. Sensitive, prone to simple melancholy, nothing more. I spent my girlhood, my adolescence, worrying myself sick over my mother and sister, trying my best to reach out to them and feeling nothing but failure when I could not help them. I didn't want that for you, Jane. You did not need that burden. You're very nurturing, Jane, just like I am. You care deeply for those you love, wanting to ease their pain. Wanting to make everyone around you happy.

"But there are some people who can't be helped. It wasn't just melancholy. It was more than that, much more. Almost dementia. Violent mood swings, from periods of elation to the darkest, deepest melancholy imaginable."

She reached a hand out to brush Jane's burning cheeks with her fingertips. "You've no idea the full extent of it. But it was always clear that neither you nor Susanna were afflicted. No, Jane. You could not have hid it from me, even if you tried." Her chin dropped to her bosom, her eyes filling with fresh tears. "This is all my fault. I only meant to shield you from it, to shield you from the burden of worrying over them. Instead, I only gave you false concerns."

Jane could barely breathe as her mother's words registered in her reeling mind. She desperately wanted it to be true—that she was not doomed to madness, that she could be a good mother to her child. To Hayden's child.

"Oh, Mama, I've made such a terrible mistake. What will I do?"

She shook her head. "I do not know. But we will figure it out, eventually. We haven't a choice."

Jane only nodded, unable to speak.

Hayden shrugged in frustration, feeling like a fool. For the second straight day, he had spent the better part of the afternoon roaming the woods between his home and the Tollands'. He'd learned that Jane still remained there, having not yet left for Essex. More than anything, he wanted to storm over there and demand to see her, but he knew he must carefully consider his situation before he did anything rash. Still, he walked the woods, knowing that she liked to do so herself. He hadn't any idea what he'd say to her if they did meet, but he was drawn to the woods nonetheless.

Before, he'd thought a marriage in name only a perfect solution—a fine idea, and the only logical arrangement for a man like him. But now, after knowing Jane these past months, he knew he would never be satisfied with such a bargain. He wanted her. And his wanting went far beyond lust.

It was more than simply wanting her in his bed, than wanting to taste her skin upon his lips, to join his body with hers. No, he wanted to possess her—heart, body, and soul. To gaze at her across his table each night, to fall asleep with the scent of her lingering on him, to wake up to her beautiful face. To share his life, his dreams, even his failures with her. Nothing else would suffice.

He loved her. The thought terrified him—made his palms dampen and his heart race dangerously fast. He knew he put her in peril, loving her as he did. But would simply withholding the declaration of his love protect her? It seemed unlikely.

Then what further harm could come from it, his mind urged, from declaring his love, taking her as his bride? Devil take it, her very life was at stake. Yet even as he thought the words, they lost their potency. Perhaps it wasn't true. Perhaps his circumstances had been nothing more than bad luck, as Emily insisted. He'd never before doubted the curse, not till Jane Rosemoor had come into his heart. Was it only desperate wishful thinking that allowed him to consider other possibilities?

He shook his head and paused, surveying the landscape spread before him. Even at summer's end, the woods retained their lush greenness. Evergreens. Sustaining, everlasting. Like his love for Jane, a love that would know no end. He could not push her from his heart if he tried. But what to do? She would not have him. She believed she was cursed herself, doomed to madness if she bore a child. It was ridiculous. She was perhaps the sanest woman he knew. He reached for a small, gray rock and turned it over in his palm. The surface felt rough, yet its weight was reassuring. He ran a thumb across the uneven planes, considering his options.

He could declare his love and hope to convince her that she was in no danger of going mad. Hell, even if she did go mad, he'd love her still. He could hope the odds were in his favor, and that he would at last break his own vile curse. That he could, for once, claim what he desired above all else. Someone to love, someone to love him in return.

Or he could do nothing. He could spend the rest of his days second-guessing his decision, bereft of love, filled with uncertainty. Away from Jane. He shrugged as a heavy sigh escaped his lips.

The latter was insupportable, the coward's choice. He could no sooner do nothing than he could grasp the moon in his hands. She might refuse him a third time, yes. Possibly. But the chance that she might not was worth the risk. *She* was worth the risk.

His mind made up, he pulled back his arm and released the stone, sending it flying through the air with a whistle.

Now he just had to figure out how he was going to go about convincing her—no easy task when the woman in question was Miss Jane Rosemoor, the most wonderfully maddening, delightfully bull-headed woman he'd ever met. He couldn't help the grin that slowly spread across his face in antici-pation of the challenge that lay before him.

Reaching up to straighten his cravat, he turned back toward Richmond Hall, his step light, his pace brisk. He would begin with a letter.

My dearest Miss Rosemoor,

Word has reached my ears that you remain in res-idence with the Tollands, and I hope this letter finds you well. Although I have no right to make such a request, I find that I must discuss an urgent matter of importance with you, and in due haste. As you must know, the morrow brings Ashbourne's annual Feast of St. Mary's fair, and everyone for miles about will gather on the village green for the festivities. I write in hopes that you will forgo the merriment and remain at home to grant me an audience. I pray that this can be accomplished without overmuch difficulty.

With my highest esteem,
Westfield

Jane looked up as the page fluttered to the bed beside her. Whatever could this mean? Why would he wish to meet with her, and so furtively? Had he somehow learned her secret? No. She shook her head. He could not know. No one knew besides her mother, not even dear Emily.

Believing her weakened by emotional strain and besieged by a gastronomical malaise, Emily fretted about her like a mother hen, insisting she remain abed and refusing to tolerate any talk of their departure. Jane had agreed to remain in Derbyshire for a sennight, no more, as she regained her strength for the journey home to Essex. Yet only a single day had passed before Hayden's manservant had arrived, bearing the missive that now lay beside her on the coverlet.

Emily had brought it to her discreetly—and reluctantly. Her fury at Hayden had not yet dissipated.

Jane had held it in her palm, her unfocused eyes staring at his seal for more than an hour before she'd gathered the courage to break the wax and open it.

She closed her eyes and released the breath she hadn't realized she'd been holding in. At last the words sunk into her consciousness, and a flame of anger seared her breast. Her eyes snapped open at once, her cheeks burning with emotion. He was a married man. What was he thinking, ordering her to remain home and receive his call while everyone else set out to enjoy the day?

What matter could be so urgent as to require him to leave his new bride's side and seek out the company of another, one he'd known in an intimate way? Had his estimation of her sunk so low that he thought perhaps they could enjoy one last romp before she removed to Essex? With his highest esteem, indeed, she huffed, worked now to a fit of pique.

Before now, she had no intention, none whatsoever, of going to the fair. She had planned to remain abed, refusing to venture out in public where she might encounter the earl and his new countess.

But now she must go. She must insist that she felt much improved, and claim that the fresh air and merriment afforded by the fair would improve both her mood and her health. She would not sit home, awaiting his call as he requested.

She smiled a bitter smile, proud of her own fortitude as she straightened her spine and rose from the bed, reaching for the treacherous page. She dropped it into her washbasin and reached for her candle, tipping it toward the edge of the paper. She pulled back her hand as it lit, curling inward as the orange flame licked at the words, erasing them, reducing them to nothing more than a pile of ashes.

Chapter Twenty-one

Jane wrapped her lace shawl tightly about her shoulders, watching as Emily stood beside her in the front hall, wringing her hands in obvious agitation.

"Are you certain you're well enough to go, Jane? I don't mind staying home and keeping you company. Cecil can go on to the fair with Auntie Eliza."

"Dearest Emily, I promise you I am well enough. The fresh air will do wonders for my health, I assure you."

"Of course," Jane's mother added with a nod. "The sunlight and festive mood will surely help restore the bloom to her cheeks."

"Are you certain?" Emily's eyes darted to Jane's mother, then back again to Jane. "Perhaps you'll find the crowd tiresome. Everyone from the district will be in attendance, you know. Everyone," she repeated, and Jane knew full well her meaning.

"I know," Jane said softly, wishing she could put her cousin's troubled mind at ease. "But truly I shall be happy to spend some time outdoors, and a fair sounds like a wonderful diversion." She tied her bonnet's ribbons beneath her chin as Cecil sauntered into the front hall, an ebony walking stick tucked beneath his arm.

"Come now, ladies. I've had the carriage sent around. Shall we set off?"

Emily nodded, her brow still puckered with concern. "I suppose so."

Their party descended the front stairs as the carriage clattered to a halt before them. The warm, scented breeze stirred the hem of Jane's gown as a liveried footman handed her up. She settled into her seat, Emily and her mama joining her, but Cecil remained in the drive.

"I'll ride behind as I'm likely to stay past dusk," he called out. "Certainly a fair is no place for ladies after sundown."

Emily nodded in agreement, and the conveyance set off with a lurch at Cecil's signal. Jane leaned back against the squabs, smoothing down her skirt's soft lawn fabric. Her bodice was stretched taut against her sensitive breasts, the band of fabric beneath them uncomfortably tight. Her waistline hadn't yet begun to thicken, but even if it had, her gowns' high waists would effectively conceal it for many weeks. How long could she hide such a secret? Her heart rate accelerated at the thought, and she forced herself to take a few deep, calming breaths. She looked up at her mother and Emily, both gazing out the carriage's dusty window, lost in their own thoughts as they turned into the lane.

What would Hayden do when he arrived at the Tollands' home and found her gone? Would he accept that she did not wish to see him again, or would he continue to press for a meeting? Jane's fingers rose to her temples, attempting to gently massage away the tension that remained there despite her efforts as the carriage rolled briskly toward the village.

She dropped her hands to her lap and lowered her gaze to her slippers as she crossed one ankle over the other. She could barely sit still. Shifting in her seat, it took every inch of her reserve to remain there in the carriage, headed away from Emily's home, when she knew Hayden would no doubt arrive there shortly. Dear Lord, but she wanted to see him again. Like the pull of the tide, she felt physically drawn back—toward Hayden—despite all rational thoughts to the contrary.

He was a married man, her mind repeated. He might not have given Miss Upshaw his heart, but he'd given her his name. Someday the woman would bear him a child—his heir—while her own child would not know him, would not know the protection of his name. What kind of life would her child have—an outcast, never accepted into society, unable to make an advantageous match? Of course Lucy had also been born on the wrong side of the blanket, and things had turned out well for her—she was married to a marquess, accepted into the *ton*.

Oh, they thought she didn't know, Colin and Lucy, guarding their secret from her all these years. But she'd always known that Lucy was her sister—half sister, she corrected, and it was clear that Colin had learned the truth the year of Lucy's come-out. Only her mother and Susanna remained shielded from the truth, and Jane would make certain it stayed that way. Indeed, secrets could be kept if carefully guarded. But who would save her from ruin, as Oliver Abbington had saved Lucy's mother?

William Nickerson's handsome face immediately came to mind. Years ago he'd pleaded for her hand, offered her his life's devotion if she'd accept his suit. Now he loved Miss Adare instead. But if the girl's family truly opposed the match, he hadn't much hope of marrying her.

Besides, Jane knew there were things she could

do—female ploys she could utilize—if she truly wanted Nickerson to marry her and not Miss Adare. Would it take much effort to seduce him? He was a gentleman, after all, and Jane had no doubt that, once lured into anything more than a chaste kiss, he'd marry her without the slightest hesitation. Jane sighed. Of course, she'd never even consider it. She couldn't. It went against her nature to cruelly and manipulatively use a friend in such a fashion. She wouldn't be able to live with herself, and they'd all be miserable. No, there was no one to save her.

Her mama had suggested that she and Susanna leave at once for the Continent and return after the child's birth, allowing Susanna to claim the child as her own. Perhaps it was for the best. No doubt Susanna would agree to the plan, effectively saving her sister's reputation. At least Jane would see her child raised in a happy, secure home.

Her hand involuntarily moved to her abdomen as her breath hitched in her chest. "I'm so sorry," she whispered.

"Sorry?" Emily asked, her worried gaze immediately flitting to Jane across the width of the carriage.

Jane dropped her hand at once. "I didn't realize I spoke aloud. I was only woolgathering." Her mama reached for her hand and gave it a reassuring squeeze, and Jane returned the pressure. She must convince them that she was well enough to return to Essex posthaste. She could not risk seeing him again. Her fragile resolve simply could not sustain such temptation. No, she must leave before the sennight passed. There was nothing more to be done. And then she would submit to her mother's plan, as distasteful as the notion seemed. She simply had no other choice.

* * *

Hayden stepped out of the still-steaming tub and into his dressing gown, shaking the excess water from his head as he did so. Droplets fell onto the marble-tiled floor at his feet, glistening in the midday sunlight that streamed in through the open window.

As soon as he helped Hayden shrug into a dressing gown, the valet reached over to close the sashes with a frown. Phillips possessed an almost maniacal fear of drafts around his bathing master, even when the draft in question was nothing more than the warm, late-summer breeze. Hayden couldn't resist a chuckle.

He strode into his dressing room, not bothering to cinch the belt around his waist. In minutes, he'd stepped into a pair of fawn breeches, pulled on his stockings, and shoved his still damp arms into his shirt, fastening the buttons that ran halfway down the front with quick, precise motions. He tucked the shirttails into the waistband of his breeches and reached for his dark gray waistcoat. The valet put his cravat around his neck and Hayden watched his reflection in the cheval glass as the man deftly knotted it and smoothed down the starched folds before holding out Hayden's dark blue coat.

"Thank you, Phillips." Hayden shrugged into the proffered garment.

"Very well, my lord." Phillips nodded toward the window, the heavy drapes pulled back to reveal the glorious day. "A fine day for the fair. Will you be adding to your stables today?"

"I'm afraid not," Hayden answered, pulling on a gleaming pair of Hessians. "I've already sent the new governess ahead with Madeline, but I shan't be going to the fair myself."

Phillips's bushy gray brows drew together, but he said nothing.

"No," Hayden continued, his heart singing gaily in anticipation, "not this year. I thought instead to secure a mistress for Richmond Park. It's time these halls saw a countess again, don't you think, Phillips?"

He almost laughed aloud at the manservant's stunned expression.

"Indeed?" was all the stone-faced valet said.

"If only I can convince the lady in question, that is."

Phillips arched one brow. "I wouldn't suppose you'd encounter any resistance, my lord."

"Ah, but you do not know the lady in question. Yes, I'm likely to have a rough time of it." Hayden smoothed his hands down one sleeve, then the other, adjusting his cuffs and then straightening his coat. In three long strides he went to his dressing table and opened the lid of the mahogany box that held his most precious possessions—his mother's and sister's jewels. Reaching into the velvet-lined chest, he retrieved the ring that he knew belonged on Jane's finger—a single, oval sapphire surrounded by diamonds. A Moreland family heirloom, passed down from one generation to the next. His mother had worn it faithfully right up until her death.

He had not given Dorothea one of his mother's jewels as a token of their betrothal agreement. Instead he'd purchased a ring for her in London—a simple ruby, which Lord Pemberton had sheepishly returned to him before Hayden had left Surrey.

Long ago, he had chosen one of his mother's jewels for Katherine, a cluster of aquamarines in delicate gold. She had been buried in it; he had made certain of it. The fragile ring had been lovely, yes, and well suited to Katherine. But, he thought, slipping the heavy sapphire into his pocket, this particular jewel was more befitting a countess. *His* countess. His jaw tightened as he closed the box's lid and turned to face Phillips.

"Wish me luck," he said, clapping the valet on the shoulder.

"As you wish, my lord," Phillips muttered, unable to conceal his astonishment beneath his usual mask of decorum.

Hayden grinned as he headed toward the door in long strides and hastened down two flights of stairs to the front hall. He donned the hat that Mrs. Pierce handed him, pulling the curved brim low over his eyes as he stepped out into the bright August sun. A groom stood in the drive, Hayden's favorite mount saddled and waiting beside him.

"Vlad, old boy," Hayden called out as the white dog loped to his side. He reached down and scratched Vlad behind one ear, his chest tightening as he remembered the dog's role in saving Madeline's life. He turned back to the door. "Mrs. Pierce, have Cook find Vlad a meaty bone."

"Of course, my lord," the housekeeper replied. "Come, Vlad." She motioned for the dog to follow, and Hayden reached down to ruffle his thick coat before the animal loped off into the house.

Hayden took his crop from the groom and swung up onto the enormous bay's back. With a nod, he set off. As he reached the end of the drive, he tapped his mount's flanks with his crop and the beast responded with a bound, breaking into a graceful gallop.

Only when the Tollands' house came into view, its yellow stone façade rising up between the treetops, did he heed the knot of tension that bunched the muscles in his neck. This time, he realized, she *must* accept his suit. He would not take no for an answer; he would not leave her side till she allowed him to slip the sapphire on her finger. He patted his pocket, reassured by the jewel's outline against his coat's fabric.

Minutes later, he confidently strode up to the door, which swung open at his knock.

"My lord," the housekeeper said as she bobbed a curtsy. "I'm afraid Mr. and Mrs. Tolland have gone to the Feast of St. Mary's fair in the village."

"I thought as much. It's actually Miss Rosemoor I've come to see. Will you tell her I'm here? I believe she is expecting me."

The housekeeper shook her head with a frown. "But, my lord, Miss Rosemoor has gone to the fair with them."

The blood rose in his face. "Are you certain?"

"Yes, my lord. They left almost an hour ago, along with Lady Rosemoor."

"Lady Rosemoor?" Who the hell was Lady Rosemoor? Jane's mother? Sister-in-law?

"Yes, we've had the pleasure of Miss Rosemoor's mother's company these past few days. But I'm afraid there's no one at home today, Lord Westfield."

"Very well, Mrs. Smythe." He reached up to tip his hat. "Good day."

"Good day, my lord."

He spun around in frustration. *Damn it.* She was going to make this as difficult as possible, wasn't she? He should have expected it. Well, he could be equally difficult. He would not make it so easy for her to avoid him.

He called for his horse. If she had gone to the fair, then he would go to the fair, too. If she refused to face him in private, then, by God, she'd be forced to face him in public.

Chapter Twenty-two

"What did you win, Jane?" Emily asked with a laugh, and Jane held up the porcelain fairing she'd won tossing rings on the green—a painted trinket box depicting a lady's dressing table, complete with miniature fripperies and adorned with a winged cherub.

"Something to remember your time here in Derbyshire by," Emily added. Jane smiled sadly in reply, fighting the urge to touch her abdomen. She would no doubt have a sufficient reminder of her time spent in Derbyshire. She idly fingered the fairing before tucking it into her reticule and drawing the bag closed.

"What shall we do next?" Jane's mother raised one hand to shield her eyes from the sun. "Another game of skill, perhaps?"

"I'll be off to inspect the horses," Cecil said, nodding toward the gathering crowd by the main road. "I'm hoping to add another stallion to my stock today."

"Very well," said Emily, offering her cheek for his kiss. "I think the theatrical performance is soon to begin in the square. I've heard the lead actor is splendid—puts Kean to shame. Shall we see what all the fuss is about?"

Jane and her mother nodded, and the three

women set off toward the tent in the center of the village square. The warm breeze stroked Jane's cheek as they made their way through the throng, the air thick with music and merriment.

Children dashed this way and that, ducking under their parents' arms and squealing with glee at each amusement encountered. A man in a tall hat and military-styled red coat, its gold buttons glittering in the sun, amused a crowd gathered about his organ; an identically dressed monkey delighted the children, young and old, with its antics. Peals of happy laughter rose up from another group of children clustered around a pair of puppeteers, their marionettes animatedly depicting a children's tale.

The scent of roasted chestnuts and sugared cakes filled the air, and Jane suddenly felt ravenous. She stopped before a tent where several women in crisp aprons served up sweets. "If you don't mind, I'd love a cake first. They smell positively delicious."

"They do, don't they?" Emily said, inhaling deeply. "I'll have one, too. Lady Rosemoor?"

"Oh, indeed. How can I resist such a temptation? Wait right here and I'll fetch them." Jane's mother reached into her reticule and retrieved a coin before hurrying off to the counter.

"Jane, look." Emily rose up on her toes and pointed to a colorfully decorated tent across the walk. "The Romany Gypsy tent. Oh, I must get my fortune told!"

"Your fortune?" Jane asked with a frown. "Surely you don't believe in such nonsense."

"Oh, but I do. The Romany Gypsies are known far and wide for their ability to see the future. Aren't you the least bit curious?"

"Not particularly," Jane muttered, her stomach

knotting. Her own future would surely hold no happiness—why should she wish to glimpse it? A ruined woman with a fatherless child—that was all her future held. A lifetime of wanting, wishing for something she could never have.

Her dour thoughts were interrupted when her mother reappeared at her side bearing three cakes wrapped in waxed paper. "Here you are, girls." Lady Rosemoor bit into one and smiled delightedly. "Mmmm, delicious."

"Aunt Eliza, I was trying to convince Jane to come with me to the Gypsy tent to have our futures told."

"Gypsies?" her mother exclaimed, clapping her hands together. "Oh, what fun! Come now, Jane. It's bound to be more entertaining than the theatrics." Her lips pursed, as if remembering her daughter's plight, and she looked to her with concerned eyes. "You needn't have your own fortune told, of course."

"Very well," Jane acquiesced, having no intention of entering the tent and opening herself up to such sorrow.

Fifteen minutes later Jane stood restlessly outside the tent, nibbling her cake distractedly as she waited for Emily to emerge.

"I can't wait to hear what she sees in my future," her mother said, trying her best to peer into the slit between the tent's flaps. "I wonder if I shall find love again, with your dear father gone. Do you suppose I should ask her?"

"I haven't any idea. Do they allow you to ask questions, or do they simply . . ." Jane's words trailed off as her roaming eye landed on a woman in a honey-hued muslin gown. Miss Upshaw. Lady Westfield, she corrected herself.

The woman stood between two tents, furtively

looking about as if to make sure she remained unseen. Yet from where Jane stood, awaiting Emily to emerge from the Gypsy tent, she was afforded a clear view of the woman. She watched in utter fascination as a man appeared, his back to Jane, and wrapped his arms about the woman in a passionate embrace. What held Jane's stunned gaze and widened her eyes with amazement was not the fact that the couple indulged in such scandalous behavior in a public place, but that the gentleman was no more than a head taller than the petite woman—without a doubt *not* Lord Westfield.

Jane swallowed hard, unable to tear her eyes away. The pair separated, and after a brief exchange of words that did not reach Jane's ears, the anonymous man dashed off and the cuckolding Lady Westfield moved away. Jane gasped, desperate to escape before the horrid woman spotted her. She could not face her. Not now. Not ever.

"Jane? Dearest?"

Jane looked up at her mother, realizing with a start that she was speaking to her but unable to make her lips form a reply. Just then, Emily rushed out of the tent, smiling broadly.

"Oh, Jane, it was wonderful. Madame Cosmina is truly gifted; you must reconsider—"

"I'll go next," Jane blurted out, shouldering past her mother and into the dimly lit tent as expeditiously as possible. She could not risk an encounter with Hayden's wife.

Reluctantly, Jane handed over a coin and settled herself into the chair directly across from the gaudily garbed woman who proclaimed herself Madame Cosmina with a thick, Eastern European accent. After dropping the coin into a box, the fortune-teller reached for Jane's hands. With an impatient sigh, Jane stripped off her gloves and placed her bare hands in the woman's old, gnarled ones. Madame Cosmina's eyes fluttered closed, and Jane couldn't help but impatiently avert her gaze from the woman's lined face, worn with age. Jane's breathing became shallow in anticipation, her palms dampening uncomfortably.

A full minute of silence ensued before Madame Cosmina spoke. "I see fear, great fear."

A shudder began at the nape of Jane's neck and worked its way down her spine. She shifted uncomfortably in the rickety chair as a lump formed in her throat.

"This thing you fear, this worry . . . It will never come to pass," she hissed.

Listening to the words despite herself, Jane felt her stomach do an uncomfortable flip-flop.

"No, you fear for naught. You have been spared."

"Spared?" Jane croaked, then immediately wished she'd remained silent.

The old woman nodded. "You will know of what I speak."

A hope sparked in Jane's breast. Was it possible? Her mother's counsel had assuaged her fear of madness, but was this woman confirming it? Could the Gypsy truly see the future? Or did she simply dole out vague, pithy statements that could be interpreted any which way by gullible patrons desperate for happy news?

Jane took a deep breath, steadying her nerves. The latter, of course. She'd let her imagination run wild, nothing more. The spark extinguished.

"I see happiness in your future," the Gypsy continued. "A great love."

"I'm afraid you're mistaken, madame. There is no love in my future." Now Jane knew that the woman did not possess the gift of foresight. It was impossible.

"Oh, but you are wrong, miss. Quite wrong. The man I speak of will love you above all else. You, and the child you carry."

Jane gasped sharply, snatching back her hands and rising so quickly that the chair she'd sat in toppled to one side. "You are mistaken," she repeated, her voice tremulous. "I've had enough of this nonsense."

With shaking hands, Jane retrieved her gloves and hurried out, the pain in her heart all but taking her breath away. How could the Gypsy know? The question echoed in her mind. What sort of sorcery did the woman practice?

Jane paused as she stepped back out into the sunlight, valiantly attempting to rein in her emotions as her eyes readjusted to the day's brilliance.

"Dear Lord, Jane, you're as pale as a ghost. What did Madame Cosmina say to you?" Emily laid a hand on her forearm, peering up worriedly into her face.

"Nothing worth the coin I paid, that's for certain. Just a bunch of stuff and nonsense, and none of it worth repeating."

"Emily's right," her mother said, reaching for Jane's hand. "You look unwell. Perhaps we should go. Do you mind terribly, Emily? I fear that Jane has overtaxed herself today."

"Of course I don't mind. Come, Jane." Emily threaded her arm through hers. "Let's find our carriage and be off at once."

Jane nodded in reply and allowed herself to be led back across the green, through the milling crowd, toward the waiting carriage.

"Mrs. Tolland," a feminine voice cried out, "have you met Richmond Park's new vicar?"

Jane turned toward the voice and saw Mrs. Tanner from the shop, standing with a slight, dark-haired man wearing an ill-fitting jacket. He was handsome nonetheless, in a boyish, inconspicuous way.

"New vicar?" Emily turned to watch the pair hurry across the lawn toward them. "I had no idea there was a new vicar at Richmond."

"Indeed, he's only come in the last week or so with his new bride, isn't that so, Mr. Banks?"

"Indeed it is. I owe a great deal of gratitude to Lord Westfield. A fine man. A fine man, indeed."

"Mrs. Tolland, this is Mr. Jonathan Banks. Mr. Banks, Mrs. Cecil Tolland."

"Delighted to make your acquaintance, Mrs. Tolland. I've already met your husband today, whilst I was securing a new mount for my wife."

"Allow me to present my cousin," Emily offered. "Miss Jane Rosemoor of Essex, and her mother, the Dowager Viscountess Rosemoor."

"A pleasure." He bowed to them with a smile. "My wife is off enjoying the theatrical production at the moment. I hope you'll have the opportunity to make her acquaintance soon. She's so far from home, and I know she longs to make some friends in the district."

"Oh, the poor dear," Mrs. Tanner interjected with the shake of her head.

"You must pay us a call as soon as convenient, then," Emily offered. "I'd enjoy it very much."

"Thank you, Mrs. Tolland. Indeed we will. Well, I won't keep you ladies any longer."

"Very well, then, Mr. Banks. Good day." Emily

nodded toward the vicar and shopkeeper with a smile.

Mr. Banks tipped his hat in reply. "Shall I escort you back to the festivities, Mrs. Tanner?"

"Why, thank you, sir." Mrs. Tanner laid her hand in the crook of his elbow with a smile. "Such a gentleman," she said with a giggle. "Good day, ladies."

"Oh, dear." Emily bit her lower lip as she gazed off toward the line of waiting carriages.

"Whatever is wrong?" Jane asked, filled with trepidation.

"I think perhaps we should make haste to our carriage." Emily reached for Jane's arm and steered her across the lawn, Jane's mother huffing to keep up as they bustled toward the waiting conveyance.

"Mrs. Tolland," an unmistakably masculine voice called out as they neared the road. A familiar voice. "Off so soon?" Jane's heart accelerated. *Hayden.*

Her chest tightened—she could barely breathe, and she felt perilously light-headed. Yet she could not allow her expression to betray any emotion or the slightest trace of agitation. Not with her mother by her side. If only she could get away, dash right into the safety of the carriage, and not look back. But she could not. Instead, she remained rooted to the spot, silent as he arrogantly strode over to join them.

"Miss Rosemoor," he added, bowing to her, the infuriating man. "I'm glad to see you have not yet returned to Essex."

"Good day, Lord Westfield," Emily interjected brightly. Too brightly. "You must meet Miss Rosemoor's mother, the Dowager Viscountess Rosemoor. Lady Rosemoor, I present Hayden Moreland, the Earl of Westfield. His estate, Richmond Park, is just across the wood from our home."

"A pleasure, Lady Rosemoor." Hayden bowed gracefully, doffing his hat with the sweep of one powerfully muscled arm.

"It is indeed a pleasure, Lord Westfield. Your gardens at Richmond Park are reputed to be lovely beyond words. I'm sorry I won't have the opportunity to see them before we leave for home."

"I am very sorry to hear it." He replaced the tall hat on his head. "Perhaps you could extend your visit? It would be my pleasure to show you my gardens. They are indeed lovely this time of year."

"I'm afraid we cannot. We've tarried here too long as it is. Jane has been missed most dearly."

"Hmmm," he replied, turning his attention to Jane, his eyes raking up her form, eliciting a shiver. "I imagine she has been. Miss Rosemoor, I called at the Tollands' earlier today, hoping to have a word with you before your departure. I was disappointed to find you not at home. What providence to find you here, though, isn't it? Would it be too much to ask for a moment of your time? I think you'll agree that we have some matters to discuss." He held out his arm to her, but Jane did not move to take it.

"Some matters of a *personal* nature," he added. "Perhaps we could stroll on ahead?" Again, he offered his arm.

"A poor idea, indeed, Lord Westfield." The words flew from Jane's mouth before she had time to consider them. "I saw your wife back by the Gypsy tent, and you would do well to locate her at once and keep her close by your side."

"Wife?" His dark brows flew together over a furrowed brow.

"Mrs. Tolland?" a voice called out. Jane looked up in surprise as the young vicar ambled back toward their party, a woman on his arm. Even from the distance separating them, Jane sensed something familiar about his companion. "I've found Mrs. Banks and hoped to introduce you before you left," Mr. Banks said.

Jane dropped her gaze and fiddled with her reticule, refusing to meet Hayden's probing stare. She heard Emily gasp, and looked up to see her cousin's eyes widen to alarming proportions and her mouth fall open in unconcealed shock.

Curiously, Jane turned toward Mr. Banks again and found herself gaping, too. Her heart slammed against her ribs, her breath caught in her throat. *What on earth?*

It made no sense—no sense at all. Lady Westfield held Mr. Banks's arm, smiling up at him unabashedly as she approached Lord Westfield. *Her husband*, for God's sake.

"Lord Westfield," Dorothea murmured sweetly. "How lovely to see you."

"Mrs. Banks, Mr. Banks." Hayden nodded to the pair.

Jane looked to Hayden, assessing his reaction. He did nothing but smile absently and brush a stray blade of grass from his sleeve, completely unaffected. She shook her head, the sound of blood rushing to her temples positively deafening her. "I—I don't understand," she stuttered, her own voice sounding muffled to her ears. "Your wife—"

"*My* wife? You thought . . ." he trailed off with a rueful shake of the head. "Devil take it, of course you did. I must apologize. I thought word had sufficiently spread that my marriage did not proceed as planned."

"It didn't, Lord Westfield," Emily said, the color rising in her cheeks. "We were under the impression that Miss Upshaw had become your wife."

Dorothea's subsequent tinkle of laughter pricked each and every one of Jane's nerves. "How very silly of me! It's my fault, I'm afraid. Why, when I saw Miss Rosemoor in the shop I just assumed that she'd heard the news of my marriage to Mr. Banks. When I said Lord Westfield had made me the happiest woman alive, I was speaking of his kindness to Mr. Banks. To us," she amended. "I had no idea you did not know—"

"I most assuredly did *not* know, Miss Upshaw." Jane shook her head in confusion. "Mrs. Banks, I mean. Oooh, what difference does it make?" With a swish of her skirts, Jane stormed past the gaping group and accomplished the carriage as quickly as she could, Emily and her mother trailing behind.

"You must excuse us," Emily called out over her shoulder.

Jane clambered inside in abject humiliation, her cheeks aflame and her emotions churning. She settled herself onto the leather bench and chanced a glance out the carriage's window as Emily and her mother climbed in and silently took their seats. She could only huff indignantly at the sight of Hayden grinning up at her. "Go away," she shouted down to him, then winced at her own childish behavior.

"And you said you didn't indulge in fits of temper in public," he called out.

"Oh, how dare you? You arrogant, insufferable man," she cried, instantly regretting her words as he threw back his head and laughed heartily.

"Jane Rosemoor," her mother hissed, her face scarlet. "You'll tell me at once what this is all about."

Emily smiled and patted her aunt's hand. "Later, Auntie Eliza. Drive on," she called out, rapping on the door.

* * *

Hayden could only smile as the carriage lumbered off down the road. She was a challenge, no doubt, the most worthwhile challenge he'd ever encountered.

And how remarkable that she hadn't yet heard of his betrothed's change of heart and subsequent marriage to Mr. Jonathan Banks. Hayden had told his housekeeper upon his return to Richmond Park, and he assumed that by now his entire staff knew the full details and had sufficiently spread the news throughout Ashbourne—throughout Derbyshire, for that matter. What an inopportune time to learn of Mrs. Pierce's unexpected discretion.

He watched as the Tollands' carriage disappeared around the bend in a cloud of dust. What to do now? Jane was obviously disinclined to receive his calls and would cut him to the quick in public before allowing him to say his piece with any civility. Worse still, he now had her mother to contend with. No doubt he would have to win her over, as well.

No time to waste. He dashed to his horse, tied up on the village green, and hastily unhitched him. In one fluid motion, he leapt upon the bay's back and took up the reins. Swinging the stallion's head around toward the lane, he dug his heels into its sides. "After that carriage, Andromeda."

As if it understood its master's command, the horse lunged forward, quickly gaining a full gallop in pursuit.

Only when the carriage's shiny exterior came into view did Hayden rein in the horse. A trickle of perspiration made its way down the side of his face, and he reached inside his breast pocket and removed a square of linen.

Doffing his hat, he mopped his brow as the high afternoon sun shone down on him, warming him, sending ripples of heat through the thick air. He tipped his hat back on his head and stuffed the handkerchief back into his pocket as a trio of sparrows zipped past his ear, chirruping gaily. The breeze stirred, bringing with it the sweet, piquant scent of honeysuckle. Hayden took a deep, fortifying breath before quickening the horse's gait to catch up to the carriage.

There was no turning back now. It was time to lay his unexpectedly lively heart on his sleeve, if that was what it would take to have her hand. Her heart.

Jane looked up in surprise at the sound of an approaching rider, the steady clip-clop of hooves gaining on the carriage's right. She leaned forward in her seat, as did her mother and Emily as the rider appeared beside the carriage's open window.

All the breath left her lungs in a rush, and she sat back against the squabs with a thump as Hayden tipped his hat and bowed from his mount. Whatever was he doing? What game was he playing, toying with her like this? It had not passed her notice that, even as Miss Upshaw had wed another, he had remained silent. Moreover, it was clear that it was Miss Upshaw who broke off their engagement; if her and her husband's inability to keep their hands off one another in so public a place as a fair was any indication, theirs was clearly a love match.

If Miss Upshaw hadn't called off the wedding, no doubt the woman would be Lady Westfield right now, and not the new vicar's wife. Jane had to learn the news in the most uncomfortable of circumstances, and there he'd stood, laughing at her discomfiture like the arrogant beast he was.

Of course, it briefly occurred to her that this had been the meaning of his missive—that he'd meant to call on her to deliver the news personally. And yet . . . it had been too late, hadn't it? She'd already run into Miss Upshaw—Mrs. Banks—and been led to believe that he'd married her and returned triumphantly to Richmond Park. Why had he waited? Why had he let her suffer?

"Good day, ladies," he called out. "Lovely day, isn't it?"

Jane clasped her hands in her lap, trying to quell their trembling.

"Miss Rosemoor, if you don't mind, I must entreat you for a word. Right now."

Her gaze flew to the window.

"Now?" Jane's mother called out. "Have you lost your wits, Lord Westfield? I must ask you to cease this nonsense and let my daughter be."

Jane swallowed a lump in her throat. Did her mother realize the truth? Had she recognized that Hayden was the father of the child she carried? Anger stirred in her breast. She could *not* let her mother force him to marry her. He would hate her for it. Just because he hadn't married Miss Upshaw didn't mean he'd changed his mind about *her*, about loving her. He still had his silly curse to contend with, after all, and he was a stubborn man.

The carriage lurched forward a bit, and Hayden disappeared from view. Moments later, the sight of him sitting atop the magnificent horse reappeared in the window. Jane couldn't help the jolt of attraction that surged through her at the fine form he cut in his finely tailored blue jacket and gray waistcoat, his firmly muscled thighs outlined in tight-fitting fawn breeches. The brim of his tall beaver hat cast a shadow on his face, almost concealing his eyes, but his perfectly trimmed whiskers high-lighted his chiseled cheekbones and proud jaw, his full, sensual lips parted into an easy smile.

"I must apologize for my outrageous behavior, Lady Rosemoor, but your stubborn daughter leaves me no choice. I am firmly in possession of all my wits, I assure you. She's refused my call, ignored my pleas, and I'm left with no other alternative save publicly declaring my love to her, here on the road in the most indecorous manner."

Jane sucked in her breath, her eyes widening. De-claring his love? Did he say *love*?

Jane's gaze flew to her mother's, and she was sur-prised to see the dear woman smile, tears dampening her eyes. She winked at Jane—actually winked—then leaned out the window with a scowl. "Hold your tongue, young man. This is most inappropriate."

"Indeed it is, madam. Yet what choice have I? Pray, you must let me continue. My regard for your daughter is honorable and true, and I must declare it to her at once. Miss Jane Rosemoor, I love you with all my heart. You are, without a doubt, the loveliest, most maddeningly wonderful woman I've ever met. You've shown that you are my equal in every way, and my esteem for you knows no bounds. I can no longer live without you. You would be be-stowing me the greatest favor imaginable if you would agree to be my wife, though Lord knows I don't deserve you."

Jane watched in astonishment as Emily sup-pressed a giggle with a gloved hand.

"You've shown me love and laughter, opened my eyes to new possibilities, to chances worth taking, a life worth grasping. I must know at once if you return my affections, my dearest Jane."

Jane couldn't breathe, much less speak. Never in her life had she been rendered so utterly flabbergasted, so completely speechless. What of his claim to heartlessness? What of his curse?

"Please, Jane," he implored, his voice softer, thick with emotion. "Do not make me suffer so. Your answer?"

Tears welled up in Jane's eyes as her gaze flitted to her mother, now weeping openly into her handkerchief, and then to Emily, grinning from ear to ear, her cheeks rosy and damp.

She knew she loved him with all her heart—all her soul—but could he truly mean these words that she'd not dared to hope for, not allowed herself to dream of hearing? She no longer feared the familial madness, but could she risk her fragile heart? She thought then of the babe growing inside her. Would Hayden forgive her for deceiving him so?

At once all her doubts washed away in an exquisite rush, and her heart picked up its pace in anticipation. Yes, her heart cried. *Yes.*

She stood on unsteady legs and rapped on the roof. "Stop the carriage!" she cried.

Chapter Twenty-three

The carriage swayed to a halt, and Jane flung open the door and leapt out, barely grabbing on to the footman's hand before her slippers touched the ground. Picking up her skirts, she raced around the carriage, just as Hayden swung down from his mount and opened his arms to her.

She closed the distance separating them and flew into his welcoming embrace, her eyes misting with tears of joy. Pressing her face against his coat, she breathed in his familiar masculine scent, feeling as if she might burst from happiness.

"Well? Have I your answer?" He stepped back from her and reached for her hands, clasping them tightly in his as his gaze sought hers.

Jane felt lost in those gray-green eyes, swimming in their depths. The love in his gaze enveloped her, cloaking her in their warmth and sending shivers of delight straight down to her toes.

He doffed his hat and dropped to one knee, still clasping her hands in his. "Marry me, Jane Rosemoor. My heart will not rest easy till you say yes."

"Oh, yes," she said at last, her vision blurring as the tears began to flow. "Yes. I love you with all my heart, Hayden. Surely you knew?"

His lips curved deliciously into a smile, his eyes alight with obvious joy. In a single motion, he rose and pulled her to him, his mouth hungrily taking hers.

Cheers and applause broke out from the carriage, and Jane found herself laughing against his mouth. His lips retreated, his laughter joining hers as they turned toward the carriage and watched as Emily and Jane's mother leaned out the window, waving their handkerchiefs with delight.

Hayden retrieved his hat from the ground and bowed exaggeratedly in reply.

A flutter of nerves in Jane's stomach reminded her of her deception, and she swallowed hard. She knew she must tell him that she lied to him; she must have his forgiveness before they could wed. She tugged on his sleeve and leaned close to his ear. "We must talk," she whispered. "You might wish to reconsider your offer after what I must confesss."

He nodded. "Lady Rosemoor, allow me to see your daughter home."

"Yes, Lord Westfield," her mother replied with a sniffle. "Of course. I'll be expecting you shortly so that I can get to know my future son-in-law. Oh dear, Colin will be miffed to learn he was not here to give his approval."

"Colin?" Hayden asked.

"My brother," Jane supplied. "The Viscount Rosemoor. You haven't asked his permission, you know."

"I'll write to him at once, Lady Rosemoor. Better yet, I'll invite him to Richmond Park and ask him for Jane's hand in person. Would that make you happy, Jane?"

"Very happy." She'd missed her brother.

If Hayden would still have her after she confessed her secret, then she would marry him right away, in the rectory at Richmond Park. She could not wait much longer to become his wife. She'd waited a lifetime for him, after all.

"Drive on," Hayden called out to the driver with a nod, and the carriage lurched off. He took her hand in his and led her toward his horse.

"Come, ride with me. I'll take you to the lake, and we can speak there. But I fear we should speak quickly, lest your mother comes looking for us. I don't want her to think I'm out compromising you. Again," he added, one dark brow arched. "Much as I'd like to."

Jane laughed. "Believe me, the pair of them will be standing at the front window, awaiting our return with bated breath."

"I'm sure you're right. Let's be off at once, then."

Jane nodded her assent and allowed him to lift her up onto the horse's back. He climbed up behind her and settled himself into the saddle. He took up the reins in his right hand, wrapping his left arm about her and pressing her tightly against him as they set off.

Minutes later, the shore of the lake loomed ahead, and he reined in the bay. He swung down gracefully, then reached up for her, folding her in his arms as he lowered her gently to the grassy lawn below. Taking her hand in his, he led her toward the steep knoll that sloped down to the shimmering water.

At last he turned to her and spoke. "Thank you, Jane. I don't know how you've forgiven me my first proposal. I was an insufferable clod." He shook his head. "And everything that's happened since . . ." He looked off to the horizon, a shadow crossing over his eyes. "Either I'm the luckiest man alive, or you're the most forgiving woman in all of England. Or quite possibly both."

"I understood your reasons, Hayden. I know what it's like to feel cursed, not in control of your own fate. I've finally come to see that my own fears were largely unfounded. Yet in a way, I'm almost glad that I suffered them nonetheless. Otherwise, I might have accepted a lackluster marriage long ago and not waited for the true love of my life. *You.*" She reached for his hand, and he brought it to his lips. "But what of your own fears, Hayden?"

He sighed heavily. "Cowardly fears they were; nothing but an excuse to shield myself from life's pleasures. I suppose I convinced myself I didn't deserve happiness. All these years, Emily swore it was nothing more than a series of unfortunate coincidences, these tragedies that have plagued me. But loving you has changed me. I no longer fear that which I cannot control. My heart tells me that I am meant to spend my life with you. *That* is what I trust."

"But you cannot trust me," she said quietly.

"Of course I can." He smiled down at her. "I'd trust you with my life."

Jane's lungs burned as she took a deep, ragged breath. Would his feelings for her change when he learned the truth? "I've deceived you, Hayden." One hand rose to cover her mouth, then dropped to her side. Her cheeks blazed with shame. "I've concealed something from you, something unforgivable."

"Unless you confess you've secretly eloped with William Nickerson, then you have no fear of my not forgiving it, Jane."

He had no idea of the enormity of it. She reached for his hand and placed it on her abdomen, covering his hand with her own. "I'm carrying your child."

She saw his mossy eyes widen, his mouth fall slack. "You're *what*?" He pulled his hand away as if burned.

Hot tears sprang to her eyes. "I cannot say it any plainer. I'm carrying your child, Hayden."

"But how? There was only that once, and you wrote me—"

"I lied." Her throat ached miserably.

"You . . . you lied?" he sputtered, backing away from her. His hands, visibly shaking, rose to his temples. "And you were just going to let me go ahead with my marriage to Miss Upshaw while you knew you carried my child? Why, Jane? Why would you do such a thing? Didn't you think I deserved to know? Did you think me so cold, so cruel, as to cast you aside?"

"Of course not," she countered, shaking her head vehemently. "I knew you'd do your duty—that you'd marry me and hate me for it. I thought you'd be forced to watch helplessly while I went mad; that I'd be nothing but a burden to you, a shameful secret. That my child would be forced to grow up with a father who'd refuse to love him for fear of losing him."

"Him? Did you say 'him'?"

"Well, of course I have no idea whether the babe will be a him or a her. I couldn't very well say 'it,' now, could I?" she snapped.

He raised his brows, a hint of amusement in his eyes. "I suppose not."

"I realized I'd made a mistake—a terrible mistake—the moment I saw Miss Upshaw in Ashbourne and thought you wed. But don't you see? I thought I was protecting those I love. You, Hayden, and this babe." She laid her palm flat on her stomach. "Indeed, I made a grave mistake," she said softly. "One I will always regret. I doubted you, when I should have known better."

He closed his eyes and inhaled sharply. "No, Jane." He opened his eyes, and his gaze met hers. "I gave you no reason to think differently. I was a betrothed man and still I took you to my bed, used you in the worst way possible. I should have married you the very next day. None but a rogue and a coward would do otherwise."

"I would never have agreed to it. At the time, I believed myself doomed to madness. I thought having a child would threaten my sanity. You see, it was only after I thought you'd wed Miss Upshaw that my mother at last allayed my fears."

"I could have tried to convince you otherwise. Hell, I could have forced your hand, if need be." He spun around, his back to her. With an oath, he kicked a rock and sent it arcing through the air. "How could I leave you to suffer so?" His voice was hoarse, laced with grief, and it tore at Jane's heart.

Slowly, tentatively, she moved toward him, fitting herself against his back. She laid her cheek between his shoulder blades and reached for his hands, easing them from angry fists and lacing her fingers through his. Moments passed before his rapid, ragged breaths began to slow, and his racing heart calmed. Jane gently squeezed his hands, and a tear slipped down her cheek when he at last returned the pressure.

"We've both made mistakes, Hayden. We've acted out of fear and raced to conclusions that need never have been reached. But look where it has brought us. Right here, right where we should be. Perhaps fate knew we would need a hand; that we needed to face the certainty of life apart before we'd ever agree to a life together."

His shoulders seemed to sag, and then he dropped her hands and turned to face her. "You are the single most extraordinary woman I've ever known." The burning intensity in his eyes nearly took her breath away.

"And you are the most wonderfully forgiving man I've ever known. You're going to make a fine papa." A smile curved her mouth at the startled expression her statement elicited.

And then his lips began to twitch. A smile began at the corners of his mouth and spread outward—a dazzling smile, lighting his eyes and animating his features. With a whoop, he whisked her off her feet and into the air, spinning her around and around till the landscape began to blur.

At last he lowered her, cradling her against his muscled chest with a groan. His lips sought hers even as his hand stroked her stomach through the fabric of her gown.

He kissed her deeply, passionately, with a fiery intensity she barely recognized. His tongue parted her lips, probing the warm depths, seeking out her tongue in a sensual, seductive dance. Her limbs went limp, and she clutched at him desperately as his hands rose to untie her bonnet and cast it aside.

She gasped as his lips left hers and moved to her jaw, her temple, her throat. His hands released her hair from the pins that held it in place, and she shuddered as she felt the silky locks brush her back.

He tenderly combed his fingers through her hair, fanning it across her shoulders. "So very beautiful," he murmured. "You've no idea how I've longed to see you once more with your hair down, framing your lovely face. I thought I'd go mad, remembering the way it felt between my fingers, soft as silk." He brought a lock to his lips and kissed it reverently.

"All is forgiven, then?" Jane peered up at him, a smile dancing at the corners of her mouth.

"Of course. Now I know for certain I am the happiest man alive. A child. My child!" He swept her off her feet once more before setting her back unsteadily on her feet. "Madeline. We must tell Madeline at once. She's going to be beside herself with delight. She adores you, you know. It seems to run in the family."

"Not until you return me to Emily's and allow me to set their minds at ease. Then we can go straightaway to Richmond Park and tell her, my lord."

"My lady."

"Jane," she countered.

"My very dearest Jane," he corrected.

She looked across the lake's rippled surface to the far side of the water and saw the stone walls of Richmond Park rise up in grandeur from the solid, Derbyshire ground. *Home,* she thought. At last, she'd found the place she belonged. Here, in Hayden's heart.

Joining hands, they turned back toward the waiting stallion, toward their future, a future without the faintest trace of fear, a future filled with love and laughter and the patter of tiny feet.

With a happy sigh of contentment, Jane gazed lovingly at the prideful, arrogant, delightfully stubborn earl who would be her husband, and knew with certainty that she was indeed the luckiest woman alive.

Epilogue

Jane sighed contentedly and snuggled against the warm body pressed against her back, her eyes fluttering open in the dim light of dawn. She felt Hayden stir against her. His arm slid from her shoulder, his fingers tracing the curve of her breast and the slope of her hip before moving lower to cup her bottom.

"Good morning, Lady Westfield," he whispered huskily in her ear.

"Mmmm." Jane smiled a sleepy smile. "And what a lovely night."

"It was, wasn't it?" His breath was warm against her neck. "Not one I'll soon forget. Wouldn't the *ton* be shocked to know what a wicked, wanton woman lurks beneath my countess's perfectly proper façade?"

Tipping her chin down, Jane nipped playfully at his fingers with her teeth.

"I always thought you sharp-tongued," he teased, reaching around to clasp her. With one sharp tug, he pulled her on top of him, her long body stretched out over his. "But sharp-toothed, too?"

She rested her chin on his chest, gazing up at him with eyes full of love.

She'd never tire of simply looking at him; of watching the way his eyes shifted from green to gray, depending on the light or his mood. She'd never expected such happiness in her life. Each day became more precious than the one before it, replacing life under a veil of fear with a lifetime of happy memories. That she'd come so close to letting him slip through her fingers—to letting love slip away—still made her heart race and her palms dampen, even now.

She would remain eternally grateful to fate for setting things right, for this was the life she was meant to lead. She smiled at her husband, basking in the lustful heat of his gaze, admiring the way the gray at his temples made him appear more noble, more distinguished than before.

She moaned softly, suddenly aware of his arousal, pressing urgently against her belly. He grinned down at her wickedly, and she found herself sliding down his smooth body, fitting herself over him, and giving in once more to the passionate tides of seemingly unquenchable desire that had all but overtaken her these past hours.

As she began to move atop him, she was filled once more with the delicious knowledge that she had indeed found her match, the one man above all else who could make her overcome her fears, who would love her despite them.

Gasping for breath, Hayden watched his sated wife roll off him and lay back upon the pillow. "Mmmm," he murmured, reaching for her hand and bringing it to his lips as the hammering of his heart finally began to subside. "I'll never tire of this."

He propped himself up on one elbow and gazed at her lying naked beside him, a smile on her lips and her skin flushed pink from their lovemaking.

Tenderly, he brushed back the chestnut strands that clung to her damp forehead.

"Nor will I," she replied. "I'm always amazed by the . . . well, variety." The color in her cheeks deepened deliciously, and Hayden felt a miraculous stiffening in his groin yet again. Dear Lord, he felt like a boy of eighteen, not a man well past his prime. What was she doing to him? Enchanting him, no doubt. As always.

A hazy light filtered in through the heavy drapes, casting an ethereal silver glow across their bedchamber. He smiled at the familiar sight of her effects scattered across the room. A delicately carved dressing table sat beneath one window, holding a silver brush and mirror set engraved with her initials alongside other female fripperies of which he had no idea of their exact purpose. Her lilac gown still lay in a heap on the velvet chaise longue where he'd deposited it last night after pulling it over her head in his haste to undress her. Even the air was perpetually filled with her scent—exotic, spicy. Perhaps someday he would examine her dressing table and learn the exact source of such a heady, intoxicating scent. Or perhaps he'd allow it to remain a mystery forever.

A tray of barely touched food sat on a table in the room's corner, for the most part ignored since the maid had deposited it there. Instead, their appetites had taken on a far different nature since they'd come upstairs immediately following the wedding breakfast yesterday. How many hours had they remained secreted away? And how many times had they made love in that time? He'd long since lost count.

"Hayden?"

He looked over at Jane, who pushed herself to a

sitting position, her long legs stretched out before her and crossed at the ankles. He couldn't help but rake his gaze up the length of her limbs, smiling appreciatively at the glorious sight.

"It was beautiful, wasn't it?" she asked, her sapphire eyes aglow. "The wedding, I mean."

"It was, indeed. And you, my sweet, looked lovely." He traced a finger down the curve of her shoulder and across one rose-tipped breast, delighting in the way the skin puckered to his touch.

"I'm always happiest with everyone I love here, under this very roof."

"I know you are. We should arrange for it more often. I'm thoroughly enjoying the fruits of your good humor."

"Madeline was the most beautiful bride I've ever seen. I know she'll be happy. It's obvious they're very much in love, and Mr. Leighton is a fine man."

"I completely agree. He'll make her an excellent husband. I'd never have let him have her if I hadn't been convinced of it."

"But the children will miss her so. Anna has spent the past few days sulking in her room, poor girl. Alexander will never admit to it, but I'm certain I saw tears in his eyes when Madeline walked down the aisle. And the twins were nearly hysterical when the wedding carriage pulled away." She laid her hand on his forearm, the heavy sapphire on her finger reflecting the points of lights in the candelabra by the bed. The candles had burned low; nothing but a stub of wax remained on each silver arm, the flames flickering in their final throes. "I know her new home is only as far as the village, but it just won't be the same without her here. I'll miss her terribly."

"And so it begins." He sighed heavily. "One by

one, all the sparrows will fly the nest. Then we'll be left with no one to amuse ourselves with but each other."

Her eyes began to dance mischievously. "It will be perhaps a bit longer than you think."

He raised one brow. "Is that so?"

"Indeed." She smiled a smug smile of self-satisfaction, one he recognized instantly for what it was. "I'd say we can count on another eighteen years of chaos at least."

"Have you something to tell me, Lady Westfield?"

"Nothing but the news that we shall be blessed once again in seven months' time. I wanted to be sure before I told you."

"Each time you share such news you make me the happiest man alive all over again. Have you any idea how much I adore you, Lady Westfield?"

"You've a lifetime to show me, haven't you, my love?" Her lips brushed his seductively, her breath warming his cheek.

"Indeed. I'd give you the moon if I could."

She shook her head, her mouth curving into a sweet smile. "I've no need for the moon. Only your heart, Hayden." She laid her palm flat on his chest, covering the place where his heart beat furiously against his ribs.

He covered her hand with his own. "It's yours, Jane. Forever."

"And you said you were heartless," she teased. "Just goes to show, I was correct all along and *you*, my lord, were mistaken."

"In case you have not noticed, you were incorrect on several counts yourself. You've borne four children and yet you remain as sane as the day I met you."

"Humph. It isn't at all polite to point out a lady's mistakes, now is it?"

He roughly pulled her into his lap and pressed his lips into her lavender-scented hair. "Waspish woman."

"Arrogant brute," came her muffled reply.

"I wouldn't have it any other way."

"Nor would I, Hayden. Not even for the moon."